A
Simple
Murder

A
Simple
Murder

ELEANOR KUHNS

MINOTAUR BOOKS
NEW YORK

A SIMPLE MURDER. Copyright © 2012 by Eleanor Kuhns. All rights reserved. Printed in the United States of America. For information, address St. Martin's Press, 175 Fifth Avenue, New York, N.Y. 10010.

ISBN 978-1-250-00553-3

To my family, especially all my Children; my own and all those who've lived with me. You've enriched my life.

Acknowledgments

Thanks to my great editor, Kelley Ragland, without whom this book would have been poorer. Her help and suggestions have been invaluable.

A
Simple
Murder

Chapter One

By late afternoon William Rees was past Rumford and heading southeast, almost to Durham and the coast. Time to start searching for a place to stay, he thought, eyeing dusk's purple fingers clawing the rutted track. He'd look for a likely farm where he could camp for the night. Maybe some kind farmer would allow him space in a barn. Hollowed out by fury for most of the day (damn his sister, how could she push David, Rees's little boy, out?), Rees was tired enough now to fall asleep in the wagon seat.

The cluster of buildings that was Durham appeared suddenly from a bracelet of woods and farms. He plunged into the small village. Choose a road, any road, he thought, noting the possibilities branching off the central square. And he saw a tavern, The Cartwheel, if no generous farmers offered him the use of a barn. He turned onto the road doglegging south and soon after spotted a white clapboard farmhouse, rising from a thin screen of trees on the western slope. A weathered red barn rose behind it, squatting on the edges of the fields wrested from the rocky soil. Rees directed Bessie onto the narrow bridge spanning the muddy creek. Perhaps anticipating fresh water and oats and the comfort of a stall, she jerked into a weary trot.

The house was a narrow clapboard, the boards weathered

gray, with a small porch jutting from the front door. At the sound of hooves striking the stony drive, the farm wife stepped out from the front door and stared at Rees curiously. He pulled right up to the small porch and clumsily climbed to the ground. Driven by rage and fear, he'd pushed on without a break all day, and now his body punished him for it. He staggered, awkward with stiff joints and muscles, up the stairs toward her. A tiny woman with gray hair, she appeared younger close up. "Pardon, mistress," Rees said, pulling off his dusty and travel-stained tricorn, "I'm on my way to the Shaker community and I wonder if you might have space in your barn where I could sleep tonight." Wiping her hands upon her apron, she glanced at the canvas-shrouded loom in the wagon bed.

"You a weaver?"

"Yes, ma'am. I'm not looking for work right now though." He paused and then, thinking she was most likely a mother, he burst out, "My son ran away from home." Fatigue and the emotional stew of anger and fear made him more talkative than usual. "My sister said he went with the Shakers." The woman's expression softened.

"I've lost family to them," she said. "Of course—"

"What do you want here?" demanded her husband belligerently, stepping out from the house behind her. Much darker than his wife, he was black of hair and eyes.

And black of nature? Rees wondered, eyeing the other man's scowl. Most farmers were hospitable to a traveling weaver.

Putting her pale freckled hand upon his mahogany-dark tanned arm, his wife drew him inside. Rees clearly heard the word "Shakers." A few moments later the farmer came back outside. "You can sleep in the barn," he said, pointing with his chin at the red structure. "What's your name? Mine is Henry Doucette. My wife, Jane."

"Will Rees," Rees said, extending his hand. "Thank you."

"Your horse looks all in," Doucette said, casting a critical eye over Bessie. "You're welcome to an empty stall."

Rees nodded his thanks and climbed back into the wagon. With the day's journey finally nearing its end, both Rees and Bessie allowed fatigue to overtake them. Rees wasn't sure they could make even the short trip across the yard to the barn.

Rees got Bessie settled in with fresh water and a nosebag of oats. When he returned to his wagon, he found a boy of about twelve waiting for him with a napkin-covered dish and a jug of water. "My stepmother sent this up for your supper," the boy said, thrusting the dishes into Rees's hands. Although fair-haired, the boy was almost as darkly tanned as his father, right down to his bare feet. And of an age with David, Rees thought.

"Thank her for me," Rees said, staring down at the plate in grateful surprise. "This is very kind of her. What's your name?"

"Oliver. She says stop by tomorrow morning and she'll give you some breakfast," the boy said with a flash of white teeth.

"Thank you." With an awkward nod, the boy fled back down the hill at a run.

Rees sat down on a seat of fresh straw, his back to the wagon wheel, looking upon the green valley before him. The road on which he'd arrived unwound like a silvery ribbon in the last rays of sunlight. The lowing of the cattle sounded from a nearby pasture and Bessie's contented whicker floated out from the barn. Peaceful. Dolly would approve. He sighed. Eight years since Dolly's death in 1787, six of them spent as a traveling weaver. Two years he had struggled to keep his farm going without Dolly—two solid years. But he couldn't do it without her. And since he made more money weaving than farming, he'd offered the management of his land to his sister and her husband in exchange for raising his David with their own kids. He'd thought his eight-year-old son would be safe with them while he worked. Sighing, he lifted off the napkin and dug into the stew. For five years and more he'd gone home intermittently. Not often enough, he saw that now, and he'd do his best to make it up to David.

When he tried to sleep, the rage he'd tamped down during the day flared up again, hotter and fiercer than before. He'd begun yearning to see David again after his experiences on the western frontier, during the Rebellion two years previously, and as soon as winter ended he headed north. Several profitable weaving commissions delayed him in Massachusetts, so he arrived home to Maine the summer of 1795, a year later than he expected, but he rode home with a strongbox almost too heavy to lift.

Caroline greeted him with hostile surprise. "We weren't expecting to see you until winter," she said. She did not at first admit that David was gone. Instead she forced him to ask several increasingly agitated questions until he realized the truth.

Then, when he exclaimed in furious disbelief, "David's gone? How could you allow that to happen?" she and her husband stood shoulder to shoulder and defied him.

"He's a man grown," Sam said. "We couldn't stop him."

"He's not yet fourteen," Rees snapped.

"There's nothing for him here," Charles, his oldest nephew, said. Rees glared at the boy as he added, "Let him seek his fortune elsewhere." Neither of his parents reprimanded the lad for his unmannerly behavior.

"He couldn't wait to leave," Caroline said. He knew then that David was simply an inconvenience. He pressed them again and again until they were all shouting, but all they would say was that they thought David had gone off with the Shakers. Rees flung out of the house he and Dolly had shared and raced toward Durham and the Shaker settlement near it.

For most of that day, as he traveled south, he replayed the

fight with his sister in his mind. Each time he formulated increasingly cutting remarks. He should have reminded Caroline that he owned the farm; in fact, he carried the deed with him in the strongbox, right next to his leather sack of coins. He should have threatened her and her family with eviction. But all he could think of just then was David. He kept remembering the little boy who had followed him so trustingly into the barn to help with the milking.

Now, staring at the starry sky outside the barn, Rees understood that his sister and her family felt his farm belonged to them. So, as soon as he felt sure of his son's safety, Rees must return to Dugard and make his sister understand the farm belonged to Rees and would someday be David's. And then, whispered a little voice, Would they leave? Or would they fight him on it?

Suddenly aware of his pounding heart and of the blood throbbing in his ears, Rees took several deep breaths. He forced himself to relax, listening to the lowing of the cattle and the faraway rooster crow. Gradually his thoughts scattered, and as the moon climbed into the sky he finally slept.

He awoke when Oliver clanked by with the milk pail, so early the sun just peeked over the horizon. Mist filled the valley below and dampened Rees's clothing. He sat up and yawned, his eyes gritty with insufficient sleep. Cows mooed and Oliver's soothing voice carried clearly to Rees's ears.

Stumbling to his feet, he went into the barn and fetched Bessie. He hitched her to the wagon and they began trundling down toward the house. Mrs. Doucette popped out with such suddenness Rees knew she'd been watching for him.

"Come in for breakfast, Mr. Rees," she called out, flapping her hand at him. He pulled to a stop but declined to enter the house; he didn't want to be drawn into a long conversation. Only when he knew David was safe would Rees relax. He did accept a bowl of mush and a cup of coffee, eating quickly in his seat on the wagon. "If you come this way again, Mr. Rees, and plan to stop for a few days, I could use your help with some weaving," she said.

Rees nodded. "Wool or linen?"

"Both. But more wool than linen."

Rees didn't expect to be in the area for very long but he said politely, "Of course. I'll be glad to help." She smiled.

"Now, for Zion. Just follow the road out front. When it splits, turn left. That will take you directly into the Shakers' community."

Rees followed her directions and reached the divergence in the road very shortly thereafter. The main road continued, straight as an arrow. He turned left. At first trees hemmed in the track in walls of green, but forest soon gave way to orchards and then orderly fields. Men in dark clothing and straw hats bent over the green fuzz visible from the road. Rees thought he smelled the sea's faint salty tang in the air, and white flocks of gulls screeched above. The Shaker farm stretched from well inland almost to the coast.

The road cut through the center of the village, a scattering of red, brown, and yellow buildings dominated by the large white meetinghouse at this end. Few people walked the street, mostly women, and they avoided Rees's eyes. He pulled up in front of a yellow building, since he saw nothing like a general store, and waited for someone to notice him. Since he'd visited several religious communities he knew they usually discouraged visitors.

It was so quiet he could almost hear the dust of his passing dropping back to the ground in tiny whispers. If he hadn't seen the women walking to and fro he could almost imagine this place abandoned. Where were the sounds of normal life, of the normal chatter that went with a cluster of people? Where were the voices of children? There must be children. Although the Shakers themselves were celibate, they were famous for taking in orphans and the unwanted.

"Good morning to you," said a male voice very unexpectedly by Rees's side. He jumped and turned. A man had come around the side of the building. Dressed like the other men in dark pants, broad-brimmed hat, and linen shirt, he had clearly left some task in the barns. The smell of horses and cows eddied out from him, especially from his boots, in a pungent wave. Both hair and beard were a startling white. "I'm Elder White. What are you doing here?" Not hostile but not friendly either.

"I'm William Rees. I'm looking for my son. I'm hoping he is here."

"Are you planning to take him away, if he is?" Elder White asked.

"No," Rees said in surprise. "Not if he doesn't want to come with me." Elder White stared at Rees for another disturbingly long moment.

"What's his name?"

"David Rees. He's thirteen, almost fourteen, and has red hair like mine."

"He's already fourteen," White said, his tone faintly patronizing. (What a poor father you are, you don't even know the age of your son.) "He's in the fields right now but will return soon for the midday meal. Please join us. You must be hungry after your long journey." His speech rolled out in formal, almost stilted cadences. "You may speak to your son afterward, if he wishes, under my eye." Rees stared at him. What was this man expecting? That he would kidnap David and carry him away? Rees nodded in reluctant agreement. Elder White continued to wait and Rees realized he must verbally agree.

"Very well," he said ungraciously.

Then the Elder said, "I'll show you where to wash up. You may stable your horse across the street." He pointed at the stables and waited patiently while Rees released Bessie from the traces. While he led her into the stable, two men, silently directed by the Elder, hauled the wagon after them. Rees left his mare in their capable hands and returned to the yellow building.

They went inside. A series of doors lined the left side. Elder White opened the first one; it led into a small room with two identical cots, two chairs hanging on wall pegs, and two small wooden chests. Matching jugs and basins sat upon them. Elder White nodded to the right side. "I will send someone with fresh water," he said and withdrew. Rees stood awkwardly in the center of the room for the few moments it took for a Sister to appear. She replenished the water and withdrew so quickly Rees had no image of her face.

He scrubbed his hands and face, wondering whose possessions he made use of, and rejoined the Elder waiting in the hall. As they walked to the end, the clang of a deep-throated bell reverberated throughout the village. White put Rees into a small room with a second door opposite. "Wait here," the Elder said and withdrew. The tantalizing aromas of roast beef and fresh baked bread drew the water into Rees's mouth and he suddenly realized he was very hungry. He cautiously opened the door into the dining room. Except for many tables, each with a necklace of chairs, the room was empty. He quietly closed the door, the sound echoing through the uninhabited room.

A few more minutes passed. Gradually the Shaker Brothers began sifting into the room. Each one looked at Rees curiously but no one spoke, not even to ask him what he was doing there. Then David entered in the company of a young man with brown curly hair. When Rees cut through the male barrier, David threw his father a furious glance and retreated to the other side of the room. "David," Rees said hopefully.

"We do not speak unnecessarily," one of the older men said, turning upon the weaver. Rees felt heat rise into his neck; he felt like a kid being reprimanded by his teacher.

A bell tinkled inside and the Brother closest to the door opened it. Quietly the throng entered the dining hall. From another door the linen-capped Sisters entered, just as silently as the men. Rees tried to approach David but he scuttled away. Rees stopped, wounded. Elder White caught Rees's eye and sternly pointed at one of the tables. Rees hesitated, fighting the urge to protest. But he obeyed. If he were to have any chance of speaking to David, he must not allow himself to be expelled from the village.

Elder White led prayers, much shorter than Rees would have expected in a religious community, and they sat to eat. Sisters brought laden trays from the kitchen to each table: roast beef and potatoes and gravy and the fresh bread Rees had smelled outside in the hall. He choked down a few bites, watching David all the while. Even the children ate in an unnatural silence, as well behaved and as self-contained as the adults.

After a delicious vinegar pie ended the meal, Elder White dismissed his community. He collected Rees from his table and they went into the hall and up the stairs. The Elder's quarters contained an extra room fitted out as an office with a table and several chairs. He directed Rees to sit. "Please wait here," White said and left again. A few minutes later he returned with David. Rees stood up abruptly, the chair clattering to the floor.

"David," he cried. "Thank God you're safe." David's sullen expression softened for a moment and then hardened once again.

"I'm not leaving," he said flatly. "I am not going back to that farm."

"I didn't come to take you away," Rees said. Awkwardly he moved forward to hug his son but David's belligerent stance warned him off. Where's my little boy? Rees wondered. As a little boy David greeted him with wild cries of delight and ferocious hugs. But not recently, Rees realized, not for several years. And now he stood eye to eye with Rees, a reddish fuzz fringing his chin, and with the dour expression of a stranger. But it was David's gray eyes that made Rees's heart turn over; they were Dolly's eyes staring out of David's masculine face. "I wanted to see you and know you were safe."

"Well, you've seen me now," David said. "I'm safe. I plan to stay here. You can go away again." Rees swallowed painfully.

"I'm sorry, David. I-I didn't know."

David stared at his father from eyes as flat and cold as a winter pond. "May I be excused now?" he asked Elder White.

"Of course," said the Elder gently. He waited until David had left the room before turning to Rees. "You are now assured of your son's safety and his desire to remain with us?" Rees did not reply immediately. He heard the thread of disapproval running through White's tone. Guilt sparked a burst of temper. How dare this man, this minister, condemn someone he didn't know?

"I think I'll bide hereabouts for a while," Rees said. The Elder gestured him from the room and down the stairs. "Just to be sure he's happy." White heard the break in Rees's voice and looked at him sharply.

"Hmmm." He paused on the porch outside. "Well, we have no room for the casual visitor but you might find a bed in Durham." Rees nodded, recalling the Doucette farm. He'd drive north, back to that home, and take on Mrs. Doucette's weaving. He knew he could expect an invitation to spend the night in the barn. And once in Durham he would rent a room at the tavern. "You can visit your boy as often as you like."

"Thank you," Rees said. "Thank you. I know, well, I should have visited home more often." Shame wrung the admission from him.

"God forgives," White said. "Surely David will too, eventually."

Within the hour, Rees and Bessie were back on the road, heading north. They reached the house just at dusk, a little later than his arrival the evening before. Mrs. Doucette came out upon the porch, smiling and waving when she saw him. "You found our barn that comfortable?" she teased. Rees smiled.

"I decided to accept your job. I'll carry your yarns back to Durham with me."

"I'm glad to hear it," she said. "I'll ask Oliver to stable your horse in the barn. You come inside and wash up for supper."

So Rees stiffly climbed down from the wagon, trying not to groan with the burning in his legs. As he stumped painfully up the front steps, Oliver grasped Bessie's bridle and drew her up the hill toward the barn.

Rees left his boots upon the porch and walked inside. The main room was kitchen, dining room, and parlor all at once. The large oaken table where meals were prepared also served as the dining table and was bracketed by eight chairs. Five dark-haired children occupied five seats. Rees thought Mrs. Doucette did not seem old enough to bear so many children. Rees looked at the three remaining chairs. "Mr. Doucette isn't here," Mrs. Doucette said quickly. "A farm meeting in Durham. Sit down, please."

Rees obeyed, awkwardly perching on a corner of an empty bench. Although he dealt with women regularly, he felt uncomfortable sitting at another man's table with that man far away. But when Oliver stumped in, his hands and face still wet from washing, and they all sat down to Grace, Rees lost his awkwardness.

Six children, three on each side of him, and all watching his every move, proved as effective a chaperone as any duenna. Mrs. Doucette placed a large pewter dish before him. The children ate from worn wooden plates.

Once the simple supper of stewed chicken and biscuits was over, Mrs. Doucette bundled the two youngest to bed. "Please don't leave yet," she said to Rees. "I'll give you the yarns when I return."

"Very well," said Rees. He moved the kettle over the fire to heat water for washing dishes.

"My father never helps," Ruthie said disapprovingly. At seven, the eldest after Oliver and the only daughter, she already behaved like a matron. "He says it's women's work."

"I'm not married," Rees said. "I've had to learn."

"But you have a son," Oliver said.

"Yes. About your age, I think." In the sudden sharp pause Rees realized they were wondering about his wife and family. "My wife died," he explained.

"I'm sorry," Oliver said.

"It was a long time ago," Rees said. "Come on," he said, pulling Ruthie's brown braid teasingly, "you can help me wash the dishes and surprise your mother. And I'll tell you a story. Once upon a time, a young Indian maiden was sent to live with her auntie in another village." Rees hoped he could remember this tale. Many years had passed since Philip, Rees's Indian tracker, had told it to him. Fortunately, this audience was not a critical one. The youngest stood stock-still, listening with big eyes and a finger in his mouth. Even Ruthie was so caught up she stopped moving with a dish in her hands and had to be reminded on her way.

When Mrs. Doucette came downstairs Ruthie was just putting the last plate into the cupboard. Mrs. Doucette stared around in astonishment. "Oh my, oh my."

"Mama, there was this Indian princess," Ruthie began, running to her mother.

"Later, child," Mrs. Doucette said, smiling at Rees over Ruthie's brown head. "Let's help carry the yarns out to Mr. Rees's wagon. It's getting late and will soon be bedtime for all of you."

"I'm not tired," her five-year-old said flatly, ruining his declaration with a jaw-cracking yawn.

Mrs. Doucette led the way into a small room off the kitchen, little more than an enclosed porch, that contained her spinning wheel. She had rolled the spun yarns into balls and piled them upon a square of canvas. Even Rees found it too heavy to lift. But the children eagerly grasped a corner and, with Ruthie holding a lantern so they could see, they half carried and half dragged the canvas up the slope to the barn. Mrs. Doucette, whose skinny arms proved surprisingly strong, and Rees hauled it into the wagon.

"I'll return the canvas," Rees said, panting. Mrs. Doucette nodded.

"Good night, Mr. Rees," she said. The family started down the hill, the lantern throwing a soft glow on the ground ahead of them. Rees looked up at the sky. Only a faint lavender streak glimmered above the horizon and the stars were beginning to appear overhead. He threw his blanket upon a bed of straw and lay down. The moon was climbing into the sky and he thought the hour must be about nine o'clock. Sighing as he recalled the anger in David's eyes, he rolled over and prepared for sleep.

Chapter Two

Once again the clatter of Oliver's milk pail, this time accompanied by Henry Doucette's shouting, awakened Rees. He'd overslept and the sun already peeked over the horizon. He quickly fed and watered Bessie and hitched her to the wagon. When she pulled, the wagon resisted and then jerked forward, heavy with the yarn. As Rees drove down toward the house Mr. Doucette shouted again; he was behind the stone wall that wandered up the hill. Each rock had been painfully wrested from the soil and put into place. Rees viewed the hundreds of stone walls that banded Maine as monuments to the struggle involved in farming this rocky soil.

The aroma of fresh bread and the line of freshly washed clothing dancing on the line told Rees that Mrs. Doucette had been awake and working for hours. Ruthie came out with coffee and new bread and jam for Rees's breakfast. She lingered while he ate, until her mother cried, "Ruthie. Let Mr. Rees eat in peace. I apologize for my ill-mannered little girl, Mr. Rees." She came out and perched upon the top step. "We all got a late start what with stories and all. And my husband didn't come home until after ten." That explained Mr. Doucette's shouting then. "Just leave the plate on the step," Mrs. Doucette said as she pulled Ruthie inside.

Rees left his empty plate and cup upon the top step as instructed, shouted a thank-you through the open door, and drove down to the road. Although the air was still pleasantly cool under the trees he could feel the day's heat building. He reached Durham just after eight. Since it was Saturday and the farmers were bringing whatever they had to sell to market, wagons clogged the main road and townspeople thronged the boardwalks.

Why was everyone staring? A young boy pointed at him, then another. It seemed as if everyone was looking at him. The arrival of four armed men who surrounded the wagon came as something he almost expected. He knew he couldn't make a break for freedom; in these crowded streets he would not succeed. His heart hammering, he pulled Bessie to a stop.

"Mr. William Rees," said one of the men, a short redheaded man wearing a storekeeper's apron. A toothpick clamped between his lips rolled from side to side.

"Yes." Rees heard the resignation in his voice. A perpetual stranger in every town, he was accustomed to hearing himself accused of everything from chicken stealing to rape. The last had involved a young girl afraid to tell her parents she was pregnant by one of the farmhands. And during his stint in the army he'd been accused of murder. To save his skin, he'd done his own investigating and found the killer, finding his gift for investigating crimes along the way.

"Step down from the wagon, please."

"What is this about?" Rees's heart began to thunder in his chest. On shaky legs, he climbed down and kept his hands in full view. Some of these men looked itching to shoot him. Keeping his hands elevated, he turned to face the shopkeeper. Despite the apron, Rees had no difficulty recognizing this man as the sheriff. He looked at Rees with blue-green eyes as cold as the ice on a frozen pond. A crowd that included several Shaker men began to gather.

"Murder, Mr. Rees. Elder White laid a charge against you this morning for the murder of one of his community."

"Murder!" Rees gasped, his stomach churning. "Who was murdered?"

"A young Shaker woman."

"We hang murderers," spat one of the sheriff's companions, motioning at Rees with his musket.

Any one of these men, caught up in the heat of the moment, could shoot him here, on the spot.

"Yes," agreed the sheriff grimly, and Rees knew he was only inches away from hanging. "But don't be hasty, Willie. We have no proof he's guilty, not yet anyway."

"I spent last night at the Doucette farm," he said quickly. "Look in the wagon, under the canvas. I'm a weaver. That's Mrs. Doucette's yarn."

"Mr. Henry Doucette?" asked the sheriff.

"And Oliver and Ruth and Jacob and Mrs. Doucette too of course."

The sheriff's toothpick rolled from side to side. "Maybe we should check that out," he suggested, looking at the burly deputy with pockmarked skin and scummy teeth. With a nod, the man took off.

The sheriff looked at Rees thoughtfully; Rees met him stare for stare. "I'm Sheriff Coulton. And the proprietor of the general store. Your horse and wagon will be kept behind the store for the time being and you'll be confined to the local jail while your story is verified." Rees sighed, torn between irritation and relief.

"Very well," he said.

"Come with me, please, Mr. Rees." Coulton grasped his arm.

At almost a foot taller in height and fifty pounds and more in weight, Rees knew he could break Coulton's hold and escape. But he wouldn't; he still planned to stay in these parts, at least until he set things right with David. And surely, when Sheriff spoke to Mrs. Doucette, Rees would be freed.

Like jails everywhere, this one was small, dark, and pungent with the combination of urine and vomit left by brawling farm boys. Rees hesitated, steeling himself. He feared enclosures of all kinds, even the ones inside his head. His first impulse was always to run. He closed his eyes and took in a deep breath; he wouldn't leave David again, not now anyway. He stepped inside.

"Have you eaten?" Coulton asked as he closed the door and clanged the lock shut.

"Mrs. Doucette fed me," Rees said, looking around for the cleanest corner in which to sit.

"It'll take a few hours to sort this," Coulton said. "Mean times you can contemplate your sins." His face disappeared and Rees settled down for the wait.

Dinnertime came and went and the sun crossed the zenith and began descending through the afternoon sky. Coulton finally reappeared mid-afternoon. "The Doucette family verified your whereabouts last night," he said, scraping the key into the lock. The door swung open and Rees plunged into the golden sunshine. His hands began shaking as the steel that had kept him together began to dissolve.

"Mr. Rees?" Elder White waited a few feet away. Rees looked at him blankly. Returning from the refuge he went to in his mind always took a few minutes. What was he doing here? White met Rees's gaze, his expression sheepish.

"Mrs. Doucette and all the children confirmed your story," Sheriff Coulton said. His eyebrows rose as he added, "Something about an Indian princess? Henry Doucette, though, although he admitted you slept there, seemed less enthusiastic. He's a jealous man. If he thinks you're cozying up to his wife I'll be finding your body facedown in a ditch."

"Thank you for the warning," Rees said. "So, who is the girl who was killed?"

"I think you should speak to Elder White," said Coulton, spitting his used toothpick to the ground. Now Rees saw a trail of them, like crumbs leading from the witch's house. With a nod, the sheriff crossed the dirt road and started back to the center of town and his store. Rees looked at Elder White.

"Pray forgive me, " he said. Rees did not reply. "Violence does not occur among us. To have something so bestial, so obscene happen on the heels of your arrival . . ."

"What happened exactly?" Rees asked.

"The sheriff didn't tell you?"

"No. Anyway, I would prefer to hear it from you."

"One of our Sisters was found murdered last night. We think it must have happened after evening services." White paused, his face contorting with grief and horror. "She was a new member. . . ."

"I am so sorry," Rees said nodding, knowing he sounded curt. He didn't understand why the Elder had approached him.

"Your son says you have some gift for making clear the darkness surrounding tragedies of this sort." White sounded unusually tentative. Rees stared. How did David even know? But his surprise was quickly submerged by joy. David couldn't entirely hate his father. "Would you be willing to stop with us? In Zion? And puzzle this out for us?"

"In Zion?"

"Please. I feel I must compensate you for my foolish accusation and your spell in jail."

"I'd require a room large enough for my loom," Rees said. "And for a wagonload of yarn. I accepted a weaving commission from Mrs. Doucette and I mean to complete it." Elder White did not hesitate.

"Of course," he said. "Hands to work, hearts to God—that is our way, Mr. Rees. We would never interfere in someone's labor." He hesitated. "Does that mean you accept?" Now Rees hesitated. Looking into a murder meant laying bare all the secrets, and all the strong emotions that came with them. But Elder White had been kind and maybe Rees could elevate himself in David's eyes.

"Yes," he said. "I planned to remain in the area for a while anyway." At that Elder White exhaled a breath.

"Thank you. Do you know the way? If so, I will go on ahead to make the necessary preparations."

"I remember," Rees said. The road went straight to Zion, off the left fork; of course he knew the way. "I'll collect my horse and wagon from the sheriff and be along directly." With a nod, the Elder headed for his buggy and the gray that pulled it. Rees turned and walked back into the town center and Coulton's general store.

When he entered the dim interior, the sheriff, apron-clad, was already presiding over the counter. "You come for your horse and wagon?" he asked.

"Yes. Before I go, though, I'll take some of those crackers and some cheese if you have it. I missed dinner. Do you starve your prisoners so they will come in and purchase something?" Coulton's startled glance melted into a grin.

"That's it, of course. Although I did offer, a couple of hours ago." He brought out a wax-coated wheel and cut off a slab with a wicked sharp knife. Rees picked up a handful of slightly stale crackers. "Gratis," Coulton said. The weaver ate walking up and down the aisles. Piles of barrels and boxes filled the aisles and he could scarcely squeeze around the merchandise. Sacks almost hid the back door to the stables. "I hope you don't leave us too soon."

"Well, you're in luck then," Rees replied. He understood the subtext of Coulton's remark. Despite the Doucettes' testimony, the sheriff still suspected him. "I'll be stopping with the Shakers."

"For how long?"

"At least until the killer of that young woman is caught," Rees said. Coulton blinked and his toothpick popped out of his mouth.

"He will be, I assure you, without your help," he said. Rees shrugged. David had suggested he help and he would not disappoint his son.

"Such a shame, a young woman with her life ahead of her."

"I wouldn't know," Coulton said.

"How was she killed?" When the sheriff did not reply, Rees added, "Since I'm the accused, I think I have a right to know."

"You were accused," Coulton corrected him. "I guess all is forgiven; not many receive an invitation to stay in Zion." Rees smiled noncommittally. "Hmmm." Coulton came to a decision. "Keep your eyes and ears open. Someone may know something."

"I will," Rees said. An easy promise to make, especially since he didn't promise to confide everything he learned to the sheriff. "How was she killed?"

"Hit over the head. Skull cracked like an eggshell."

"Was the instrument recovered?"

"No." Coulton spread his hands in frustration. "No. Could

be a rock I suppose. And Elder White took the body for burial so I haven't even had a chance to look at the wound."

"Is that their way?" Rees asked. "A rapid interment?" He knew if they hadn't buried the girl, he must hurry to examine her. And find out if Elder White was hurrying her into the ground so as to prevent awkward inquiries. Coulton smiled mirthlessly.

"You'll have to find out, I figure. You'll be there. They won't even answer my questions."

"Was she interfered with?" An ugly question but unfortunately the first thing one thought of when the victim was a young and pretty woman.

"No one suggested it. Maybe you'll discover the answer to that as well."

"Maybe," Rees said. He looked at the crumbs of cheese and cracker littering his shirt. He'd finished every scrap of food, almost without tasting it.

"You'll find your mare in one of the stalls in the stable out back," Coulton said. "The wagon is in the barn. Here, I'll let you through the back door." He guided Rees through the maze of boxes and bags to the door at the back. It opened into a storeroom even more cluttered than the store, and from there into the stable yard.

"Thanks for taking care of my Bessie," Rees said.

"You're welcome. She's not a foal, but your mare is a good 'un, sweet-natured and docile. I like horses. Been around them my whole life." As Coulton went back to the store, Rees looked Bessie over carefully. Not only had the sheriff fed and watered her, he'd curried her as well and her coat shone.

"Well, well," Rees said, looking around at the stall. Bessie had enjoyed much better accommodations than her master.

He hitched Bessie to the wagon and started out. By now afternoon was well advanced and he expected the two-hour journey would take him into early evening and milking time. But Bessie, fresh from her rest in Coulton's stables, maintained a smart trot almost the entire distance, and they reached Zion with a few minutes to spare. Elder White was waiting in the street for them.

He instructed Rees to put Bessie and the wagon into the stables and then brought him inside the Dwelling House. His room would be the same one he'd used before but now the second bed, chest, and chair were gone. Fresh hot water waited in the jug for Rees to wash his hands. "Prayers will begin shortly," White said, "and then the dinner bell will ring for supper. Before then, I would be obliged if you would attend me in my office."

So now I'll find out about the particulars, thought Rees with a nod of acknowledgment.

White, strong from a lifetime of labor, helped the weaver carry the loom and the canvas full of yarn inside. It was an easier job with two men, and after reminding Rees of the location of his office, he went upstairs. Rees crossed the street to the stables but discovered some enterprising young men had already put away both Bessie and the wagon. So he went back inside, washed his face and hands, and followed Elder White to his office.

The Elder opened the door to Rees's knock. "I considered putting your loom in the weaving shed," he said. "But as our weavers weave for everybody in the community and you take paid commissions I thought it best to keep you separate."

"I'm pleased with the accommodations," Rees said. "And I often work late at night so I prefer keeping my loom close at hand." The Elder took a chair from a wall peg and bade Rees sit down.

"Although I am sure Sister Chastity welcomed going home

to Mother, the manner of her passing is a sad tragedy for us all," Elder White said. Rees waited. "In fact," the Elder continued after a pause, "I believe the sheriff suspects one of our little Family is guilty."

"It is his job to think of every possibility," Rees said, and then wondered why he was defending the man. The sheriff put him in jail. "Do you know of anyone who dislikes Sister Chastity? Enough to harm her?"

"Of course not," White said immediately, outraged. "We abhor violence of any sort. The interactions among our family members are entirely harmonious." Rees did not contradict the other man although he didn't believe him. Such heavenly harmony was not possible among the sinners on earth; people were people. He was certain that if he dug beneath the smooth serene surface presented by the Brethren, he would find the same rivalries and petty jealousies, the same illicit passions he saw everywhere. But he didn't say any of this aloud. He intended to discover the killer, and that task would prove much simpler with Elder White's cooperation. Unless Elder White himself had killed the woman? Rees spared a moment's consideration of that possibility.

Since White also did not speak, the two men sat in silence. The Elder seemed to be waiting for something and a few moments later the door opened with a little click. A woman entered and White rose to his feet.

"Eldress Agnes Phelps," he said to Rees in introduction. Another ladder-back came down from the peg. The three sat in a circle, carefully far enough apart to prevent any accidental touching of knees. As Rees sat down he examined the new arrival.

She was a small, fine-boned woman with large blue eyes. Rees thought she must have been a beauty as a young woman, but now her blond hair was mostly faded to gray and loose skin hung around her neck in turkey folds. Neither the severe bun nor the linen cap covering her hair flattered her, baring a high forehead scored by discontented lines. She eyed Rees without smiling, weighing him and finding him wanting. Her eyes flashed imperiously to Elder White. He cleared his throat.

"Your son told us you have some experience resolving, um, the sort of difficulty we now face." Elder White smiled suddenly at the man sitting across from him. "He was confident and most persuasive." The burst of joy that swept through Rees prevented him from speaking for a moment.

"I do," he said finally. "Rather too much in fact." When the Elders waited Rees added, "I identified my first murderer while serving in the Continental Army. Since then, I've made several stops where unsolved crimes demanded attention. A case of arson that resulted in the death of a farmer—that was a disgruntled farmhand. The murder of a young girl on the frontier. A deserter who murdered a friend to protect his secret."

"We fear Sheriff Coulton will settle upon one of our members as an easy choice."

"It's possible one of your members *is* the guilty party," Rees pointed out. Neither Elder White nor Eldress Phelps contradicted him. Of course they must already have considered that possibility. "I'll be glad to do my humble best," Rees added after a moment of silence, "but I must speak to everyone here, women as well as men. Then, if none of your Family is guilty, I'll search farther afield."

"With the Sisters I must be present as well," Sister Agnes said, her voice slow and quiet. Did anyone else hear that undercurrent of icy contempt?

"No," he said. "Neither you nor Elder White can be present. Your community members may not be willing to speak openly in your hearing."

The two Elders exchanged a look. The Eldress repeated, "You may not speak to any of our female members alone."

"Isn't there any woman you know whom you trust, who might be willing to act as chaperone," Rees said. "Even Mrs. Doucette . . ."

Again the two Believers exchanged a glance. "We'll discuss this," White said. "In the meantime, you may begin speaking with the Brethren. Is there anything else you need?"

"The ability to wander at will on your property. I want to look into every barn, every shed."

"Of course. You may wander everywhere the Brethren go. They'll answer you openly and honestly; a commitment to honesty is one of our beliefs."

As it is to most of those who lie to me, Rees thought, hiding his thoughts with a smile.

"But you must not touch or speak to any of our Sisters without the chaperone present," Sister Agnes said, even more forcefully than before.

"Then give me a place, or places, and opportunities to speak to them," Rees said. "Another woman will know far more about Sister Chastity than any of the Brothers." That made sense and both Elders nodded in unison.

"You may, of course, participate in our unions and our services," Eldress Phelps said, softening her tone. "And there may be . . . we might know someone who will help."

"I'll make myself available to discuss your progress at any time," White said. Rees nodded. The Eldress was by far the stronger of the two, so usually they worked together in concert. But a thread of competition infused this relationship as well, and sometimes Elder White must thrust himself forward. Few men would behave differently.

"I'll keep you apprised of my activities," Rees promised. He did not guarantee full disclosure. Religious or no, one or both of them might also be guilty. "And what did you think of Sister Chastity?"

"I spoke with her only once," White said in surprise. "At the occasion of her joining the Family. I barely retain a memory of her."

Rees watched the subtle shift of the Elder's eyes away from his own and knew he lied. White remembered the young woman all right; this must be pursued at a later date. "And you?" Rees said, his gaze moving to Eldress Agnes. She hesitated for a long moment, gathering her thoughts. When she spoke, Rees saw her choosing each word with care.

"She left an unhappy marriage and brought her two children with her. I found her somewhat flighty. But I never doubted her desire to sign the Covenant and join our Family. Although one does not want to accuse unjustly, I wonder if her husband followed her here."

"He did try to take the children two weeks after her arrival," White agreed, almost blurting it out in his relief.

The sudden clang of the dinner bell sounded throughout the village. " 'Tis time for prayers," said Elder White. "We must be prompt."

"Sister Chastity's past life will be a good place to start," Rees said, putting out his hand to stay them. "Tomorrow I'll apply to you for her full name and the direction of her husband." White nodded as he rose from his chair and turned to hang it upon a peg. "One final thing," Rees said since the Elders seemed prepared to hurry from the room. "Has your Sister been buried yet?"

White turned, his expression grim. "No. Not yet. That is our sad duty tomorrow."

"I must see the body myself," Rees said.

"Must you?" the Eldress cried out, genuinely distressed.

"I wouldn't ask if it weren't so very important," Rees said firmly. "I want to examine the wound." The Elder hesitated.

"She is laid out in the icehouse. Tomorrow morning the women will wash and wrap her."

"Then I must see her tonight."

"Very well," White sighed. "I'll take you after supper."

"Very good," Rees said, throwing his chair upon the peg. He followed the Elders downstairs.

Chapter Three

❧

While the Elders went to the Meetinghouse for prayers Rees walked around the village. He stepped through the Dwelling House and paused. Shakers were approaching from every direction, streaming toward the meeting, a dozen men and a handful of women. Rees followed the path in the opposite direction, to the left around the Dwelling House. A brick kitchen, separate from the residence, was just behind the dining room at the other end of a dirt path. Two gardens, a kitchen garden and an herb garden, beautifully neat and well tended, sprawled to one side. Paths led to the right, and to additional small buildings, and then straight east, to fields and barns and stables. Rees went back inside the Dwelling House and the waiting area to wait for the others to arrive for dinner. He didn't know how long prayers might last and whether he had the time for further exploration and he didn't want to be late. Punctuality was a virtue among the Shakers.

He spent twenty minutes, maybe half an hour, alone before other men began appearing. Now that Rees knew he would be spending a few weeks or more here, he paid more attention to them. The majority of the men were either older or boys just coming in adulthood. Few were Rees's age, what he thought of as the prime of life. That made sense, he thought; men of his age were concerned with families and the living needed to support them. David came in with the same curly-headed young man of yesterday. If Rees had not met his son yesterday, after the several years' break, he would not have recognized the boy. He was sunburned from working outside and dressed as all the other men were, in dark breeches and white linen shirt. This time David offered a small nod. Rees felt a glow of happiness light in his belly. If David had recommended him to Elder White he could not entirely hate his father. And maybe he even wanted to keep his father close by for a time. Rees felt happier than he had for a long time. A few minutes later Elder White arrived. The tinkling bell chimed and the doors opened for supper.

Quietly everyone found their seats, eighteen men on one side, about thirty women on the other. David sat at a different table today, with the children instead of the men. When everyone was seated, Elder White rose to his feet. "This is William Rees," he said. "David's father. He will be stopping with us for a little while." Everyone nodded politely but no one spoke.

The Sisters began bringing out huge platters of food. Rees paid more attention today; he hoped this meal was a sample of what he might expect. Hash, made with the leftovers from dinner's roast pork, was chopped with herbs, onions, and potatoes and smothered in a rich brown gravy. Hominy, flavored with marjoram and rosemary, along with hot bread fresh from the oven and colorful piccalilli completed the meal. Rees ate until he thought he would burst. And then dessert, a cake made with the last of the dried apples. If he continued eating with such gusto Rees feared he would burst his breeches.

When dinner ended and the Believers separated, drifting away to evening chores, Elder White said grimly, "Come, Mr. Rees. I'll show you the springhouse." He collected a lantern and they set out through the golden late-afternoon sun.

They circled around the Dwelling House, angling toward the small buildings at the back. "Smokehouse," White said, pointing to the small structure nearest the kitchen. "Weaving shed." That sat across from the smokehouse. "Sister Chastity was found here. We think she may have decided to work late."

"I'll want to come back here," Rees said. He didn't expect to find anything on the rough gravel but would look nonetheless.

The path paralleled the main street; Rees caught glimpses of it through the buildings, and finally the lane circled around to meet it once again. Elder White crossed the small bridge over the rushing stream and plunged into the trees on the other side. Although late-afternoon rays gilded the road and the treetops, here underneath the trees it was already dark. The springhouse was visible, barely, and Rees knew it would be shadowed and gloomy inside, despite the one small window. White lit the lantern and handed it to him.

"I'll wait out here," he said.

Rees went inside. The fast-moving water underneath the floor and the sawdust-covered ice blocks kept the interior temperature in the fifties. The faint greenish light struggling though the small window did not provide more than a ghostly light, like swimming underwater. Rees shivered. He wished he'd brought his coat. But he stopped thinking about his discomfort when he saw the body lying on the ice blocks in the center of the room.

She looked peaceful, and someone had straightened her limbs. Rees held up the lantern so the candlelight fell fully upon her face. She looked younger than he expected, barely out of her teens. Few lines marked her forehead and a childlike roundness remained to her cheeks. He knew she was probably in her twenties, but life had used her gently. The light struck red and gold sparks from her curly hair, and although it had looked dull in the gloom Rees now suspected it was actually a bright coppery red. Rees wondered where her linen cap was and swung the lantern from side to side until he finally found it, lying on the sawdust floor. When he picked it up he knew why the woman who laid her out had not replaced it upon her head; clotted blood stiffened the back of the linen. Rees suddenly wished he had not eaten so much supper. Closing his eyes, he took several deep breaths until he steadied once again.

Turning her over and watching her limbs flop limply forward brought on another spasm of nausea, but it passed when he had settled her upon her stomach. He bent over the wound. As the sheriff had said, she had been struck from behind, but the injury was not upon the right side. The blow had cracked the bone on the upper left as though she'd turned toward her attacker. When Rees ran his fingers over the wound he clearly felt a depression surrounded by cracks radiating outward. Oddly, the walls of the depression felt smooth, as though the weapon that had struck her was round and even. Rees could not imagine what that could be. He wiped his fingers upon his handkerchief and turned her over once again. He wondered if she had known the person behind her.

He examined her hands. The recent calluses bore fresh blisters; underneath them the skin was baby soft, the nails well cared for. Sister Chastity had not been used to manual labor before joining the Shakers; those hands certainly did not belong to a farmer's wife.

Although her clothing was made of the sturdy homespun used by the Shakers, her stockings were silk, finely spun, and Rees suspected they were of French manufacture. When he turned up the hem of her plan homespun skirt he found her hidden underskirt was made of the same silk. Sister Chastity had not resisted the lure of such pleasures; he suspected she had not even tried very hard. How had she managed to hide this worldly vice from Eldress Phelps?

He spent a few moments gazing into the still face. Despite the ashen pallor, she was a pretty girl and he couldn't believe celibacy would hold much attraction for her. Certainly she must have longed for male attention. Maybe she found it, Rees thought, staring at the silk stockings.

He went back outside. Shadows made Elder White just a darker blur beneath the trees. "She was so young," he said. "And she leaves two little ones besides."

"She is a very pretty woman," Rees said. "Barely more than a girl." He handed the lantern to the other man.

"I met her only once, at the signing of the Covenant," White said quickly. "She committed herself completely to the tenets of Mother Lee." Rees thought of the silk stockings but did not mention them. There seemed little point now.

"Tomorrow I'll take her name and the directions to her husband's farm," he said. "I'll want to speak to him." He looked at the darkening sky. "And I'd like to look at the place she was found again, please."

"She lay upon the stones just outside the weaving shed," White said with a sigh. "But she was struck last night and with the dew and the many feet that have trodden there today, I doubt much remains . . ." Nonetheless, after they crossed the bridge, he veered right, onto the path to the shed.

The setting sun streamed across the fields in long golden bands but the path outside the weaving house lay in shadow. Rees opened the door and peered into the shed. Windows, with real glass, circled the room; even now sunlight bathed the interior in brightness. All the looms and spinning wheels backed up to the windows so that the Sisters could work comfortably. As

Rees looked at the light pouring through the windows and the large well-built looms, he felt a flash of envy. For a weaver, these were as close to perfect working conditions as possible.

When he closed the door, cutting off the last rays of sunset, the path seemed very dark. White handed Rees the lantern. He knelt upon the path and in the spill of candlelight examined the stony track. This was Maine and stones of all sizes littered the ground. Even with the lantern it was almost too dark to see detail. "Where exactly did she lie?" he asked White.

"I do not know," the Elder said. "She was removed from the path when I saw her."

Rees gently began turning over the stones. He found a large one stained brown, probably with dried blood. Rees went for his handkerchief and then remembered he'd wiped his fingers on it. "May I trouble you for a rag in which to wrap this stone," he said. White dashed into the weaving shed and returned with a practice cloth. Rees wrapped the stone and stowed it in his pocket.

With that as his guide, he deduced the location of her head and began working backward until he found a deeply scuffed section. Her attacker had struck her here and she had fallen forward. But other than a few smudges left by booted feet no mark remained of the Sister's killer.

"What time would she have come out here?" Rees asked.

"Half-past eight or later," White said. "She was in union before that."

"Then how could she see?" Rees protested. "The sun would have already set and weaving by lantern light, while possible, is difficult." White shook his head.

"Eldress Phelps says Sister Chastity was unskilled as a weaver. We believe she came here to practice." Unconsciously Rees shook his head. Unlikely. The shed would have been too dark, even with the lantern. And an unskilled weaver would surely have found the work impossible in so little light. Rees thought again of those silk stockings. "She was a very motivated new member," White insisted. Rees frowned but did not argue.

"Maybe so," he said.

In silence, the two men followed the path back to the Dwelling House. As they approached the yellow structure, White said, "You are welcome to join us tonight at union."

Rees, who thought the day had already been too full, said, "I'll be pleased to join you some future evening. But today has already been busy and very tiring, so I hope you won't take offense if I decline." Elder White nodded.

"Of course. I'll send someone to your room with fresh hot water."

"Thank you," Rees said gratefully, wondering if he still stank of the jail.

"If you'll put your clothing outside," White added, confirming Rees's suspicions, "the Sisters will wash them. They'll be returned to you. Do you have clean clothing to wear? If not, we'll be happy to lend you breeches and a shirt."

"Thank you," Rees said. "I do have clean clothing with me." He'd never taken his satchel inside so when he hurled himself angrily into the wagon after his argument with Caroline it was still under his seat. White nodded and opened the door into the Dwelling House. As Rees turned into his room, now dim and shadowy with dusk, the Elder went up the stairs.

Rees took a chair down from a peg and sat down to remove his boots. A tentative knock announced the arrival of his hot water by a gangly twelve-year-old. Rees pulled the curtains and lit a candle to bathe by. The smooth slip of hot water and lavender soap across his body felt like heaven and he lingered over his ablutions until the water went cold. As instructed he put his dirty clothing outside the door. Then he lay down on the bed, just to rest his fatigue-gritty eyes for a moment.

He awoke at dawn the following morning. The rising sun peeked around the curtains, throwing bars of gold onto the opposite wall. Rees pulled out clean clothing from the satchel stored under his bed. When he looked outside the door he found a new jug of hot water, now cooled to lukewarm. As he quickly washed his hands and face, the bell began to ring for breakfast.

Afterward Elder White called him aside and handed him a slip of crumpled paper. "Mr. Parker owns a farm in Surry, due south of Zion."

"Does he even know of his wife's death?"

Elder White hesitated. "I sent a letter to him," he said. "Along with a general letter to any family she might have remaining. I must rely on Mr. Parker for delivery of that message as I know nothing of her birth family. But I suspect Mr. Parker hasn't yet received that package. You might find yourself breaking the sad news to him. Do you know how to reach Surry?"

"Yes," Rees said, tucking the paper into his pocket. Surry lay on the direct route from Massachusetts north into the District. He had driven through the town more times than he could count.

"I understand the Parker farm is both large and productive. Sister Chastity sacrificed many comforts to join us." That explained the new calluses and silk stockings. "We will bury her this afternoon, before evening chores," the Elder added heavily. "Will you attend?" Rees wondered if the young woman had living parents who would mourn her passing. Would her estranged husband grieve?

"Of course," Rees said. He would mourn her for the sake of her children and for the young life cut off so suddenly.

He left the Elder's office and went downstairs, planning to begin warping his loom. But when he opened the door, he surprised one of the Sisters busily sweeping the floor. He stopped short and she uttered a scream and dropped the broom. As she prepared to flee he held out his hand.

"Wait. I don't want to interrupt your work. When would it be convenient for me to return?" She stopped and her hand rose to cover her mouth, but not before Rees saw the harelip. With her hand shielding that imperfection, her pale luminous skin and bright blue eyes made her lovely. "I've taken a weaving commission from Mrs. Doucette," Rees said quickly, trying to put the girl at ease. "I'll need to schedule times to weave."

"Jane Doucette?" Her speech was mushy but understandable.

"Yes." How did she know? He watched some of her tension evaporate.

"After breakfast until ten thirty," she said. "I'll clean your room last."

"I'll make myself scarce after ten thirty," Rees agreed. "And it won't be every day. I know I'll have errands to run." After several moments of awkward silence, he realized he was standing in front of the door, barring her escape. Hastily he moved aside and she darted past him. As she fled through the door he said to her back, "What do they call you?"

"Mouse," she replied to his surprise.

"Not Hope or Faith?"

She turned around and asked shyly, "Is it true what they say; you're here to find Sister Chastity's killer?"

"Yes, it's true," Rees said.

"Good," she said fiercely. "Good." Although her hand continued to hide the split lip, her cheeks rounded and rose and Rees thought she offered him a tentative smile. He smiled back.

"I'm very pleased to meet you, Mouse," he said. She ducked her head at him and trotted down the hall. Rees closed the door and turned to the loom. First, he needed to assemble the pieces.

Elder White reminded everyone at dinner's end that the funeral would take place immediately. Rees felt the chicken he'd eaten turn handsprings in his stomach. Although the expressions around him ranged from indifferent pity to genuine sorrow, no one looked at all guilty. "Did you know her?" Rees asked the old man beside him. The bearded gentleman looked at Rees for a moment, considered reprimanding him for speaking, but chose to answer instead.

"I did not."

After dinner they walked in a group from the Dining Hall to the large white Meetinghouse at the end of the street. Men and women divided, entering by opposite doors and sitting upon wooden benches across from one another. Elder White and Eldress Phelps sat in the open space between the pews with Sister Chastity in an open plain pine coffin between them.

The Sister, née Catherine Parker, was garbed in Sunday white. Except for the coppery curls visible around her linen cap, she was as completely white as a marble effigy. All marks of her violent death had been erased and she seemed peaceful and very very young.

Elder White rose to his feet to speak first. "Although our Sister was only lately come among us, she exemplified the most worthy of our ideals. Even her name, which she chose when she signed the Covenant, speaks of her commitment. Our small family is much diminished by our loss. However, in the midst of our sorrow, we can rejoice that she is returning home to Mother."

As Elder White returned to his seat, Eldress Phelps rose in her turn. Mouse, and a few other Sisters, had begun to weep.

"She willingly struggled to learn those tasks she did not know," the Eldress said. "Although rather more light-minded than was proper and too talkative, Sister Chastity possessed a cheerful disposition." As she spoke, slowly and with many pauses, Rees grew increasingly certain she had not liked this young woman. "I received instruction from this Sister as well as offering it," the Eldress continued. "She taught me patience and forbearance. I believe that, because of Sister Chastity, I am better fitted for the Ministry. I will miss you, Sister."

When the Eldress returned to her seat, no one moved or spoke for several minutes. In the silence, Rees could hear sounds of suppressed sobbing. He marked the sorrowers in his mind; they must know Sister Chastity best of all. But when two of them, identical in their Shaker garb except for the hair visible around the caps, spoke, their eulogies were as bland as vanilla pudding. Rees could have done as well without knowing the girl at all.

Finally, one of the Brethren rose and spoke of her skill in baking and another of her excellent and careful darning. When no one else rose up, the funeral was deemed complete. Six muscular Brethren came to the front to pick up the coffin and bear it to the burying place. Rees fell into step with the other men, following the coffin from the Meetinghouse. They carried the box to the back; that was traditional enough. But only the recently dug grave in the copse of trees betrayed the purpose of this space; no headstones nor crosses marked the final resting places of the departed. When the coffin slipped into the earth

and the Brethren covered it, Elder White planted a small sap-
ling in the mounded soil. Rees looked around at the trees trembling in the light breeze and realized many of them, if not all,
marked the graves of those who had gone home to Mother. They
served as living memorials. Rees approved, preferring the dancing saplings to cold stone.

Chapter Four

The next morning, Friday, Rees set out immediately after breakfast for Surry and the estranged husband of Sister Chastity. He was not eager to make this trip. If Mr. Parker did not know of his wife's death, and Rees expected that to be true since he had not arrived at Zion to demand his children, the conversation with him was bound to be an emotional one. Rees's annoyance with Elder White, who should have been making this journey, was tempered with the knowledge that he would have wanted to speak to the husband in any case. Besides, the day was fair and Bessie frisky, eager to prance out upon the road. After the first few minutes Rees began relaxing into the ride.

They rattled over the small bridge and through the trees that fringed the stream. Rees could see a small building in the left distance where laundry flapped in the breeze. Beyond it lay the small copse of trees that marked the end of the Shaker property. The thickly forested triangle of land on the right occluded the Surry road, screening Zion and its main street from travelers. Within a few minutes, he pulled out onto that road, heading due south. A small dirt lane looped away to the right, heading northwest, but after that Rees saw no signs of habitation for many miles.

For a time the road wound around the shoulder of a western

hill, the granite bedrock forming a wall on the road's right edge. The stream that meandered through Zion now rushed down a gorge on Rees's left. Fields began appearing on the opposite bank; he was coming into Surry. He stopped the wagon for a moment. From the bottom of the streambed, fields gradually sloped upward to a sun-splashed summit. Small black-and-brown-mottled cattle dotted the green, so far away he could not hear their lowing over the rushing water below. With that bucolic scene before him, he drank the ale and ate the bread and cheese he had brought with him.

He turned Bessie around. They rode down the last slope, turning right in the puddle of sun at the bottom and saw Surry spread out in the shallow valley below. He stopped at the local tavern for directions to the Parker place and set off again, this time angling northwest along the banks of the Surry River. Within minutes he began to see fields full of the black-and-white cattle described by the barkeep. Hundreds of dairy cattle, all fat and sleek. No wonder the man laughed when Rees asked about the Parker farm; he was clearly the largest and richest landowner in the area. When Rees rode up the drive to the farmhouse, it sparkled blindingly with new white paint. A black servant, standing on the side porch and shaking a small rug, shouted, "Cyrus, Fetch Mrs. Hollister. Mr. Parker has a gentleman visitor."

Stiff, his knees and hips locked into place, Rees staggered clumsily from the wagon seat. As he climbed slowly up the porch steps an older woman with dark hair scraped back into a tight knob under her cap came through the door to meet him.

She eyed Rees suspiciously. "Yes?"

"My name is Will Rees. I must speak to Mr. Parker on a matter of great importance."

"About what?"

"I'm sorry but that's for Mr. Parker."

"Mr. Parker is in the fields right now. He won't leave his work without a good reason." She came forward to the top of the step as though to bar his way. With the sun's full light upon her, Rees realized Mrs. Hollister was still a young woman, younger than the severe hairstyle would have her appear. A few smile lines gave character to her face and her plump lips were rosy and alluring. Rees looked at her, imagining her without the mobcap and with her hair loosened and spilling over her shoulders. Oh yes. Now he wondered about the real relationship between Mr. Parker and his housekeeper. She stared back defiantly, her face turning pink, but without any of the deference of a housekeeper.

"I have news of Catherine Parker, his wife," Rees said, emphasizing the last two words. Mrs. Hollister paled, her hand rising to her white throat.

"You aren't one of those religious quacks, are you?"

"No, I am not a Shaker," Rees said.

"She wants to come back, doesn't she? Well, they're divorced so she can't."

"I think any decision must rest with Mr. Parker, don't you?" Rees said.

Wordlessly she pointed to the chair on the porch. Then she hurried back into the house, and a moment later Rees heard her calling, "Jack, Jack. Go find your master. Tell him it's important. Run."

Mrs. Hollister may not have wanted to welcome the messenger from her master's wife but her upbringing would not permit rudeness. A few minutes later, she invited Rees inside, to the parlor, and offered him a glass of lemonade. "No thank you," Rees said, standing awkwardly in the center of the floor. He wished he'd removed his muddy boots at the door. He was afraid to step on the flowered carpet, afraid to sit in the delicate furniture, afraid to move lest he leave a spot of mud behind him. He could easily imagine Catherine Parker sitting in here, her refuge from the dirty chaotic world of the farm outside.

Through the lace upon the windows, Rees saw Mr. Parker ride up on a glossy bay. A few minutes later his boots thudded up the front stairs and into the central hall. "Mr. Rees?" Mr. Parker halted at the door. "Please come into my office. I don't know why Edna put you in here." Rees joined his host with alacrity. He knew why the housekeeper had put him in what was clearly Catherine's space; she wanted him to feel unwelcome. "That parlor . . . more appropriate to a city house than a farm, but Catherine insisted." Rees nodded. True enough, although this farm was a rich one. Mr. Parker may have been in the fields, but, looking at his spotless boots, Rees doubted he was doing anything more than supervising his laborers from the saddle. The image of Elder White's calloused hands rose into Rees's mind; on the Shaker farm everyone worked.

Parker gestured Rees into a room on the other side of the house. The uncarpeted floor was clean but badly scuffed and stacked ledgers covered every available surface. Parker scooped away one pile from a chair and motioned Rees into it. Parker himself sat down in the desk chair and looked at Rees for a long silent moment.

"Did Edna offer you something to drink?"

"Lemonade."

"You need a man's drink. Whiskey or ale?"

"Ale, please."

"Edna," Parker bellowed. "Edna."

She knew what he wanted. When she appeared a moment later she carried a tray with a pitcher of ale, two glasses, and a plate of small cakes. Parker poured out a glassful and pushed the pitcher toward Rees. "You must be thirsty. It's a long way from Durham." After a heartbeat he added, "What is the message from Catherine?" Rees put down his glass, suddenly losing his appreciation of the very fine ale. Parker said nothing and Rees saw that the other man was neither excited nor worried about the message. Instead he looked wary.

"I'm sorry," Rees said. "Your wife is dead."

"What! That can't be!" Clearly Parker had not expected this. "What happened?" Tears of shock and maybe grief rushed to his eyes. Leaping to his feet, he stalked around the room until he mastered his emotions.

"No one is quite sure," Rees said. "She was found lying on a path, with a severe injury to her head."

"Severe injury?" Parker drained his glass at a gulp. "Those mealymouthed bastards killed her?"

"I, um, even the sheriff doesn't know for sure," Rees stammered, startled by the depth of Parker's fury.

"Of course one of them did it," Parker declared. "It's not natural, how they live."

"Why did she join the Shakers?" Rees asked.

"She didn't want to be a wife and mother." Blood reddened his cheeks. "We quarreled about it. And instead of telling her to go home and care for her family, they offered her an escape. And then she took my children with her."

"How long since you've seen her?"

"Not since the autumn," Parker said angrily. "But I went to Zion about six weeks back. Wanted my children." He spun around. "Can I take them now?"

"Perhaps," Rees said. The estrangement between husband and wife and the distance argued against Parker as the murderer, but his desire to reclaim his children provided a strong motive.

"Well, you can tell that . . . that Elder I'm coming for them.

He better have them ready to go, not even try to keep me from them. I want them to grow up properly. Catherine only took them to hurt me." He sighed. As his anger seeped away he just looked tired. "Catherine was so beautiful. Have you seen her?" Rees shook his head. "Her hair was the most beautiful shade of gold and copper. But she was always too delicate to be a farmer's wife. She hated being around the animals and wept when we butchered in the fall." He shook his head. "She named my daughter Lavinia. Lavinia! A farmer's daughter should be named Jane or Sally, not Lavinia." He sighed again and for a moment he stared into space. "Did she suffer?"

"No," Rees said, although he couldn't guess. "She was going back from the weaving shed—"

"Weaving!" Parker shook his head again. "I certainly can't imagine my Catherine warming a weaving bench."

"Sheriff Coulton will probably ride out here to ask you a few questions," Rees said.

Parker shrugged. "I haven't been alone at all for this past week. The sheriff is barking up the wrong tree if he thinks I'm the guilty man. I've nothing to hide." His eyelid twitched, a faint spasm, but Rees saw it. Well, Parker had something to hide. But what? Edna the housekeeper?

Although they talked for a few more minutes, Parker added nothing further.

Rees rode away from the farm wondering about the quarrel that had prompted Catherine Parker to become Sister Chastity in a Shaker community. Mr. Parker did not seem cruel or stingy; witness her dainty pink-and-white parlor. Yet she'd surrendered all her comforts to escape. And Rees didn't think Parker was the killer. Of course, he'd been fooled before.

———

The next morning after breakfast, Elder White approached Rees. "May I see you for a moment?" he asked. Rees followed him to his office. When both men were seated, Elder White said, "Eldress Phelps and I discussed the matter of the chaperone and we believe we've found someone suitable. Sister Agnes spoke with her and she is willing to be of service to us. They will be along directly."

"All right," Rees said, looking at the other man in surprise. He didn't understand the hesitation in Elder White's voice.

"I feel I must explain something to you," White said. "So you fully understand." He held Rees's gaze for a moment. "Her name is Lydia Jane Farrell. She lived among us, as our Sister. She made a mistake. You shouldn't . . . It would be rude and unkind to question her about her separation from the Family. Through it all, we have remained on good terms. She knows us from the inside, yet our prohibitions no longer apply to her. And she is willing to help."

"Very well," Rees said, now more curious about the woman than before. The Elder rose to unhook a chair from its peg on the wall. Rees leaped up to fetch the second one. At that moment Eldress Phelps's confident knock sounded upon the door and she came in.

The woman who followed appeared to be a Believer. The bertha all the women wore around their shoulders topped her dark claret-colored dress, cut in the same simple style as the Eldress's, and she wore the square linen cap upon her head. In the sunlight the hair revealed at the cap's edges sparkled with red highlights. She met Rees's gaze straightforwardly from eyes as dark a blue as the ocean. She did not smile.

"William Rees, weaver. Lydia Jane Farrell," Elder White said.

"It is a pleasure," Rees said. Miss Farrell inclined her head but did not speak, her demeanor polite but not friendly.

"When do you want to begin speaking with the Sisters?" Eldress Phelps asked Rees.

"Monday, I think," he said. Tomorrow, Sunday, would be devoted to Services.

"You may use this office," suggested Elder White.

"I believe if we speak to the Sisters as they work, they will speak more freely to us," Miss Farrell said. Elder White blinked in surprise. Rees turned to look at the young woman curiously. She smiled slightly and went on. "We may discover much more of importance. Calling them into the office will surely alarm them and make them too uncomfortable to speak."

Both Elder White and Eldress Phelps looked at Rees. He hesitated a moment. Miss Farrell's easy assumption of authority rankled; still her idea was a good one. "Yes," he agreed. "I think that might be best." For a moment everyone stared at him, Miss Farrell more astonished than the others. Rees wondered if she'd expected him to protest. He smiled at her innocently, flustering her and raising a pink flush into her cheeks.

"Very well, Mr. Rees," she said. "I will meet you outside the Dwelling House at eight thirty Monday morning." Rees inclined his head in acknowledgment. With polite nods all around, Miss Farrell withdrew.

She left behind a silence thick with unspoken remarks. Rees suspected at least part of the reason for her separation from this Family was her outspokenness. Harmony rested in part upon obedience and he couldn't see Miss Farrell easily curbing her impulses. "She is . . . mercurial," Eldress Phelps said at last. "But she will be of great help to you."

"No doubt," Rees said. Excusing himself, he retreated to his bedchamber. The early-morning sun streaming through the windows brought heat as well as light; he threw up the sashes to catch a breeze. Other than the sounds common to a farm—the mooing of a cow, a rooster's crowing—the village was silent. Peculiarly silent. The Shakers did not shout or banter or argue. Rees found the silence disturbing.

He finished drawing the threads through the heddles, sleyed the reed, and tied off the warp. He wove a few practice rows to test the tension. The clacking of the treadles and the swish of the shuttle flying through the warp broke the unnatural silence. Rees relaxed into the rhythm, losing all track of time. A sudden tentative knock upon the door sent him leaping to his feet.

"I'm sorry, Mr. Rees," said Mouse through the door. "But it is eleven . . ."

"Of course," said Rees, finishing the row and resting the shuttle upon the top of the loom. He brushed his hand over the smooth twill; Mrs. Doucette would be pleased.

As Mouse bustled in with her broom and assorted cleaning supplies Rees headed for the door. But he didn't go through. Turning, he said, "Mouse, you know I am looking into Sister Chastity's death with the blessing of Elder White and Eldress Phelps?" She nodded. "The Elders have found someone to accompany me, a Lydia Jane Farrell. Do you know her?" Mouse nodded again. "Do you trust her?"

"She keeps bees," Mouse said. "She was a Sister once, a few years ago." She hesitated, trying to decide how much to confide. Rees waited quietly, knowing that pressing her would only drive her into silence. "She is opinionated and outspoken but she was always kind to me."

"Very well. You wept at Sister Chastity's funeral. Did you know her well?"

"Of course. We all work together. We shared a room when she first arrived."

"And what did you think of her?" Rees asked.

Mouse remained silent for several moments, her face working. Rees sensed many comments unsaid. He suspected Sister Chastity had not been kind; nothing about Catherine Parker suggested a woman tolerant of imperfection. "She learned the tasks quickly," Mouse said at last, "but she was always prone to loud chatter. Eldress Phelps spoke to her more than once about gossiping. And here am I . . ."

"This is not gossip," Rees said quickly. "How am I to find the killer if I don't know about the victim?" He paused to let that sink in. "The other Sisters who were weeping, who are they? You sat next to a fair-haired girl and in the row before you were two other Sisters, one dark and the other freckled." And plain, but Rees chose not to add that.

"Oh, that is Sister Tilly," said Mouse absently. "She weeps to see the mice cleared from a kitchen. She weeps because she is tenderhearted; Sister Chastity was never very patient with her." Mouse's flash of perceptiveness surprised Rees and he looked at her with renewed attention. "Marguerite Languedela'or sat next to her. We are not supposed to make special friends but Marguerite and Chastity . . ." Mouse hesitated and then continued more slowly. "They never snapped or were cross with one another, but they mocked the rest of us behind our backs." Mocked *you*, Rees thought.

"And the fair-haired girl?"

"Sister Anne. After Chastity left my room, she shared with Anne. I never sensed any particular warmth between them, but still . . ." Sudden tears flooded her eyes. "Those poor children."

"I know," Rees said. And poor Chastity. Despite her faults she did not deserve to have her life snatched from her. "Will another roommate be assigned to Anne now?"

"Maybe," Mouse said.

"Thank you, Mouse," Rees said. "If you think of anything else, please tell me. I value your insight." A flush of surprised pleasure lit her cheeks.

"Oh, but after next weekend I won't be assigned to cleaning the rooms of the Brethren," she cried in dismay. "I'll be in the kitchens."

"Will you? Why?"

"We all rotate the jobs. All work is equally valued by Mother. Only the Sisters assigned to the children remain with them forever. How I wish . . . But Eldress Phelps thinks I might scare them." Although she did not weep, her eyes were filled with a deep aching sorrow. An accident of fate had barred Mouse from a home and family of her own and now Eldress Phelps had removed Mouse's only other chance to give her love to children. Rees wondered if the Eldress knew how cruel that appeared.

"I'll be speaking with almost all the Sisters and the Brethren," he said awkwardly into the uncomfortable silence. "We will speak again." With a nod, Mouse turned away and Rees quietly withdrew.

Chapter Five

After a rainy night, dawn blew in cool and damp. The watery sun that tried to pierce the clouds did little to warm the air. Rees joined the Believers on their way to the Meetinghouse, understanding that he was privileged to witness their service. Although the Shakers had welcomed visitors in their early days, they did so no longer, and Rees's invitation came about only because of his unusual status.

He followed the men through their door and sat in the last bench. Most of the Sisters, all twenty-five dressed in white, sat on the other side. Lydia Jane Farrell stood out, a crow among the doves, in her indigo gown. For a time no one spoke or moved. Then Elder White rose and began addressing his flock with sporadic homilies. Then the benches were pushed back and although Rees saw no signal the congregation burst into song. The Shakers formed themselves into two circles, the women a pale center for the outer rim of darker-clad men. With the Sister circle revolving one way and the Brethren turning in the opposite direction, the knot began to move around the hall. Rees stared incredulously as the members began moving in a synchronized hop, their hands gesturing and their voices chanting wild airs. Religious fervor held them totally in thrall, oblivious to all others in the room. Even Mouse was so caught up she did not hide her split lip.

Rees glanced at Miss Farrell, her back pressed against the opposite wall, her expression one of longing. She turned suddenly and hurried out, her hand pressed to her mouth.

Impulsively Rees followed. He did not immediately see her when he reached the street; he saw no dark form hurrying down the wooden sidewalk. Then a movement in the alley between the Blacksmith and Meetinghouse caught his eye. Rees sped after her, not pausing to consider what he might say when he reached her.

When he whipped around the Blacksmith's he saw her at the top of the slope. She had removed her white linen cap and loosened her hair. Her dark-red braid dropped onto the dark gown like a rope of gold. As it unplaited it transformed into a shining fall of burnished copper.

She whirled suddenly, staring at him in fury. Rees, lifting his hands calmingly, backed up a few steps. "Are you following me for a reason?" she demanded.

"I just wanted to ask you a few questions," he said, wondering why the hell he'd run after her.

"Monday is not soon enough?"

"I don't want to ask you anything in public," Rees said. She eyed him for a moment, her expression going still and cold. "Did you know Sister Chastity?"

"No. I saw her a few times, that's all." She seemed surprised by his question. "She arrived after I was already . . . gone. Why?"

"I'm curious about her. I want to know what she was like. One never knows what will affect the investigation, what will provide the key that makes everything clear."

"It was not any of the Family," she said.

"I'll see," he said. Everyone had the same opinion, but Rees was not so convinced.

"Elder White and Eldress Phelps bade me assist you. I'll tell you everything I've heard." Rees nodded and looked around for a large rock, a plentiful commodity in Maine. He sat down. She did the same and for a moment they both sat in silence. Rees looked at the path, beaten by many feet, winding up the hill behind her. He wondered if she lived back there, with the bees mentioned by Mouse.

"The other Sisters did not care for her," Miss Farrell said. "Sister Chastity was a gossip, and not a kind one. Anyone with an imperfection, like Mouse, came in for cruel slurs. Mouse shared a room with her, did you know that? Chastity was so taken with her own consequence, and so cruel to Mouse, that Eldress Phelps stepped in and moved Chastity to another bedchamber."

"Is it possible one of the Sisters disliked her enough to kill her?" Rees asked.

"Certainly not!" she said.

"One of the Brethren then?"

"Contact between the Sisters and Brothers is very limited."

"But not impossible," Rees said, noticing she had not really answered his question.

"I don't want to believe any of the Shakers capable of this terrible sin," she said, her expression agonized.

"Likeliest, they are all innocent," Rees said. "I'm speaking to others as well. Did you know she had been married?" Miss Farrell looked at him in surprise.

"No. Was she divorced then?"

"And there were children," Rees went on.

"I didn't know. How terrible," she said.

"Is there anything else you can tell me about Sister Chastity?"

Miss Farrell settled back upon the rock. "It's common knowledge that Eldress Phelps was unhappy with Chastity's work. She knew little, and, although was becoming a fair weaver, the quantity of her work declined. Especially in the last few months."

"Why was she allowed to join then?" Rees asked in surprise.

"The Believers accept all of God's children," she said. "And I believe she brought a healthy portion, with more promised in the future."

"More promised," Rees repeated. Miss Farrell nodded.

"We all share what we have. I brought my dowry. Elder White returned it to me when I left the Family."

"So you believe Elder White to be honest and trustworthy?"

"It is not what I 'believe.' He *is* honest and trustworthy." She looked at Rees with dislike. He nodded but not in agreement. After traveling the road for more than six years, he had learned to be cautious with leaders. Even the honest ones would sacrifice fair dealing on the altar of position. If that were not true of Elder White, he would be a rare man indeed. "Is there anything else?" Lydia Jane asked. "I have chores . . ."

"Nothing right now," Rees said, rising to his feet. He offered her his hand but she shook her head in refusal and stood up unassisted. "I'll rely on your insights as I speak to the Sisters," Rees added. Her mouth quirked sardonically but she did not contradict him.

"Until Monday," she said.

"Miss Farrell?" She turned. "Thank you." She nodded, her expression softening, and started up the slope. For a moment Rees watched her stride away. Lydia Jane Farrell was a beautiful woman, but prickly. He sensed a turbulent stew of emotions swirling beneath her plain dress, and despite Elder White's warning Rees burned with curiosity about her past. What had happened to embitter her so?

———————

He walked back to the village. As he approached the Meeting-house the sound of the service—singing, confused acclamations, chanted shouts—had increased in volume. Rees turned toward the Dwelling House. It was not his nature to wear his feelings on his coat and he couldn't imagine surrendering himself to the rapture. Anyway, Mrs. Doucette's weaving waited.

As he crossed the street he saw a familiar tall lanky body exit the cow barn—David. Like a pigeon called home, Rees turned toward his son. He struck out on the dirt track that led to the pasture and followed David back into the shadowy interior of the cow barn. It smelled of hay and cattle, although, except for the animal at the end, none were inside.

"There, there," David crooned. Rees followed the sound to the back and peeked over the stall wall. The black-and-white heifer lying in the bed of straw looked at him with dull eyes.

"What's wrong with her?" Rees asked.

"I don't know," David said. "It might be mastitis. Brother Levi will know. I'll ask him when he returns . . ." His voice trailed off.

Rees watched his son stroke the cow's soft nose. "She's calm with you."

"Brother Levi says I have a gift," David said with a flash of pride.

Rees relaxed upon the wall and said, "He may be right." This was the first time in many years David had not flown into a rage at the sight of him. Rees reminded himself to be easy. "She would not be so placid with me."

David ran his hands gently over the cow's udder. "Hot and dry." He dipped a rag in the bucket of fresh water and began sponging the affected organ.

"I believe you will make a fine farmer one day," Rees said. David glanced up at him.

"Better than you," he snapped, with some of his usual resentment. Rees nodded.

"That is true." Mollified, David returned his attention to the heifer. Rees felt as though he'd narrowly missed catching his leg in a bear trap.

"When I lived with Uncle Samuel and Aunt Caroline," David said, "I spent most of my days in the fields."

"Surely you spent some time milking," Rees said. The herd he'd left behind had been Dolly's pride. She'd commanded top dollar for her cheese.

"Not since I turned ten," David said, rising to his feet. He dumped the water just outside the door. Rees trailed after David as he went to the trough to refill the pail. "I think Uncle Sam sold the herd soon after that," David said, looking at his father, eye to eye.

"What!" Rees shouted, shock wringing the exclamation from him. David jumped and water sprayed out in a shining arc. "He had no right. Those were Dolly's."

"Maybe you should have been paying more attention," David said, dipping the pail back into the water. "To everything."

"My sheep?"

"Aunt Caroline spins the wool so the sheep are safe."

What other changes had Samuel and Caroline made? Rees wanted to ask but didn't dare; he and David were getting along well right now and he didn't want to spoil it.

"You suggested to Elder White I look into Sister Chastity's death," Rees said.

"Yes."

"How did you know I had some experience in untangling such puzzles?"

"When I was a little boy, you used to come home from your journeys and tell Mom all the funny or interesting things you saw on the road. I guess you never saw me there, listening."

"I didn't expect you to remember," Rees said in a hushed voice.

"It was the best time of my life," David said, meeting his father's gaze. Rees saw a shadow of a young boy's pride in his father still shining in David's eyes and shame roughened his voice.

"I won't let you down," he said. David said nothing and after a long uncomfortable silence Rees jumped back to his investigation.

"Did you know Sister Chastity?"

"Spoke with her a few times," David said. "We are a small Family. Through the course of a week, one pretty much speaks with everyone. I saw her at union a few times. But I was beneath her notice." He clamped down on his lower lip.

"The name she chose indicates her avocation," Rees said, carefully not looking at his son. "Do you know her children?"

"I've met them," David said. "They're just babies."

"How do they feel about being taken from home?"

"They want to go home, that's all they talk about," David said. "They cry all the time for their father. Sister Chastity made little time for them. Everyone knows that." Rees nodded. Mr. Parker had the truth of it; his wife took the children mainly to hurt him. "Here comes Brother Levi," David said. Rees turned. The brother was hurrying up the track to the barn. The energetic service in the Meetinghouse had flushed his cheeks pink but all his concentration was now fixed upon the ill heifer. He brushed past Rees without a glance. Rees followed him into the barn. Despite his Sunday garb, Levi dropped to his knees beside the cow.

"I bathed her udder with cool water," David said. Levi smiled at him.

"I'm sure that made Buttercup more comfortable. What is your diagnosis, lad?"

"Mastitis?"

"Yes, I think it is," Levi said. Rees realized he was only a few years older than David. "We'll clean out her stall. Scrub down the walls with vinegar. Fresh clean straw on the floor. She's a good strong lady; she should weather this. Throw out her milk—"

"But her calf?" David interrupted in distress. "He's not fully weaned yet."

"Well," Levi said, "if he's too young for weaning we will have to bottle-feed or cull him from the herd."

"I'll do it," David said. "I'll bottle-feed the calf."

"I'll discuss it with Brother William," Levi said. "And we will keep Buttercup in here, away from the rest of the herd. We don't want any of the others to come down with this." David nodded in emphatic agreement.

For the first time Brother Levi noticed Rees. He glanced at David in perplexity. "This is my father," David said. Levi's expression transformed from surprise to interest to concern.

"You aren't leaving us, are you?"

"I'm not taking him away," Rees said. "He'll make his own decision when the time comes."

Levi looked both faintly relieved and pleased. "He's gifted with livestock," he said. David ducked his head, his cheeks coloring.

The sudden clang of the dinner bell sounded across the fields and interrupted the sudden silence. "You go along," Levi told David. "I'll finish here."

In a companionable silence David and Rees started toward the village. David stopped at a barrel to scrub his hands and face. When Rees joined him David said, "There is no dirt in Heaven. That's one of the things they say here." Rees nodded.

"Everything is well-ordered."

"Thinking of signing the Covenant?" David asked, darting a sly glance at his father. Rees shook his head.

"I wouldn't mind the work, although I don't care much for farming," he said honestly. "But I wouldn't be able to participate in Services. Do they always last the day?"

"Yes." David smiled. "Today Brother William excused me so I could care for Buttercup."

They grinned at each other in complicit understanding. He was his skeptical father's son after all.

They separated at the door and found different tables. Warm with accomplishment, Rees sat down. He and David were no longer strangers and now he glowed with a cautious hope they would eventually become friends.

Chapter Six

On Monday morning Lydia Jane Farrell was waiting for him outside the Dwelling House as promised, Eldress Phelps standing by her side. In her linen cap and black shawl Miss Farrell looked exactly like the Shaker Sisters, and Rees wondered again why she'd left the order. She met his gaze unblinkingly, without warmth or friendliness.

"Whom do you wish to speak with first?" she asked.

"I think the woman who laid Sister Chastity out for burial," Rees said.

"Sister Clementine," Eldress Phelps said. "She is in the laundry this week." She nodded at Lydia.

"This way please, Mr. Rees," Miss Farrell said. As they left the porch Eldress Phelps went back inside the house.

Rees and Lydia walked to the end of the street and across the bridge. When they turned left and started for the meadow, Rees could not resist a quick glance at the springhouse. Screened by trees, it was just a flash of white behind the green.

They followed the stream toward the meadow where laundry danced on the lines. As they neared the laundry house the hot steamy smell of wet wool and heated irons rose up to envelope them. Rees admired the ingenious system of tubes that carried the hot wash water to the stream and away to the ocean.

"Come on," Lydia Jane said impatiently, standing by the open door. Rees hastened to join her. The heat eddying out from inside caught him unawares and he stumbled back so quickly he almost fell. Miss Farrell shook her head.

"Sister Clementine," she called. "Sister Clementine." A few moments later a stout black woman plunged through the door, gasping in relief as she met the cooler air.

"Sister Clementine," Rees said. She inspected him with bright curious eyes.

"You the weaver man?" she asked. Her speech rolled slow and syrupy from her mouth.

"The same," Rees said. "And Miss Farrell is my chaperone."

"You looking to who killed Sister Chastity."

"Yes. Eldress Phelps said you laid her out?"

"That I did, poor soul. I always lay out those who're going home to Mother."

"I wanted to ask about her underclothing," Rees said, acutely aware of Lydia Jane standing behind his left shoulder. She gasped.

"And why is that?" Clementine looked at him sharply.

"When I examined her I noticed she wore silk stockings." When Clementine's gaze flicked toward Lydia Jane, Rees added quickly, "She won't betray this confidence, will you, Miss Farrell?"

"No."

"Silk stockings and a silk underskirt are not normally worn by the Sisters, I believe," Rees said.

"No. And her petticoats and chemise were silk too. I just thought she was having a hard time putting away worldly luxuries." She sighed. "I decided to bury her in them. God will understand."

"You're thinking she was on her way to meet a man," Lydia Jane accused Rees.

"I am considering it," Rees said.

"Was she . . . ?" Miss Farrell's cheeks flamed and she looked at Sister Clementine pleadingly.

"Not that I could see. Of course I wasn't looking." She and Rees exchanged a complicit look and she added compassionately, "Surrendering to the pleasures of the flesh ain't for everyone."

"Did you know her?" Rees asked.

"Oh, I saw her sometimes, in passing you know, as Family often do, but not to speak to," Clementine said. Rees suspected Chastity ignored the older black woman or worse. "You need to speak to her roommate and the Sisters she worked with."

"You were kind to her, at the end," he said. He could just imagine Chastity's behavior toward Clementine, a politeness made up of equal parts condescension and patronization.

"The dead wants their dignity," she said, "and I try to give it to them." Her gaze rose from Rees's face to a point high above his head. "Storm coming," she said. Calling to the Sisters inside the shed, and moving much more rapidly than Rees would have thought a woman of her bulk could, she surged into motion. She stripped the lines, flinging sheets and clothes and pegs into a basket. The two other Sisters, still in their teens by the look of them, tumbled out to help.

"We'd better go if we are to make it back before the rain," Lydia Jane said. Thunder rumbled in the distance and a few drops splattered the ground. "Hurry." She took the lead, flying over the path to the footbridge. The first few drops increased to a gentle patter. As Rees and Lydia Jane crossed the bridge the skies opened and the rain began falling in sheets. Now they ran full out. Despite their speed they reached the Dwelling House soaked to the skin. Panting, Lydia took her sodden linen cap off her head and examined it ruefully. Rees grinned at her companionably.

"I'd like to speak to Sister Anne too," he said after he caught his breath. Miss Farrell shook her head.

"I don't know where she is working today. And before you ask, I don't know where Eldress Phelps is either so I can't ask her. You must cultivate the virtue of patience, Mr. Rees. She'll keep until tomorrow."

"I beg to differ," Rees said, stung. "In these cases, speed is of the essence. People forget or move away—"

"Not here," she said. "Until tomorrow then." She darted into the rain and with her hands shielding her head she ran across the street. Her wet skirts flapped and clung around her legs. Rees watched until she disappeared from sight, admiring the lithe motion of her body. Then he went into the Dwelling House to change from his wet clothing.

Mouse had already finished inside, folding down the bedding to the foot to allow the bed a good airing. Rees changed to dry clothing and, after a few moments of restless pacing, settled down upon his bench. Automatically his hand went for the shuttle and his feet worked the treadles. He did not think he would have cared for Sister Chastity. She sounded selfish and self-centered, exactly the sort of person who would not tolerate the Shakers' austere lives. So why did she come here? And why did she stay? There must be some overwhelming reason.

Rees worked steadily until the dinner bell sounded, so lost in his own thoughts the sudden loud clang levitated him from the bench. He finished his pattern, hearing the footsteps outside change from just a few to a steady stream, before rising to join them. He cast a quick glance at the cloth. The tension was identical to the length finished yesterday, and the weaving even and smooth. He expected no less of himself.

When the men entered the Dining Hall, Rees was surprised to see one table already occupied. Mr. Parker sat alone, Sister

Chastity's ex-husband, uncomfortable but determined. As soon as his children saw him they raced straight to him with cries of joy. One of the Sisters followed and tried to persuade them to return to the children's table, but they clung to their father's sleeves like burrs and refused to move. Finally Elder White gestured the Sister away and the little family group ate together amid the larger Shaker community. They provided the only conversation in the room; childish treble punctuated by Mr. Parker's baritone. Hearing it brought a smile to Rees's face.

After dinner he walked Mr. Parker out to the street and waited with him while his vehicle was brought around. No plain wagon for the Parker family; this was a coach. And almost as elaborate as something Rees might see in Philadelphia or Boston. A driver sat high up in the box, but he jumped down to stow the children's luggage in the back. Squealing with excitement, as though all the sounds they'd saved up from the last several quiet months were bursting from them now, they ran to the coach. But the little girl ran back to hug one of the Sisters, both of them sobbing. Mr. Parker shook Rees's hand and climbed up beside his children. With a lurch the coach started forward. The little girl leaned out to wave at the Sister. The driver spun the coach around and a sheet of mud sprayed Rees's breeches and white stockings. And the Parkers were off.

"Damn," Rees said involuntarily, looking down at the brown slurry streaking his clothing. He would have to change again. He returned to his room to put on yesterday's dirty, but dry, stockings and wiped off his shoes. Then he went in search of Elder White, curious about the conversation that had passed between the Elder and Mr. Parker.

White proved elusive, not present in his office nor in the Dwelling House. The Brother in the Blacksmith's directed Rees to the stables next door and he finally ran the Elder to ground in the tack room. Here the Brethren engaged in leatherworking and Elder White was inspecting the variety of whips, whiplashes, bridles, and other leather items. Rees inhaled the sweet smell of fresh leather, seasoned with the aromas of hay and horses.

"Is the leather of Shaker manufacture?" Rees asked as he stepped into the small enclosure.

"No," Elder White said. "We have no tannery. Not yet anyway. We must finish the grist mill first." He turned from his examination of the whips. "And what brought you out here, Mr. Rees?"

"I have another question," Rees said. Elder White raised his eyebrow encouragingly. Rees paused and cleared his throat. Discussing money was awkward. "Regarding Zion's finances." He hesitated.

"And why would you ask about that?" White said.

"Part of the inquiry into Sister Chastity's death," Rees replied.

"She knew nothing of our finances," White said. Rees plowed on.

"Converts bring their worldly possessions to the Shaker community. Isn't that right?"

"Of course. That is not a secret."

"If they have nothing?"

"We do not turn them away. We do not seek to profit from our members but communal sacrifice supports all of us." His quiet tone did not disguise his condescension. Rees felt blood stinging in his cheeks.

"What happens if one of the members leaves?" He knew what Lydia Farrell had said but now he wanted to hear the answer from Elder White.

"We return to them whatever funds they brought," White said. He permitted himself a small smile. "Of course. You are inquiring into the dowry Sister Chastity, who came to us as Catherine Parker, brought. Mr. Parker left it under her control. I offered that sum back to him but he refused it." Rees did not mistake the faint gleam of triumph in White's eyes.

"Is it common to accept one half of a married couple?" Rees asked. He sounded disapproving, even to himself.

"Not common, no. But she showed us a document from a lawyer indicating the couple's intention to divorce and a letter from Mr. Parker giving her both custody of the children and control of her portion." He paused and then added honestly, "I do not believe Parker expected her to bring the children to our community, however."

"No, I think not," Rees said. "Parker would never have surrendered his children so easily." Catherine's death saved him the trouble of fighting for his children, as well as benefiting the Zion community.

"Was Mrs. Parker's portion a substantial amount?" His blunt and impolite question brought the Elder's eyebrows up but he answered, his tone stiff.

"Fair to middling. Usually our members bring small amounts but we have had a few large gifts. And we have been promised—" He stopped abruptly, a spasm of distress twisting his features. Rees scented another secret. He knew it might have nothing at all to do with the murder, but he was curious nonetheless. And he would discover the mystery, eventually. Elder White seemed to reach the same conclusion. "One of our Family brought us a pair of blue roan horses. We are breeding them with some of our other stock. . . ." His voice trailed off as he directed Rees's gaze outside to the paddock behind them. Rees walked to the back door and peered into the misty green world outside. Mixed in with the bays and chestnuts were three silvery blue roan, two adults and a leggy colt. Even from this distance he could see the characteristic black spots speckling the adults.

"Beautiful," he said.

"Unfortunately, the mating of the roans does not always produce a viable foal. We were lucky this time."

"You own a large herd," Rees said, trying to count the moving backs.

"Fair to middling. The Family has been fortunate," White said. "Look, your Bessie is among them. She seems happy."

"I suppose," Rees said, observing that Bessie looked like a tinker's packhorse among that august group. Elder White returned to his inspection of the leather whips and after a moment Rees left. He could think of no more pertinent questions at the moment. He could only wonder at the motives that encouraged converts to hand over everything they owned. He knew he would not be so willing to hand over his few pennies and the farm he meant for David.

The skies cleared overnight and the next morning when Rees met Miss Farrell outside, the air felt warm and steamy. Her cheeks were already flushed with heat and Rees felt damp and uncomfortable. "I spoke with Eldress Phelps," she said. "Anne is working in the kitchen this week. Do you still want to speak with her?"

"Yes," Rees said with a nod. "And I'll probably want to speak to that Sister Marguerite as well."

"I thought you might." Lydia Jane smiled. "I obtained the assignments of several of the Sisters so we won't waste any time today. She's in the weaving house."

"Good," Rees said. He could not criticize her foresight but her self-confidence irritated him. It was unfeminine. How could she be so beautiful, so attractive, and so forthright? Lydia smiled at him and he knew she understood his mixed emotions perfectly. "To the kitchens first," he said.

They circled the dwelling and approached the kitchen door.

Heat from the fire blazing in the fireplace blasted to the outside. Rees peered through the door. Pies and several loaves of cooling bread adorned the oak table in the center. Brightly polished copper pans hung from hooks in the ceiling. As a winter scene, this would have appeared cozy, but in the heat of the summer it was hellish. The faces of the Sisters inside were scarlet and glistening. One Sister began stirring down the fire but Rees felt no drop in the temperature at all. Already perspiring, he jumped back. "I am not going in there," he said. Without a word, Lydia Jane stepped inside. A few minutes later she returned, Sister Anne in tow. Both were flushed and Anne's clothing was damp. She lifted her face to the breeze.

Rees removed himself to a bench a short distance from the kitchen and after a brief hesitation Anne followed, sitting daintily on a nearby boulder. For a moment Rees and Anne regarded each other. So fair the roots of her hair scarcely showed against the white of her linen cap, Anne had the porcelain skin and round blue eyes of a French doll. Rees thought she could not be more than twenty. "I wanted to talk to you about Sister Chastity," Rees said. Her eyes immediately filled with tears.

"I know," she whispered.

"How long did you share a room with her?" Rees asked.

"Maybe five months." She looked into the distance. "She and the children came last fall but she shared with Mouse at first."

"How did you find her?"

"Weepy at first. But of course she must have been homesick. I know she really wanted to join our Family." She spoke with passionate conviction.

"Why? Why did she want to join this community?"

"She didn't say. Except that she agreed with Mother Lee about marriage and that she wanted a celibate life." Rees shook his head dubiously.

"Did you ever see her slip out at night, after she thought you were sleeping?" Miss Farrell asked abruptly. The girl's cheeks flushed and she nodded.

"But only once or twice," she said. "I thought she was going to the weaving house to practice." She bit her lip. "She couldn't have been meeting a man. She was . . . skittish around strange men." Rees shook his head in disagreement. That didn't mean she wasn't meeting her lover.

"Did you hear her return?" Lydia Jane asked. "Was it immediately? Or later?" Rees frowned at her but she ignored him.

"I don't know," Anne confessed. "I was always asleep by then."

"Did she bathe before going out?" Lydia persisted. "Change clothes?"

"Yes," Anne whispered. "Maybe she was visiting the children."

"But surely she could do so during the day," Lydia said without rancor but very firmly. "Did she visit them during the day?"

"I don't know," Anne confessed.

"I know you're trying not to gossip," Lydia said. "But murder is far more serious than that. She was your friend and you want to protect her. But you're only protecting the one who killed her."

"I don't know if she met anyone," Anne wailed, fresh tears springing to her eyes. That at least was the truth.

"Perhaps not," Rees said. "But you have to tell us everything. All of it." Anne nodded and wiped her eyes with the corner of her apron.

"I really did not know her well," she said. "She didn't confide in me. In fact we rarely spoke. I don't know what she did at night; she might have visited her children," she added with a touch of defiance. "I surely don't understand why anyone would kill her."

"Nor do we," said Miss Farrell. "But you are helping us find out." Anne sniffled and nodded her head. Rees and Lydia Jane looked at each other in silent agreement. They would learn no more from Anne today. All three rose to their feet. But as they prepared to part Rees suddenly asked, "Do you know if she had any family?"

"No. Except for her husband. Oh, but she did have a brother. He lives near the Parker farm. I don't think Sister Chastity and her brother got on. He never visited and she said she never wanted to see him again." Rees leaned forward in excitement.

"Do you know her maiden name?"

"I'm sorry, I do not," Anne said.

"Eldress Phelps will know," Lydia Jane said. "I'll ask her."

They watched Sister Anne hasten back to the kitchen, glad to be away from them. "I'm not surprised she knew so little," Lydia Jane said. "I expect Chastity said as little as possible to this innocent child."

"What do you know?" Rees asked suspiciously.

"Know? I know nothing. But I have heard a few things. Nothing certain, just . . . whispers."

"Just whispers. In a murder investigation. In future please tell me these whispers, no matter how insubstantial. And also, I am conducting this investigation. I don't want you jumping in with your own questions."

"You didn't stop me," she pointed out. Rees frowned. He didn't want to admit she'd proven more successful at teasing out nuggets of information than he had. She sighed. "Very well. I didn't mean to thrust myself forward. I just thought you might not know the routine. And you might not feel comfortable asking some of them." Rees said nothing, galled beyond endurance by her perception. She was right. "Anyway," she said, softening her tone and trying to placate him, "the Sisters will speak more readily to me than to you. That is why I'm accompanying you, is it not?"

"Yes," Rees said, hearing the sourness in his tone. He took in a deep breath and released it. "In future, please try to restrain yourself. I look like a fool." He wished he could speak to the Sisters without her; he was too conscious of her standing at his shoulder. And then when she jumped in on his questions . . . it was maddening.

"I'll try," she promised. "Are we going to speak to Sister Marguerite now?"

"I am," Rees said. "You will stand quietly by my side."

With a smile she whirled around.

"This way."

Chapter Seven

Marguerite Languedela'or sat alone in the weaving shed, the southern window behind her left shoulder. The late-morning sun slanted across the steadily lengthening cloth, unbleached tow-colored linen. But the weaving was smooth and even, and, when bleached white in the sun, it would be made up into snowy white towels and other articles much prized by housewives in the area who would pay top dollar for such fine work. Rees admired her skill.

Lost in her work, the Sister did not note their entrance. For a moment Rees stood there, watching her as she threw the shuttle back and forth. Her dark hair formed an ebony band around the cap and was clearly visible through the translucent linen. Then she glanced up, her blue eyes startling against her white skin. She did not move for a moment. Then, carefully and precisely, she placed the shuttle in the center of the woven piece. "I've been expecting you," she said in a husky voice. She was so tightly controlled she barely moved her lips.

"I am talking to everyone who knew Sister Chastity," Rees said. Marguerite nodded impatiently.

"I knew her no better than anyone else," she said, her gaze sliding away from Rees.

"You wept at her funeral."

"It is just so sad, so tragic, a young woman with children, dying so young. And so horribly." Rees identified the slight accent and exotic cadence; Sister Marguerite was French.

And that explained the beautiful weaving. Before the Revolution, France so prized their weavers they were not permitted to leave the country. And she hadn't referred to Chastity's death as "going home to Mother."

"Did she ever speak of her husband?" Rees changed tack.

"I told you, I barely knew her. We did not speak." Her shoulders tensed as she coiled herself even more tightly. "I did not even know the names of her children."

"Everyone I've spoken to," Rees said, "has told me you and she were close friends and that you spent significant time with her."

"We spoke only about our work," she replied, biting her lower lip.

"You mock Mouse," Miss Farrell interjected. "You tease and humiliate her." Rees turned to Lydia, prepared to frown, but her remarks finally elicited an emotional response from Marguerite.

"She is a monster," she said.

"You tease and humiliate other Sisters as well."

"I don't know why you criticize me." Marguerite angrily puffed out her breath. "You are not a member of our Family, and that is by your own foolish behavior." Rees watched the blood drain from Lydia Jane's face, leaving it a livid white. His admiration of Marguerite's beauty was rapidly turning into dislike.

"I daresay your friend Sister Chastity told you about Lydia," he said. Marguerite sniffed.

"I would not speak to you at all were it not for Eldress Phelps. She instructed all of us to answer your questions so I am doing that. It is all gossip, which is forbidden." Rees stared at her but she would not meet his eyes. Afraid but also a liar.

"Sister Chastity was your friend," he said. "Don't you want to find the man responsible?"

"Of course. Murder is a sin. But I know nothing. Look to her husband. Or to her brother. I know nothing." As tears filled her eyes, she picked up the shuttle and began weaving once again. Rees tried to pry additional information from her but to every question she replied, "I know nothing."

"Do you know the name of her brother?" Lydia Jane asked. "Or Sister Chastity's maiden name?" Marguerite glanced up in contempt.

"Lewis," she said. "That is no secret. And now, you are interrupting my work." She began weaving again, ignoring them completely.

Rees and Lydia Jane walked back outside into the sun. "She knows more than she says," she said.

"Indeed," Rees agreed. "And she's a liar. I believe she doesn't know the names of Chastity's children but I question everything else she said."

Lydia nodded. "But she knows the name of Sister Chastity's brother, something Sister Anne did not know."

Rees stared down at her. "That's true."

"And she's frightened."

"Yes," agreed Rees. "But of what or whom? Elder White? I doubt it. What do those little whispers tell you?"

"Only that they were close friends." Lydia worried at her lower lip with her teeth. "But that's important too. Special friends are discouraged. They're too disruptive. We are friend to all and to none." Rees nodded. He understood. He still remembered his sisters Caroline and Phoebe banding together against him, giggling and shooting mocking glances in his direction. When he ran at them, his mother scolded him. Catherine Parker and

Marguerite no doubt had employed the same tactics, albeit more subtly, against Mouse and the others they disliked.

They walked in silence for a moment. "Eldress Phelps is at the dairy house today," Lydia said. "Shall we ask her about Chastity's maiden name? We should make sure Marguerite is not lying about that as well."

"Very well," Rees said. "You know, I don't think Marguerite is afraid of Elder White. She'd eat him for breakfast. I can't think of anyone in Zion who would frighten her." Lydia nodded.

"She must know people outside the Family then." She spoke quietly, without her usual vehemence. Rees looked at her. Marguerite's nasty remarks had found their mark, tearing open an unhealed wound. Lydia looked away from him but not before Rees saw regret and sorrow in her eyes.

"Don't think I didn't notice you jumping in with a question of your own," he said.

"She was telling you nothing," Lydia said in a more usual tone. "I know her. I had to throw her off-balance." She slanted a sideways glance at him. "Are you planning to scold me?"

Rees sighed. "I should." But once again she'd elicited more information than he could have alone. Embarrassing but true.

"She was honest when she blurted out her opinion of Mouse," Lydia said. "And that revealed her as the shallow and evil person she is."

"I know," Rees said. Lydia nodded, her satisfaction plain. "We'll talk to her again, after we know more."

"I wouldn't trust her if she told me the sky was blue," Lydia muttered. Rees glanced at her. No love lost there.

The brick dairy sat in close proximity to the kitchen gardens, but on the other side near the path to the barns. Stone steps led down to the brick floor below. Rees and Miss Farrell stood outside, waiting to be noticed, while Eldress Phelps watched the final disposition of the pannikins. Some milk went to the ice-house but most remained here to be churned into butter or transformed into different types of cheeses. Rees saw Mouse churning, her face grimacing with boredom. When she saw him she waved.

"Sister Hannah," scolded the Eldress, sounding as though her patience had already been sorely tried. She glanced up to see what was distracting her charge. "I'll be out directly," she said. "Sister Hannah, you may begin patting the butter into the molds."

Rees looked around for a bench. Since he saw none, he sat down at the base of the oak tree shading the dairy house. After a moment Miss Farrell joined him.

"It feels strange not to be working," she said.

"Do the Believers work all the time?" Rees asked.

"'Hearts to God, hands to work,'" she quoted. "That is our creed." She glanced at him sideways. "Mouse likes you."

"I like her too," Rees said, noting her surprise.

"She's . . . timid with most people," Lydia said. They sat in a companionable silence for the few moments it took Eldress Phelps to come up the steps and approach them. They both rose self-consciously to their feet. She paused before them, her hands clasped in front of her. Although nothing in her stance indicated her annoyance at this interruption of her work, Rees felt it just the same.

"I'd like to visit Sister Chastity's brother," Rees said. "Do you know her maiden name?" Eldress Phelps looked at him in surprise and chagrin.

"I did not know she had a brother," she said. "Perhaps Elder White knows."

"Thank you," Rees said. Interesting. "I expect I'll be able to find out."

"The dinner bell will ring soon," Eldress Phelps said. "Every-thing must be scrubbed by then. Please excuse me." She turned and disappeared into the dairy once again.

"She didn't know," Lydia said, still wondering.

"Clearly, Chastity kept much to herself," Rees said. "Her brother's existence is not commonly known."

"But Marguerite not only knew about him, but she knew his name," Lydia said. They exchanged a glance. "What are you going to do next?"

"Speak to Mr. Lewis," Rees said. "As Surry is a distance, I expect it'll take the entire day. And I still must speak to most of the Brethren."

"You believe Chastity was meeting one of them," Lydia said, her voice a mixture of regret and something else. Envy?

"It makes sense, doesn't it?" Rees asked. "They're here, close to hand and available."

She nodded but said stubbornly, "It's still possible it was a man from town, isn't it?"

"Of course," Rees agreed although he thought it unlikely. "I'll have to speak to each of the Brothers in any case."

"We have union three times a week," Lydia said. "The Sisters and the Brothers meet and engage in conversation. I believe one is being held tonight. You might participate in a few of them. That will give you an opportunity to study several people all at once."

"Good idea," Rees said. He couldn't imagine anything more boring, but it would introduce him to several members of the Family. "I'll speak to Elder White after dinner." He recalled the Elder inviting him to these occasions during their meeting.

"When are you planning to go to Surry?" Lydia asked.

"Tomorrow or Thursday," Rees said.

"I'd like to accompany you, if I may."

He stared at her in horror. "No. It is not appropriate."

"I rarely travel, even to Durham, and sometimes I begin to feel smothered, like I can't breathe." Rees did not reply. He understood. It was that feeling that kept him on the road. "When I was a Sister, of course it wasn't permitted, but I'm just a single woman now."

"Wouldn't you be the subject of gossip?" Rees asked.

"Yes. If they knew. Perhaps you could meet me at my cottage and we could leave from there?" She stopped and stared at him, holding her breath.

The sudden reverberation of the dinner bell saved Rees from making an immediate reply and gave him a few moments to mull over her plea. That feeling of being smothered and confined was an old companion of his and he understood how desperate she must feel. Besides, the trip was long and some company would be pleasant. When the dinner bell ceased its deafening clang, Rees said, "Very well, you can come. But only if you promise not to jump in with your questions when I'm speaking to Mr. Lewis."

"I don't know if I can keep that promise," she said. "You wouldn't expect that of a male partner. Would you?"

Rees glanced at her, startled. "I probably would," he said truthfully. Although that kind of impertinence was more annoying coming from a woman. She stared at him in astonishment and then her expression softened.

"I know I speak my mind more often than I should, as a woman." Her lips tightened at some unpleasant memory.

"I am the investigator," Rees said. "I ask the questions. And I don't work with a partner. Usually."

"You must, here in Zion. What if I adjust my cap or swing my skirt to warn you one of my questions is coming?"

Amusement and annoyance warred within Rees; amusement won. "I'd rather you keep silent. But if you're going to blurt out a question, touch your cap and I'll be warned." He already regretted his good deed. She exasperated him sometimes, but he was beginning to enjoy her company, even though he wished he didn't.

"Go north toward Durham," she said, marking the short distance remaining to the Dining Hall. "A little ways out you'll see a track on your left. Follow it to the top of the hill."

"Very well," Rees said.

She veered away from him, her long stride sending her skirts flapping. She was as fleet as a deer, Rees thought in admiration, watching her vanish around the corner of the Dwelling House. When she disappeared from sight he joined the throng heading for the dining room.

"Of course I am delighted you want to attend our union," Elder White said when Rees caught him after dinner, though truthfully the Elder looked more surprised than delighted. "Why are you interested?"

"I thought I could meet some of the Brothers," Rees said. "I doubt I need to speak to all of them."

"Of course not," White agreed. "Most of them didn't know her at all. Have you learned anything from the Sisters?"

"She has a brother in Surry. Do you know her maiden name?"

"I'm not sure I knew she had any family besides her husband. That's why I sent two notes to Mr. Parker; so he could send one on if necessary. Why?"

"I plan to drive down to speak to him."

"I see." White hesitated a moment. "You should know that not everyone attends every union."

"I understand," Rees said.

"Very well. If you'll meet me in the hall just after eight o'clock, I'll show you to the room."

Rees waited for Lydia for twenty minutes after dinner. He thought she might come to the village again, but, although he loitered around the main street, she did not appear. Disappointment soured his mood and he didn't feel like going inside and weaving. Drifting aimlessly toward the cow barns he wondered how David was getting on. The boy had not come to dinner; probably hovering over a sick cow.

As Rees expected, he found David inside the stall. The sharp smell of vinegar overwhelmed even the odor of cow; David had followed Levi's instructions wholeheartedly. Rees peered over the wall. His son, forehead planted firmly on Buttercup's flank, was milking. He glanced up at his father.

"I heard you come in."

"How is she doing?"

"Better. I think we might save her."

"Maybe that's what happened to my herd of cattle," Rees suggested, not believing it for a moment.

David said scornfully, "They were healthy. Uncle Samuel doesn't like cattle. Too much work. And Aunt Caroline isn't like Mother, who took pride in her cheese. Caroline wants to be a fine lady."

"What about the fields?" Rees asked, unable to resist asking, but trying to keep the anger from his voice.

"He let the fields of flax go fallow although he still grows corn and wheat. Aunt Caroline has the vegetable garden." Rees said nothing although rage and grief exploded inside of him. His heart began hammering in his chest. "I talked to Sister Chastity's children before they left," David said, sitting back on his heels. He gently wiped down Bessie's udder and teats with a cool cloth. "They wanted to go home with their father. I asked if their mother visited them often and they said only once in a while and then only with Sister Marguerite. I don't think they liked her very much."

"Thank you," Rees said. Sister Marguerite had lied again.

"Do you know Sister Marguerite?" Rees asked.

"Only slightly," David said. "She ignores most of the Brethren. She's not even polite. She never goes to the unions. I don't know why she's here; she doesn't like any of us."

"She is a skilled weaver," Rees said. And she liked Catherine Parker. For a moment both were silent. "What about your schooling?" Rees asked. David looked at him incredulously. "Well, I haven't seen you heading off to class."

"I'll attend school in the winter," David said. "All the boys go in winter. The girls are going to school now. But didn't you know? Uncle Samuel took me out of school years ago. I was ten. He said farmers didn't need reading or figuring."

"But you have to be able to read," Rees said, stunned.

"I know how to read. And how to figure," David said. "I don't know. Maybe he's right. But I surely didn't like taking Caleb's place."

"Caleb? He doesn't work there anymore?" Rees heard his voice rise into a squeak.

"No. Uncle Samuel turned him out. Caleb was getting on, you know. His legs bothered him and his hands were all crippled up." Rees turned and punched the side of the stall. Even then he thought he might burst from the rage inside. He turned back to find David staring at him, appalled. Rees inhaled a deep calming breath.

"Where is Caleb now?" he asked very quietly.

"He's dead. After spending several nights outside and in barns he got sick. Your lawyer friend Mr. Potter took him in and Mrs.

Potter tried to nurse him back to health. Caleb seemed to get better . . ." Remembered pain choked him and tears filled his eyes. Rees pretended not to notice. When David spoke again, his voice was hoarse and trembling with the effort at control. "He seemed to get better and then suddenly he died and I didn't even get to say goodbye."

Rees stood there, silenced by guilt and grief and shame. David smeared his sleeve across his face, trying to rub away the tears. When he looked at his father again, although neither blame nor anger colored his expression, Rees hated himself.

"I am so sorry," he said. "I am so sorry." He'd thought David blamed him for Dolly's death, and maybe he did, but Rees's neglect was now revealed as more recent and immediate.

"After that, I was Caleb," David said. Rees didn't know what to say. He wanted to scream and swear and throw things at the barn walls. He wanted to punish Caroline and Samuel for not being the kind of family he thought they were. But most of all he was ashamed of his inattention and all-consuming self-absorption.

"Am I interrupting something?" Brother Levi paused in the barn door and stared at them. Rees could not have been more embarrassed if he'd been caught kissing a woman not his wife.

"We were discussing the murder of Sister Chastity," David said, proving he could think on his feet.

"I'm angry," Rees said, turning to Brother Levi. "Did you know her?"

Brother Levi blinked and struggled to recall. "Fair hair?" he hazarded.

"Red actually," Rees corrected.

"I thought her name was Sister Lydia," Levi said in perplexity.

"Miss Farrell does have red hair," Rees agreed. "A darker red. Sister Chastity was lighter. And curly."

Levi shook his head.

"No, then, I didn't know her." Turning to David he asked a question of much more importance. "How is Buttercup?"

"Much better. I just milked her." As Levi dropped to his knees by the heifer's side, Rees withdrew to the barn door. Unless Levi was a practiced deceiver, and Rees doubted that, this young man could be erased from the list of possible killers. Buttercup was of far more interest to him than any woman.

Rees caught David's eye and without another word spoken they agreed to continue this discussion at a future time.

Rees walked back to his room and his waiting loom. With several hours still remaining before supper, he could finish many ells of cloth. Despite all the interruptions, he was burning through Mrs. Doucette's supply of yarn and probably, within a few weeks, would finish the lot.

He squeezed out another hour after supper and then spent several minutes waiting in the hall for Elder White. They went upstairs and into one of the Brethren's rooms. The furniture had been pushed aside and a double row of chairs, close enough for conversation but not close enough for any inadvertent touching, were lined up in the center of the room. Rees stood awkwardly to one side, wondering what he should do. Sit down? Or continue to prop up the wall? Elder White motioned to him, rather impatiently, and Rees moved to the farthest chair just as the Sisters began filing in. Mouse was among them. Her eyes brightened when she saw him and she made a beeline for the chair opposite.

"What are you doing here?" she whispered from behind her shielding hand.

"Taking a look at the Brethren," he replied softly, although no one was really close enough to hear them. Mouse dropped her voice so low even Rees could scarcely understand her.

"You think Sister Chastity might have been meeting someone? Maybe even was expecting a baby?"

Rees stared at her in amazement. "How can you think these things?" he whispered, darting furtive glances at the Shakers several seats away.

"We all knew of Sister Ly— I mean, Miss Farrell's tragedy." For a moment the impulse to shake the story from Mouse was almost overpowering. Rees forced himself to sit back in the chair. This was not the place to press Mouse, not in the midst of a crowd.

"I had not heard of any tragedy," he said. "Will you tell me another time?"

"We aren't supposed to speak of it," Mouse said. Her translucent white skin flooded with rose. "I thought, because you and Miss Farrell . . ."

Rees bent toward her, lowering his voice to the merest thread of sound. "Does everyone know this tale?" he asked. Mouse shook her head.

"No. I know more than most because Brother Charles is my cousin." Now the rose darkened to crimson. She looked at him, mortified. "This is why we are forbidden to gossip," she moaned. "My tongue runs away with me."

"Miss Farrell had a baby?" Rees guessed. "But then, where is it? She doesn't have a child now."

"She had a little girl," Mouse said, tears flooding her eyes. "But the baby died."

Rees stared at her. He thought of Lydia's sorrow, and pity and shame rushed through him. "I didn't know. Where is Charles now?"

"He went on a buying trip a few months before the baby was born," Mouse said. "He never came back."

And that explains the bitterness, Rees thought. Suddenly

conscious of someone's eyes upon him, he turned his head. Elder White was watching from the other side of the room. Rees smiled guiltily, aware he had been prying into Lydia's past against all instruction. Turning back to Mouse he asked, "Did Sister Chastity ever attend unions?" Mouse screwed up her face in an effort to remember.

"I don't recall ever seeing her here," she said. "But she didn't like any of us."

In a sudden rush, a Brother Rees did not know plunged into the chair beside him. An older man, he promptly picked up the newspaper and disappeared behind it. Rees glanced around at the other Brethren. The blacksmith, a lanky fellow with brawny arms, perused a farming circular in the seat on Rees's other side. Some of the other Brothers conversed pleasantly with the Sisters across the aisle rather like old married couples who have long ago said everything they needed to say.

"Who is everyone?" Rees asked Mouse.

"Well . . ." She looked down the row. "That is Brother John at the far end. Some say he would be a perfect successor for Elder White." Rees looked at the elderly man's austere expression, the deep grooves bracketing his mouth hinting at a sour disposition. "The next two, Zeb and Zeke, are brothers, twins, I think. They came from the New Hampshire community. Brother Michael is new. Some say he is a Winter Shaker and will soon leave us." Rees looked at Michael. A young handsome man with luxuriant dark hair and a mustache, he seemed the type to appeal to a young woman. Rees couldn't see him surrendering to this celibate and simple life for long.

"Did you ever see him speaking to Chastity?" Rees asked. Mouse nodded.

"A few times. But he spoke mainly to Sister Marguerite." She added disapprovingly, "In French." Rees moved Brother Michael to the top of his "Important Persons" list.

"Brother William is next," said Mouse. "He is one of our Deacons. Like me, he was raised by the Believers but in New York. Not at Sabbathday."

"Sabbathday?"

"A Shaker community north of here."

"Oh." Rees recognized William; he worked everywhere on the farm. Short and stocky with his freckled fair skin burned red by the sun, he chatted pleasantly with the Sister across from him. William looked like the farmer he was, not someone who would appeal to the rarified tastes of Chastity.

"There are a few other men," Mouse said "Many fewer than there are women." Rees nodded in understanding. As a man, he would not find celibacy appealing.

"I've met Brother Levi," he said.

"He almost never comes to union," Mouse said. "I think he cares more about the animals than any person." Rees grinned at her, pleased to hear his own opinion spoken by another. He looked around again, catching himself yawning. He wasn't the only one. Several of the Sisters hid yawns behind their hands, tired by their long days full of hard physical labor. And Rees had to rise early to travel to Surry tomorrow.

"Did Miss Farrell attend these unions?" he asked Mouse. She nodded.

"Always. The men, some of them anyway, vied for the chair across from her. She is so very beautiful." She clamped her hand over her damaged mouth. Rees did not know what to say. Instead he turned to look at the Brethren sitting in the row beside him, his gaze moving from one to another. Could Sister Chastity's lover, and killer, be among them?

Chapter Eight

Immediately after breakfast the next morning Rees hitched Bessie to his wagon and started out. Finding the small track without difficulty, he followed it up and around the knoll until he reached an even smaller track on his left. He ascended into an explosion of colors and scents; flowers of every hue crowded the space, pouring their perfumes into the air. Rees climbed down from the wagon and stared around in a daze.

"Up here, Mr. Rees." Miss Farrell stood at the top of the slope, so surrounded by flowers her head appeared to be floating among them. Rees slowly climbed the remaining incline, following a path made of flat stones, until he stood beside her.

She had put off her white cap, exchanging it for a straw bonnet with sky blue ribbons. "You seem surprised," she said.

"I am," Rees murmured, looking around. Roses trellised up the side of the small cottage and hung over the lintel in a shower of pink. Lydia looked embarrassed.

"Even when I was a Believer," she said, "I was permitted to grow flowers. The bees require them." She gestured to the right, and Rees saw, lined up upon a small elevation, several rows of white hives. And now that he looked around, he realized bees were everywhere, humming through the flowers. "When I left the Family," she said, "Elder White allowed me to remain here in exchange for the honey these bees produce. Several of the Brethren built this cottage onto the shed."

"I'm sure they appreciate your honey," Rees said. She smiled.

"I'm sure they do. And I appreciate a place to live." She looked around once more. "Shall we go?" She handed Rees a large and heavy basket. "Something for lunch," she said. "Surry is a distance."

Once they rejoined the larger track, Miss Farrell directed Rees to the left, and through dense forest. They came out very suddenly onto the Surry road.

For a time they rode in silence, Miss Farrell looking around her with pleasure. Rees did not interrupt her excited contemplation of the trees and occasional farm on either side of the road. After Mouse's revelations of the night before, and seeing the wealth of perfumed and beautiful flowers around her cottage, Rees looked at Lydia differently. Despite her plain Shaker garb and the modest image she sought to project, she showed herself to be a creature of her senses. She had not been able to surrender carnal love and a family of her own. Hell, she hadn't been able to give up flowers; she engaged with the world around her with all her senses. With each new facet of her personality, he thought anew how unsuited to the life of a Shaker she seemed.

She caught his wondering glance and said, "I haven't been outside the village for over two years. Everything seems so new and fresh."

"Why did you join the Shakers?" Rees blurted. He had not intended to ask such an unforgivably rude question. For a moment she remained silent and he wished he could retract it.

"The celibate life appealed to me," she said at last. "I was engaged to marry and my fiancé elected to marry my best friend."

"Ah," Rees said. "You were hurt so you took your dowry and ran away to the Believers."

"Why do you ask?" she challenged him.

Rees struggled to find an answer that would not sound either disapproving or patronizing. "You are so full of life. So vibrant."

She blinked in surprise and then she smiled. "A compliment as I live and breathe. It's true I found the quiet and harmonious life not so pleasant as I expected," she said. "But I have my bees and my cottage. And even a little money. One of the Brethren takes my honey to market in Durham every now and then." Her voice trailed off as a spasm of unhappiness crossed her face. Curiosity burned through Rees but this time he bit his tongue.

They rode for the next few hours or so in silence. About three-quarters of the way toward Surry, Miss Farrell said, "Shall we stop for something to eat? We'll be coming to a dirt road on your left. It leads to a pretty place." Again that mysterious silence. Prompted more by curiosity than by hunger, Rees nodded.

The lane was almost invisible and Rees would have missed it if not for Lydia's quick shout. When he turned in, the trees crowded close upon them, scraping the wagon's sides. Grass, weeds, and small saplings carpeted the ground underneath; no one had traveled this way for some time. When they reached the end of the track, the trees gave way to a rocky bluff overlooking the sea. Gulls shrieked overhead and the smell of the ocean, salt, and rotting fish rose up to the bluff.

Rees jumped down from the wagon. Miss Farrell didn't move. She looked around, her expression haunted. "Miss Farrell," Rees said, lifting a hand to assist her to descend.

"I haven't been here for several years," she murmured. "It looks just the same."

"Miss Farrell?" Rees spoke a little louder this time. She looked down at him. Disdaining his help, she hoisted her skirts above her ankles and jumped down. Rees, unsure whether he should be insulted or amused, fetched the basket from the wagon bed. Instead of choosing a group of rocks that formed a natural table and chairs, Miss Farrell selected a grassy patch just above the cliff. Rees approached the edge cautiously. The bluff dropped directly to a small rocky beach, soon to be under water. They could see across the ocean all the way to the earth's curve. With a sigh, Lydia spread out the small coverlet and began laying their food upon it.

"Did you grow up near here?" Rees asked. She shook her head.

"I grew up in Boston. A . . . friend brought me here a few times. He often visited a cousin who lived in Surry." She put down the crock of beans with an unexpected thud. "It was a long time ago."

Rees knew better than to pursue that topic. He helped himself to a plate of baked beans and a square of steamed brown bread. She handed him the honey and they ate in a companionable silence, watching the ocean's colors change with motion and sunlight.

"Maybe your friend knew Sister Chastity," Rees said.

"She hadn't come into our Family then." She stopped, her cheeks whitening. "Maybe," she said, shaking her head unhappily. "Maybe."

"So, where is he now?" he asked, pressing her just a little. Maybe she would confide her sorrow. "I'd like to talk to him."

"I don't know," she said. "I haven't seen him or spoken to him in over two years." Rees couldn't bear to look at the agony in her eyes.

"Maybe his cousin knows," he suggested.

"His cousin moved away," she said. "But maybe." She rose suddenly to her feet and smoothed out her skirts, her fleeting willingness to speak about herself over.

They finished their meal in silence.

"Thank you for lunch," Rees said, watching her pack up the leftovers. She nodded silently and Rees thought she might be on the verge of tears.

Almost an hour later they reached Surry. Rees stopped again at the tavern to ask for directions. The barkeep recognized him. "Ah, now you want the Lewises," he said. "Last time it was the Parkers. You've come too far. Go back up the hill. You'll see a gate at the top. That's the Lewis farm."

Rees pulled up at the top of the hill and stopped where the road curved left, heading north. The weathered gate was pulled open, giving access to the rickety wooden bridge that spanned the stream tumbling below. A long dirt lane looped through the sprawling fields on the other side. Lydia threw a nervous glance at Rees.

"I know this gate," she said.

"Are you sure?" He turned to stare.

"I think this is where I came with Charles; this is where his cousin worked."

"We keep coming back to a connection between Catherine Parker's family and Zion," Rees said.

He crossed the bridge and rode a distance down the road. When he saw a man laboring over the young wheat, he stopped to ask if this was the Lewis farm. The field hand pushed back his straw hat, revealing a white band above his brown face, and stared at them curiously. "Yes, that it is. Farmhouse yonder." He pointed toward the ocean, in the direction Rees and Miss Farrell were already heading, and bent back to his work.

The fields continued for a good distance before they reached the house. Rees drove the wagon up to the porch. He couldn't see the ocean behind the house but he could smell salt. The house's wooden clapboards were battered gray. Barking furiously, a dog raced up to the wagon, giving news of their arrival. Rees waited. A few moments later a young woman came to the porch. She snapped her fingers at the dog.

"Jupiter, down Jupiter." The dog lay down but watched suspiciously as Rees jumped from the wagon. "May I help you," the young woman said. Rees thought she was probably no more than sixteen and very conscious of her manners.

"I'd like to talk to Mr. Lewis," he said.

"Whom shall I say is calling?"

"William Rees. And this is . . ." He turned to introduce Lydia Jane but stopped suddenly. An unmarried man and an unmarried woman traveling together; what would these honest folk think?

"His wife," Lydia Jane said instantly with a flash of a wicked smile.

"Come in please, Mr. and Mrs. Rees. I'm Betsy Lewis." She appeared unaware of his hesitation.

Rees helped a grinning Lydia Jane down from the wagon and they followed Miss Lewis inside. Miss Lewis showed them into a family parlor, sturdy hand-hewn furniture, rag rugs upon the floor, and an eight-shed loom in one corner. Rees stepped over to examine the loom but no more than a few moments passed before a plump motherly woman appeared in the door. Although only a few years senior to Lydia, Mrs. Lewis already sported threads of silver in her brown hair.

"Mr. Rees?" she said.

"I've come to speak to Mr. Lewis about his sister Catherine," Rees said, choosing his words carefully. Mrs. Lewis nodded.

"Mr. Parker gave us a letter with the sad news from Elder White." She spoke calmly with no trace of grief.

"She was murdered," Lydia said. Rees shot her a furious glance.

"I know. Mr. Parker told us."

"When I spoke to him he seemed mystified," Rees said.

"Much of Catherine's behavior was mystifying," Mrs. Lewis replied with a touch of acid. "I doubt my husband will be able to tell you anything," she added as hoofbeats sounded outside. They all sat quietly until Mr. Lewis entered. As Rees rose to shake hands, he scrutinized Catherine's brother. He resembled her, although he was of a sturdier build. His light hair was more gold than red from the sun and the skin that had been so white on her was bronzed on him.

"Mr. Rees," he said, looking at the weaver curiously.

Lydia leaned forward and whispered something to Mrs. Lewis. She nodded and said, rising to her feet, "Let me prepare some refreshment." Lydia followed demurely. Rees wondered what mischief she was planning now.

"I don't know what I can tell you," Mr. Lewis said. "Cathy and I weren't close as children and I hardly saw her after she married. And when she left her husband for that crazy religion, well, I haven't spoken to her since." Anger colored his tone and then he remembered again that she was dead. He turned away.

"Do you know her husband?" Rees asked, choosing a neutral topic.

"Of course." Mr. Lewis swung around. "Aaron and I grew up together. He took it hard when she left."

"Why did she leave?"

"I don't know." Lewis shrugged. "She was always a girl of queer starts."

"Do you know of anyone with whom she quarreled?"

"Everyone?" Lewis said with a grimace. "She thought well of herself. She was better than the rest of us simple farmers, you know. Still, I can't imagine anyone hurting her. It was a trivial fault." His voice cracked.

"Did she own anything of this farm?" Rees asked, thinking of his own sister. Lewis stared.

"Of course not. My parents left me this farm. They gave her a dowry. She took it to her marriage."

"And she didn't choose to come home when she left her marriage?" Rees asked again.

"No. This wasn't her home," Lewis said roughly. "She was always spoiled and demanding and she couldn't wait to leave. Well, what do you know, she wed the largest landowner in the district. You would think she'd be happy, but not her. The next thing you know, she's up and left him. I wouldn't have allowed her to come back. A married woman stays with her husband." He sighed, all the air rushing out of him. He looked smaller somehow, deflated.

"But you loved her," Rees said. Lewis nodded.

"She was the baby, you know. She always wanted more, but I don't think any of us knew what that more was."

Mrs. Lewis, pushing a heavily laden tea cart, appeared at the door, Lydia following with a plate of sliced cake. "Come to the cart now," Mrs. Lewis said. They all gathered. Cups and plates went around and Rees was offered a choice of coffee or tea. Since the war, when tea was the drink of the enemy, Rees had drunk coffee and he selected it now. For a moment he occupied himself in doctoring his beverage. Lydia offered him the sliced pound cake. Rees eyed her suspiciously. Unusually quiet, she wore the expression of a cat at the cream.

"Have I met you before?" Lewis asked her suddenly. "You seem familiar."

Her composure fled in an instant and she stared at him in dismay. One hand plucking her skirt, she said haltingly, "I visited here once several years ago."

"With her cousin," Rees said quickly. "They were asking after another relative."

"Oh yes, I remember. You wanted to know about one of my

laborers. Did you ever find him?" Lydia shook her head. "And did you know my sister, Mrs. Rees?" Lewis asked her.

"Only slightly. We live by Zion but we are not members." And she looked at Rees with a smile.

"Was she happy there, do you think?" Lewis asked. Lydia hesitated.

"Yes, I think so," she said finally. Rees couldn't tell if she was lying and Mr. Lewis seemed satisfied. "She did not deserve her death."

"No," Mr. Lewis agreed. He turned away again, his handkerchief fluttering. Mrs. Lewis went to him and put her hand upon his elbow. They stood like that for a few moments, turned toward the window and the bright sunshine outside.

"I apologize," Mr. Lewis said.

"It is a terrible thing to lose a loved one. I know," Lydia said. It was the correct thing to say. Both Mr. and Mrs. Lewis smiled at her.

"We wish we could tell you more," Mr. Lewis said. "The truth is, I've seen very little of my sister for the last ten years. I regret that now."

"I know," Lydia said again, reaching out as though to touch his hand. "All the things we would like to have seen, but now there is no longer, and will never be, the opportunity." Rees found himself nodding. He sometimes wondered if Dolly had ever understood how much he appreciated her. He knew he hadn't told her enough.

"We really must be going," he said. He didn't want to think of Dolly right now. Lydia Jane shook her head reprovingly at him.

"Of course," said Mr. Lewis. "Will you return and let us know what you discover?"

"We will," Rees promised.

"Thank you for the refreshments," Lydia said in her turn, and Mrs. Lewis smiled at her.

"I'll walk you out." She preceded them through the house to the front door. "Thank you for coming," she said. "He is more distressed than he wants anyone to know. Identifying Catherine's killer will ease him." Lydia pressed Mrs. Lewis's hands warmly between her own before descending the steps to the wagon. Mrs. Lewis watched them climb into the wagon and waved as they started down the drive. Only when they turned onto the road did she close the door.

"Is it your wife you still grieve for?" Lydia asked suddenly.

"That is none of your business," Rees said, snapping at her.

"You're right," she said. "So many secrets. They keep people apart, don't they?"

"What are your secrets?" he asked. She was silent so long Rees turned to look at her.

"I don't think they are secrets," she said at last. "Most of the Family don't talk but I'm sure they know at least some of my past." She sighed. "I fell in love with one of the Brothers, Charles Ellis, and got pregnant. Before we left the Family to live on our own, Charles wanted to make one last selling trip. He'd promised Elder White, you see. But he never came back. When my pregnancy became obvious, I had to leave the Shakers. Elder White was so very kind. He set up the cottage for me." She sighed again. "I never told anyone Charles was the father; that at least is still a secret."

"And what happened to the child?" Rees asked.

"She died a few months later." Lydia's voice trembled. Rees waited while she fought for control. "I don't know why. Punishment for my sins, I suppose." Lydia wiped her eyes with her fingers.

"My wife, Dolly, David's mother, died eight years ago," Rees said. "I still miss her sometimes."

"There's been no one else since her?"

"No. I travel and— No." Rees managed a lopsided smile. "David holds me responsible, of course. He has some reason for that."

"You must have loved her very much," Lydia said. Rees shook his head.

"I was a boy," he said. His feelings for Dolly would always be conflicted. He hadn't intended to wed so young but David was on the way. Through the years he'd grown to appreciate Dolly's good sense and acerbic wit and he knew she loved him. "She was a good wife." He directed a sideways glance at Lydia. "Very opinionated. I know she'd like you."

"No doubt I'd like her too," Lydia said with a smile.

They crossed the bridge and started up the hill toward Durham. "I'll begin talking to the Brethren," Rees said. "I wish I knew who she met that night."

"Oh," Lydia said. "I forgot. I talked to Mrs. Lewis while we were in the kitchen. She said Catherine did not like men. She left her husband because she didn't enjoy . . ." Color boiled into her cheeks, down her throat, and even into her ears. Rees stared at her. "Her wifely duties," Lydia choked out. "Catherine didn't like them. That's why she ran away."

"Well, that explains why she elected to join the Shakers," Rees said, trying to grasp this information. "They would never press her to marry."

"And why she chose the name Chastity," Lydia said. "Maybe she really was just practicing her weaving."

"Maybe," Rees said doubtfully, recalling the silk underclothes. "Or maybe she found a very special friend." Lydia looked at him, her eyes widening in shock. He nodded. "We need to speak to Sister Marguerite again."

Chapter Nine

By the time Rees drove Lydia Jane to her cottage and himself to Zion and rubbed down Bessie the supper bell had rung. He sprinted the last few yards and arrived inside flushed and panting, just as Elder White began saying Grace. Rees quickly slid into a seat at a table with Brothers Levi and William. They nodded slightly in greeting; he nodded in return, and tried to catch his breath.

As the Sisters began bringing around the food Rees realized he was trembling with hunger. Neither the picnic shared with Lydia Jane nor the coffee and cake taken with the Lewises had been a substantial meal, and anyway, he'd eaten them hours ago. He was glad the Shaker customs spared him the necessity of making polite conversation; in the quiet he was able to ponder Lydia Jane's revelations, both about her own past and about Catherine.

Rees stole a glance at Marguerite. She ate daintily, as she did everything, and in her cap with the dark hair pulled back she appeared serene and as virtuous as the other Sisters around her.

Lost in his thoughts, he did not note the passage of time and dinner ended before he expected. He rose, groaning, to his feet. Blisters from the reins dotted his fingers and cramps fired up and down his legs. He usually did not drive for so many hours at once. Levi shot off toward the cow barns but William made an effort to walk beside Rees as he left the Dining Hall.

"You are looking into our dear Sister's death," William said, his effort at conversation clumsy.

"Yes," Rees said. "Do you know something about it?"

"I regret I do not. I spoke to her only once. She seemed happy here though. I just don't understand what she was doing beside the weaving shed. Work had finished for the day."

"I heard she was practicing."

"That late at night? It is too dark to see. Even I know you can't weave in the dark," William said. Rees nodded in agreement.

"You seem happy here," he said. "Wouldn't you prefer a farm of your own? And a wife?"

"No," William said. "This is a good life for me. And all for the glory of God." Rees nodded, unable to think of any response to that. Fatigue made him dull.

"You wanted to speak to me?" he said.

"I wanted to suggest you talk to Brother Michael," William said. "I think he was friendly with our Sister. I saw them several times, just talking. I don't believe there was anything improper. He works with the flax in the barn near the weaving shed and he may have seen something."

"Would he be there that late at night?" Rees asked. William looked confused.

"Of course not. I mean he may have seen something another time. Maybe someone from town spying on the Sisters." Rees looked at him dubiously. "It has happened," William said seriously. "And Chastity and Marguerite are both lovely." Rees thought it just as likely Michael was spying upon the women but he did not say so.

"Thank you for your suggestions," Rees said, thinking of one of his mother's expressions: Don't teach your grandmother to suck eggs. People always presented the simplest ideas as though he was incapable of thinking of them himself. "I will speak to Brother Michael as soon as I can." William inclined his head and lengthened his stride.

"Wait," Rees said as William began to pull away from him. "One more question. Did you know Charles Ellis?"

William spun around, his face blank with surprise. "Of course. We shared a room for a little while. Why do you want to know?"

"What happened to him?"

"No one knows. Brother Charles and Brother Ira went on a selling journey for us: wooden boxes, honey, whips, some seeds. It is common enough. They never returned. We lost all our goods, all the money for what was sold, a sturdy wagon and two horses, a matched pair of blue roans."

"That sounds a serious loss," Rees said. William nodded.

"Grievous. But the worst loss of all was our two Brothers. Charles, you see, was the Deacon before me. He would surely have become an Elder some day. And Ira was just a boy, only a few years older than your son." Rees's heart clenched inside his chest. "He was so proud to be assigned the task," William said. He shook his head sadly.

"Did you notice anything different about Charles that week?" Rees asked. "Was he excited? Or troubled in any way?"

"Excited, yes, that I recall. But he was excited by the trust placed in him by Elder White. Troubled?" William stared into the distance, rubbing his hand over his freckled jaw. "He kept saying when he returned there would be changes. I don't know what he meant by that. Maybe he would finally sign the Covenant.

But I am sure he meant to return. Those that claim he ran away, stealing our wagon and horses and money, are just wrong." Rees nodded, scenting several mysteries in this last impassioned speech.

"And he never knew Sister Chastity?"

"She came after. Unless he met her on the road? But that would only have been for a few moments at most. Is that important?"

"Everything is grist to my mill," Rees said. An acquaintanceship between Charles Ellis and Catherine Parker might be important, but how well they knew each other and whether that was important he could not tell. "At some point, the answer will present itself."

"You are more of a Believer than you know," William said, throwing a grin over his shoulder. "You trust in God to lead you to the answer."

"I never thought of it like that," Rees replied with a chuckle.

As William crossed the street, Rees turned into the Dwelling House and went into his room. This morning's wash water was tepid but Rees scrubbed his face and hands anyway. He took off his shoes and socks and thought he would lie down for just a moment. When he woke again darkness had fallen and the house was so quiet Rees knew everyone was asleep. Turning over, he went back to sleep.

He woke to the sound of rain dripping from the eaves; the Brethren would be pleased. After several days of dry sunny weather the fields needed the water. He went outside to wait for Lydia Jane under the portico but she never came. Was she embarrassed? Or sick? Or maybe he'd offended her? Although his first impulse would have sent him running up the hill to her cottage, the depth of his disappointment scared him. Somehow, without noticing, he'd begun relying upon her. And he enjoyed her company. He must take himself in hand. Since he knew he would be leaving within a few weeks he mustn't allow these incipient feelings to blossom. She was nothing but a temporary assistant; he must keep reminding himself of that. And now, instead of chasing after a female, his time would be better spent interviewing Brother Michael.

Clapping his tricorn firmly upon his head, Rees darted out into the rain. He sprinted toward the weaving house and the red barn behind it. As he dashed past the shed door he heard the clacking of treadles. Several Sisters worked the looms today. Marguerite sat on her usual bench. Rees almost paused. But he did not want to speak to her with so many Sisters, weavers and spinners both, in earshot.

Rees reached the barn just as the skies opened up. Only Brother Michael was inside working. The wooden heckler was too heavy for most women and usually required two men to operate. Brother Michael, therefore, had opted not to struggle with it alone. Instead, he was switching the flax, the rhythm and strength of his arm as he slammed the board down upon the stalks betraying years of practice. He did not at first see Rees and for those undisturbed moments the weaver watched the play of emotions across the other man's face. Brother Michael did not exhibit the serenity touted by the Shakers. Whatever his thoughts were, they called forth both fear and anger. Rees wished he knew who or what caused such strong emotions.

He stepped out of the shadows, wondering if Marguerite had warned Michael about him. When the lad jumped and almost dropped the sheaf of stalks in his hand, Rees guessed she had. "What are you doing here?" Michael gasped, leaping backward.

"I just wanted to ask you a few questions," Rees said. Brother Michael looked even more alarmed.

"I know nothing," he said. Rees looked at Michael sardonically.

"Marguerite coached you, I suppose. You don't even know what I plan to ask."

"I tell you, I know nothing," Michael said again.

"I know you spoke to Sister Chastity, more than once," Rees said. Despite the cool air, perspiration beaded Michael's forehead.

"Just to say hello and goodbye and how are you," he said. Rees approached the young man. Michael pressed his back against the wall, a wide rim of white circled the irises of his rolling eyes.

"Why are you so frightened?" Rees asked. "Surely not of me?" Of course not. But someone had Michael sweating in terror. "You never slipped out of your bed at night to meet Chastity?" Rees asked. Michael's eyebrows rose. With his dark hair and bright blue eyes, he seemed familiar, yet Rees knew they had never met.

"Me? Of course not. I barely knew her. And she would never be interested in me." The quick denial sounded sincere. And he didn't sound afraid now. "I only said hello a few times." Rees caught the faintest whisper of an accent: French. He studied the boy more closely.

"Are you Marguerite's brother?"

"No." But his gaze shifted away. Rees noted the dark sweep of his eyelashes on his pale cheeks, eyelashes a girl would envy.

"Yes, you are."

"No, no, no."

"Her cousin then." Rees suddenly wondered what startling question Lydia would interject. He missed her. Taking her with him to the Lewises had been a mistake; they'd bonded.

"No."

"I don't understand," Rees said. "The Shakers accept families. There is no reason they would deny a brother and a sister membership. Why won't you tell me the truth about this?" Michael shook his head obdurately. Before Rees could press him further, several Brothers came into the barn. Michael gladly turned his back on Rees and began flogging the flax against the wall, the thuds loud in the silence. Rees hesitated a moment but, although no one stared, their covert looks did not welcome him. As the other men began working around him Rees retreated outside. Still pouring down in sheets, the rain quickly soaked him to the skin. Well, that was a waste of time. He stamped back to the Dwelling House through the mud.

He was dripping and cold and very irritable when he reached his room. He dropped his sodden shoes outside by the door and changed into another shirt and a pair of breeches. Both were old, worn thin, but at least they were dry. Since the thrifty Shakers would never light a fire in late June, no matter how cold, he threw his blanket over his shoulders. He pulled his moccasins, the only dry footwear he had left, from his satchel.

As he ran his thumbs over the smooth leather he began to smile. The moccasins, a gift from Ruth McBride, always brought her to mind. A wise woman and a midwife he met on the western frontier, she'd become a good friend, and an assistant when he began looking into a murder there. She had a habit of quoting appropriate bits from the Bible. What would she say to him now? Probably something about patience. He slipped the moccasins on his feet. Calmer now, Rees began to think more clearly. Perhaps Elder White could speak to Brother Michael, put the fear of God into him? Rees nodded and sat down at his loom. That might work. He would offer Michael one more chance first.

———

The rain passed overnight and by morning the sun was trying to tear a hole in the clouds. Through his windows, Rees could see the muddy morass the road outside had become. He wondered if the Brethren would try to work in the fields today, or remain inside until the soil dried.

Although his shoes were still damp and a little stiff, Rees put them on. He planned to follow Michael to the barn after breakfast and attempt one more informal interview before using Elder White's authority as a club. But he found Lydia Jane waiting for him in the front. Puffiness and a faint redness around the eyes betrayed a long bout of weeping, but she seemed composed now. She offered him a faint smile.

"I had to walk around the long way," she said. "The hill is a mud slide." Despite the pattens that elevated her above the road, mud had splashed the hem of her dress.

"I didn't expect to see you today," Rees said. He sounded accusing. He softened his tone. "Are you all right?"

"It was raining yesterday," she said as though that explained everything. "What are we doing today?" Rees stared into the distance for a moment.

"Talking to Sister Marguerite. And perhaps Brother Michael again."

"Again? Did you speak to him without me?" Hurt and disappointment flashed across her face.

"I tried to speak to him," Rees said. "Tried. He was stubborn. And I'm sure he's hiding something." Lydia's expression relaxed.

"I thought of something yesterday," she said. "I think I know the last name of Charles's cousin Patrick. You know, the one who worked on the Lewis farm."

"What is it?" Rees asked eagerly.

"O'Riley or something similar. Patrick wasn't an Ellis, you see. His father was an Irish groom."

"I wonder if the Lewises would recognize that name," Rees said. Lydia smiled.

"Maybe the weather will be better tomorrow," she said.

"Maybe. We could get an early start," Rees said. He glanced at Lydia and was pleased to see she had lost that white, stricken look. They smiled at each other.

"Let's find Marguerite now," Lydia said. "I expect she is in the weaving shed."

They fell into step together, treading gingerly around the deeper puddles. Rees welcomed the path outside the shed. Graveled, it offered drier footing and they were able to reach the shed quickly. Rees peered inside. Without the sun shining through the windows, the interior was dark and shadowy. Only a few Sisters worked here today, and most of them were spinning. Sister Marguerite did not sit at her usual bench.

"Where is she?" Lydia asked, gesturing to the empty seat.

"She was here just a moment ago," said one of the women. She wrinkled her forehead and added disapprovingly, "Brother Michael waved at her and she went outside to meet him."

Exchanging a quick glance, Rees and Lydia hurried outside and started up the slight incline to the barn. The water streamed down, cutting furrows in the mud. Rees's feet slipped and sank in. He grasped Lydia's hand to keep her upright and even then she almost fell. When they were almost at the top, Sister Marguerite and Brother Michael appeared in the barn door. Rees looked at the boy's rolling eyes; he looked like a spooked horse. Marguerite crossed her arms and glared at them.

"I want to ask you a few questions," Rees said as gently as he could. Clearly the boy was simple.

"Leave him alone," Marguerite said with fierce protectiveness.

"It would be better for Michael to answer a few questions now rather than in Elder White's office," Rees said. "And I have more questions for you." Without uttering a word, Michael turned and fled. Rees, who'd been half-expecting such a move, jumped forward to follow but Marguerite barred his way. Rees stopped short before he knocked her over.

"Leave him alone. He knows nothing about Chastity."

"Call your brother back," Rees said. "Please." She widened her eyes at him in surprise.

"It is not forbidden or improper for a brother and sister to join the same Family," she said defiantly.

"No. But then why lie about it?" Rees asked. "Did you or your brother admit to anyone you're siblings? " Marguerite said nothing. She stared away from him, over the long wet fields.

"He has had . . . some trouble in his life." She looked at Rees. "I don't want sheriffs coming to me, looking for him." And Michael was respectful enough, or scared enough, of his sister to agree.

"But he's here, in Zion?"

"I couldn't let him starve, could I?" She sighed. "I'm the only one he has." Rees looked at her. Now he knew how to pry out the truth.

"I think Chastity was sneaking out to meet Michael," he said.

"She was not! Michael and Chastity did not . . . they were not . . ."

"Why are you so certain?" Rees pressed. "What do you know?" He thought she might break and he leaned forward, looming over her.

"Mr. Rees, Mr. Rees." One of the young boys raced across

the field shouting after them. He slipped suddenly and fell, but rose again, his shirt and dark breeches smeared with mud. "Come quickly. Elder White wants you." Rees groaned in frustration.

"Very well," he told the boy. He turned to face Marguerite. "I'll return to speak to you," he said. She sniffed contemptuously. Offering a hand to Lydia, which she refused, Rees turned to hurry after the young messenger. They slipped and slithered across the loose mud. Lydia followed more slowly, picking her way cautiously over the furrows.

Elder White waited under the portico of the Dwelling House, in company with another man. He looked familiar but Rees didn't recognize him until he stepped out of the shadows: Mr. Lewis.

"Mr. Rees," he said, striding forward with his hand extended. "Mrs. Rees." He nodded at Lydia Jane. Elder White's eyebrows shot into his hair and Rees hid a smile. "I found something I think you need to see. It's at the farm." Lewis's grim expression wiped away all of Rees's amusement. "The dogs found them."

"We were planning to drive down tomorrow in any case," Rees said.

"We? Pardon me, ma'am," Mr. Lewis said to Lydia Jane, "but this isn't something a lady should see." She met his gaze unyieldingly. Mr. Lewis looked at Rees. He shook his head. He knew better than to battle this out with her, especially in public.

"We'll both be there, first thing tomorrow," he said.

"Very well." Lewis looked at Rees intently. "You'll need your wagon and a length of canvas." Apprehension clenched Rees's belly.

"Well, I've got chores waiting," Lewis said. "Tomorrow then."

He nodded at both Elder White and Lydia Jane and mounted his horse. Mud splashed the mare all the way up to her withers from the journey north, and when he wheeled her around a spray of the muddy slurry added another coat. He cantered south on the main street, mud flying in all directions. Elder White gazed at both Rees and Miss Farrell in concern but he said nothing, and after a moment he turned and went back inside the Dwelling House.

"Your reputation is ruined," Rees said. Lydia smiled sadly.

"It already was, long before I met you," she said. "Should we try again to speak to Marguerite?"

"Yes."

But when they walked to the barn Marguerite was gone and none of the Sisters in the weaving shed had seen her.

"She's hiding," Rees said. "She doesn't want to talk to us." He wanted to shake that young woman. Lydia nodded.

"She knows something," she said. Rees looked down at his damp and muddy shoes and the dirt on his white stockings. They were his last relatively clean pair.

"We'll try again after tomorrow," he said. "I need to find canvas." And see about laundry. He was not above washing his stockings in the basin, if he had to.

"I'll wait at the end of my lane just after breakfast. Don't think about leaving without me."

"I wouldn't dare," Rees said, only half-joking. She frowned at him. Picking up her skirts, she hobbled across the muddy street.

Rees spent an unsettled night wondering what exactly Lewis had found; something so terrible the farmer did not want to describe it. And he thought Rees would be interested. And would need canvas and a wagon. Reluctantly Rees came to the conclusion Lewis had uncovered a body. But whose? Knowing this, could he now persuade Lydia Jane to stay home? But then he would have to tell her what he suspected and she would be absolutely determined to come. Unlike most women, she hated being seen as weak. Rees smiled ruefully. In that way, she reminded him of Dolly and he knew how angry she would have been if he had tried to protect her.

Chapter Ten

He still hadn't completely decided whether he would stop for her the following morning. But when he saw her waiting, straw hat on her head and a light shawl in case the rain started again, he couldn't pass her by. He pulled up and jumped down to help her with the basket. "I wasn't sure you would stop for me," she said when they were both settled in their seats.

"I know how you would react," he said. She permitted herself a small triumphant smile.

The roads were muddy, the going slow, but they traveled as rapidly as they dared. They did not stop for a picnic today but ate sitting in the wagon seats. A powerful urgency possessed Rees and, feeling he'd already wasted yesterday, he was eager to reach the Lewis farm as soon as possible.

They made better time the nearer they approached Surry. The sky lightened, the sun came out, and the last few gray clouds gave way to fluffy white puffs high in the sky. Lydia dropped her shawl into her lap.

They reached the gate to the Lewis farm just before noon. An old man, his face leathery and seamed by a lifetime in the sun, waited for them by the gate. "You the weaver?" he asked. Rees nodded in surprise. "Mr. Lewis asked me to show you what was found," the man said. "You're going to have to leave the wagon on the other side of the bridge." He gestured to the weedy shoulder of the dirt road. Rees nodded and slapped the reins down upon Bessie's back. They drove over the wooden bridge and Rees pulled over. The man closed the gate behind them and loped over the wooden bridge and up the road to the wagon. Rees jumped down. He circled the wagon to assist Lydia but before he reached her she had climbed down on her own. For the first time, the man acknowledged her presence. "You're going to have to wait here, missy."

"No, I am not," she said. The man glanced at Rees. When he said nothing, the man shrugged and pulled a long dirty tan object from his shirt. "This is what the dog found," he said.

"Bone," Lydia said indifferently. But Rees saw her white knuckles clenched around the edge of her shawl. He held out his hand and took the bone. An arm bone, both knobby ends ragged with chewing. As he'd feared, the dogs had found human remains. Rees put it carefully into the wagon.

"We have to hike in." Again the laborer looked at Lydia. She stared back defiantly. "The way down is rough and muddy," he warned.

"I'll manage."

With a slight shrug, it was no skin off his nose, the man turned toward the junction of the bridge truss and the road. He half-walked, half-slid down the slope and began picking his way through the tumbled boulders by the stream. Rees offered Lydia a hand but she proudly refused it, bundling up her skirts so she could scramble across the rocks.

Although the bank edging the stream was not very high, it was steep. They had to angle their way across the slant, choosing a path over the boulders and around the mud puddles. Finally they reached the streambed, a large expanse of jumbled stones.

"Not much farther," the man said over his shoulder. Lydia nodded, her lips clamped into a tight line. Her shoes, stockings, and hem were soaked with mud but she didn't pause or hesitate as she jumped from rock to rock.

The bluff to their right gradually flattened out, circling a stand of trees and then ending at the bottom of a long meadow dotted with cattle. One cow glanced at the interlopers incuriously and went back to cropping the grass.

"Boy brought the cattle down to this pasture, saw something across the river," the farmhand said. He gestured to the steep eroded bank on the other side. The road ran along the cliff top, high above. Rees realized he knew this spot; he'd looked down upon this pasture from the road above on his first trip to Surry. "Follow me," the hand said. He crossed the river at a shallow place, jumping from stone to stone, until he reached the opposite bank. Rees glanced at Lydia and then followed. When he reached the middle of the river he saw, and recognized, a partially uncovered skeleton crumpled at the bottom of the bluff.

"Lydia," he shouted, "stay there. Stay on the bank." She shook her head and jumped to the first of the stepping-stones. Her long hanging skirt touched the water and darkened as the water wicked upward through the fabric. She clutched a fold and lifted up the skirt but didn't pause. Rees turned and hurried ahead.

The soft earth of the bluff had slid down to the rocky bank below, revealing the bones. Rees saw ribs and several long bones, but he could already tell this skeleton was not complete. Many of the smaller bones were gone, still buried or carried off by scavengers. He went closer. Caught up against a rock, the all too human skull grinned at him.

"Oh no," Lydia said, moaning and jumping onto the rock beside him. "Oh no. It's Charles. It's Charles." With an agonized scream, she ran toward the skeleton.

Rees grabbed her skirt and yanked her back. "No. You'll disturb the bones. I need to look at them first."

"It's Charles," she cried, trying to jerk her skirt free. "It has to be Charles." The farmhand looked at her and shook his head.

"No place for a woman," he said.

"If you don't stand on this rock without moving, I swear I'll tie you to a tree with your own shawl," Rees said. Her white-rimmed eyes were wild. "I mean it." She glared at him but, after a moment, she inhaled a deep shaky breath. Rees cautiously loosened his fingers from the rough weave of her skirt. When he felt sure she would not hurl herself at the bones, he jumped the last rivulet of water and knelt by the torso.

The shattering on the dorsal sides of the bones left no doubt the body had been pushed from the bluff above. And it had been a body. Other than the movement caused by weather and the dislodging of the bones by small animals, the proximity of the bones left no doubt they had come down encased in a human skin.

The farmhand picked up a hat. Although faded gray, it was still recognizable as the flat-brimmed straw hat favored by the Shakers. He handed it to Rees. Charles's hat? Rees tossed it over to Lydia. Although she did not scream, she hugged the hat to her chest, tears streaming silently down her cheeks.

Rees knelt by the bones. First he looked at the skull, chewed but intact, and then he worked his way down to the chest. Several of the ribs bore jagged grooves as though gouged by something sharp. Rees whistled silently and sat back on his heels. He recognized those marks: knife wounds. "We need to bring these bones back to Zion," he said. Then he realized he'd left the canvas in the wagon. "Damn."

"What's the matter?" Lydia said. He realized she had come up behind him and was hovering only a few feet away.

"We forgot the canvas."

"Here, take my shawl. And I have an apron as well."

Rees carefully lifted the rib cage, the spine, and a piece of the pelvis from the earth and wrapped them in the shawl. The other half of the pelvis was shattered. The joints had disarticulated but the hip joint and long leg bones lay below the hips almost as they would have in life.

"This doesn't make sense," Rees said. The spill down the bluff would have separated them all. He ran his fingers over the dirt around the pelvis and pulled up a scrap of earth-darkened cloth. Someone had wrapped the body in a shroud before dumping him. Rees swallowed; he did not like the image forming in his mind.

"Look," said Lydia. She slid a thighbone from its sheath of dirt and held it up. The top end was twisted, deformed, the lower edge of the bone bowed out. Walking must have been agony.

"Did Brother Charles limp?" Rees asked.

"No," Lydia said, her face whitening. "But Brother Ira did. He had to walk with a crutch . . ."

"Well then, " Rees said. "We may have found Brother Ira." Now, with a quick rustling movement, Lydia knelt by his side. She ran her fingers over the twisted bone and turned to Rees with tears brimming in her eyes.

"Oh no," she said. "He was only seventeen." Rees stowed the bone in the shawl with the others. "Could it have been an accident?" she asked, wiping the tears from her eyes. "But why then didn't Charles come back and tell us?"

"I don't know," Rees said. He thought of the knife cuts on the ribs but would not, could not tell her about those. "I need to talk to Elder White and Sheriff Coulton. Here, help me pack up the rest of the remains." Lydia took off her apron and they piled all the remaining bones into it. "In what season did Charles and Ira disappear?"

"Fall," she said. "We'd already begun collecting seeds. And Brother Charles had taken some to sell. Why?"

"Just curious." Rees now knew why the body hadn't been discovered. With autumn, the cattle left the summer pasture and went into the winter one closer to the farmhouse. No farmhand would come down here after that. And the body, wrapped in something dark and gradually buried under a layer of leaves, would soon become invisible. It might never have been discovered but for the subsidence of this bluff and the weather that eventually revealed the white bones.

Rees tied up the shawl and knotted the ends around his shoulders. The apron made another sack, lighter than the first one. Rees decided he would just carry it. They began the hike back to the wagon and the road. With the weight of the bones dragging at him, he found the scramble over the rocks difficult. He began to lag behind the others. Lydia finally came back but he refused to surrender the apron sack. Not to a woman anyway. She would not leave his side, so they hiked out together.

They reached the wagon mid-afternoon. As Rees carefully put the bones into the wagon the farmhand said, "Mr. Lewis asked me to invite you to noon dinner."

"That's kind of him," Rees said. "I hope they haven't held dinner for us. But I'll be glad to stop and speak to Mr. Lewis."

"I'll go on ahead then," said the farmhand. "He asked me to stop by when you finished." He cut into the trees edging the road and disappeared from sight. Rees guessed that walking directly across the fields would prove the shortest route.

When Rees had everything secure to his satisfaction, he climbed into the wagon seat. Lydia had scrambled up before him. He looked at her, noting the sunburn reddening her nose and the streaks of mud liberally decorating all portions of her face and dress.

"I'll be glad to wash," Lydia said wearily. "And my shoes . . ." She held up one foot. Although sturdy, the shoe had been hard used today. "I don't know if they will be wearable after this."

"This trip had to be done," Rees said, urging Bessie forward. They pulled out onto the rutted road. "Anyway, I'm sure the Lewises will allow us hot water. And maybe a bite of bread and cheese as well," he added.

Both Mr. and Mrs. Lewis were waiting on the porch when Rees pulled up to it. As soon as Mrs. Lewis saw Lydia Jane, her muddy clothing and sunburned face, she flew down the steps. "Oh, you poor dear. Was it awful?" She put her arm around Lydia's shoulders and supported her inside.

"Is it one of the Shakers?" Lewis asked, once the women had gone ahead into the house.

"I believe so," Rees said. "A few years ago two of the men went missing. Now Zion can put at least one of them to rest."

"Did they take that curve too fast? Was it a wagon accident? I've seen a few wagons tipped. Far as I know, though, no one's ever gone off the side."

"No," Rees said. "I saw no sign of a wagon." He recalled the knife cuts once again. "No, I'm fairly certain this was not an accident."

"What a shame." Mr. Lewis offered Rees a mug of ale. When Rees, who was beginning to tremble with reaction and fatigue, drank it all in one gulp, Mr. Lewis refilled the mug. "You think this has something to do with my sister, don't you?"

"I don't know at this moment. But they are both Shakers, in this community, both murdered. It is likely," Rees said.

Lewis shook his head and they sat for a moment in companionable silence. Then he drained his own glass of ale.

"I hope you and your wife will stop with us for dinner," he said at last.

"I'm happy to accept," Rees said. "But I hope you didn't hold your meal for us." Mr. Lewis smiled but said nothing, so Rees knew they had.

Mrs. Lewis and Lydia chose that moment to appear at the door of Mr. Lewis's office. Lydia's hands and face glowed pink from an enthusiastic scrubbing and she had brushed away as much of the mud from her dress as possible.

"Dinner will be served shortly," Mrs. Lewis said.

"Are those remains the cousin you were looking for?" Mr. Lewis asked Lydia. His wife frowned at him.

"No," Rees said. "Someone different."

"Oh." Mr. Lewis frowned in confusion. "But one of my laborers did have something to do with the Shakers."

"We think her cousin," Rees said with a nod in Lydia's direction, "was named Patrick O'Riley or something like that." Pretending Patrick was Lydia's relative instead of Charles's was easiest.

"O'Riley," Mr. Lewis said. "That doesn't sound familiar." He glanced at his wife.

She shook her head. "There was an O'Reardon," she suggested tentatively. "But that was many years ago. And he wasn't a farmhand. He worked with the horses."

"That's right. I remember now. He was a wizard with them, like so many of these Irish are. He worked as a coachman for some wealthy family in Boston before coming to us."

"I think it was Philadelphia," his wife said.

"Wherever it was. All those coachmen own beautiful silver-headed whips. I daresay, in Boston or Philadelphia," he added with a nod to his wife. "It is a symbol of their status. I hope he landed on his feet. He was a pleasant fellow."

"What did he look like?" Rees asked.

Lewis shrugged. "Don't rightly remember."

"Ginger-headed," his wife said, adding darkly, "but he kept company with that troublemaker."

"Red hair isn't much to go on," Rees said, tugging on his own fiery mop.

"Maybe it isn't important," Lydia said.

"And dinner is ready now," Mrs. Lewis said, rising to her feet. "Mr. Rees, I have a place for you to wash in here."

After dinner, Rees and Lydia returned to the wagon. Rees offered her a hand and this time she accepted it. Rees looked at her. She did not seem well. Despite her smiles and affectionate leave-taking from Mrs. Lewis, Lydia was pale under the sunburn. She waved at the Lewises as Rees turned the wagon, but when she was out of their sight, her smile disappeared. "Are you tired?" he asked.

"A little," she admitted. He did not think that "tired" was the best word; drained was closer to the mark. But she said nothing further until the wagon clattered over the bridge to the main road. "It's just such a shock," she said. "Ira's bones. I never knew what happened to Charles. Now I think he must be dead."

"We don't know that for sure," Rees said.

"Of course we do. I know he wouldn't just leave me, and he would never harm Ira. We should go back to that place and search again. We might find Charles's remains."

"We'll look another day," Rees promised. He knew Charles could as likely have killed Ira and made off with both wagon and money as fallen victim to the killer himself. But Lydia couldn't hear that, not today. He glanced at her. Most likely she wouldn't hear anything; she'd withdrawn into herself and sat in a desperately unhappy silence. He wished he knew how to console her.

Rees pushed Bessie as hard as he dared. Still, they didn't reach Zion until early evening, well after milking time at four. His earlier urgency had returned and now he had one goal, to tell the sheriff about these bones and to turn them over to Elder White for burial. After hiding the bones behind his loom, he unhitched Bessie, rubbed her down, and put her in her stall. Leaving her with a nosebag of oats, he backed the wagon into its assigned space. He was rushing, trying to finish so he could find Elder White before supper. As Rees stepped out into the road, he saw the Elder, his white hair glistening in the sun, walking up the road from the Meetinghouse. Rees ran to meet him.

"I have something to show you," he said. Elder White looked at him, his gaze traveling from Rees's freckled and sunburned face down to his muddy shoes and back again. "Something important."

"What is it?"

"You need to see it," Rees said.

"Very well."

Rees led him into his shadowy bedchamber. He pulled Lydia Jane's apron and shawl from behind the loom. Kneeling on the floor, he carefully untied both packages and spread the contents on the floor. Elder White stared and then turned away, looking faintly green.

"Why do you have those remains?" he said.

"I found them in Surry, caught in a mudslide," Rees said. "They belong to Brother Ira."

"That can't be? And how could you possibly be sure of that?"

Rees held up the twisted thighbone. "Miss Farrell told me

Ira limped. Look at this. He must have been in great pain all the time."

Elder White turned around and stared at the bone in Rees's hand. Slowly, reluctantly, he began to nod. "He must be given a Christian burial," he said.

"Of course. But I want Sheriff Coulton to see them first."

"Why?"

"Because it looks as though Brother Ira was stabbed to death, murdered," Rees said. And when the Elder looked ready to argue, Rees uncovered the ribs and pointed to the deep jagged gouges in the bone. Elder White collapsed upon the bed.

"Dear God, what wickedness is this? That poor child never did anyone any harm," he said.

Rees nodded. "I know. I'll bring them into town tomorrow and show them to the sheriff. I think he should know, particularly in light of Sister Chastity's death."

"They can't possibly be connected," Elder White said. "He's been gone two years and more."

"And yet he was found on Sister Chastity's brother's farm. Furthermore, two violent deaths in one community," Rees said, "how can they not be connected? Once I understand one, I will understand both." Elder White looked at Rees in silence. For the first time, he truly looked old.

"It is almost time for supper," he said, rising heavily to his feet. "We will have to talk more later." With one final glance at the bones spread out across the floor, he walked slowly to the door and went out.

Rees began bundling the bones back into the wrappings. He had just finished stowing them behind the loom when a tentative knock sounded upon the door.

"Yes?" he said.

"Mr. Rees? It's me, Mouse. Elder White thought you might want fresh water for washing."

"Very well," Rees said, sweeping his eyes over the room. When he was sure nothing looked out of the ordinary, he opened the door. Mouse staggered in, carrying a steaming pail of water. Rees took the pail from her and splashed the water into his basin.

"Did you know Brother Ira?" Rees asked. Mouse looked at him in surprise.

"Of course. I knew him well. He was an orphan a few years older than me. He was always kind to me. We were the same, you see. Damaged." Her blue eyes shifted away and then came back to Rees's face. "He disappeared with Brother Charles. Why? Have you found him? Is he all right?"

"I don't know," Rees lied. Mouse stared fixedly at him.

"What's wrong? You know something." As she continued to stare into his face, comprehension dawned in her eyes. "Ira is dead, isn't he?"

"Why do you think so?" Rees asked.

"Because he didn't come home. He had nowhere else to go. And now you're asking about him." Tears welled in her eyes. Rees slowly nodded.

"I think it is likely. I found something . . . but please, say nothing. Not to anyone. You understand? At least until I know something certain."

"Of course," said Mouse. "I understand. And I'll pray you are wrong." She shook her head, sniffling. "He was so excited, so proud when he was chosen to accompany Brother Charles on his journey. It meant Elder White trusted him, you see."

"And Brother Charles?"

"He was proud too." She smiled. "He kept telling me, 'Change is coming, Mouse. Change is coming, cousin. Everything will be different when I return.'"

"And what did that mean, exactly?" Rees asked. Did Charles intend to finally sign the Covenant or marry Lydia? Mouse shrugged.

"I don't know. So where is Charles?" she asked. "They left together."

"No one knows," Rees said. Mouse caught his tone.

"You can't think he hurt Ira? Why, he wouldn't. Charles was a good man. Or do you think somebody . . . ?" She looked at him in horror.

"I don't know," Rees said. "But I'll find out, I promise you that." Mouse looked into his face and shivered.

"I believe you," she said. "Remember, Mr. Rees, some things the Lord keeps for himself. Vengeance is one."

But not justice, Rees thought.

"I remember," he said. "Will you tell me everything you know about Charles, so I—" The clang of the supper bell sounded through the village, interrupting him. Mouse nodded at him and hurried away. Damn! He couldn't guess when he would find the chance to speak to her again.

Chapter Eleven

Morning came too soon. Rees pulled himself heavily out of bed. His legs and arms ached, he had a blister on his right heel, and his face stung. Sunburn probably, like his hands and arms. And he dreaded this trip into Durham. If the need were not so great he would postpone it.

Bessie, it appeared, felt the same. When Rees went to fetch her and hitch her to the wagon, she balked. Usually a docile animal, she reared and he had to lean hard on the reins. "Let me help," David said, sprinting to his side. Between the two of them, they forced her between the traces and Rees harnessed her. "Going out again?" David asked, a sulky edge to his voice.

"Going to Durham. I'll be back later this morning," Rees said. "How is Buttercup?"

David's face lit up. "Doing so well Levi says we might release her into the herd soon."

"He seems knowledgeable," Rees said.

"He knows everything about cattle," David said fervently. Rees felt a flash of jealousy. Surely David should admire his father so wholeheartedly. "I'll have a great herd of milk cows of my own someday," David said.

"I know you will," Rees said. He touched his son's shoulder. "I'll see you later, I hope."

"I'll probably be in the barns."

One of the Brothers motioned and he hurried away. He did not look back at his father and Rees felt unexpectedly abandoned. This was the first time David had ever walked away from him. As he climbed into the wagon seat, Rees suddenly understood how David must have felt watching his father drive away, over and over, and shame overtook him.

Sheriff Coulton was performing his other role, that of shopkeeper, when Rees arrived in town. He parked the wagon in the store's yard and carried the bags around to the front door. Coulton, swathed in his white apron, presided over his store from the counter as a few ladies roamed the aisles.

"I need to speak to you," Rees said, leaning forward to whisper. The sheriff put a fresh toothpick in his mouth and gestured for Rees to continue. "Not here," he said. "I have to show you something." Coulton did not move. "This is important," Rees said fiercely.

"Very well. Let me find my wife." Coulton disappeared through the door that screened the living quarters from the shop. A few moments later he reappeared, Mrs. Coulton in his wake. She eyed Rees suspiciously. He nodded politely, wondering why Coulton had married such a plain woman. She was taller than he by at least a head and bulkier, with brawny arms. Her shock of black hair framed a face with muddy skin and protuberant black eyes. She turned her hostile gaze upon Rees. Did she ever smile?

"We'll be in the storeroom," Coulton said. "Call me if you need me." She smiled at him lovingly, the curve of her lips unexpectedly attractive.

The sheriff led the way into the crowded storeroom. "I need

something to spread this out upon," Rees said, looking around at the bundles and casks and barrels all tumbled together with no discernible order. Coulton glanced around as well, and rolled over a barrel of flour, standing it bottom end up.

"Will this do?" With a nod, Rees untied the knots in the shawl and spread it out upon the bottom.

Coulton stared. As he picked up one of the bones, he said, "Are these human?"

"Yes. And I think these belong to Brother Ira, one of the Shaker Brothers who went missing about two years ago, on a selling journey with Charles Ellis."

"Charles Ellis? Where did you find the remains?"

"On the farm belonging to Catherine Parker's brother. That is, Sister Chastity's brother," Rees said. Coulton masticated the toothpick for several seconds.

"So, you think the two deaths are connected?"

"I do. I think this body was dumped there. And look at this." Rees carefully unwrapped the ribs and pointed out the knife wounds. Coulton ran his fingers over the gashes.

"The boy was stabbed to death. It takes a lot of strength to do this kind of damage. And the killer stabbed him several times. But how do you know these are the bones of the boy Ira?"

"Because he was lame. See this." Rees showed Coulton the twisted thighbone.

"Hmmm," said Coulton.

"I think Charles Ellis may have stabbed the boy," Rees said.

"No. He couldn't have," Coulton said. "I knew Ellis. He was a good man. Not a killer. And this . . ." He pointed to the gashes striping the bones. "This is powerful anger. Someone wanted to make sure Ira was dead. Ellis was a peaceful man."

"Mmmm," Rees said. "So, maybe someone is killing Shakers?"

"Many of the farmers were angry with the Shakers when

they purchased that farm," Coulton said. "There were a couple of incidents: fires and the like. But that's past now."

"Is it?" Rees asked.

Coulton looked at Rees and shook his head ruefully. "Maybe not. I'd like to keep these overnight, if I may. Take another look at them." Rees hesitated.

"I promised Elder White he could bury them."

"Of course he wants to," Coulton said with a touch of asperity. "But he can certainly 'send them home to Mother' a day later."

"Very well," Rees said, handing the bundle to the sheriff. Coulton cast a curious look at the shawl and the apron but said nothing as he carefully rewrapped them in the canvas.

"Let's go to the Cartwheel for a drink," he suggested. Rees looked at him. It was late for breakfast and early for lunch and Coulton didn't strike him as a drinking man. "I don't often get out of the store," Coulton explained carefully.

"Or away from the wife," Rees guessed with a nod of assent.

They slipped out the back door and cut through the yard to the alley on the other side. When they met the main street, the tavern was directly opposite, and all without Mrs. Coulton knowing.

The Cartwheel was crowded, despite the hour, and raucous with male voices. Coulton greeted most of them and Rees saw a few quickly slip out. He recognized the publican as Simon Rouge, one of Coulton's deputies. "Sit here," Rouge said, gesturing to a table near the bar. To the men already comfortable there, he suggested they find another table; they immediately removed themselves and Coulton and Rees sat down. Sustained by the heavy Shaker breakfast, Rees accepted only a beaker of ale. The sheriff took whiskey.

"I don't believe Ellis had anything to do with the boy's

death," he said. Rees did not argue, although he wondered at the sheriff's passion, and after a moment Coulton asked, "Any luck finding the girl's killer?"

"No. No one seems to have liked her much, but no one hated her either. There's still one Brother I want to talk to. . . . Did you know Charles Ellis well?"

"Only slightly," Coulton said.

"What do you mean?" Rouge cried. "You knew him like a brother."

"I knew Charles Ellis Senior well," Coulton said, controlling his annoyance with difficulty. "But his grandson, Charles Ellis Junior, grew up in Boston."

"He visited here all the time," Rouge said.

"Sometimes," Coulton said.

"All the time. But then, maybe you wouldn't know," Rouge said. "You didn't even live here then." An angry flush surged into the sheriff's cheeks and Rees thought for a minute Coulton would punch the other man.

"Well, did he visit?" Rees asked Rouge.

"Yes, he did, when he got older. His father, Hiram, was estranged from old man Ellis. Once he moved away, Hiram never saw his father again. But Hiram's son Charles was on good terms with his grandfather. The old man doted on the boy, left him everything. There was some problem with that when Charles joined the Shakers. But that's ancient history."

"Did Charles have family around here?" Rees asked.

"Not that I know of," said Coulton.

"Mouse," said Rouge. "Hannah Moore. She's a cousin. Or second cousin. Something."

"Let's get back," Coulton said abruptly. Rees looked at him. Coulton was trying to smile but scarlet suffused his cheeks and neck.

"Wait," Rouge said. "Mr. Pennington was in here earlier. He lost his best mare." Rees slowly sipped his ale. He wanted to hear what else Rouge knew. "Sounds like those horse thieves are still around." Coulton nodded and threw a few pennies on the table.

"My wife's waiting," he said. "I'm sure Mr. Pennington can find me in the store." Rees followed him into the sunlight. "The problem with some people is they think they know everything."

They slipped down the alley and very quietly returned to the storeroom. They were in there no longer than a few seconds when Mrs. Coulton flung open the door and looked, seeing her husband with relief.

"I'm leaving now," Rees said. "I'll return tomorrow for the package."

"I'll have it ready."

Rees went out to his wagon and climbed up to the seat. He suspected Mrs. Coulton knew her husband's secret, that he slipped out once in a while. Since she'd given Rees the devil eye she probably blamed him for it.

The sheriff arrived unexpectedly the following morning, so early Rees had not finished breakfast and had to be fetched out of the Dining Hall. He waited in his buggy, staring around curiously. Rees saw to the second when the other man spotted him approaching; he was at least a head taller than almost everyone else and his hair blazed bright as a new penny.

"What are you doing here?" Rees asked in surprise. The sheriff climbed down. In deference to the steamy weather he did not wear a jacket, but his shirt was freshly ironed, his tricorn was lined up exactly to the center of his forehead, and his polished shoe buckles threw off blinding flashes of reflected sunlight. He took a fresh toothpick from his pocket and jammed it into his mouth.

"Thought I'd save you a trip," he said as he pulled the canvas-wrapped bundle from behind the seat. Rees stared at him doubtfully; this was a long trip for a favor.

"Won't your wife mind?" he asked. Coulton ignored the question.

"The, um, apron and shawl are in there too," he said. "Your lady friend might want them back." Rees felt the heat rising up his neck and into his ears and scolded himself for it. He was no schoolboy with a crush on the girl sitting in the seat ahead of him. Lydia was his assistant and, despite their friendship, only for the time he spent in Zion at that.

"I think," Coulton said, returning to the matter at hand, "someone lost his temper with the boy. Maybe you're right; maybe Charles was planning to make off with the wagon and the goods. I just find that hard to believe since the Charles I remember did not have a temper. Or," Coulton went on, "since you believe the murders of these men and the Shaker girl are related, maybe it was a lovers' quarrel. That I would believe; Charles always liked the ladies."

"I don't think so," Rees said. "It doesn't sound as though they ever met." He did not think Charles killed Ira so he could steal the wagon and the horses either. Maybe he was a thief, but he didn't seem like a killer. And why was Coulton really here?

"This is a pretty farm," the sheriff said, looking around.

"You haven't been here before?" Rees asked. Coulton shook his head.

"No. Although I'm supposed to serve as sheriff for this farm too, Elder White has made it clear I am not welcomed. I will of course respect his wishes. But I'm curious. And I had an errand out this way . . ." Rees nodded; he understood curiosity. "Where was the girl's body found?"

"Tie up your horse and I'll show you," Rees said. Coulton immediately threw the reins over the rail and joined Rees in the road.

They walked over to the weaving shed. Coulton dropped onto his knees on the path. The long pale fingers furred with ginger hair skimmed over the rocks, turning them over until he found several stained with a dark brown substance. Rees thought it could be blood or just as easily dried mud.

Suddenly Lydia Jane hurtled through the weaving shed's door. She threw Rees a glance in which excitement and triumph were equally mixed before hurrying away. Moments later Marguerite Languedela'or appeared at the door. Her gaze passed over the two men without interest but she stared after Lydia. Was she worried? Concerned? Maybe both. Rees wondered what Lydia Jane had wormed out of her.

"Do you know what killed the girl?" Coulton asked, interrupting Rees's train of thought.

"No," Rees said. "Something heavy and round. No sharp edges."

"Again, the killer must be very strong," Coulton said, rising to his feet.

"I think he brought the weapon with him," Rees said. "And carried it away. I found nothing the right shape here in Zion."

"Find the weapon, find the killer," Coulton said. Rees didn't think it would be that easy, and anyway the sheriff's quick assumption of authority irritated him. "It seems you've reached a dead end."

"At the moment," Rees said, his voice sharp. He didn't like the condescension in the sheriff's voice. "I'm sure something will present itself." It must; he would redouble his efforts.

They walked back to the sheriff's buggy and shook hands. "If I can help you in any way," the sheriff said, "please tell me." Rees smiled noncommittally and watched the sheriff drive away. Instead of turning around and driving back to Durham, he continued on through the village, south to Surry. What was that all about? Rees filed it away for future consideration, when he had the time to mull it over. But not now. Now he had to learn exactly what Sister Marguerite told Lydia. He trotted back to the main street and across to the alley by the smithy.

Rees had watched Lydia descend this path several times but this was the first time he climbed it. He passed the rocks they'd used as seats. The path veered right, climbing another slope with Lydia's cottage visible at the top. Tangled wildflowers gradually gave way to cultivated garden flowers: lavender, roses, and tickweed, and a flagged path leading up to the cottage door.

"Lydia Jane," Rees called, his gruff voice an interruption to the somnolent drone of the bees. No answer. He stood at the back door of the cottage and repeated her name. Still no answer. A flicker of white caught his eye. When he climbed the small incline and circled the knot of saplings he finally saw her.

Dressed completely in white, she stood by the hives, bees flying all around her. Her glittering auburn hair, tumbling unbound down her back, wore a moving snood of bees. She kept her eyes closed. Rees froze. Although Lydia seemed unafraid of stings, Rees could think of nothing else. They stood silently for a few moments and then Rees coughed and her eyes flew open. She looked at Rees and then, moving very slowly and deliberately, she shook the bees from her hair. Putting the white hood over her face, she slid the rectangular, wax-coated screen back into the hive. Slowly she approached Rees. He retreated.

By the time she reached the cottage, most of the bees had flown back to the hives or disappeared into the thicket of blooms.

Lydia Jane removed her gloves and hood. "To what do I owe the pleasure of your visit?" she asked.

"You spoke to Sister Marguerite?" he asked.

"I did," she said

"Well, what did she say?" Lydia smiled and moved past him toward the cottage. "Lydia, please. I'm trying to find a murderer."

"And I," she declared, spinning around, "am trying to help you."

"You aren't my partner," he said, and wished he could retract those words as soon as they tumbled from his mouth. He watched the hurt and anger settle over her features.

"I thought I was," she said, her eyes flashing. "Certainly that is what Elder White believes. But even if I am not, common courtesy would decree that you at least tell me you plan to leave the village before I walk down to meet you and wait an hour."

"You knew I meant to bring the bones to Sheriff Coulton," Rees said. She held herself still for a long moment. When she looked at him, he saw disappointment in her eyes. Disappointment in him.

"This has been a difficult time," she said at last. "Questioning the Sisters. The shock of discovering Marguerite's sin. Then Ira's bones." She shook her head. "I need a period of calm and ordered reflection. I'll speak with you another day." She went inside the cottage and closed the door.

"But what did Sister Marguerite say?" he shouted through the door. It remained tightly shut, the window next to it as well. He paced back and forth for a few minutes before finally surrendering and stomping back down the hill. What was the matter with her? He didn't understand. He plunged down the hill, his boots skidding in the dirt. But by the time he reached the bottom he was calmer. Maybe he should have told her his plans; after all, they had found the bones together. But still, wasn't she being unreasonable?

He hurtled around the corner of the Blacksmith's shop and almost slammed into Elder White. The Elder glared at him reprovingly. Then he saw Rees's expression and his disapproval went to alarm. Rees recognized the Elder's interpretation of his quarrel with Lydia and went hot with embarrassment. The two men regarded each other for a moment. Rees broke eye contact and spoke very quickly.

"I have the remains. Sheriff Coulton brought them to me this morning. I can give them to you for burial." Elder White inclined his head and fell into step with Rees.

"I will not identify these remains in the service. We can't know for certain they belong to him," the Elder said. Rees turned to stare at him. "And identifying them as Ira's will raise questions about Brother Charles. That I do not want to do."

"But we should be asking questions about him," Rees protested. Elder White shook his head.

"Gossip will accuse him," he said. "I can't allow that to happen." As Rees drew in a breath to argue, Brother William came flying up the path from the paddock.

"Elder White, one of the blue roans is missing."

"Are you certain?" he cried, wheeling around. Rees turned as well and followed them to the paddock.

Rees could see no difference in the number of horses milling around inside the fence, but White did not even have to count them. "Smoke is missing," he said.

"There's something else," William said. "Brother Michael didn't sleep in his bed last night." Rees scowled, angry at himself. Why hadn't he followed the boy and questioned him?

"Was he at supper last night?" Elder White asked. Brother William shook his head.

"I didn't see him. But he may have been."

"I should tell the sheriff," Rees said.

"No," Elder White said. "It's just a horse."

"Maybe he ran because he killed Sister Chastity and now he thinks I know," Rees said. Both Shakers flinched.

"Very well," Elder White said. "But I'm not interested in punishing the boy."

"Sheriff Coulton may have a different view," Rees said dryly. Like murder, horse stealing was punishable by hanging.

Chapter Twelve

For the second time in as many days, Rees hitched Bessie to the wagon. The recent rainstorms had broken the heat spell and, although sunny, the air was cool with a fresh strong breeze. Bessie broke into a canter of her own accord. As they neared the Doucette farm, Rees impulsively pulled her into the drive and up to the house. Mrs. Doucette and Ruthie were pegging out clothes on the line in the back. Ruthie waved shyly. Mrs. Doucette came out from behind a sheet.

"Why Mr. Rees," she said in surprise, coming through the grass to greet him. She straightened her mobcap with one sun-browned arm. "I just baked a fresh pie; a little bird must have told me you were coming." Rees looked down from his perch on the wagon seat.

"I'm not staying," he said. "I just wanted to promise you I'm working on your yarn. It's taking a little longer than I expected, the interruptions have been constant, but I'll finish soon."

"I'm not worrying about the yarn, Mr. Rees," she said. "Are you sure you won't stop for a piece of pie?"

"I regret I can't," Rees said. "I'm on my way to see the sheriff."

"He's a good man," she said. "Have you met his wife?"

"Yes," Rees admitted. "You also?" She nodded and they shared a glance of complete understanding.

"She is my sister-in-law, Henry's sister. She doesn't like me very well."

"It's a shame when families don't get along," Rees said, thinking of Caroline.

"No one can wound you more deeply," she agreed. "Please stop by on your way home for a slice of pie."

Rees lifted a hand in farewell. He turned the wagon and within a few minutes he and Bessie were driving toward Durham.

The sheriff was back in his usual post at the counter. Rees wondered again what errand had taken Coulton out so early and got him home again so quickly. "Why Mr. Rees, as I live and breathe. Twice today. What an unexpected pleasure," Coulton said, rolling his toothpick to the other side of his mouth.

"One of the Shaker horses has been stolen," Rees said, leaning over the counter.

"Hmmm. And here I thought all of them were paragons of honesty and virtue," the sheriff replied.

"How do you know the horse was stolen by a Shaker?" Rees asked suspiciously. Had Coulton heard something and was that why he'd visited Zion this morning? Was he keeping back information from Rees? Of course he was, just as the weaver kept some things back from the sheriff.

"I don't. But he was, wasn't he?" The sheriff pinned Rees down with his sharp gaze.

"Yes. Well, we think by someone living there. Brother Michael. But I don't know if he has signed the Covenant yet."

Coulton stared at him. "You sound just like them," he said.

"And Elder White doesn't want Michael punished," Rees added. Coulton burst out laughing.

"Horse stealing is a hanging offense, even on Shaker property," he said. "And we've had a rash of missing horses. Anything else missing?"

"Maybe. Elder White hadn't checked his office yet."

"All right." The toothpick went from side to side. "Tell the Elder we'll help him hunt. But if we catch the boy, I make no promises about hanging or otherwise."

"I want to talk to him first," Rees said. "Please, don't hang him before I ask him a few questions."

"Why? You think he might be connected to that girl's murder?"

"I do. It makes sense, doesn't it?" Coulton stared into space for a long moment. He didn't look convinced.

"Very well," he said at last. "I'll give you your few minutes with him. Before we hang him," he added with a grin. Rees felt fairly sure the sheriff was joking.

"Glass of ale before I go?"

"No, thank you. I want to organize the search," Coulton said. "I'm sure I'll see you again. Soon."

"No doubt," Rees said. He returned to the bright sunshine and climbed into the wagon. It must be almost eleven; he would accomplish no weaving before dinner. And of course he still had to deliver Ira's remains to Elder White. He was far too busy.

He slapped the reins down and Bessie jumped forward. They drove out of Durham at a rapid clip and within twenty minutes were nearing the Doucette farm. Rees saw Henry Doucette through a break in the trees, stamping toward the front porch. Even from this distance he looked angry. Rees blessed the impulse that had prompted him to stop earlier.

Rees reached Zion just before dinner. After caring for Bessie, he went to his room to wash up. Some kind soul had put hot water in his jug within the past hour so it was still pleasantly warm. Rees plunged in his hands. And the Shaker soap, there was something about the Shaker soap. Just as Rees picked up his towel, a diffident knock sounded upon the door. Rees opened it, curious. Elder White stood outside.

"Will Sheriff Coulton help us?"

"He said he'll organize a search," Rees said, wiping his hands. "But he wouldn't promise not to send Michael to trial." Elder White, frowning in distress, stepped inside and shut the door behind him. "He promised you'd have an opportunity to intercede on Michael's behalf, however. And I'll have a chance to speak to him first."

"If he is accused of murder, then of course he must be tried and convicted," Elder White said. "But not for taking the horse. He should be allowed to make restitution in some other fashion."

"That is a discussion for you and the sheriff," Rees said. He pulled the loom from the wall and brought out the canvas-wrapped bundle. "These are the remains." Elder White lifted his arms reluctantly. He flipped back a fold of canvas and stared at Lydia Jane's shawl underneath. When he raised his horrified gaze to Rees's, the weaver squirmed.

"She is . . . an assistant," he said. "We merely had a difference of opinion." He did not think Elder White believed him.

"I do not want to see her come to harm," he said. "I am trusting you in this, Mr. Rees."

"I promise you, she won't, not with me," he said. He wasn't sure he believed his own words and Elder White, clearly dubious, kept his anxious gaze upon Rees for a moment longer. Finally the Elder moved toward the door but he turned with his hand on the knob.

"I'll make the announcement tonight," he said. "As I told

you earlier, I will not identify these remains as Ira's. I ask you not to as well. Even here the gossip and speculation will spread like a disease." He shuddered.

"I won't say anything," Rees agreed, wishing he hadn't talked to Mouse. "But I think your people will talk and guess anyway." Elder White nodded in unhappy agreement and went out. Rees pushed the loom back toward the wall. As the dinner bell began its clamor, he too left the room, shutting the door quietly behind him.

After dinner Rees sat down at the loom. As he picked up the shuttle he began organizing his thoughts. Tomorrow, if Lydia would not tell him of her discussion with Marguerite, he would press the girl himself. Michael was her brother; she must know something, maybe even guess where he might hide. And Charles Ellis, now he was a puzzle. Despite fathering a child with Lydia, possibly murdering a boy, and disappearing with a wagon, cash, and two valuable horses, he was considered almost a saint by everyone to whom Rees spoke. He shook his head. From the outside where he sat, Charles Ellis appeared a charming and self-centered rogue. Why did everyone want to believe him innocent? Even Lydia, whose judgment Rees was growing to appreciate. He firmly pushed down all thoughts of her and turned his thoughts toward Sister Chastity. What possible connection could she have with Charles?

Rees wove all afternoon, until the supper bell rang, producing several yards of smooth twill-patterned cloth. And Mrs. Doucette's sack of yarn was still three-quarters full.

He joined the Brethren waiting at the Dining Hall door and claimed the first empty seat he saw. Elder White said Grace and then waited for the slight rustle of people settling themselves to subside. "I do not know how many of you are aware of this," he said, "but Mr. Rees, the guest residing with us, found the remains of some poor traveler. We do not know, and we cannot know, to whom these bones belong. You may hear a rumor that they are the remains of Brother Ira." Gasps and whispers stopped him from continuing. He waited until all was silent once again. "Maybe. We can't know that. We do know these remains belong to some poor unfortunate who fell into a ravine and died alone." Rees glared at the Elder.

He's as close to lying as he can be. It is Ira and he didn't die alone. He was stabbed, dumped over the side, and buried in loose soil.

"We know nothing about this young man," Elder White went on. "Except that he possessed a soul. So we will send him home to Mother, as we would one of our own." He sat down abruptly. And Rees knew that, whatever the Elder might say, he too believed the bones were those of Brother Ira.

Rees waited for Lydia the next morning, shawl and apron in hand, but she did not appear. Finally, impatiently, he bundled the two articles together and started up the slope to her cottage. He met her descending. They nodded at each other and then looked quickly away, just friendly acquaintances. "I thought you might want to speak to Sister Marguerite," she said. Rees handed her the wad of cloth.

"Michael stole a horse and ran away," he said. Lydia looked up sharply, sucking in her breath.

"Do you think he killed Sister Chastity?"

"He says not." Rees paused, thinking. "I'm not sure," he finally admitted. "There's something odd about him."

Lydia nodded "Marguerite says he's always been slow. But he loves horses."

When she did not continue Rees said, "What else did she

say?" Lydia shook her head uncomfortably, her expression troubled. "I need to know if I'm going to be asking more questions."

She hesitated a moment longer and then looked at him challengingly. "Come up to the cottage then. We can sit down."

Now Rees hesitated. "I'm not sure that is wise," he said. "If Elder White sees us . . ."

Lydia shrugged. "I think you're scared of me."

"Elder White spoke to me," Rees said. But Lydia was right; the intimacy of sitting down beside her, just the two of them, terrified him. And excited him.

"He is a kind man," she said. "But we have a lot to talk about and we can't do it standing on a hillside." She turned and led the way up the slope. After a moment Rees followed, knots forming in his stomach.

Although small, the cottage was well built, as all the Shaker structures were, and carefully planned. A large fireplace dominated the back wall, the fire banked to a few glowing embers. A small table, scrubbed white, sat to the right of the fireplace just in front of the back door. On the other side of the cottage a woven curtain partially screened a small bed. Windows flanked the front door on either side and through them Rees could see the rainbow blooms outside. Built-in cabinets and drawers lined the walls. Lydia Jane gestured Rees to the table. She stirred up the fire to start the kettle boiling and put a plate of honey-sweetened cookies on the table.

"Sister Marguerite," she said as she sat down across from Rees. "Well, she admitted Sister Chastity came out at night to meet her. Often." Scarlet flamed into her cheeks. Rees stared at her.

"She admitted they met?"

"They were very close," she said, staring at him intently.

"Chastity and Marguerite? They . . ." He ran out of words.

He'd suspected but hearing blunt confirmation of this possibility staggered him. With an embarrassed nod, Lydia rose to pour hot water into the teapot.

"Just so. Well, that doesn't matter. The point is Chastity was not meeting a man. She and Marguerite met in the weaving house. Nothing is ever locked and in the evening, after everyone is in bed, the weaving house is secluded and private. That's why Chastity was found just outside; she was leaving the shed." Rees leaned back in the chair and stared at the ceiling.

"Was Marguerite still inside that night?" He waved away the cup of tea.

"Yes. They always left singly."

"What did she hear?"

"That's it; nothing." Lydia's forehead wrinkled. "She says she went out and Chastity was lying on the ground."

"Didn't she go for help?" Rees cried, horrified.

"She says she was afraid to," Lydia said. "All those unwelcome questions, you know. She was afraid she would be asked to leave Zion." She paused and added, "And she probably would be. She begged me to say nothing."

"And will you keep silent?"

"I don't know," Lydia said. "I paid a heavy price for disobeying the rules. I know it is uncharitable of me to think that . . ." She sighed. "I wonder sometimes, would Charles have stayed with me? Or would he have finally signed the Covenant?" Rees knew what he thought but kept silent with an effort. "I know this," Lydia said, leaning forward and staring intently at Rees. "He did not kill Brother Ira and take the wagon and run. There was no reason to. And if he did not, then someone killed them both and Charles's body is somewhere out there. We just haven't found it yet. We need to look again in that bank."

"We might search and search and never find it," Rees said. He paused, not wanting to ask the question but needing to hear the answer. "You miss him, don't you?"

"Sometimes," she admitted. "And some days I can't even remember his face. And that is worst of all." Rees nodded. Sometimes he remembered only Dolly's gray eyes; the rest of her face was a blur.

This time the silence extended for several moments. Rees broke it. "I need to talk to Marguerite about Michael. He is her brother, isn't he?"

"Yes," Lydia said. "Her younger brother. She admitted that much." Rising to her feet, she banked the fire and put the cookies into the jar. Rees went outside and waited by the door. Then they walked down to the village together.

Marguerite was not in the weaving shed today. A young girl, who stared in disbelief at Rees and Lydia Jane standing together, directed them to the dyeing shed at the back of the red barn. Once they passed the barn Rees could follow his nose; the stink of fermenting indigo was both pungent and unmistakable. Several Sisters, including Marguerite, were scraping the indigo precipitated to the bottom of the final vat into bricks and laying them out to dry. She worked in an unhappy fury. When she saw Rees and Lydia approach her expression darkened into a grim rage. With a quick look at Rees, Lydia moved to Sister Clementine and spoke in a soft whisper. Clementine glanced at Rees before settling her sympathetic gaze upon the French woman.

"Sister Marguerite," she said in her soft southern voice, "these here people want to speak to you."

Although the Sister obeyed, approaching them with downcast eyes, her stiff shoulders betrayed both anger and fear. As they moved out of earshot of the other women, she muttered, "I told you everything."

"I just have a few more questions," Rees said. Marguerite moved her shoulders fretfully. "When you were hiding in the weaving shed, and Sister Chastity was outside, did you hear anything?" Marguerite shook her head. "You must have," he said impatiently. "The killer didn't fly over the path. You must have heard footsteps." Marguerite looked away from him, shaking her head. Rees glared at her with a mixture of anger and scorn. "She was your friend," he said, "but you won't help us. Your brother stole a horse and ran away and now the sheriff and his deputies, not just the unarmed Shakers, are looking for him. Yet you won't help us. I can only believe you don't care about either of them."

She turned back to him, her eyes wide in her suddenly ashen face. "The sheriff is involved?" she gasped. Rees nodded.

"I'm trying to help you," he said. "And Michael. Why won't you trust me?" She stared at him.

"I think you are a good man," she said at last, "but you are rushing into something you don't understand. You trust the wrong people. It is not safe to tell you anything."

"Is Michael safer now than he was?" Rees retorted, his voice rising.

Tears flooded her eyes. "No. He was as safe here as he could be. But you frightened him, Mr. Rees. You did that. You frightened him into running away."

"Well then, tell me everything you know and maybe I can find him before the sheriff and bring him back." She shook her head slightly, but not in disagreement.

"You must understand," she said, "when I was in the weaving shed I closed the door so no one would see me. I did hear footsteps, but faint. And someone spoke to her but so softly I could not hear the words."

"Could you recognize the voice?" Rees asked. She shook her head.

"I cannot even tell you if it was a man or a woman. It was just a soft undertone." She shrugged. "And he must have been wearing a cloak. I heard a . . . slither like a snake." Rees considered that for a moment but he couldn't see how it helped. "When all was quiet, I peeked outside. And there she was, my dear friend, lying on the path." She choked back a sob. Rees waited while she fought her emotion. "I lit my candle and that's when I saw the blood. I screamed but no one heard me and I was afraid to scream again. When I knelt beside her I could see she wasn't breathing. I said her name over and over but she wouldn't wake up." Rees kept his eyes upon her and she blushed. "I know you judge me, you think me cold and heartless for leaving her there, but I knew if I called for help Elder White would wonder what we were doing there and would expel me. Where would I go? How would I live?" She looked up at Rees pleadingly. "Don't you understand? I have no one but Michael. It would be the streets for me."

"Yes, I see," he said with unwilling sympathy. There was nowhere else for her. She buried her face in her hands and wept in unrestrained sorrow. "Let's talk about Michael." She nodded, her shoulders shaking, but did not look up for another few moments. Then she wiped her face on her apron and took a deep breath. "Why did he come here?"

"He loves horses. He got into some trouble and needed a place to stay. I knew it would be safe here and the Shakers ask no questions."

"He didn't just steal a horse here," Rees said in sudden understanding. "That's what he does; he's a horse thief. Of course you don't want the connection between you known. He must have sheriffs all around the country after him."

"He is my brother," she explained simply. "I swear to you, Mr. Rees, he is not a killer." Rees thought of the boy, high-strung and trembling, and nodded.

"I believe you," he said. "But why was he so scared of me. I meant him no harm." Marguerite looked away from him for a long moment and he thought she was preparing to lie. But when she turned her eyes were full of tears.

"He saw someone he knew," she said. "They wanted him to help steal some horses."

"The blue roan?"

"I don't know. But he did not want to do it. He worked with the horses here. He didn't need anything else."

Rees thought that made a certain sense; Brother Levi seemed cut from the same cloth. "Where was he supposed to take the horses?"

"Southern Kentucky, I believe. I'm not sure though."

"Did he tell you whom he met in Durham? Or where he would go for help?"

"No. My brother told me very little and I did not want to know."

That Rees believed completely. "Thank you," he said. "I'll do my best to protect your brother." Marguerite looked at him sadly.

"I do not believe you can. When he left Zion, he put himself out for the wolves to find."

As Marguerite walked slowly back to the dye vats, Lydia said, "What do we do now?"

"I'll have to tell Sheriff Coulton," Rees said. "He may be able to track Michael, maybe even as far as Kentucky. And I must look into Charles Ellis. He's connected to this somehow." Realizing too late what he had said, he looked at Lydia apologetically.

She smiled at him, although it was a forced smile, and said, "He's dead. I know it. He loved too many people here to leave. Not just me, Mr. Rees, but all the family that remained, both blood and Shakers. And he loved Zion." She swept her arms around at the barns and fields. "He would not leave all of this." Rees did not want to argue but he thought it just as likely Charles had chosen to make a new life somewhere else. "I know he's dead. We need to search that streambed again."

"We can do that," Rees said, "but there's no guarantee Charles's body would be put with Ira's. And that stream runs all the way from Durham to Surry and beyond."

"We must try," she said stubbornly.

"Very well," Rees said. He touched her shoulder lightly, to comfort her. "But not today. After I speak with Sheriff Coulton, I plan to spend the rest of my today weaving. Mrs. Doucette is waiting for her cloth and I haven't woven even one-half of her yarn yet. Do you want to assist me with that?" She looked startled and then she smiled.

"No, Mr. Rees," she said. "I think you can do that without me. Besides, you would find me a poor weaver." This time the smile she gave him was genuine and Rees knew she'd forgiven him. "But maybe the day after that?"

"Maybe." He smiled at her before turning serious once again. "Listen, can you imagine why someone would kill Charles? You knew him and everyone else here. Did he have enemies?"

"Of course not. It wasn't Charles the killer was after, couldn't be. It must have been the wagon and the horses and the money from the sale of goods."

"A robbery?"

"Yes. It does happen. And if Charles and Ira had good fortune, they might have been carrying as much as a hundred dollars." Rees whistled. A man could set himself up as a wealthy landowner with that kind of money. A robbery certainly seemed a plausible motive. But then why take such pains to hide Ira's body?

"Was it known when Charles and Ira were due to arrive back in Zion?"

"Yes," Lydia said. "Not to the exact hour, or course. But Charles sent word from Surry that he would be back the next day."

"Everyone knew that?"

"Of course. We were all so happy," she added wistfully.

Rees carefully did not voice his thoughts. While it was possible some opportunistic robber saw a chance to steal from the Shakers (but how would he know how much money they were carrying?), it did not seem likely. Someone knew the exact route and time of their arrival and lay in wait; that meant it was someone they knew. Rees's money was still on Charles, but it could be anyone in Zion or possibly in Durham as well. And the effort to conceal Ira's body suggested the killer lived here and planned to remain here.

Chapter Thirteen

Lydia did not ask to accompany Rees to Durham and he would not have agreed anyway. He did not need a chaperone in Durham. Certainly he would miss her company and her always trenchant opinions, far more than he cared to admit, but it was time to make some distance. He was getting too attached. Besides, he did not believe she would want to accompany him. The discovery of Ira's bones had cut her old scars open again and she'd retreated inside herself. Rees felt that withdrawal keenly. With a mixture of jealousy and pity, he saw her old feelings for Charles surface, and her grief as he died for her once again. She would only prove a distraction, Rees told himself, as his awareness of her feelings, and his own for all his struggle to diminish them, kept him from concentrating on the investigation at hand. Better to create some distance, he repeated, especially before his inevitable departure in a few weeks.

They did not speak to one another again, and once they reached the village, they separated. Lydia climbed the path behind the Blacksmith and Rees went to the paddock for Bessie. A few minutes later David found him in front of the stables hitching the mare to the wagon. "Any news about Brother Michael?" he asked.

"I'm on my way into Durham to talk to the sheriff now," Rees said. "Did you know him well?"

"No. I didn't like him much. He boasted."

"Boasted about what?"

"Horses. He claimed he had a big farm down south with a large herd of horses." David shook his head. "No one believed him. And none of the Brethren would be impressed anyway. They don't care how many horses a man owns. A man's worth is not measured in his possessions," David intoned, sounding so like Elder White Rees laughed involuntarily.

"That is not polite," he said. David grinned unrepentantly, Dolly's eyes sparkling in his tanned face. Rees's heart turned over.

"I wasn't surprised to hear he stole one of our stallions," David said. "He wanted the blue roans. He talked about interbreeding them with the Canadian pacers." He stopped and after a moment he said tentatively, "May I ride to Durham with you?" He looked as though he expected his father to refuse. Guilt swept over Rees.

"Of course," he said. "You're welcome to join me." Looking as though he couldn't believe his good luck, David jumped into the seat. Rees climbed up more slowly, recalling the day when he too could spring into a wagon seat. They took off in silence, but then Rees could not keep quiet. "You know," he blurted, surprising himself as much as David, "I didn't mean to abandon you. I thought you were somewhere safe. I had to make a living and—"

"But why couldn't you make a living as a farmer?" David said.

"I can't. I feel penned up. And there are bad memories for me in Dugard." His voice faltered. "I still miss your mother."

David stared straight ahead. "I won't go back there," he said. "Not with them there."

"The farm belongs to us," Rees said. "You and I."

David turned to face his father and said sharply, "They don't think so."

"I know. I have to think about the best way of dealing with that. I don't want to just evict them. Caroline is my baby sister."

After a few moments of silence David said, "Let me help you find Sister Chastity's killer."

"You have been helping."

"No. I mean more. I can talk to people too."

"It's too dangerous," Rees said.

"Sister Lydia helps," David said. "Isn't it dangerous for her?"

"She is my chaperone," Rees said. "I can't speak to the Sisters without her."

"I can help search—"

But Rees shook his head again. "No. The man who killed Sister Chastity may have also murdered Brother Ira. Maybe Charles Ellis. He won't hesitate to kill you too." He glanced at his son. David's lower lip protruded like a sulky child's. But his curiosity warred with his disappointment and after a few moments he said, "Didn't Brother Charles and Brother Ira go out on the selling trip over two years ago? Sister Chastity didn't even know them."

"I know. But I think the killer knew them all," Rees said. *And still lives here.*

Although he did not say that aloud, David reached the same conclusion. Turning to stare at his father in alarm, he said, "He probably knows us too." Rees sat in a stiff silence, reluctant to lie but unwilling to concur and further frighten his son. David nodded in understanding. "Of course he does."

As they approached the Doucette farm, Rees saw the opportunity for a more neutral topic of conversation. "I'm weaving for the wife on this farm," he said. "Nice woman. And nice children . . ." As he spoke a musket shot rang out, high over their heads, but terrifying. Bessie bolted and almost ran the wagon into the ditch. Rees, who'd half-leaped from his seat in surprise, struggled to pull her back onto the road. The wagon came to a stop with one wheel on the grassy verge, across the road from the Doucette driveway but only a few feet closer to town. Henry Doucette was standing near the end of their lane.

"Are you crazy?" Rees shouted, standing up in the seat.

"Stay off my property," Doucette bellowed, waving his musket threateningly.

"Henry, Henry," his wife said, trying to lean on his arm and wrest the gun from his grasp at the same time. He slapped her away and leveled the musket at Rees and David once again. "Damn Shakers. Stay away from me." The slurring of his words and his unsteady balance told the tale: he was drunk. Mrs. Doucette rose to her feet once again, and, with her mouth set determinedly, she jerked the musket from her husband's hands. He almost fell over.

"Give that back," he demanded. She turned and sprinted up the drive, surprisingly fast despite her skirts. Doucette reeled after her in pursuit. Rees sat down, his trembling legs too weak to support him. He picked up the reins but sat there a moment longer. His hands didn't have the strength to grasp the leathers.

"We'd better go," David said, his voice trembling on the edge of hysteria. "He might come back." Rees nodded and slapped the reins down onto Bessie's back. She jerked forward and the straps almost slipped through his fingers. David half-turned to stare back at the driveway; he didn't face front until they were well out of range of any musket ball. "Why was he shooting at us?"

"Your clothing," Rees said. "At least I think so. You look like a Shaker." David stared down at his clothing.

"Next time I drive this way," he said with a breathy gust of laughter, "I'll wear rags." Rees laughed too, nervously and too loudly for such a weak joke. But it released the tension. "I heard some of the farmers didn't like the Brethren," David said when they'd both settled, "but I didn't think anyone would try to kill them."

"Fortunately for us," Rees said, forcing himself to speak calmly, "Mr. Doucette was not trying to kill us. He fired over our heads. We were never really in any danger."

But David *is* in danger as long as he wears those clothes, Rees thought. I'm going to wring Doucette's fool neck, first chance I get.

Coulton was not standing in his usual place, king of the store counter. Instead Mrs. Coulton stood there, unsmiling and watching her customers suspiciously. "Is the sheriff here?" Rees asked. She glared at him and Rees thought she would refuse to answer. He stared back, almost eye to eye. She was tall for a woman, and she carried herself with an awareness of her height and physical strength. Not for the first time, Rees wondered what the pleasant sheriff saw in his wife. Her gaze slipped over Rees and touched upon David. She leaned over the counter.

"What are you doing here?" she asked Rees in a fierce whisper. David, his eyes wide, turned to look at his father.

"I'll look for the sheriff myself," Rees said and turned to the back door. As they hurried down the crowded aisle, he said to his son, "I see she doesn't like Shakers either." Even while Rees missed Lydia's pungent remarks, he was glad she hadn't witnessed the prejudice David had just experienced.

They found the sheriff in the back storeroom. Ledgers and scraps of paper surrounded him but he gladly pushed them aside.

Despite the open window and door, the little room was hot and stuffy and stank of horses. "Let's talk outside," he suggested, jumping to his feet.

"Any sign of Michael?" Rees asked.

Coulton shook his head. "Nobody has seen him, not recently anyway. The string of horse thefts around here that you heard Deputy Rouge mention have stopped. At least for the time being. But I had news of thefts all up and down the eastern seaboard. That sounds like him I think. He's a professional. I've no doubt he's fled to another state by now."

"Maybe Kentucky," Rees said. "This is my son. David, tell Sheriff Coulton what you told me." As Coulton turned to face the boy, David repeated his story. The sheriff listened without interrupting, the toothpick dancing from one side of his mouth to the other.

"Kentucky, huh? Tell Elder White he won't see his horse again." He stared up into the sky. "I didn't see him as a horse breeder though."

"Does Mr. Doucette breed horses?" David asked suddenly.

"Not that I know of," Coulton said in surprise. He glanced at Rees for clarification.

"We were riding by his property when he started shooting," Rees said. "He fired over our heads. He was too drunk to hit anything."

Coulton sighed. "Again? Every now and then he gets liquored up and starts shooting. He hasn't hurt anyone so far as I know. Not yet. I'll ride out to his farm and have another talk with him." Coulton shook his head in disgust.

"Do you have a map of the area?" Rees asked. Coulton nodded.

"Inside." He preceded Rees back into the small close room. "What do you want it for?"

"I want to take a look at the stream. Since I found those bones, several people have wondered if Charles Ellis was also murdered and buried somewhere along there." Coulton rummaged through a pile of paper stacked upon the flat end of a barrel.

"Seems like a long shot to find a body that's been buried two years." He pulled out a roll of parchment and flattened it over the heaps of paper on his table. "This is Durham," Coulton said, stabbing at a circle with one blunt forefinger. Rees peered at it. Durham lay further inland than he supposed. The Surry road did not veer toward the coast until it approached Zion. "Your stream," Coulton pointed to a thin line, "runs alongside the road from Durham until here, where it turns east and cuts through the Shaker farm." Rees nodded. It came down across the village road, under the springhouse, and past the laundry house. "It curves here," Coulton went on, "and runs parallel to the coast for several miles. The Surry road, as it bends southeast, meets the stream somewhere around here and they run together through Surry and southward after that."

Rees peered at the line. And past the Lewis farm. He pointed to the stream after it made its turn by the Shaker laundry. "How easy would it be to bring a wagon to it?"

Coulton shook his head. "I don't know. I've never been there. But I would guess, not very. Anyway, the Shakers have all of this cleared for fields."

Rees bent over the map and studied it. He had never seen this portion of the stream either. If it were not so out of the way, he would wonder if maybe Charles Ellis had never left Zion after all. He straightened and allowed the map to snap back into its loose roll.

"Yes?" Coulton looked past Rees, who whirled around. Mrs. Coulton stood just outside the open door, listening. Rees wondered how long she'd been standing there, watching them. He involuntarily shuddered.

"I can't find the candles," she said. "And Deputy Rouge is here, wanting to speak with you."

"I'll be right out," Coulton promised. He turned questioningly toward Rees.

"That's all I wanted," Rees said, looking around for David. The boy had escaped the suffocating little closet and was sitting outside on a barrel. "I'll leave this way," Rees said, stepping through the back door.

"If I hear anything about your Brother Michael, I'll get word to you," the sheriff promised and shut the door behind them.

Chapter Fourteen

Rees stiffened when they approached the Doucette farm on the way back and David gripped the sides of the wagon seat so tightly his knuckles went white. He watched the Doucette driveway intently as though he expected Mr. Doucette to fly out firing his musket. Once they rode past the driveway, he exhaled with relief and relaxed.

"Are you going to search the stream?" he asked after a few minutes.

"I thought I'd walk over and look at it after dinner," Rees said. He didn't expect to find anything, least of all the body of Charles Ellis, but now he was curious.

"Please, I want to come with you," David said, turning his pleading gray eyes upon his father. Rees couldn't bear to disappoint those puppy eyes. When he did not immediately refuse, David said, "It's on Shaker property. I'll be safe there. With you." Rees hesitated and as the seconds ticked by David began to look hopeful.

"Very well," Rees finally said. "If you can be excused from your chores. And we will not set foot outside the borders of Zion. Understand?"

"Yes, yes," David agreed eagerly. "I understand."

They drove into Zion and unhitched Bessie. While David

took her to the paddock, Rees pushed the wagon into the stables. While they were so occupied, the dinner bell rang and Believers began streaming toward the Dining Hall. Rees and David joined the throng, David sprinting off to talk to Brother Levi. Rees caught up to Elder White and said, "I spoke to Sheriff Coulton. He says he thinks Brother Michael has fled. I regret to say you will probably not recover the horse." Elder White looked at Rees in surprise.

"Is he sure? Brother Jacob said he thought he saw Michael over by Piper Lane yesterday."

"I thought . . . he seemed sure," Rees said. "Is Jacob?"

"No. The man he saw wore farmer's clothing and perhaps Jacob was deceived by a passing resemblance."

"Probably," Rees said. But as he went into his room to wash his face and hands he wondered. If the sheriff only supposed Michael had fled, based on the sudden cessation of disappearing horses, he could be wrong. And Brother Jacob right. In which case Rees must speak to Coulton and warn him as soon as possible.

After dinner David and Rees met outside the Dwelling House. The sun blazed down, burning Rees's unprotected forearms. He unrolled his sleeves as they walked briskly to the end of the street and crossed the wooden bridge. No laundry fluttered on the drying lines today and Rees could see past the laundry shed to the rocky cliff on the other side of the stream.

As they followed the streambed it deepened from a gully to a gorge. By the time they reached the bend in the stream, seen now to have been caused by an enormous boulder, the walls leading down to the rivulet of water below was at least fifteen feet high. "Let's go down," David said, and plunged down the steep slope. He slipped on the loose scree and almost fell, landing on the rocky bank with his foot and leg plunging knee-deep in the water. Shaking his head, Rees remained on top; he would leave all adventurous feats to the boy.

Rees walked along the edge, dodging the trees that clung thickly to the lip, although his questions had already been answered. No wagon could penetrate the screen of trees, even if it could escape notice as it trundled past the laundry shed. They would find nothing here.

They walked for some time. From his elevated vantage point, Rees watched David's coppery hair as he scrambled over the uneven ground. The sun-splashed stream was wider now, and faster, and Rees suspected that at the center of the pools the water dropped to a depth of several feet. As the gully cut through the steep craggy slope, the water tumbled over boulders, settled into large pools, and dropped as small waterfalls. Impenetrable verdant forest on both banks formed a screen too thick to see through. This was wild country, and Rees thought that if a body were hidden here, it would likely never be found.

After an hour or more of walking, Rees called a halt. "Come up here, David," he said.

"But the stream continues," David protested.

"Yes. But there is no way to bring a wagon through here and even a horse would have difficulty."

"We should follow it to the end," David said stubbornly.

"David," Rees said. David looked around, ignoring his father.

"Maybe we should pick it up closer to the road," he said.

"Maybe," Rees said, "but not today." He waited for David to try and persuade him but the boy didn't. He would though, Rees knew that; he'd inherited stubbornness from both parents. When David scrambled up the slope and joined him at the top, they started home.

They reached the center of Zion at mid-afternoon. David shot off toward the barns but Rees, tired and sore, limped to his room. Blisters swelled up on his heels and his legs ached from the unaccustomed exercise. He stripped off his shoes and stockings and hobbled to the ewer to wash away the dirt and sweat from his face and hands. Although the trees had shaded him from the sun, the bites of both black flies and mosquitoes spotted his arms like a rash. David was probably covered with them too.

He felt too tired to sit down at the loom and work but he forced himself. More important even than the livelihood it provided was the promise he'd made to Mrs. Doucette. As he threw the shuttle he gradually relaxed and after a few moments his mind began to float free. He thought of Lydia crying, "He's not dead," and Sister Marguerite, "He's my brother," and Coulton assuring him the boy had fled. But Elder White said sonorously, "Brother Jacob saw him," and David said, "We need to search the riverbank because he's hiding there."

The clang of the supper bell woke him. He'd fallen asleep with his head on the warp. Rees straightened up, his back aching in protest. His right hand, numb at first, began to tingle and a sharp pain in his right cheek marked the imprint of the shuttle. Since vanity was a sin, there were no mirrors, but when Rees touched his cheek he clearly felt the grooved point, like the prow of a ship, left by the shuttle. Standing, he tottered to the chair and sat down to replace his shoes and socks. Sleeping had exhausted the time meant for weaving, but at least his unconscious mind had thrown up a suggestion for further investigation.

Rees awoke next morning to both heat and humidity. The sky glowered down with the threat of rain. He'd overslept, not awakened even by the breakfast bell, and the singing and chanting from the Sunday service already floated through the window. He put on his soft moccasins so he would not further injure his blistered feet, and walked to the end of town. He crossed the wooden bridge but instead of turning left, toward the laundry house, he turned right. He started up the incline.

On a weekday, he could expect to hear the sounds of hammering as the Brethren worked on the new gristmill. But today all was silent, except for the sounds of rushing water. On this side of the main street, the stream descended in a series of drops. The water was not deep but it traveled fast, in a rush of white foam. When Rees reached the top of the first more or less level point, he was panting.

The stream took a sudden turn to the right. The water dropped from a high ledge into a small but fast-moving waterfall. The mill's paddle wheel, already in place, turned slowly with the force of the water.

"Do you like our mill?" asked Lydia from behind him. Rees spun around in surprise. She smiled tentatively. Rees grinned at her.

"It's too far away from the village," he said.

"Oh, it not just for Zion," she said. She pointed at the path under their feet. "If you keep following this you'll reach the Surry road. Elder White hopes the farmers around us will bring their grain harvests here to be ground."

"For a group that turned away from the world," Rees observed, "they are remarkably clever businessmen." Lydia nodded.

"We can walk up to the mill," she said, pointing to a narrow bridge over the stream and the path on the other side.

"I'd like to see it," Rees said. She whirled in a flutter of skirts and walked quickly across the bridge. Rees hurried to catch up. The path on the other side went up a much steeper slope. They arrived with the unfinished mill just ahead of them and a mill-pond to the left. The water seemed calm until it reached the lip of the cliff where it spilled over in a great rush. Breathing hard and sweating, Rees turned around. They were so high he could see the end of Piper Lane where it connected to the Surry road. Anyone walking there would be clearly visible. Brother Jacob *had* seen someone; Rees could now be certain of that.

A distant rumble of thunder and a flash of lightning warned of the rapidly approaching storm. Lydia looked at the sky and pointed toward the black clouds boiling in from the west. "We'd better go back," she said, but it was already too late. Big fat drops of rain began pattering down around them. They ran for the mill, and in those few seconds, the rain became a torrent.

Only some of the roof was on. Rees and Lydia Jane huddled in that protected section. The sounds of crashing thunder and beating rain made speech impossible. The sky outside grew so dark Rees could barely see Lydia's face. A sudden bolt of lightning split the sky, illuminating everything in a garish white light.

"This won't last long," Lydia shouted. Rees nodded, turning to look at her. She stood very close, close enough to touch. They both realized it at the same time and backed up self-consciously. But now Rees was hyperaware of her. He imagined he could feel the heat emanating from her body and that he could smell her hair. He gripped one of the crossbeams upon the wall with all his strength and focused upon the odor of sawdust and damp earth.

Since Dolly's death he had met many women and become friends with a few. Carnal connections had been rare and meaningless. But Lydia . . . Rees stared into the darkness, knowing if he looked at her he would grab her and press her to the wall. He'd never wanted anyone as much as he did then. At the same time, although he hungered for her, desire was not all he felt. Lydia was different. For the first time he could see himself remarrying, something he never thought he would do after Dolly. And knowing how much pain and sorrow loving could bring, he wanted to turn and run, grab his wagon and Bessie and flee the village. He sucked in his breath and fought for control.

The storm passed over, the rain diminishing to a steady drizzle and the sky beginning to lighten. Gray daylight and cool wet air poured in. Lydia's presence no longer seemed so intimate, but Rees still knew he had to get away. His hands hurt. He unclamped them from the beams. Deep red grooves scarred the palms and splinters flecked his fingers.

"We should leave," he said, surprised by his normal-sounding voice. She nodded. He saw her disappointment and wondered, flushing with embarrassment, if she had sensed his desire and welcomed it.

They silently left the mill, stepping into a silvery drizzle. The cooler air brought by the storm raised goose bumps on Rees's arms. As they went down the path, a shaft of sun broke through the clouds. "A sun shower," Lydia cried, turning up her face in delight. It was too much for his already overwrought senses.

"Excuse me, I've got work to do," he said. With a hastily muttered farewell he hurried down the path and away from Lydia. If it were not a Sunday, he would have hitched Bessie and fled the village, searching the stream down toward Surry or driving around Piper Lane. But ride around investigating on a Sunday? Elder White would not accept it. Rees wasn't sure he could escape scrutiny hiding in his room and weaving but he planned to try.

As he settled into weaving's rhythm, his mind began working independently. He thought about Lydia Jane first. He realized that he loved her. She had crept inside him, become part of him so that he couldn't imagine life without her. But he also knew he couldn't settle down again. He could never be just a farmer, and the wandering required by his work would only cause her unhappiness. It had killed Dolly, bringing home the illness that brought death to her and the babe in her belly. That pain and guilt would never leave him. His only choice was to leave Zion, so he must hurry and finish looking into the deaths.

Shoving all thoughts of Lydia from his mind, Rees turned his attention to the murders. Was Sister Chastity connected to Ira and Charles, and if so, how? Where exactly was Charles? Dead? Or alive and living a good life somewhere else? Lydia was so convinced of his death she'd half-persuaded Rees as well, but that might not be true. Again he thrust the thought of Lydia from him. If Charles was indeed dead, where were his remains? Rees thought of searching the area between Durham and Surry and his heart quailed. The great area of fields and forest would be close to impossible to search. Even an examination of the stream would take time, more time than he could spend.

Then there was Brother Michael. Recalling his dream, Rees wondered if the sheriff was wrong and Michael was hiding in the area. But why? The answer jumped into Rees's mind: because he wanted the other two blue roans in the Shaker paddock.

"I've got it back to front," Rees thought. Tomorrow he would walk over to Piper Lane and take a look around.

Chapter Fifteen

Monday dawned hot and bright, the thundershowers of the previous day just a memory. Rees slipped out of the Dining Hall through the back door so he could avoid Lydia. Although ashamed of his cowardice, he just couldn't face her, not today.

"Where are you going?" David asked, falling into step.

"Just walking to the end of the village," Rees said. "Thought I'd take a look at Piper Lane." David said nothing but he matched his long stride to his father's. They crossed the small bridge and continued on to the end. Trees grew thickly on both sides of the street, screening the fields on the left and hiding the village from passersby on the Surry road to the right. Rees started across the road. Piper Lane lay maybe twenty feet south of him.

With the sudden loud crack of a musket, Rees dropped face-down on the ground. Someone was shooting at them again.

"Down," he shouted to his son. But when he turned, David was running and already halfway to the copse of trees at the back. Rees scuttled into the forest on the point and peered through the tree trunks to see if he could spot the shooter. He saw movement upon the bluff on the southern side of Piper Lane but could not identify the person.

It was just barely possible it was a hunter, but Rees didn't believe it. Durham was not the frontier where the men went out mornings to hunt squirrel; this was farming country. Slipping from tree to tree, Rees approached the road. The shooter couldn't see him either. But as he neared the Surry road, another shot sounded through the forest. Rees stopped moving. He didn't expect his attacker to hit him easily; muskets were notoriously inaccurate, but he saw no reason to take chances either. Clearly, this was no hunter. Someone perceived Rees as a threat and would keep him pinned here as long as they could. And that someone could be Michael, but Rees knew better than to assume that was the case.

And there was David. Rees turned around but the boy had gone to ground somewhere and was invisible. Rees began to scrabble backward, toward Zion's main street. He still did not see David. When he reached the end of the tree break Rees took in a deep breath. Then he sprinted across the road toward the trees on the other side as fast as he could. The shooter did not fire. Rees didn't know whether he was out of sight, out of range, or whether the shooter had fled.

David was lying on the ground in the copse of trees. Mud, leaves, and twigs clung to his hair and clothing as though he'd propelled himself through the forest headfirst. Tear tracks streaked his dirty cheeks. Rees dropped to his knees beside him.

"Are you all right?" Rees asked.

"Fine." David rolled over to look at his father.

"Probably just a hunter." Rees tried to sound reassuring.

"He was shooting at you," David said.

"Probably just a hunter," Rees repeated.

"Don't lie to me," David said. Rees met his son's steady gaze.

"Yes, someone was shooting at me. If I had to guess, I'd say it might be Michael. If he hasn't run off. He could be over there waiting for his chance to steal those blue roan horses."

David took in a deep breath. "What are you going to do?"

"Ride into town and tell Sheriff Coulton."

"I want to come with you."

"No. I don't know if Mr. Languedela'or is just warning me off or really trying to hit me. In any case, he will be as likely to miss me and hit my companion. I can't lose you, David."

David looked at him. "You lost me for six years."

"I thought you were safe. And I always planned to go home and fetch you," Rees said. "Dolly's own mother told me I'd be ready to remarry in a year. But grief doesn't disappear on schedule. I missed your mother so much I could barely take care of myself. I wouldn't have been able to care for a child."

"Don't you understand?" David cried, his eyes moistening. "When Mother died you left me an orphan. You chose to disappear. And you almost never came back." Rees looked away in shame.

Thrusting himself to his feet, David ran out of the copse of trees, instantly disappearing from sight.

Rees slowly stood up, his heartbeat just now returning to normal. He started after David but realized the boy would be too angry to talk. He hesitated, realizing he could see the path in front of the weaving shed from this vantage point. Trees screened him from the village street and fringed the stream. But he could peer through the trunks and even see a corner of the building. Struck by inspiration, Rees looked around him. Pushed to one side was a pile of old horse droppings and the clear imprint of buggy wheels. Now he saw how the killer accomplished Sister Chastity's death. He had pulled in here to wait, probably more than once while he learned her routine. Nobody would have seen him. Then, that night, after dark, he'd left his buggy and his horse here and walked across to hide in the trees beside the stream. When he saw Chastity leave the shed, he ran up the path, struck her, and retreated. He'd have moved very quickly. Had Chastity seen him? Maybe, but Rees thought probably not. She would surely have screamed or reacted somehow to the sight of an unfamiliar man. A few minutes more and he would have been back in his buggy out on the Surry road heading home.

Rees cursed himself for a fool; this he should have seen earlier. But he still didn't know why. Or who. Not Michael; he saw Chastity every day and had no need of a buggy to spy upon her. And Rees still couldn't see a solid connection between Chastity and the earlier deaths, though he was sure it was there. The only thing he knew for certain was that passions had not cooled in the intervening two years, much like his own grief, which the intervening years had barely blunted.

Rees jogged into the village, intending to hitch Bessie to the wagon and drive into Durham. Alerting the sheriff must be his first priority. But as he started toward the stables, Brother William waved at him. "We've been looking for you," he said, eyeing Rees's sweat-stained and dirty clothing in disapproval. "Where have you been?"

"Working," Rees said. He did not want to confide the entire story to the Shaker, and possibly see it spread through Zion, terrifying everyone. "Why do you want me?"

"Eldress Phelps is looking for you. You have a visitor."

"The sheriff?"

"I don't think so." Turning, William motioned to Mouse, who was standing just inside the Sister's door into the Dwelling House. She waved shyly at Rees and then disappeared. "Wait here," William instructed before hurrying away to his own chores. Rees waited under the portico and a few minutes later Eldress Phelps and Mrs. Doucette came downstairs.

"I've come for my cloth," she said softly. Rees looked at her intently but saw no bruises or marks upon her. He had feared Mr. Doucette would strike her in the battle over the musket.

"It's still on my loom," Rees said, "and I haven't finished all of the yarn." Thankfully, after the long day yesterday, only a few skeins remained to be woven.

"Give me what you've finished," Mrs. Doucette said. "I'll pick up the remainder some other time."

"Very well. Give me a few minutes to take it off the loom," Rees said.

"I'll bring her back up stairs to finish her tea," said Eldress Phelps. She smiled at Mrs. Doucette but Rees detected a pronounced irritation in the glance she directed at him.

He washed his hands carefully and dried them before touching the cloth. Cutting the warp and knotting it took only a few minutes, but unrolling the woven product from the beam was a more lengthy process, even for someone with his experience. He worked as quickly as he dared but more than thirty minutes passed before he had it neatly folded on the bed. He changed his shirt before picking up the cloth and carrying it outside. Mouse again waited by the door.

"So, you are the messenger," he teased. Behind the concealing hand, she smiled.

"I am excused from the kitchen while I do this," she said. "It's an easy job."

Mrs. Doucette came quickly down the stairs and Rees handed her the parcel. "Oh, this is lovely!" she exclaimed. "You are a fine weaver. How much do you want?" She took out her purse. Before Rees's eyes, she metamorphosed from a sweet housewife into a hardheaded Yankee trader. Rees named a price he knew she would not pay and for a few moments they haggled. They finally settled upon a sum slightly more than he expected and she extracted the appropriate coins from her bag.

Rees looked them over carefully. They were mostly English pence and shillings but with a French sou and a Spanish real mixed in. He stowed the money in his pocket and carried the bundle of cloth to the buggy. As he offered her his hand to assist her into the seat, she turned and said, "Please forgive my husband for shooting at you, Mr. Rees. He took against the Shakers and although he is now more accepting, sometimes . . ." Reddening, she looked away from him.

"That was my son on the seat next to me," Rees said, now understanding why she'd come to Zion to see him. "He isn't a Shaker, not yet anyway, but they kindly took him in and clothed him."

"I thought it might be. I'm sorry. He was firing over your heads. I know that doesn't help." Rees said nothing. "He isn't a bad man," she burst out. "But he was born very poor. He was a driver for a rich house in Philadelphia and struggled to save the money to buy this farm." Rees still said nothing. A poor upbringing did not excuse the rudeness and hostility with which Mr. Doucette greeted everyone and everything. With a sigh, Mrs. Doucette climbed into the wagon. Skillfully handling the ribbons, she turned the wagon around and drove away. Rees watched the buggy crest the slope and disappear over it.

When he turned, he found Eldress Phelps standing at his elbow. She met his gaze with frowning disapproval. "You do not seem to be progressing in the matter of Sister Chastity's death," she said. "How much longer do you expect it to take?"

"I don't know," Rees said. She made him feel like a naughty boy. Any moment the switch would come out from behind her back.

"You are disruptive here. You encourage idle conversation and you bring the violence and disharmony of the outside world inside our borders. You flaunt your unchaste interest in the opposite sex. I want you to leave." Rees stared at her with dislike.

"If Elder White asks me to leave, I will," he said. For a moment they stared at each other, eye to eye. Then she turned and walked away. Rees let out his breath in a gust. He knew he could expect a visit from Elder White now. And he would probably agree with the Eldress; she was by far the tougher of the two.

Only a few hours remained until dinner. Rees thought he might just make it to Durham and back if he hurried. He put the money earned from Mrs. Doucette in the strongbox hidden in his room and raced to the stables.

He quickly harnessed Bessie and they drove rapidly to town. He thought he might catch up to Mrs. Doucette but, although the dust of her passing still hung over the road, he didn't see her. When he glanced up the driveway he saw the buggy parked in front of the porch.

He whipped into Durham and pulled into the stable yard at the back of the store. When he went inside he found the sheriff in his usual spot. "I thought I might be seeing you," Coulton teased. "It's been at least two days since your last visit."

"Michael Languedela'or is still in the neighborhood," Rees said. Coulton, his eyes widening, shook his head.

"He can't be that foolish. Why would he stay here, when everyone is looking for him?"

"Because he wants the blue roan? Listen, Sheriff," Rees said, leaning over the counter, "one of the Shakers saw him near Piper Lane. And when I went over to investigate, someone shot at me."

"What!" Coulton's shocked expression darkened to anger. "Did you see him?"

"No. I saw movement in the trees but I couldn't identify him, not at that distance."

"Then how do you know it was Michael?" Coulton asked. Rees shrugged.

"I don't know, not for sure, but it makes sense. Who else would it be? This isn't the frontier west of the Alleghenies," Rees said. "We don't commonly carry our muskets. Michael is on the run. Maybe he saw me and he panicked."

"Michael is not a killer," Coulton said. "I know he didn't kill that girl."

"How do you know that? Do you know him?"

"I've met him," Coulton said. "He's been in to the store. He charmed my wife." Rees, who found the image of Mrs. Coulton charmed hard to imagine, looked at the sheriff in surprise. "Besides, there was a farm meeting the night she was killed. He was there, along with that young man with a head of brown curly hair."

"Levi. Why didn't you say something before?"

"I didn't remember the exact night. It was my wife who recalled the date to mind. Wait here, please." Turning on his heel, he marched to the door that separated the living quarters from the store. Rees heard the rumble of conversation.

"Of course not," Mrs. Coulton said sweetly. "I will always tell you the truth . . ." Embarrassed, Rees walked outside to the front porch and paused to watch the traffic. A few minutes later Coulton appeared at Rees's shoulder.

"I'll ride over there this morning and check on it. No one else will shoot at you, I promise you that."

"Hmmm," Rees said. "This is the second time I've been shot at in two days."

"Maybe you should leave town," Coulton suggested, only half-joking.

"I plan to ride down Surry way soon," Rees said. "Take another look at the streambed."

"Why? Do you expect to find Charles Ellis buried somewhere along there?"

"No," Rees said. "But Miss Farrell is so convinced he's been murdered she's succeeded in persuading me."

"I'm here, Patrick," Mrs. Coulton said, tying on a large white apron. She looked at Rees with some antipathy before turning her gaze upon the sheriff. "When will you return?"

"I don't know," Coulton said. "Soon probably. I don't expect to find anything. No one lives there anymore." He glanced at Rees. "But I want to reassure Mr. Rees here."

They walked together into the stable yard. While Rees climbed into the wagon, Coulton backed a gelding out of his stall. "I'll let you know what I find," he called as Rees drove the wagon to the gate. Rees responded with a wave as he pulled out into the street and started for home.

By the time Bessie was unhitched and turned loose in the paddock, the dinner bell had rung. Rees walked into the Dining Hall several minutes late, after Elder White had said Grace. Everyone stared at him; everyone but David, who purposely looked away. Rees crawled into the first empty seat he saw and fixed his eyes upon his plate. Quietly the Shakers returned to their meals. Rees relaxed. As the meal progressed, he tried to catch David's eye but the boy wouldn't look at him. Resentment and fury were written upon his face and Rees thought in despair that it was as though the last few weeks had never happened. He tried to meet David after dinner and engage him in conversation, but the boy rushed out as soon as the meal concluded. Rees didn't have a hope of catching him.

All the Shakers, busy and content, hurried out to their chores. It was not their way to engage in idle conversation so no one stopped to speak to him. He went to his room. The remnants of the cut warp on his loom hung in ragged forlorn strings; he just didn't have the interest right now in starting a new one. Unhappy and restless, he walked outside, and before he knew it his feet had carried him behind the Blacksmith's and up the slope to Lydia's cottage. He found himself outside her door, staring at it in chagrin, unable to knock or turn around and retreat down the slope. He couldn't believe he had sought her out.

He saw a flicker of movement inside the window. Lydia flung open the door and stared at him in surprise. "You look like a lost puppy," she said. "What's the matter?"

"It was a mistake to come," Rees said.

"Well, you're here now," she said, "and you look as though you could use a friend." She gestured him inside and pointed at the table. When he didn't immediately sit, she sat down and waited, folding her hands together and resting them upon the table.

"I've been shot at twice in as many days, once when I was walking with David—"

"Shot!"

"Yes. Once by Henry Doucette and once by persons unknown."

"He must have been tipsy," she said. "He does that sometimes. Did he swear and curse the Believers?" Rees nodded. "I pity his poor wife."

"I think Brother Michael shot at me the second time." She stared at him.

"But Marguerite said he'd fled south."

"That's what the sheriff told me too. But Brother Jacob saw a man he identified as Michael. When I went over to investigate, someone shot at me. Twice. It makes sense the shooter would be Michael."

Lydia nodded, but a troubled frown creased her forehead. "He never struck me as anything but peaceful," she said. "And where would he find a musket? He didn't own one."

"I don't know," Rees admitted. "But someone local is helping him. Maybe that person gave Michael the musket." Lydia shook her head doubtfully. "Anyway, David was with me." She stared at him, her mouth rounding in horror.

"Oh no," she said. "He wasn't hurt, was he? No, he couldn't have been. You wouldn't be here."

"No, he wasn't hurt. Scared more like. He accused me of abandoning him." Rees sneaked a glance at Lydia Jane. She did not contradict David's accusation.

"What did you do then?" Rising to her feet, she stirred up the fire and moved the kettle over the flame.

"Nothing," Rees said in surprise. "He raced off. And I noticed buggy tracks in the stand of trees. I think Sister Chastity's killer hid in those trees and watched her. At the first opportunity, he ran up behind her and struck her down." When Lydia did not speak, he added, "It could have been anyone."

"You are so single-minded," she said. He stared at her in astonishment. "Look at this from David's point of view. You pursue him here, make an effort to befriend him, and then you veer off into an investigation of Chastity's death. You spend little time with him. I know that. I've seen it. And when you allow him to accompany you, and he is frightened and angry, instead of comforting him, you're distracted by buggy tracks."

"But now I understand how Sister Chastity's killer reached her," Rees protested, stunned by the direction this meeting had taken. "I'm that much closer to discovering her killer." Lydia plunked a cup of tea onto the table in front of him.

"You focus on something and pursue it to the end, without pausing to notice the people around you," she said. "I'm sure you've been very successful unraveling puzzles such as this one. You're always the outsider in every village and you move on when your task is done. No connections. No succumbing to grief or to the grief of others. But David is your son. Doesn't he deserve better?" Rees took an angry swig of the boiling liquid and choked as it burned first his tongue and then his throat.

"What should I do?" he demanded. "Give up my search for Chastity's killer? Let him escape justice?"

"Of course not. But you need to do something to prove you care about David or you really will lose him forever." Recalled grief reddened her eyes. She looked down at the table and sipped her own tea. Rees put his cup down with a loud thud and pushed it away. He hated tea.

"Don't you have any coffee?" he asked. She frowned at him.

"You're David's only family, except for the relatives from whom he fled. And he is yours, Mr. Rees." Rees almost flung himself out the door in a temper. He hated being told what to do. Instead he inhaled a deep breath and forced himself to speak calmly.

"I apologize for my behavior," he said. "Of course there are some important things I need to do for David. Recover the farm from those selfsame relatives, for example. But I know if I pause in my search the killer may escape. I can't waste time."

"Charles and Ira have been dead two and a half years. The dead can wait. It's time for you to concentrate upon the living." She paused and then burst out, "I wish I still had my child, Mr. Rees, but once they're gone you can't wish them back." Her voice broke and tears filled her eyes, but she retained her composure.

Rees stood up. "I think I should go," he said. She nodded and made a pass over her eyes with her apron. He walked to the door but turned around. "Is that why you haven't rejoined the Shakers, because of your daughter?" She nodded.

"I expected to settle down with Charles. I bore the child and as soon as I held her I knew I couldn't give her up. Not to the Sisters, not to anyone."

"But then she died."

"I kept expecting Charles to return," she said simply. "I thought we would raise a brood of our own." She sighed. "It is a peaceful and simple life here; I still may sign the Covenant again someday. But I don't want to give up the joy of having children of my own." Rees nodded. She would wait, hoping to marry and raise a family of her own, as long as she could. He went out and started down the flagged path. He had run to her, expecting solace, but instead he'd brought out someone else's pain. It had affected him more deeply than he wanted to admit. But as he stomped down the path, he realized he'd also found an answer of sorts; it was time to go home.

A search of the barns, outbuildings, and finally the pastures took some time but Rees finally discovered David weeding a distant field. When David saw him coming he stood up, looking ready to run. Only the eyes of the men around him held him in place. "I'm planning to drive home," he said to David. "I need to deal with Caroline and Samuel. Will you ride with me?"

David stared at him incredulously. "Really?"

"Really."

"Uncle Sam might shoot you."

Rees's first impulse to contradict David died a quick death. Of course Sam would want to keep the farm and Rees stood in the way. If he died, or disappeared, they could do whatever they wished with the property. Surely Caroline would object; she would not want him dead. But Caroline had years of practice in avoiding uncomfortable questions.

"Maybe," he said, saddened and angry all over again. "That's all right. We'll talk to Mr. Potter. This problem needs to be solved and we might as well do it now."

"Yes," David said. "Yes. I want to come."

"We leave tomorrow at dawn," Rees said and walked back to the village to inform Elder White.

Chapter Sixteen

❧

They left just as the first streaks of dawn tinted the sky. Few stirred in Durham and Rees could see only a handful of burning candles. Then they were on the Rumford road, heading northwest. They spent the first night in a field, the small campfire a cheerful glow in the darkness. Rees cooked bacon and beans in his battered skillet. "This is fun," David said, stretching out with his hands behind his head.

"Now," Rees said. "When it's warm and clear and we found a friendly farmer. It is much less pleasant when it's raining or snowing—that's the worst—and you can't find shelter and you're trying to sleep on the side of the road." David nodded, his teeth flashing in the firelight, and Rees could see the boy didn't believe him. But after the sunny day that followed, rain blew in and David allowed that trying to sleep outside was not as much fun in bad weather. Rees didn't tell him that usually he didn't have the protection of the wagon with canvas over it; he used the canvas to shroud the loom. David managed to sleep, but Rees, despite his familiarity with traveling rough, spent a wakeful night. He thought again that thirty-six was getting too old for this. For the first time he began to reconsider settling down, but the thought of the same four walls enclosing him day after day sent an icy tingle down his spine. Maybe he wasn't so old as all that.

He felt sluggish and unrested when they set out again the following morning. They rolled into Dugard mid-morning. David looked around in confused surprise. "It looks different," he said. "Smaller. Dirtier."

"You've been away for a few months," Rees said, drawing up to a water trough. The village in which he'd grown up looked alien; he'd been away a year. He washed his face and hands and brushed his tricorn in preparation for meeting with Potter. "Now, where is his office?"

They climbed back into the wagon and started down Main Street. David nodded at the people he knew. They stared back, some pointing at David in his Shaker garb. Rees didn't bother looking at the faces; he'd left too long ago and returned too infrequently to know many of them anymore. He wondered if he should have kept a few friends here, friends who might have protected David, but it was too late to think of it now.

David directed Rees to a white clapboard building on the corner of Main and Church Streets. A small sign identified the office of George Potter, attorney-at-law. Rees tied Bessie to the post and picked up the strongbox from under the seat. When he and David went inside, Mr. Potter himself came out to greet them, stretching out his hand and crying in surprise, "Will. Will Rees. How long has it been?" He looked almost as Rees remembered, except for the gray streaks at his temples.

"And David . . ." Potter held out his hand to the boy. "I knew you had a son but didn't realize he would be so grown-up." He stopped short and Rees could see him struggling to decide whether he should mention Dolly. Rees jumped in.

"It's about David, rather tangentially, that I wish to consult you."

"Well, come on in then," Potter said gesturing them both inside and up the stairs to his office. He clattered up behind them. "Coffee? Tea?" Rees gladly accepted coffee and Potter disappeared into another part of the house. The attorney practiced above his home. But the fine desk and oak bookcases reminded Rees that Potter had married a woman from a monied family; he wouldn't share space with his home for long.

A few moments later Potter returned. He pulled out a sheet of paper and dipped his pen into the ink. "Now," he said, "how might I be of service?" Rees took out the deed from the box and pushed it across the glossy desk.

"You know Dolly and I bought the farm?" Rees asked.

Potter nodded. "Yes. Your parents' farm out by Dugard Creek."

"I left my son in the care of my sister Caroline and her husband Samuel."

Potter nodded again. "Samuel Prentiss. I remember when they married."

"Yes, well, after Dolly died and I had to start traveling to earn a living, I gave them permission to live on the farm as long as they treated David like their own. They couldn't sell anything of the farm, neither livestock nor land, but I would send money." Potter held up a hand to stop the words bursting from Rees. Rising to his feet, Potter went to take the tray from the young girl hesitating in the doorway.

"My daughter," he said unnecessarily. Her winged brows and the dimple in her cheek came from her father and Rees suspected the glossy brown hair did as well. A few years younger than David, she smiled at him shyly. He affected not to notice her but his neck and ears reddened. "Thank you, Sally."

For a moment all discussion ceased as Rees and David doctored their coffee. Rees appreciated the hot beverage, but he did not care for the delicate bone china cups that felt like doll china in his large hands. David helped himself to a slab of cake.

"Pray, continue," Potter said.

"Now I find my sister and her husband have sold off most of the livestock and are selling the land. I want something written that will prevent that. The farm will eventually belong to David and I want something left of it."

"You didn't give them the property to use as they saw fit?"

"Definitely not. I never imagined they would do this. They owned only a little holding on the other side of town . . ." Potter brought the deed toward him and for a moment all was silent as he studied it. Rees angrily finished his coffee in one gulp and poured himself another from the pot. After a few minutes Potter looked up.

"I can certainly write up something. We'll deliver a copy to them. And I will keep a copy here as well."

"We?" Rees said. "Are you coming with us?"

Potter nodded grimly. "And I will inform my father of my destination."

"Is he still practicing then?" Rees asked. He could remember the elder Mr. Potter as a stern rather fierce parent who appeared elderly twenty years ago.

"He will never retire."

"Have you had dealings with my brother-in-law?"

"Not for many years." Potter bit his lip. "I've heard complaints. And I know him to be a man of choleric temperament." Rees settled back, wondering what memory caused George Potter to grimace so. "It will help if you arrive unexpectedly every now and then," Potter went on.

"The trouble is I travel a great deal," Rees said, his brow furrowing. "And I travel widely: south to Georgia, north to northern Maine, and everything in between. That's how I make my living. Could I hire you and put you on retainer to keep an eye on them for me?"

"I'm sure something might be arranged," Potter said with a

vulpine grin, his dislike of Samuel Prentiss clear. "Give me a few hours to draw up the papers and perhaps we can ride out there this afternoon." Rees nodded, not happily. He should have realized the lawyer would need time.

"Let's go to the Contented Rooster and get something to eat," David said, speaking for the first time.

"The Contented Rooster?" Rees said blankly.

"Coffeehouse," Potter explained, scribbling some notes to himself upon the paper. "You must have seen them in Boston and Philadelphia." Rees nodded. Coffeehouses were all the rage in the cities, but he hadn't expected the fashion to reach the backwoods of Maine. He pondered his finances for a few moments. He'd spent little of the money earned before going to the Shakers, where he'd been living gratis, and he'd added to the amount with Mrs. Doucette's coins, so he was, for now, a wealthy man.

"Do they have rooms to let?" he asked. This business of his, he now saw, would take time to conclude.

"I believe so," Potter said. "You know the proprietors: Jack Anderson and wife?"

"I do. Older than us by a few years?" Rees teased out a memory of a tall lanky fellow with a shock of straw-colored hair.

"That's him. He married Susannah Clark."

"Susannah?" A picture of a young girl with fair flyaway hair like a dandelion gone to seed popped into Rees's mind. He'd teased her mercilessly and, blessed with a cheerful disposition, she'd greeted all of his pranks with a cascade of giggles. Rees spared a thought for the little brat he'd been and said, "I look forward to seeing them again."

When they left Mr. Potter's office, David took the lead. "We don't need to drive," he said, flipping his hand at Bessie. "The Rooster is close by." With long-legged strides, he walked toward the center of town, cutting left down a side street Rees did not recall. All the buildings on this avenue were new and they bustled with activity: a new blacksmith, a cooper, and a brickmaker. On the opposite side of these establishments sat a sprawling house, set back a few feet from the road and with a fence and a bed of flowers between them. Rees thought he recalled a dark little tavern that used to sit in front of Dugard Pond but couldn't be sure. This was not little and could not be dark; large glass windows lined the front wall. It struck him again with sudden force how unfamiliar this village, in which he'd grown up, had become.

David plunged ahead, flinging back the white picket gate with a clatter and springing up the brick path. "David. David, lad." The greeting floated out of the open door. Suddenly shy, Rees followed more slowly.

This establishment was smaller than those Rees had seen in the cities, but that stood to reason in this small village, and only a few tables were occupied right now. Jack, at least Rees thought it might be he, came out from behind the counter. His blond hair was fading into gray and a roll of fat around his middle strained at his apron. "Are you a Shaker now, boy?" he asked David. David's response was too low to catch, but the motion of his hand at his father was clear. "Will? Will Rees?" Jack came forward, both hands outstretched. "My God, man, it's been years. Susannah? Susannah?" he shouted. Instead of shaking Rees's hands, Jack caught him into a bear hug. Rees stiffened in surprise and then awkwardly patted the other man's fleshy back.

"What's the matter, Jack?"

Rees recognized that voice. Although deepened and enriched with experience, it clearly belonged to Susannah. Disentangling himself from Jack's embrace, Rees turned to the voice. Her fair hair had darkened some and was tucked firmly under her cap. Her elfin build had swelled to comfortable womanly curves but her welcoming smile was the same.

"Willie," she cried, hugging him hard. "My old friend."

"I'm surprised you remember me fondly," Rees said. "I remember tormenting you." She laughed, a cascade of familiar chuckles that sent Rees back thirty years.

"Yes, you did," she said, her face crinkling into a broad smile. "Sit down, dear, sit down. What can I get you?"

"Apple cake," David said promptly.

"We have a nice chicken pie," Susannah wheedled. David nodded eagerly. Rees signaled his intention to have the same. As Susannah walked away Rees settled heavily into his chair. He must be getting old, he thought. Two nights of restless sleep and he felt too tired to move. And the visit to Caro and Sam still remained. He sighed.

"You'll feel better after eating," Susannah said as she approached with cider for David and ale for Rees. Jack followed close behind, carrying thick pie wedges stuffed with chicken that he placed before them. The pie tasted even better than it looked, but with a full belly came overpowering lassitude. When he next saw Susannah he asked about a room. She nodded. Yes, they rented rooms, three of them, and none occupied right now. "And," she added, looking him over, "I'll bring up a pitcher of hot water for washing." Rees waited impatiently for David to finish cleaning not only his plate but Rees's as well. Then Susannah guided them upstairs to the first and largest of the rooms.

Rees looked at the double bed with the bright quilt folded at the bottom, the chair by the window, and the rag rug upon the gleaming floorboards and nodded in approval. "I'll have Tibby bring up the hot water," Susannah said, looking around once more before she left.

David ran down to fetch the satchel of clean clothing from the wagon. As he clattered down the stairs, the maid brought in the hot water. Rees washed thoroughly. When David returned with the extra clothing and a razor in a canvas sack, Rees shaved. Then he took off his socks and shoes, his breeches and his vest. He lay out his wrinkled, but clean, shirt over a chair. He felt the need to armor himself against the upcoming confrontation. Then he lay down upon the bed.

"I am just going to close my eyes for a moment," he said.

Barely a minute later, David shook Rees awake. "It's time to go. Mr. Potter is waiting for us at the office." Rees clawed his way out of the cocoon of sleep.

"How long?" he asked David.

"Three hours," David said. "It's after two."

"What?" Rees hauled his heavy carcass out of the bed and flung off the dirty shirt. It took only a few moments to dress and another few to comb his unruly red hair and tie it into a neat queue. Then they went to meet George Potter.

As they went around the corner, Rees didn't at first notice that Bessie and the wagon were missing. But as they drew level with the office, he felt the lack and paused. "I put her and the wagon in the Rooster's stables," David said.

"I didn't mean to fall asleep," Rees said.

"Ah, good," Potter said, coming up behind them. "I hope you don't mind." He motioned to a smart black buggy with a beautiful chestnut horse hitched between the traces. "I thought we'd be more comfortable in my vehicle." Rees thought of his battered wooden buckboard and hard-used horse and imagined Potter's reaction to them.

"What a beautiful mare!" David exclaimed.

"She's part of a matched pair," Potter said, his face lighting up. "I imported her sire from England." Sensing a fellow enthusiast, he pointed out the mare's well-shaped head and legs. Rees ignored the conversation. His heartbeat had accelerated in anticipation of his meeting with Caro and Sam. They climbed into the buggy and, to the backdrop of the conversation about horse breeding, Rees pondered the points he wanted to make to his sister and her husband.

As each yard of road disappeared under the chestnut's hooves, Rees's heart thudded faster. This meeting would not go smoothly, of that he was sure.

They passed fields and Rees recognized people he knew from school, now looking like their parents as they labored. If Dolly hadn't died he might be among them, toiling in his own fields. Unnerved by that thought, Rees wrenched his thoughts back to Sam and Caro. He recognized the instant they crossed onto his land, some atavistic thrill in the blood, although signs of neglect were everywhere. The copse of trees had been allowed to expand into thick forest and the ragged cornfield was unweeded with bare patches in the rows. The fields looked almost as untended as they had when his elderly father was alive.

"Why didn't I notice this before?" Rees asked and answered his own question: because he'd always been so eager to leave again he'd purposely kept himself blind.

The buggy swept up the familiar drive, leaving a plume of dust hanging in the air, and stopped in front of the farmhouse. As Potter and David climbed out, Rees stared at the house. His parents had built high on the hill, but not on top, so the slope would protect the house from the winter winds. The side door faced south, to catch as much sun as possible. They'd always kept the front door, which faced west, curtained off for the winter. Rees and Dolly had expanded the front room and added on another room at the back, invisible from the drive. Caroline suddenly popped out of the front door, a cleaning rag hanging from one hand.

"Why George," she said in surprise. "And . . . David." Her voice faltered. Then Rees climbed out of the buggy and she blanched.

"Get Sam, Caro," Rees said. "We need to meet with you both." Caroline glowered at him, her lower lip protruding as it had when they were children, before she would fly at him screaming. Better controlled now, she simply turned and went inside, shouting for her husband. Rees followed her. When the other two made no move to follow, he turned and said harshly, "This is my house." David and Potter fell into step behind him.

They settled themselves in the small dark parlor. Used infrequently, the furniture was uncomfortable and smelled musty. Rees noticed that the fireplace had not been swept clean of last year's ashes. And Caroline had not offered refreshment as befitted good manners. She did not come inside and engage them in polite conversation but waited in the hall for Sam. Full of bluster, he stamped in from the barns, his boots stinking of manure. Gray streaked his hair and he looked every day of his forty plus years.

"What are you doing on my property?" he shouted.

"This is my property," Rees said.

Sam smirked at him. "Prove it. We live here and have for the last six years." Rees began to rise. Potter's hand clamped down upon his wrist.

"He has the deed," Potter said.

Sam's eyes widened. "That's a lie."

"I have a copy in my files."

"He gave us the farm," Samuel shouted.

"I did not," Rees bellowed in return. "I allowed you to live here while you cared for David." Potter squeezed Rees's arm warningly.

"Where is your proof?" Potter said. "Do you have anything in writing to support your claim?" Prentiss looked scornful.

"I'm here, ain't I?" Prentiss said. Rees stared at the other man in disbelief. Once he and Sam had been friends. Trusted friends. Who was this stranger? Rees turned to look at his sister. Tossing her head she moved to stand by her husband.

"You gave the farm to us," she cried shrilly. "You didn't want it."

"This farm was always meant for David," Rees said. "You knew that." Again Potter clutched at Rees to restrain him.

"Mr. Rees has the deed in his possession," Potter said. "In the eyes of the law, he owns this property. And most of us in town," he said as an aside, "know that to be true. According to Mr. Rees, in your time of residence here, you've sold livestock and land without his permission. I will recommend to him that he demand an accounting of all you've sold so that you may reimburse him for the value."

"You damn pettifogger," Prentiss sneered at him. "Stealing a man's home from under him."

Rees looked at his sister. She inadvertently caught his glance and scarlet crept up into her face. "Caro," he said. "You know I didn't give you my farm. I gave you a place to live while you cared for my son. And you may—"

"Why are you speaking to my wife?" Sam said. "Speak to me."

"I'll speak to my sister if I choose," Rees said, suddenly realizing Sam had never sat down. A big man, Sam usually loomed over people, intimidating in his size. Rees rose to his feet. At several inches taller and a few pounds heavier, he faced his brother-in-law. George Potter also rose to his feet, and after a moment David joined them. No one spoke. If Rees were in Sam's place, he would try to soothe everyone, calm them down. But Samuel stabbed his finger at them.

"We live here now. You gave us this farm," he told Rees. "Just because you don't remember, doesn't mean you can come in here and take it back."

"That is exactly what it means," Potter said. "The sheriff will be arriving to move you and your family out." Rees turned to stare at Potter in astonishment. Potter offered him a brief nod. This would never have happened, Rees thought, if he'd been paying more attention.

"Will, don't do this," Caro cried. "Where will we go?"

"You know this farm was intended for David," Rees repeated doggedly, knowing if either one apologized, he would weaken.

"You didn't want it," she said, echoing her husband.

"If Mr. Rees allows you to stay, we will have this conversation again," Potter said, looking at Rees and shaking his head. Rees sighed. This was not what he wanted.

"We kept this farm going while you traveled the roads," Samuel said. "You owe us!"

"I traveled the roads weaving," Rees said. "I sent home money. And the farm looks practically abandoned."

"Get off my property, now," Sam said. Turning to his wife, he said, "He won't do anything, Caro."

Rees looked at his sister pleadingly. "Caro," he said. She stared at him coldly. "Caro, we are the only two left. We are the only two who remember what it was like growing up here." She turned her back on him.

"You have one week," Potter said. "Then the sheriff and his men will arrive to oversee your removal from this property."

Caroline and Sam stared at the lawyer in shock and then Caro turned on her brother.

"You were always selfish," she screamed, bursting into loud angry sobs. Rees turned and walked out the front door. He wished tears would relieve the agony inside.

"I didn't want to do it," he said to Potter. "My own family. And the children."

"I know. But you can't show kindness to someone like Sam Prentiss. He's like a wolf. You'll have no trouble finding deputies; Prentiss is unpopular and people remember your mother fondly." He glanced at Rees's stricken expression. "You can always send some money to your sister, for the children."

"I used to imagine getting back at them," David said. "But this was awful." He climbed into the buggy's backseat. Rees and Potter stepped up to the front and the lawyer took the reins. "I'll keep an eye on it for you," he said. "Don't worry. We'll hire a manager and keep the farm going until David is of age. I'll draw up a list of names for you." Rees nodded. He couldn't grasp the belligerence and anger, the sense of entitlement, displayed by his sister and brother-in-law.

"Thank you," David said. "I don't mean for the farm. Not exactly anyway. From the time I was eleven or so, old enough to understand, Aunt Caro told me you gave the farm to her in exchange for caring for me. As a bribe." Rees turned to look at his son.

"What I said was the truth. They were only allowed to live there because they were caring for you. I wanted you to remain in your home."

"Caro said you didn't love me," David went on, fighting tears.

"The farm was always meant for you," Rees said. Right now he could cheerfully strangle both Caro and Sam. "I always loved you. And when you are of age, we'll go to a lawyer, maybe Mr. Potter here, and put the deed into your name." David stared.

"Would you do that for me?"

"Of course. The farm was always meant for you." David sat back, satisfied. And Rees, staring at his son, was struck by inspiration. Charles Ellis the elder left his farm to his grandson. There had to be a will. And where there are wills, there are lawyers. There has to be a lawyer who knows something about Brother Charles Ellis. As soon as they were back in Zion he would find out.

Chapter Seventeen

❧

They pulled into Zion on Wednesday of the following week. Rees stopped in the road by the Meetinghouse and looked around. Zion looked just the same; orderly and peaceful. It was mid-morning and all of the Brethren were out in the fields, the Sisters inside except for those working in the kitchen gardens. "Do you think you'll sign the Covenant?" he asked David. The boy also was looking around. He turned to look at his father. As if he'd just now decided he shook his head.

"No," he said. "I have a farm of my own. And although I appreciate everything the Believers have done for me, and all I have learned, I want my own property. And a wife and a family," he added, a pink flush creeping into his cheeks. Rees eyed his son, wondering if David had a girl in mind. But he didn't ask. Rees's battle over the farm had forever changed David's perceptions and he was prepared to forgive. If he wanted Rees to know, he would tell him.

They continued down the main road to the stables. With David's help, unhitching Bessie took only a few minutes. An hour or more remained before the dinner bell. David went in search of Deacon William while Rees stowed the strong box back inside his room.

Then he hurried up the slope to Lydia's cottage. He told

himself he was running to her to ask the name of Charles Ellis's attorney, although David had thought Mouse was more likely to know. But in truth it was a hunger to see her that drove him on. Even though he knew that seeing her would make the pain of their inevitable parting harder, he couldn't deny himself.

As soon as he approached the door, he could smell honey, a sweet cloying aroma that intensified until he could hardly breathe. When he looked inside, Lydia Jane was working with the honeycombs, pouring out the viscous golden liquid into a series of jugs. A stack of white screens beside her testified to the long hours already spent on this task. When his shadow fell across the door, she looked up.

"Mr. Rees?" she said in surprise. Her hands paused.

"I've returned," he said.

"So I see. Have you concluded your business?"

"Yes. And I thought of something. Did Brother Charles have an attorney?"

"I think so."

"What is his name?"

"Oh, I don't know. I never paid attention."

"I'm certain he used one," Rees said. "He had to, if there was land involved. And most likely the lawyer will be able to tell me a great deal about Mr. Ellis." Lydia shook her head.

"When I recall those days, I feel as though I am remembering someone else. I think now I barely knew Charles." She bit her lip. Rees nodded in agreement. He was certain Charles Ellis was someone very different from the man described to him.

"Well, I see you're busy," he said, reluctant to leave.

She smiled. "I'll see you tomorrow, Mr. Rees," she said. Disappointed, for he felt as though something should have happened but didn't, he turned and plunged down the slope. With an unhappy sigh, he sped across the road and into the Dwelling House. The dinner bell would soon ring and he wanted to wash his hands and face before then.

Lydia met him outside the Dwelling House at the usual time the following morning. "Are you sure it isn't too painful for you to investigate Brother Charles," Rees said in concern. He found her subdued demeanor unsettling. She smiled at him bleakly.

"I want to know the truth, Mr. Rees. But most of all, I need to know if he is living or dead. And if the latter, I want to know how it happened." So, she was not so convinced of his death. But Rees did not say that aloud. He suspected she herself didn't know which would be more hurtful, that Charles was dead or that he was still alive and had abandoned her.

Since Mouse had been assigned to the kitchen this week, they walked around the Dwelling House to the back. Rees peered through the door, instantly spotting the young woman washing dishes. Strings of sweat-dampened hair hung in her face, and her arms were red to the elbows from the hot soapy water. Although the morning air was cool, the kitchen was very hot; the fire had been blazing since dawn to cook breakfast. Lydia went in to fetch Mouse and she left the pan of dirty dishes with alacrity.

They sat on the wooden bench outside, Mouse blowing and wiping her arm across her damp forehead.

"I have a few more questions," Rees said.

"Of course," Mouse said. "Anything I can do."

"I assume Charles Ellis contracted the services of an attorney?"

"I don't know about my grandfather," Mouse said, "but Brother Charles did so." Rees puffed out his relief.

"Do you know his name?"

"Of course. Mr. Golightly. He still lives in Durham. Oh my, but he must be quite elderly now."

"Do you know where?" Rees hardly dared to breathe; he hadn't expected Mouse to know so much.

"On the Rumford road somewhere."

"I know you must miss Charles," Lydia said. Mouse nodded.

"He was always kind to me. And after he came to live with the Shakers we became great friends." She sighed and added shyly, looking up at Lydia from under her lashes, "I always hoped we would become friends as well."

"I know we would have if the . . . situation hadn't become so complicated," Lydia said.

"I wonder if Elder White knows about Mr. Golightly," Rees said.

"Oh no, don't question him now," Mouse cried. Lowering her voice to a whisper, she said, "The Maine Ministry is coming for a visit." Rees looked at Lydia for clarification.

"They examine the settlements to make sure they are conforming to doctrine and managing everything as they are dictated," Lydia explained. "I suppose they heard Elder White and Eldress Phelps are not following the rules."

"How so?" Rees asked in surprise.

"Every community must have two Elders and two Eldresses and two Deacons and two Deaconesses, and that's just the beginning."

"But Zion works well without," Mouse interjected.

"Hmm," Rees said. He suspected the Ministry would find the Elders here exercising undue autonomy. "How soon will they arrive?"

"This week," said Mouse. "Maybe even tomorrow." Rees

thought he should hurry his investigation forward. Who knew what changes would fly in on that wind?

"Sheriff Coulton will know where Mr. Golightly lives," he said. "I'll stop and ask for directions."

"When are you going to Durham?" Lydia asked.

"This morning, I suppose," Rees said. Lydia did not speak but she stared at Rees hopefully. He knew she wanted to join him and he nodded at her in permission. Mouse looked at him in puzzlement and the smile on Lydia's face only increased her confusion. "You've been a great help, Mouse," Rees said.

"I want to help," Mouse said fervently. She waited a moment as though he might ask other questions.

"Thank you, Mouse," Rees repeated, this time making his dismissal plain. She reluctantly returned to her chores.

When she had moved out of earshot, Lydia said, "I'll meet you at the end of the lane." She walked away, her burgundy skirts swirling around her ankles. Rees went to fetch Bessie.

As he hitched her to the wagon, David separated himself from a group of boys and crossed the street. "Are you going somewhere?"

"I'm going into Durham to talk to a lawyer," Rees said. "I expect the sheriff will know where Brother Charles's lawyer lives." David looked disappointed.

"That sounds dull," he said.

"Probably," Rees said. "But necessary."

"David, c'mon," one of the boys called. David nodded at them and said to his father, "Remember, you promised, if you go to Surry to search the stream you'll take me with you." He started across the road at a run.

Rees didn't remember promising anything but he called

out, "I don't plan to search anywhere until Brother Michael has been caught."

Bessie, tired from the long journey to Dugard Creek, balked when Rees tried to harness her to the wagon, and it took him longer than usual. When he reached the end of the lane, Lydia Jane was waiting, and tapping her foot impatiently. "I wondered if you'd forgotten me," she said.

"Bessie didn't want to come. The old girl is tired," Rees said.

They rode for a few moments in silence. Then Lydia said, "How was your visit home?"

"Not too bad," he said. Lydia turned to look at him. "I had to evict my sister." Then the whole story poured out, his tone alternating between hurt and anger. He couldn't seem to stop talking and they were almost into Durham before he wound down. Lydia put her hand upon his arm.

"You did everything you could," she said. "I know, the worst hurt always comes from those closest to you."

"But the children," Rees groaned.

"They still have two parents to care for them," Lydia said. "And, hopefully, if your sister is truly desperate, she'll apply to you." Rees shook his head unhappily. He would have given the farm to Caro, if not for David. Rees's desire for a farm was tepid at best, but Dolly? She had loved it. And David was cut from the same cloth.

They swung into town and drove through the village center to the Rumford road. Rees planned to pull into the store's yard but before he reached the drive he saw Coulton, sauntering down the street. Since he strode along without his apron, Rees assumed the man was in sheriff mode instead of storekeeper. Gesturing at him, Rees pulled the wagon to the side. "Do you expect these families to become bandits?" he joked, eyeing the sunburned farmers and their families riding through the town.

"Stranger things have happened," the sheriff said. Frowning, he glanced at Rees and then quickly away again. "Pull into the yard, please. I must speak to you." Rees stared at the sheriff in concern. Now what?

He cautiously edged Bessie back into the stream of wagons. They crawled the few feet to the drive and Rees turned in. Even walking, Coulton arrived before them. "I have news," he said, approaching the wagon. Rees waited, his heart sinking. "Bad news. You were right," Coulton said. "Michael Languedela'or was still in the area, hiding out in the forest, sleeping rough and stealing food."

"Was?"

"He threatened a farmer down Tremont way with a musket and tried to steal his horse. The farmer shot Michael to death." Through his shock, Rees gradually became aware of the hot sun beating down upon his face and of Lydia's hand clenching his forearm.

"Dead?" he said in disbelief. Coulton nodded.

"Marguerite . . ." Lydia said. "We will have to tell her."

"But I don't understand," Rees said. "Michael had a horse, the blue roan he stole from the Shakers. Why would he steal another horse?"

"We found no sign of the blue roan," Coulton said. "I suspect that horse has already been moved south. And Michael wanted to ride out of here on any nag he could find." Rees shook his head dumbly. He could never have imagined the death of that young boy.

For a moment all three were silent. Finally the sheriff said, "I thought you must have heard something. Isn't that why you're here?" He did not appear sad or regretful and Rees surmised that the deaths of many such as Michael had hardened the man. As for Rees, he did not think he would ever get used to these tragedies.

"No," Rees said. "I wanted to talk to Mr. Golightly, the attorney—"

"Hugh Golightly?" Coulton interrupted.

"I suppose so," Rees said. "Is there more than one? I want the man that Mr. Charles Ellis Senior employed."

"Mr. Ellis employed Hugh's father, Jeremiah. He must be at least ninety by now, and I am not sure he is still living. He stopped practicing a year or two ago."

"Do you know where he lived or still lives?"

"Just down this road a few miles. You'll see tall stone pillars on either side of the driveway. If you reach the northern end of Piper Lane, you've gone too far west."

"I'll drive out and check then." Rees paused. "I wonder if the son would have his father's records?"

Coulton shrugged.

Rees nodded his thanks and whipped Bessie into motion. Still wrestling with shock and disbelief, he pulled the wagon out onto the Rumford road. "He was just a boy," he said to Lydia.

"I don't believe it," she said. "That story has to be wrong. Michael was so . . . so timid. He hated guns. He crept around like a little rabbit, afraid of his own shadow. He would have stolen horses by sneaking them away, not by shooting."

"I suppose the farmer shot first," Rees said wearily. He did not relish the prospect of telling Marguerite.

They soon saw the pillars, rising up in the distance, but it took them another few minutes to reach them. Rees turned in. The stone house lay fifty or more feet from the road with pastures on either side. He recognized this as a gentleman's farm. As many hired hands worked in the barn as cattle roamed the fields. A separate stable with twenty or more stalls and a large paddock behind it sprawled to the right of the house. Rees pulled up to the rail and tied Bessie to it. A boy, barefoot and in ragged breeches, came round from the barn at the back with a pan of water. Rees turned to help Lydia but she'd climbed down by way of the mounting stone. Few of the farms in Maine boasted such amenities and Rees wondered if Mr. Golightly hailed from Boston or New York.

As Rees and Lydia ascended the stairs, a plump woman opened the door. Her face was as round as a moon under the mobcap. A cinnamon and apple aroma rushed out to greet them. "I'd like to see Mr. Golightly, if I may," Rees said.

"He heard your wagon wheels," said the woman. She gestured them into the small hall. "Perhaps you will not mind telling me the subject of your inquiry?" A certain stilted quality to her speech betrayed a rote message thoroughly rehearsed and said so many times it no longer had any meaning.

"I'm William Rees and this is Lydia Jane Farrell. We are inquiring about the last will and testament of Charles Ellis," Rees said.

"Mr. Ellis?" she said in surprise. "Wait here." She pattered off down the hall and disappeared from view. Rees looked around for a chair but nothing but a worn rag rug furnished this space.

A few moments later she returned. "This way, please." They followed her into a brick-floored hall that ran all the way to a small room at the back of the house. Rees thought it must once have been a porch, now enclosed and made over into a room. Despite the warmth of the July day, a small fire burned in the grate. Mr. Golightly wore a heavy frock coat. He stood awkwardly when he saw Lydia, leaning upon a sturdy silver-headed cane. Looking at her with great interest, he gestured them to the chairs in front of his desk and fell rather heavily into his own seat.

"Hot tea and some of your excellent cake, Mrs. Baker, if you please," Mr. Golightly said. As she withdrew, he turned to Rees and said, "How can I be of service?" His skin bore the shrunken papery texture of the very old, the veins stood out upon his hands like cords, and what remained of his white hair was as thin and wispy as cotton lint. But his bright blue eyes peered from their nest of wrinkles, still sharp and penetrating.

"A young Shaker girl was murdered several weeks ago in Zion," Rees said. Mr. Golightly nodded.

"It was the talk of the town," he said.

"Since then, I discovered human remains buried in a streambed. We believe," he gestured to Lydia to include her, "that those remains belong to a young boy who accompanied Charles Ellis, the young Charles Ellis," Rees clarified, "on a selling trip south."

"And I believe," Lydia said, "that Charles Ellis himself is dead. Probably murdered."

"You have my full attention," Mr. Golightly said.

"I wonder if there is something about Mr. Ellis that may shed some light on the deaths," Rees said.

"You are the second gentleman to inquire into Mr. Charles Ellis in the last few months," Mr. Golightly said. Rees wondered who that might have been—Elder White perhaps? "Since I read my files recently, and still have them on my shelf, I can answer some of your questions." His bright interested gaze went to Lydia once again. "The young Mr. Ellis's will is simple and quite clear. To understand it, however, you need to know the details of his grandfather's will."

"And will you share those with us?" Rees asked.

"His will is a matter of public record," Mr. Golightly said.

At that moment Mrs. Baker returned with a tray. Rees was glad to see coffee as well as tea and two kinds of cake. "Would you pour?" Mr. Golightly asked Lydia. She did as requested and passed the cake to Rees, Mr. Golightly continuing to watch her. She stiffened in discomfort and the lawyer courteously withdrew his gaze. "Charles Ellis Senior was a successful landowner, well-educated but opinionated," Mr. Golightly said. "His wife died in childbirth with number five. He hired a series of nannies to raise the four remaining children, but none of the women stayed for very long. And he did a piss poor job of raising them himself. Agnes, the eldest, married a Bristol and bore a son they named Roger. He died a few years ago. They also had a daughter. You probably know Jane; she married that Doucette fellow." Both Rees and Lydia nodded. "The next eldest daughter married a neighbor, John Moore, and produced several daughters. You must know her daughter Hannah; I believe she lives in Zion now."

"Mouse," Lydia said to Rees.

"Yes, Mouse. Hiram Ellis, young Charles's father, quarreled with his father and went off to sea at fifteen. And the youngest girl ran off with an Irish groom. She too bore a son but no one has seen or heard anything of them for almost thirty years."

"O'Riley," Rees guessed, recalling his conversation with Mr. Lewis.

"O'Reardon, I believe the fellow's name was," Mr. Golightly said. "Her father cut her off without a penny." Lydia suddenly put her arm on Rees's hand; until that moment he hadn't realized he was twitching with impatience. "Charles, of course, was his grandfather's favorite and he inherited everything. Young Roger, the girls, and whatever children resulted from the O'Reardon marriage received nothing, other than from a few minor bequests." Mr. Golightly held up his bony forefinger. "Unless Charles died without issue or joined the Shakers. In that case the estate went first to Roger. If he passed away first, then the estate went to Patrick O'Reardon. The girls received nothing. Old Mr. Ellis thought their husbands should take on the duty of supporting them. Only if all the boys were dead would the estate be divided among the surviving females."

"So Charles, if he still lives, will inherit a sizable piece of property," Rees said.

"And livestock and money as well," Mr. Golightly said. Rees glanced at Lydia, sitting frozen into stone beside him. He knew she thought the same thing he did; Charles must certainly be dead, otherwise he would have claimed his inheritance by now.

"And if Charles is dead, and Roger Bristol is dead, then Patrick O'Reardon is the only one left. But where is Patrick O'Reardon, then?" Rees muttered. There was no reply. Mr. Golightly was sitting at his desk with his eyes closed. After a moment Rees realized the elderly man had fallen asleep. "Mr. Golightly?" Rees raised his voice. The bright blue eyes popped open. "Where is Patrick O'Reardon?" Mr. Golightly paused, visibly gathering his thoughts. After a moment he shook his finger reprovingly.

"Patience, Mr. Rees. The location of Mr. O'Reardon is of no importance whatsoever."

"It isn't? Why not?"

"Because this is where the will of Charles Ellis Junior comes into effect. Upon inheriting his grandfather's estate, young Charles sat right where you are sitting now and wrote a will of his own. He did not sign the Covenant, so, in the eyes of the law, he did not join the Millennium Church. Therefore, if he is dead, his estate, which includes the property left him by his grandfather, goes in its entirety to his wife: Lydia Jane, née Farrell."

"Wife!" Rees gasped and turned to Lydia in shock. She stared at the lawyer in a mixture of shock and horror, her face ashen.

"Oh my," she said. "Oh my."

"The situation is clear," said Mr. Golightly. "As his wife, you would inherit the estate in its entirety. I would need your marriage lines to prove the marriage. And of course, we don't know that Mr. Ellis is dead."

"I have my marriage lines at home," Lydia said. She turned to Rees. "When I knew I was expecting a child Charles insisted we marry. We went to Surry . . . No one knew."

Rees, still reeling from this unexpected news, tried to pull his scattered thoughts together. "How long ago did Mr. Ellis Senior pass away?"

Mr. Golightly sighed. "Some days it seems like years, others I think it must be barely a week. But I believe it will be four years this coming January. Pneumonia took him."

"And what has happened to the farm since? Where is the livestock? Is it being farmed?" The questions tumbled from Rees, stemming from this new information.

"Charles hired a cousin to look after it. I believe most of the livestock was divided among local farmers in the meantime. Mr. Doucette took some of the cattle; the horses went to the Shakers . . ."

"What cousin?" Rees demanded. "You just went through a family tree. The only cousin left is Patrick O'Reardon." Mr. Golightly blinked.

"Why, yes, I daresay you are right. Once Charles had taken possession, I was no longer involved. I really don't know what happened."

"I haven't been in Durham for very long," Rees said, "but I know there is no one by the name of O'Reardon hereabouts."

"There was talk of the young man changing his name," Mr. Golightly said, "but that was before the old man died. I daresay, it was an effort to curry favor with him. And it would have been to Ellis in any case."

"I don't believe there are any Ellises either," Rees said. "How did Roger Bristol die?"

"A farming accident, I believe." Rees would lay odds that a human hand had something to do with the accident. "I am so happy to finally meet you," Mr. Golightly said to Lydia. "I knew your name from the will, of course. But Charles always referred to you as his red-haired Shaker girl." He smiled shakily and Rees realized the old man looked exhausted. On cue, Mrs. Baker appeared at the door. She looked at Rees and Lydia very sternly.

"Two more questions," Rees said. "When we came in, you referred to another gentleman who inquired about the estate. Do you know who that was?"

"He gave his name as Franklin. False of course. Even though I have never met him before, I knew him to be Henry Doucette. Big burly black-haired gentleman." Lydia and Rees glanced at each other. "I told him Charles Ellis had inherited the estate and mentioned that he'd left it to 'his red-haired Shaker wife.' But I gave no names. I didn't like the look of the fellow. I've heard stories. I only told him as much as I did because of the location of the Ellis farm."

"And that is?"

"Right across the road on Piper Lane. I suspect Mr. Doucette would like to purchase it. Of course, I don't think he has the money. He struggled to come up with the funds to buy his current farm. In fact, I don't know where he found that great sum."

Rees suddenly felt a tingle crawl down his spine. "And when was that?"

"About two years ago. Maybe two and a half."

"That's enough, Mr. Rees," Mrs. Baker said, moving into

the room. "Any more questions can wait until another day. Mr. Golightly is very tired."

"Come and tell me what happens," Mr. Golightly said, his voice strengthening. "I'll wonder until you do."

"We will," Rees said and gestured Lydia through the door before him.

Chapter Eighteen

Neither Lydia nor Rees spoke as they left Mr. Golightly's house and went down the steps. Rees held out his hand to assist Lydia up into the wagon seat. She accepted his help reluctantly and when she put her hand in his he felt it trembling. She did not speak until he jumped into the seat beside her. "I swear, I didn't know any of this," she said.

"Not even about the farm?"

"No. I knew his grandfather owned a large farm and that he died, but it never occurred to me that Charles would inherit it. Or that he would write a will leaving it to me." She paused and said in sudden understanding, "I think he did not tell me on purpose. If he rejoined the Shakers, the land would go to them . . ." Her voice trailed off. Rees nodded; Charles was a man of secrets.

"Why didn't you tell me about the marriage?" Rees asked. She looked at him apologetically.

"I didn't think it important. The baby was already on the way. We were married for barely a month before he went off on the selling trip. Anyway, if he signed the Covenant, we would have been separated and the marriage would have been in name only. I think I knew even then he was considering that."

"Then Elder White had every reason to keep Charles alive. I

think the Elder knew Charles would inherit and expected him to give that land to Zion." Lydia shook her head.

"Elder White would never expect that," she said vehemently. "Of course he wouldn't."

"Did the Elder know about the inheritance—that is the question," Rees said. "I think he did."

"I'm sure he did. But that doesn't matter. He and Charles were great friends," Lydia said, her cheeks scarlet. Rees did not argue. Her furious protest suggested that she struggled with her own suspicions. They rode in a tense silence to the end of the drive.

"Let's take a ride," Rees said, turning right on the Rumford road instead of left.

Lydia agreed with a nod and said, "We'll have to tell Marguerite about her brother."

"If I'm right," Rees said, "his death makes five, all connected."

"Five? But Michael was killed by a farmer. And Sister Chastity didn't even know Charles."

"I haven't worked everything out yet," Rees said. "And I admit I don't see a connection with Chastity. But I can't think it a coincidence that Roger Bristol, in line to inherit that property, died. Charles, and his traveling companion, died. Now Michael, who has some connection with horse stealing, is shot. Too many violent deaths, all spokes around the same center. And I think the center is that cousin, Patrick O'Reardon."

"But where is he?" Lydia asked.

"I don't know yet," Rees said. "But I suspect he lives around here, under another name."

This northern end of Piper Lane was a narrow dirt track just wide enough for two wagons abreast. Rees turned in. At the intersection, thick forest fringed both sides of the road, but as they traveled south the forest on the left disappeared. Fields of corn and wheat stretched to the tree line, and Rees recognized this as the Doucette property.

On the right the forest thinned but did not disappear. Saplings had sprung up and were reclaiming fields that had been cleared for planting. "No one seems to be taking care of the land," Rees said, pointing. "The fields haven't been worked for years, probably since Mr. Ellis died four years ago."

The road they followed, and the fields on either side, went up and down in a series of small hills and valleys, but always rising to a higher level. Bessie began to pant and strain. Rees realized this must be part of the hill behind the Doucette farmhouse. On the right the remnants of a driveway, now blocked by waist-high brush, swept away to a barely visible clapboard house.

"Take a look at your property," Rees said.

"Not mine," Lydia Jane said. "I don't want it." Rees pulled Bessie to a stop and they looked up the drive. Only one shabby corner of the house could be seen, weathered gray boards through the leafy screen.

"I don't think anyone is living there," Rees said, twitching his shoulders. The July sun blazed down mercilessly; he took out his handkerchief and tied it over the back of his neck.

"Do you think they buried Charles's body here?" Lydia asked in a hushed voice. Rees turned to look at her. Her hands were clenched tightly in her lap and her eyes had the watery appearance of incipient tears.

"No, I don't," he said. "If Charles and Ira were attacked on the Surry road, and certainly the discovery of Ira's remains argues that, why would Charles's body be brought all the way up here? Especially if the killer wanted to hide it?" He turned back to the farm. "Someday this land will be plowed and planted again. A body would be discovered." She looked at him for a long moment and then nodded. Rees continued staring at the farm. He didn't understand why Charles's body would be hidden at all. Nobody could easily inherit without proof of his death. That didn't make sense. Despite his confident words to Lydia, he thought this farm deserved a thorough search.

He slapped the reins down upon Bessie's back and they started forward again. They'd almost reached the crest of the hill; Bessie put on a burst of speed, and they raced through a shallow dip and surged up to the top. Rees pulled Bessie to a stop so she could catch her breath. In the sudden silence he heard the whinnying of several horses and Bessie whickered in response.

Without a pause, Rees jumped out of the wagon and ran across the road. He leaped up to the granite ledge and plunged into the tree break and into shadow and a momentary coolness. The sweet smell of cedar engulfed him. He thrust his way through the trees to the farmyard on the other side until he broke through. He faced a barn, doors open and stacked hay visible in the gloom. To his left a fenced paddock contained a handful of horses. Rees inspected them. Plump, well-brushed, and glossy, they were well cared for. But none was a blue roan.

"He is not a good farmer," Lydia said, panting up behind him. She pointed to the barn, well built but with broken, unrepaired boards. A gray tabby strolled out and sat in the sunshine to wash, watching them with feline arrogance.

Beyond the paddock, a field of corn swept down the slope until it disappeared from sight. "This is the Doucette farm," Rees said. He knew where he stood; at the top of the hill. He turned and looked all around him. To his right, in the trampled hard-packed earth, he saw the faint tracks of shod horses going down to the road. He followed the tracks, finding an almost unnoticeable path through the trees. The path came out upon the road directly across the track into the Ellis property.

Rees walked across the road and a few feet in upon the track. Horse droppings, all old ones that he could see, dotted the ground. He turned to Lydia who had trotted up behind him. "Doucette is involved in the horse stealing; I'd lay my last farthing on it." That would certainly explain how he'd managed to find the money for the farm.

"Perhaps he is just stabling his own horses on the Ellis property," Lydia suggested but not as though she believed it. Rees ignored her comment. If she had not been with him, he would have continued on all the way into the property and begun searching it. As it was, after another look at the track and overgrown fields to the left, he turned around and plodded back to the wagon.

When they were moving once again, he said, "I wonder if Doucette is Patrick O'Reardon."

"I wouldn't have said he was clever enough," Lydia replied, unkindly but accurately.

"Who would know if Doucette is his real name? Or if he has been known by another name?"

"Maybe Mouse? Mrs. Doucette is her cousin." Lydia paused. "If Jane Doucette knows. She might not, if he appeared in town as Henry Doucette."

"Not Mouse," Rees said. "And not Mrs. Doucette either. I don't want anyone to tell Doucette I'm interested in his past. As sure as I'm sitting here, he'll run." How else could he find out the truth? Not in Durham, most likely everyone there knew Doucette under that name. Sheriff Coulton? Rees pondered that possibility for a moment, finally deciding that the sheriff might not be impartial. He was too close to the situation here.

Maybe Catherine Parker's brother would know? Rees did not anticipate the long journey south with pleasure but knew Lewis would gladly help. And maybe he could combine a quick and dirty search of the stream on his return.

"At least you are less likely to suspect Elder White," Lydia said, interrupting his thoughts. Rees did not reply. Elder White had dropped to the bottom of Rees's list, but still remained upon it. White knew all the victims and he could easily participate in stealing horses from Zion; in fact, he had the most opportunity to do so. Rees didn't think it likely, but he'd been fooled before. "He is a kind man," Lydia said, her voice rising with her passion. "You can't possibly believe any of the Shakers had anything to do with any of this."

Rees thought of Chastity's silk stockings and of her relationship with Marguerite and of her brother Michael the horse thief. "Elder White is a good man," he said, "and I think the Shakers are probably as fair and as trustworthy as any man can be. But none of us are saints." Lydia shook her head at him.

"How do you sleep at night?" she asked him. "I would not want to be so suspicious of my fellow man as you are."

"And I am so often right," Rees said, only half-joking. Lydia frowned at him and shook her head.

Lydia promised to meet Rees in Zion after she'd eaten her midday meal. Once he'd deposited her at her cottage, Rees drove to the stables and unhitched Bessie from the wagon. Dinner was long past so he went around to the kitchen to see if he could cadge some bread and cheese. Mouse, up to her elbows in hot soapy water again, saw him first. She acknowledged him with a nod. When he mimed eating, she nodded in understanding and dried her hands while Rees withdrew to the bench outside. This might be an opportunity to ask a few discreet questions, as well as eat, thereby killing two birds with one stone. A few moments later she hurried out, a napkin-wrapped bundle and a jug of ale in her arms.

"Thank you, Mouse," Rees said, taking the bundle from her. One hand instantly rose to hide the split lip. Rees unfolded the napkin: buttered bread, sliced cheese, and sliced chicken breast. "I'm famished."

"Where have you been?"

"I had an errand in Durham," he replied. "How are you?" She nodded her head in surprise. "How is your cousin, Jane Doucette? I haven't seen her since I gave her the cloth."

"Fine," she said, even more surprised. "I haven't seen her for over a week." Rees struggled to find a way to ask a question about Henry Doucette without sparking her curiosity.

"Actually, the last I saw of your cousin she was attempting to apologize for her husband's behavior," he said.

"Sometimes he is a sore trial to her," Mouse said and might have said more but for one of the Sisters who glanced outside.

"Mouse! Come inside right now." The Sister glared at Rees disapprovingly. With a reluctant look backward Mouse trudged to the kitchen. As she climbed the steps, the Sister grabbed her by the shoulder and thrust her inside. The door slammed with finality.

Shaking his head, Rees began eating his meal. Like his home village of Dugard, everyone in Durham, and in Zion too, seemed to be related to one another. He kept meeting brothers and sisters and cousins and hearing about fathers and mothers and a whole raft of relatives. Most people, like Mouse, seemed to feel protected by those bonds. They knew their place. When Rees thought about his relatives and friends in Dugard he felt caged. Out on the road, he could become anyone he wanted; he wasn't just William, son of Enoch.

"Are you ready, Mr. Rees?" Lydia came up behind him and

he realized he'd been sitting staring at his bread for several minutes. He nodded and scattered the rest for the birds. "You seemed preoccupied."

"Just pondering families," he said and finished off his ale in one gulp.

Lydia had exchanged her straw hat for the linen cap and was garbed once again like a Shaker Sister. A spot of blood glistened on her lower lip and as Rees watched her she clamped down, worrying her lip with her teeth. Instead of exhibiting peace and tranquillity, her expression was anxious. "We promised Marguerite we would try and protect her brother," she said.

"I know," Rees said. He would have killed himself to keep Michael from the rope, but he could do nothing for a boy shot by a farmer in his effort to steal a horse. Michael's own foolhardy behavior killed him. But Rees knew neither Lydia nor Marguerite would see it that way right now.

They walked silently down the path toward the weaving shed. Rees peered through the open door. Marguerite sat on her usual bench, weaving intently. Fatigue etched lines into the corners of her mouth and eyes and her skin looked dry and tired. As Rees's shadow fell across her she looked up.

"May we speak to you for a moment?" Rees asked. Terror flashed across her face and she hesitated, the shuttle frozen into her hand. Then she put it on the warp. Clumsy, on trembling legs, she rose to her feet and came out to meet them.

"What do you want?" she asked huskily. In the bright afternoon light the marks of grief and weariness were even more apparent. "I've told you everything I know."

"That's not why we're here," Lydia said. "I am so very sorry to tell you . . ." She looked at Rees in appeal.

"Michael has been shot and killed," he said.

"No," she wailed. "That can't be true. He can't be dead."

Lydia grasped Marguerite's hands and held them tightly while she sobbed. Rees glanced around for a bench or other seat and, in the end, guided the two women back to the bench inside the shed. The two women sat down. "He can't be dead," Marguerite repeated. Lydia put her arm around the other woman and let her weep. Rees paced up and down upon the path before them.

Finally the storm of grief abated. She sat up and mopped her face. "What happened?" Her voice quavered and she clamped her mouth shut.

"We were told he was shot while attempting to steal a horse," Rees said. Marguerite shook her head, tears gathering in her eyes again.

"I don't believe it," she said. "He would never be so foolish. He was good at . . . at borrowing horses."

"You said before that he ran into someone he knew in Durham?" Marguerite nodded.

"Do you know the name?"

"I told you, I do not."

"We might be able to catch him," Rees said, bending down persuasively. When Marguerite shook her head, fresh tears flying from her eyes, he said, "Maybe a description then."

"He called the man the Irishman," she murmured. Rees and Lydia exchanged a glance: Patrick O'Reardon again? "My baby brother," Marguerite cried and began sobbing again.

After a few moments of pacing Rees left Lydia to console Sister Marguerite and returned to his room. He badly needed to think. During the past few weeks, he'd hurried around collecting information. Now he needed to begin putting it together, evaluating it for veracity. He knew he didn't understand the entire story and at least some of what he'd been told was half-truths if not outright lies. He didn't yet know if some of the storytellers had tried to mislead him or were just holding back secrets for reasons of their own.

His room was tidy, the bed made. He took two chairs down from their pegs and hung his warping board in their place. With one of Mrs. Doucette's remaining skeins in his hand, he began running the yarn around the board pegs. Soon in a rhythm, his mind went to another place.

A hesitant knock interrupted him and sent the skein flying from his hand. He'd left his door open, that was the Shaker way, but he wished now he had closed it. Several revelations disappeared from his mind as if they'd never been and he didn't know if he could recapture them.

"Elder White," he said, as the older man came inside.

"I am sorry to bother you," the Elder said. He paused. Rees picked up the skein and put it on the bed. Something was wrong; Elder White was not normally so hesitant. They stood in silence for several moments.

"What's the matter?" Rees asked finally.

"The Maine Ministry will be arriving within a day or two," White said.

"I knew they were coming," Rees said, and then, realizing this must be a concern to the Elder, he added, "How will they affect you?"

"I don't know. But having the Maine Ministry arrive is a very serious matter. I wondered how your search for Sister Chastity's killer was progressing?"

"I'm coming to the end," he said, exaggerating slightly. Elder White would want to know the killer was found and brought to justice; that would ameliorate the fact that the killing occurred on his watch to begin with.

"That is good," Elder White said, looking only slightly cheered. He turned to leave.

"Wait," Rees said, realizing that the Elder did not know about Brother Michael. "I drove into Durham yesterday." White looked at Rees. "The sheriff told me Brother Michael had been shot and killed trying to steal a horse."

"Oh no," White said. His face contorted with sorrow. "Oh no. I am so very sorry to hear that. I thought the lad was coming along well. He seemed to be adapting to communal living and I hoped he would sign the Covenant and become one with us." He shook his head in regret. "You must ask the sheriff to release the boy's remains to us. We will send him home to Mother."

"I'll ask him the next time I go into Durham," Rees agreed. "Maybe tomorrow." As Elder White turned to leave once again, one of Rees's thoughts popped into his mind. "Elder White," he said, "did you know that Brother Charles had inherited a farm on Piper Lane?" Elder White turned. He did not speak for a moment and his hesitation told Rees the truth. "You did know."

"Yes. That is why he did not sign the Covenant. I believe his grandfather's will disinherited Charles if he formally joined our Family. But once he inherited the farm and it was his to dispose of as he saw fit, he would have signed the Covenant. In fact, he had promised to do so once he returned from the selling trip. I understood. I would not have given him such responsibility otherwise." Rees thought of Lydia Jane.

"You never doubted he would sign the Covenant?"

"Of course not."

"And what of his will?" Rees asked. "What of Brother Charles's will?" Elder White stared at him blankly. "You must know the provisions of his will?" he persisted. Elder White shook his head.

"I did not know he had left a will," he said with such obvious surprise Rees believed him. "Did he leave a will? What are the provisions? Did he leave the farm to Zion?"

"I expect all of that to come out," Rees said. "I don't know all the provisions of the will and don't have the authority to discuss them anyway. But right now, we don't even know that Brother Charles has 'gone home to Mother.'"

"Of course he has," Elder White said. "Else he should have found his way home to Zion." On that pronouncement he left the room, but a moment later he poked his head around the doorframe again. "Will you have Michael's remains by Sunday?" Rees shook his head; today was Friday and he did not expect to ride into Durham until Monday.

"No. Maybe next week. Anyway, they might already have buried him."

"I hope not. He was one of ours."

This time when he left, Rees shut the door firmly behind him. Charles, he thought, was as much of a nexus as his cousin Patrick. What had been Charles's intentions? Marriage to Lydia or a lifetime spent with the Shakers? Whatever they were Charles lied to everyone. Including himself. Lied over and over. And that dishonesty more than anything else made Rees suspicious and wonder if Charles was still alive.

Tomorrow Rees would ride south to Surry and speak to Mr. Lewis. Perhaps he remembered the name Henry Doucette. Afterward, he would drive slowly home, inspecting the streambed, in case the remains of Charles Ellis had been dumped along the way. Just to be sure.

He spent the rest of the afternoon warping the loom and went into supper in a calm frame of mind. He soon realized that the community was in an uproar. No one spoke but people shifted in their chairs and every now and then an errant whisper could be heard hissing through the quiet. Rees looked at Brother Levi questioningly. "Maine Ministry?" he mouthed. Levi shrugged. He seemed the least affected by the tension around him, eating his supper with concentration.

But then as long as Levi had his cattle he was happy.

David followed his father from the Dining Hall into the hall but did not speak until all the Brethren had hurried off to their chores. "When are we going to search the stream?" he asked. "I heard Brother Michael was shot and killed. We don't need to worry about him anymore." Rees thought again how quickly news traveled through a community that banned idle talk.

"David, we don't know he was the shooter," Rees said.

"You just don't want me along," David said angrily. "You promised!"

"That's not true. Please understand; I don't want anything to happen to you. When we were shot at before I died a thousand deaths . . ."

"I don't believe you. You left my mother over and over. You left me, for years at a time, with your sister. You'll give me the farm, but you won't give me any of your company." Rees stared at him in shock. As soon as David flung that hurtful accusation at him, Rees felt its truth.

Even with Dolly he'd never stayed home more than three or four months at a time. The realization washed over him in a cold wave; David was right. And there was more, but Rees turned away from it.

"Very well," he said in a strangled voice, "you may come with me, David. I leave tomorrow immediately after breakfast." David stared, torn between triumph and astonishment, as his father turned and marched away. Rees did not even go two feet before he knew he had made a terrible mistake; he would be putting David's life in danger. But he did not know how to rectify it without refusing his son again.

Chapter Nineteen

When Lydia came down the hill to meet him, Rees had just begun hitching Bessie to the wagon. "Going somewhere?" she asked.

"Surry. David is riding with me." He saw disappointment flare into her eyes. "Don't try to wheedle me into taking you as well," he said. "I didn't want to take David but . . ." He couldn't confess the remainder but she nodded in understanding.

"He needs to spend time with you. And you'll be fine. Poor Michael is gone now." Rees shook his head with anxious worry. "He needs to feel he is a part of your life," she said. "I daresay he won't want to accompany you more than once or twice."

"I hope not. I don't want to put him in danger."

David came around from the Dining Hall with a basket of food. He stared at Lydia warily. She smiled at him. "Godspeed," she said. In a flutter of skirts, she turned back to the path and soon disappeared from sight around the Blacksmith's. With a sigh, Rees went into the barn for his rifle. He wasn't taking any chances this time.

Rees and David climbed into the wagon. As they approached the junction of Zion's main street with the Surry road, Rees's heartbeat sped up until it was thudding in his chest. But nothing happened and as he looked at the slopes edging the road he knew no one was there. When they reached Piper Lane Rees pulled Bessie to a stop and looked up at the bluffs on either side of the track. On the southern side, a huge escarpment of granite thrust out from the green like a gray tongue. A man traveling through the woods from the Ellis place could probably reach the ledge in less than an hour and it would give him a good vantage over the road. Even a poor shot could take a position there and fire upon someone exiting from Zion. There was no one there now. Rees's heartbeat began to return to normal.

"There is nothing to fear," David said, seeing his father's anxiety. "Michael is dead." Rees looked at his son.

"Yes, he is," he agreed. "We'll search the stream on our way north to home."

He pushed Bessie into a rapid canter. They made good time traveling in the cool of the morning upon what had become a familiar road and reached the Lewis gate just after ten. Rees turned in. Laborers toiled in the fields, bringing in the first harvest. Some of them looked up but most kept their attention on their tasks. Had Henry Doucette labored here?

They swung up the driveway to the house. Mrs. Lewis came out to greet them, welcoming them inside with a gesture. "Why Mr. Rees," she said. "More questions?"

"Only a few," he replied. Her eyes went to his companion.

"I'm sorry your wife did not accompany you. I always enjoy her conversation."

David turned his stunned gaze upon his father, who looked away quickly. "This is my son, David," Rees said.

"Of course. I am pleased to meet you, David," she said. "I would have known you for your father's son; you are the spitting image of him. Would you like some lemonade?" David nodded, still speechless with shock.

They followed Mrs. Lewis into the small parlor. "My husband is not far away," Mrs. Lewis said. "He'll be here soon."

"I hate to disturb him," Rees said. "Maybe you can answer my questions."

"I already sent the boy for him. Please sit down." Mrs. Lewis gestured them to the chairs and withdrew. She returned a few moments later with lemonade for David and ale for Rees and a plate of small cakes. As she put them on the table, Rees heard the thud of Mr. Lewis's boots approaching from the back.

"Do you have news?" he asked as he came through the door.

"I'm sorry, no, only more questions," Rees said. Mrs. Lewis cast a glance at her husband and disappeared. "Is the name Henry Doucette familiar to you?" Rees asked.

"Doucette? Indeed it is. A drunken troublemaker," Mr. Lewis said. "The last time he worked here was, um, almost five years ago. I fired him finally and he went north somewhere." Rees felt excitement's burn. Doucette as Patrick O'Reardon would provide such a clean solution.

"The last time? Did he work for you more than once?"

"Yes. Over the space of seven or eight years, I believe." As Mrs. Lewis entered with ale for her husband, Mr. Lewis turned to her and said, "You recall Henry Doucette, do you not?"

"Yes. A troublemaker. A good worker when it suited him though. He had a son."

"Oliver?" Rees asked.

"I believe that is the name," Mrs. Lewis said with a nod. "He was wonderful with his son, for all his argumentative ways with my husband. Mr. Doucette married a woman north of here, I believe. He was a little better then; at least he stopped chasing the maids." She suddenly recalled David's presence and went silent, biting her lip in mortification. Rees nodded to himself, pleased to place Henry Doucette here. Now for the next piece.

"Did he ever use the name Patrick O'Reardon?" he asked. "Or know a Patrick O'Reardon?"

"Yes," Mr. Lewis said, staring at Rees in astonishment. "How ever did you know that? We hired Doucette on O'Reardon's recommendation. Both of them were good with horses. O'Reardon was a scrapper, not a man to cross, but he wasn't a drinker."

"Didn't he marry Doucette's sister?" Mrs. Lewis asked. "She had lived with her brother and cared for Oliver, I believe."

"Yes, he did," Lewis agreed. "I never understood why. A plainer woman . . ."

"John," Mrs. Lewis said in gentle reproof.

Of course, Rees thought, paying no heed to the Lewises, O'Reardon could be using his old friend Doucette's name. He broke into Mrs. Lewis's reminiscences, "What did Mr. Doucette look like?"

"Black of hair, black of nature," Mrs. Lewis said.

"Dark eyes and hair," Mr. Lewis corrected. "A big man, almost as tall as you. Much taller and heavier than O'Reardon, but for all that I always had the impression O'Reardon was the more dangerous of the two." Rees tried to remember if anyone had ever mentioned a good friend to Doucette. He thought not.

"And what did O'Reardon look like?" he asked.

"Average," Mrs. Lewis said.

"Short," Mr. Lewis said. "Brownish hair."

"More gingery, I think," said Mrs. Lewis.

A description that could match many of the men Rees knew. "Well, thank you, again," he said.

"Are you any closer to finding my sister's killer?" Mr. Lewis asked. "Is it that Doucette fellow?"

"I don't know, but I expect it will be over soon," Rees said. He hoped it would anyway.

"Please bring your wife next time," Mrs. Lewis said as Rees and David prepared to leave.

"She was disappointed not to come," Rees said truthfully. Mrs. Lewis accompanied them to the steps.

When she turned inside, David turned and said, "Wife?"

"We couldn't explain her presence any other way," Rees said. "I'm sorry. It doesn't mean I am replacing your mother." They climbed into the wagon seats.

"I think you should marry again," David said, surprising Rees so his hands jerked on the reins. Bessie tossed her head. "Man isn't meant to live alone." A clear quote if Rees had ever heard one, and he could think of no answer to it. Since when had David become old enough to give his father advice?

Rees parked the wagon on the road and then the two hiked to the stream bank where Ira's remains had been found. David ran ahead, leaping from rock to rock like a kind of goat. As soon as Rees looked at the eroded bank he knew he would find nothing else here. David came back about twenty minutes later.

"It's all big boulders up there," he said in disappointment. "There's no place to hide anything, especially something as large as a body. If the killer dumped Charles's remains there, they would have lain in full view of the road."

"I don't think he's here," Rees said. "This wasn't a simple robbery. Either he still lives or his murderer wanted something else from him and killed him elsewhere."

Once they'd hiked back to the wagon, David insisted upon exploring south along the stream for a little while but quickly returned. The road turned west while the stream continued south. To reach the water a pedestrian would have to cross a farmer's field in full view of the house.

"We don't know that there are any remains," Rees reminded his disappointed son. He had not surrendered his suspicion Charles was alive and living elsewhere. "And if there are, they may not be hidden here."

"Where else? Most of the land, except for a few tree breaks and the vegetation around the stream, has been cleared for planting."

"We may never find him," Rees said.

They started north, stopping regularly to check the bank. There were few possible hiding places. Despite the screen of trees edging the road, most of the bank descending to the water was composed of loose rock. Nothing could be hidden there. But every now and then they found a steep but thick patch of forest. David would race down to search excitedly. Rees would follow more slowly. After a few hours of this they were both tired and sweaty, their clothing liberally stained with dirt. And they had found nothing.

"We're coming to a good place to stop," Rees said, recalling the bluff over the ocean. "We can eat there and rest a little while before we go on."

"I'm hungry," David admitted. Rees urged Bessie into a trot and soon he saw the faint narrow track that led to the bluff. They did not cross the stream and Rees wondered if it had changed direction and now flowed south at the base of the cliff on the other side of the road. Trees scraped the sides of the wagon; David flung out his arm to hold back an unusually large branch. When Rees heard the loud crack he thought the wagon's passage had snapped a tree limb. But the next loud report left no doubt as to the cause; someone was shooting at them. Again.

Rees whipped Bessie into a gallop. They raced through the trees and plunged into the open space on the top of the bluff. Whitecaps dotted the blue ocean and gulls screamed overhead.

Rees spun the wagon round and pulled Bessie to a stop near the trees. "Get down," he yelled at David as he jumped out of the seat to the far side of the wagon. He reached over the side for the rifle, linen, powder, and balls. Bessie bucked in terror and the wagon jumped and shuddered. Rees crept alongside the mare and looped the reins around a tree trunk. He hoped the shooter wouldn't think to fire at her. Killing her would strand Rees and David here and make them easy targets. David plastered himself against a wheel. Another shot cracked through the air and this time Rees heard the ball smack into the wagon's side. Quickly sheltering behind the buckboard, Rees loaded his own rifle. Praying his powder was dry, he aimed at the stand of trees across the lane, from where he thought the shots had erupted, and fired. The ball blazed out. Rees doubted he had hit anyone but maybe knowing he was armed as well would give the sniper pause. "Wait here," Rees told David and darted to the cover of a tree trunk. A few seconds later, he was on the move, hurrying from tree trunk to tree trunk, working his way toward the lane. He wanted to kill the bastard. A stray ball could have hit and killed David and that Rees could not forgive.

Another shot rang out, but this one came from the junction of the lane with the Surry road, up ahead. Rees began to hurry. The underbrush was too thick for running and he didn't dare move out of the forest shelter to the lane. When he found an opening through the trees he took another shot even though he saw no one. A few moments later he heard the pounding of horse hooves dying away into the distance. Rees hurried toward the road, reaching it within a few minutes. A fresh pile of droppings told the story; someone had waited here inside the trees. When Rees and David drove in, the shooter followed them, took up a position, and began firing. And the deeply cut marks left by horse hooves betrayed the speed with which they had fled afterward.

Although Rees knew the attacker was gone, he ran across the lane at top speed and into the trees on the other side. A few minutes of searching and he found the shooter's position; the imprint of one knee in smashed vegetation where the man knelt to take aim.

Rees took in a deep breath. His heart drummed in his chest and he was suddenly aware of his trembling legs. Think, Rees. Who knew he planned to search the stream? Lydia? Elder White? Rees could think of no one else.

"Father?" David's voice floated faintly to him. Rees plunged through the trees to the lane.

"David?"

"I'm here." His voice sounded strangely distant.

"Where?" Rees approached the wagon. Now that the shooting had stopped, Bessie was quietly cropping vegetation.

"Over the cliff."

"What!"

"Don't worry, there's a path. Come down. I think you need to see this."

Something in David's voice compelled Rees to hurry. A quick search showed him David's route, a long scramble over huge boulders leading down to the rocky shore at the base of the bluff. Since the tide was out, the upper rocks were dry. But the waves still broke over the lower stones, leaving them wet and slippery. Rees carefully picked his way around the narrow rocky beach at the bluff's foot. David, climbing up the cliff, was already halfway to the top.

"What are you doing?" Rees cried, his heart leaping into his mouth. "Get down at once."

"Look." David took his hand away from the jagged rock to point. "Look at that ledge."

Rees tore his eyes away from his son. A few feet above David, and a little to the right, a long skinny lip of rock protruded from the rock face. Snagged in the branches of a small tree was a battered Shaker's hat, outlined against the blue sky above. It would not have been visible from any other vantage point.

"Charles Ellis," Rees said.

"I think I see bones," David said, crawling crabwise across the rock. Rees held his breath as his son reached for the ledge and, in a flurry of long arms and legs, swung himself onto it. Rees moved forward and inspected the beach under the bluff, not that he expected to find anything. Whatever might have fallen to the shore would have been washed out to sea long ago. A moment later David's pallid face appeared over the ledge's lip. "There's a skeleton up here," he said. "Some of the bones anyway."

"What do you mean, some of them?" Rees asked.

"The skull is here, um, the right arm bone and some of the leg bones." When he looked over again Rees saw a distinct greenish cast to the boy's features.

"I have a canvas sack in the wagon," Rees said. It belonged to Coulton; the last collection of remains had traveled to Zion in that sack. Rees had just forgotten to return it. "I'll pass it down from the top."

"What about the man shooting at us?"

"He's gone. For now." Rees planned to carry his rifle in one hand and the bag in the other, just in case. David nodded and disappeared from view once again.

Rees made his careful way across the rocks and scrambled back up the ledges to the top. By the time he reached the bluff his right palm was bleeding and he could hardly catch his breath.

He lay on the smooth hot rock for a moment. He saw no one; so far the shooter had not returned. Rees hurried to the wagon and pulled the sack from under the seat. Then, with the rifle bumping against his side and the sack pushed before him, he crawled to the edge of the bluff. He had to adjust himself a few times until he lay directly above his son. He could just see the top of David's coppery head. He dropped the sack down, holding one end of the rope.

For a few moments David's hat bobbed up and down, disappearing under an outcropping of stone as he bent over to collect the bones. Then he tugged on the rope. Rees peered over.

"Yes?"

"Do you want the hat? And the leathers?"

"What leathers?"

"It looks like a strap cut from a piece of reins," David shouted up. "It's tying the remains to the little tree." Tying the remains to a tree? Accident? Or had the body been placed there?

"Yes, I want everything," Rees called down in return. Had the killer knifed Charles Ellis as well as Ira? The leathers argued for strangulation but Ellis was a grown man. He wouldn't allow someone to twine a leather strap around his neck, unless he was already unconscious. He would be harder to kill than a crippled boy. Maybe the bones would reveal something.

"The sack is coming up," David said from below. Rees gave a mighty heave upon the rope and the bag jerked up, much faster and much lighter than he expected. It smacked into the cliff face with a crunch and Rees shuddered. He didn't want to damage the bones; instead of pulling he reeled the sack up, hand over hand, very carefully, until he could grab the canvas and lift it the rest of the way.

Putting the sack carefully to one side, he leaned over to ask the boy how he planned to escape the ledge. He looked right into David's flushed perspiring face. He grinned at his father and hoisted himself with a little grunt to the next handhold. Rees reached over, David swung his arm up, and they joined wrist to wrist. Rees pushed up to his knees and hauled with all his strength. Scrabbling at the rock with his booted feet, David surged over the edge and sprawled beside his father. When he could speak again Rees said, "If you ever scare me like that again, I'll kill you myself."

"Thought it . . . would be . . . easier to come up," David panted. "Afraid . . . to go down."

For a moment they lay there. Rees listened carefully, alert for any sound of another's approach, but heard only the soughing of the wind and the racketing gulls. With the arrival of evening cooler air swept in upon the wind. "It will be dark soon," he said. His stomach growled, hollow as a drum. "Let's eat our dinner. We leave as soon as it gets dark."

"I thought you said the shooter was gone," David said, fear threading his words.

"He is. But we don't know but what he is waiting for us on the road," Rees said. "The end of the lane is a perfect place for an ambush. Pray God, he won't be able to see us. And if he rides back, we should be able to hear him coming." David's cheeks paled but he said nothing. "We have to take our chance now," Rees said. "If we stay the night we'll be sitting ducks tomorrow morning." David nodded reluctantly and picked up the sack. "Be careful with that," Rees said.

While David spit on his hands and rubbed them on his breeches to clean them, Rees picked his way down the ledges to the point where he could dip his dirty hands into the water. It was ice cold and the salt stung his scraped palm like fire. When he climbed back up, David had already taken out the bundle of food and was chewing lustily. Rees quickly tore off a hunk of bread and a chunk of cheese. It was manna from heaven.

After eating and draining the jug of ale dry, Rees fetched the canvas sack. He extracted the bones first, carefully laying them upon the granite. As David had said, only a few bones remained. "Everything is from the right side," Rees observed.

"The head pointed north," David said. "I think the body lay on the ledge with the right side toward the stone wall." Rees nodded approvingly.

"Yes, it seems so." He gently stroked the arm bones, untouched by birds or other animals. "All of the finger bones are present. His right arm must have been pinned under his body. Maybe the right leg as well."

"The leather strap was lying around the right arm, above the shoulder and around this bone," David said, pointing to the spinal cord. Rees noticed that his son had lost whatever squeamishness he'd felt earlier. Rees picked up the braided leather. It was clearly of Shaker manufacture.

"Was he strangled?" David asked breathlessly.

"I don't know." Rees picked up the skull and ran his fingers over it. A slight depression in the left temple caught his fingertips. He peered at the dent, almost invisible in the fading light. Although the blow might not have been severe enough to kill him, he most likely had lost consciousness. Rees ran his fingers over the depression once again. He thought this was the twin to the wound on Sister Chastity's head.

"Look," said David, pointing to the inside of the hat. Next to the dark stain, blood, Rees suspected, was a name written in fading letters: Charles Ellis. "Now why would they leave this with the body? Did the killer think it would never be discovered?" Rees stared at his son. For all these years, he'd recognized signs of Dolly in David: the gray eyes, the shape of his lips, certain expressions. Despite the boy's height and his red hair, Rees thought of David as Dolly's child. But this cool analytical reasoning was all him. Sudden emotion stung in his eyes and he put his hand on David's shoulder.

"I am so sorry I didn't fetch you away from your aunt and uncle many, many years ago," he said. David, looking startled, drew away from his father's touch. Rees sighed and took the hat from David's hands. He turned it over. Although the core was constructed of straw, it had been covered with thin dark wool to give it some added months of wear. The extra layer had likely blunted the force of the blow. "The killer struck Ellis but the blow didn't kill him," Rees said. "He fought back. So the killer wrapped the leather around Ellis's neck and strangled him. It must have taken great strength."

"But Ira?" David objected.

"Killed somewhere else and dumped like trash." Rees tried to imagine the scene. "Someone they know approaches them on the road. Suddenly the man, and it must have been a man, strikes Charles down. While he's unconscious, the killer whips out a knife and stabs Ira. Over the bank he goes. Then he drives the wagon with Charles tied to the side to this bluff here."

"He must have had a partner," David said. "That's too much for one man alone." Rees nodded.

"That would simplify everything." He sighed. "So, now I'm looking for two men."

"Why not use the knife on both victims?" David asked. Rees pondered the question for a moment.

"Because Charles has something the killer wants. He doesn't want Charles dead yet."

"Horrible!" David gasped.

"When the killer gets what he wants, he kills Charles and

hurls the body over the side, expecting it to fall into the ocean and be swept away. No, that doesn't work." Rees thought for a moment. "Surely the killer would look over the side of the bluff, just to make sure Charles's body is gone. And how careless to leave the hat, with the name inscribed inside. And what did Charles have?"

"The farm?"

"But Charles's remains are necessary to claim it. And no one has come forward." Rees shook his head in frustration.

"Maybe killing Charles was an accident," David suggested. "In a fight or something."

"Not likely," Rees said. "This place was carefully chosen. No, the killers wanted time with him. What did he know? What did he have?" Both were silent a moment. "It is ironic, though, us finding the body. If the killer hadn't ambushed us, we would never have known the remains were here."

"God meant us to find Charles," David said. "So you could identify his killer."

Chapter Twenty

As the sun dropped behind the hills to the west, shadows crept over the bluff until only the easternmost point glowed gold. Within a few seconds even that blinked out. Rees took out his pocketknife and cut a long strip of linen from the bottom of his shirt. He slit the cloth in half. Then he did the same to David's. In the last of the light, he tied the linen over Bessie's hooves to muffle the sound of her passing.

When all the light was gone from the sky, the two men climbed into the wagon. Rees compelled his son to lie down in the wagon bed. After their blunt conversation about Charles and Ira, David did not protest. They started down the lane. Even with the muffling cloth upon Bessie's hooves, the sound of her footfalls sounded loud to Rees. As they approached the junction of the lane with the Surry road, his heart began hammering in his chest. They swung onto the road. He urged Bessie into a trot, thinking that if she were moving quickly the wagon—and the driver—would be more difficult to hit.

Shadowed by the steep western hill and the trees, the Surry road was already completely dark. Rees loosened the reins, giving Bessie her head. He trusted her senses now more than his own. Nothing happened, and after an hour or so David scrambled into the seat by his father. Rees didn't protest; he needed the company. Hell, he decided, was not fire and heat but cold and a long black road with a patient killer hidden somewhere close by.

They rolled into Zion close to midnight. The sound of Bessie's hooves rattling over the wooden bridge woke Rees from his stupor. The mare walked to the stable and stopped. "Thank God," David said in heartfelt tones. He scrambled out of the wagon and hurried into the stable for a lantern. Rees staggered down from the wagon, his legs and back on fire. He caught Bessie's bridle.

"We're here now," he said to her, calm and relieved.

A sudden flare of light shot up under the portico for the Dwelling House. A moment later a lantern bobbed across the road toward them. Mouse said, "Where have you been?" Rees looked at her in astonishment.

"Why are you waiting for us?"

"I was worried." She held the lantern high so that it shone upon Bessie. David quickly stripped off the bridle. "No one knew where you were and neither one of you came in for supper. And my cousin came to Zion to tell me she saw a black horse galloping toward Surry. She thought you might be in trouble."

"Your cousin?" Fatigue slowed Rees's ability to think to a crawl. "Jane Doucette?"

"Of course. She was very distressed. She wanted me to warn you."

Something was wrong with that story but Rees couldn't put his finger on it. He was too tired.

"I put fresh water in your room just after supper and a plate of food," Mouse said. "You both look like you can use them." Rees twitched his shoulders, sore and achy from the tension of the trip home.

"Thank you," he said. "We'll talk about it tomorrow. David

and I are both dead on our feet." Mouse handed Rees the lantern and hurried back to the Dwelling House, and shortly Rees heard the quiet snick of the closing door.

They dragged the wagon inside the stable and fed and watered Bessie. Rees picked up the sack of bones from the wagon bed. "You better stay in my room tonight," he said to David. "Otherwise you'll disturb your roommates." Staggering with weariness, they crossed the street. Once inside the room, Rees put down the lantern beside the linen-covered plate. "Wash first," he said. Although the water was room temperature, it felt good to scrub away the dust and sweat from face and hands. Rees cleaned up first and sat down on a chair. He was almost too tired to eat.

"David," he said. "Don't say anything to anyone about the bones. Not to Elder White, not to Mouse, not to Levi. No one. Not until I say it is all right to do so. I need to think about what happened for a little while."

"But what if the shooter comes after us?" David objected. "Isn't it better everyone knows?"

"I doubt he's a Shaker," Rees said. "They follow rigid schedules and are always in company with one another. Escaping the scrutiny of the other members in this community would be difficult. Especially for two of them. You know that better than I do."

David nodded. "But Zion is not so separate as I thought," he said. "The murderers can come here too."

"I doubt the shooter knew you were even there," Rees said. "In any case, I think you'll be safe if you stay among the Brethren. I'll bring these remains to the sheriff on Monday."

When David finished washing, they sat down to eat: cold chicken, slices of buttered bread, only a little hard from sitting, and the first of the blueberries, all washed down with water.

Then David collapsed fully dressed upon the rug. Rees managed to strip off his breeches and his ragged shirt before falling into bed.

He awoke only once, thinking, "We saw no horse. Nobody passed us before the shooting began." Then he dropped off to sleep once again.

He awoke an hour or so after daybreak to the familiar sounds of mooing cows and a crowing rooster. Rees's first thought was for his secret cargo. He turned to look, his shoulders screaming with pain, and saw the canvas sack sitting by the bed within easy reach of his hand. Even dropping with exhaustion, he had instinctively protected his evidence. David was sprawled upon the floor, twisted into the nest of blankets, sleeping with the abandon of an exhausted child. Rees carefully pulled himself into a sitting position and then upright. His lower back ached so much he moved like an old man.

The remnants of their late-night supper sat upon the table, no food but a scatter of crumbs and the dirty plates and flatware. Mouse's thoughtfulness struck him forcefully, not just the light supper she'd slipped into the room but waiting up for them to assure herself of their safety.

"David," Rees said in a low voice. "David." He limped to the boy's side and put a hand upon his bony shoulder. "Time to get up." He shook lightly. David leaped up as though stung. "The breakfast bell will ring soon. Better wash." David stared bleary-eyed at his father, upright but only half-conscious. Rees moved painfully back to the basin. Slowly, slowly the kinks were working their way out of his back and legs. He threw some water onto his stubbled face and dried.

The bell clanged, reverberating through the room. David fled through the door, no doubt starving. Rees carefully bent over to put on his shoes, stockings, and breeches. Then he hid the sack behind his loom before slowly following his son into the hall.

The sweet perfume of maple syrup and bacon brought the water into Rees's mouth. David was already in the waiting room, at the front by the door. Rees joined the men at the back. Most of them had risen before daybreak for early-morning chores; since today was Sunday everything had to be completed before service. Elder White arrived last, his face gray with weariness. Rees looked at him curiously, realizing that the members of this community most able to act independently were the Elders. But he just couldn't see the elderly Shaker shooting at anyone. Then the bell inside rang and the doors opened and they hurried inside for breakfast.

After the meal Rees joined the flood of Brethren heading toward the Meetinghouse. But when they turned right, he went straight, into the alley next to the Blacksmith. He climbed the path to Lydia's cottage. He saw her before she saw him; she was standing at the back inspecting the hives. For a moment he watched her, dreading the task before him. She turned suddenly and saw him and the fear sprang into her face. Then she walked down to meet him.

"I thought you were away," she said.

"May I come in?" he asked. Reluctance and the awareness of bad news held her still for a moment and then she nodded.

"Very well."

She preceded him down the hill and gestured him into her cottage. "Should I sit down to hear this?"

"I think so, yes," Rees said. When she was seated he carefully lowered himself into the opposite chair. "As you know, David and I drove down to the Lewis farm." She nodded. "Mrs.

Lewis asked after you," he added. Lydia's mouth relaxed although she did not smile. "As we drove back, we stopped to search the streambed." Lydia tensed and folded her hands so tightly together the knuckles turned white. "When we stopped at the bluff for our meal we found human remains. Charles's hat was with them. Lydia, he didn't leave you. He was murdered, probably by the same men who murdered Ira." She stared at him for a moment longer and then burst into tears. Rees did not dare embrace her although he wished to. He awkwardly patted her wrist for several moments until her tears slowed.

"I'm sorry, I'm sorry," she said, wiping her eyes on her apron.

"He didn't leave you," Rees repeated, striving to comfort her.

She blew her nose and said shakily, "You don't need to lie, Mr. Rees. I know the truth."

"What truth?" Rees stammered.

"Eldress Phelps told me Charles meant to sign the Covenant upon his return. Once the estate was in his hands, he meant to sign the Covenant."

Rees frowned. "Why did she tell you that? Eldress Phelps can't know if that is even true."

Lydia managed a weak smile. "She said she didn't want me to grieve."

"I think she should mind her own business," Rees said shortly.

"So you see, Mr. Rees, the farm should transfer to the Shakers," Lydia said. "Charles always meant it to." Although Rees thought Charles had intended to sign the Covenant, now that Lydia said so he had to argue.

"Just because Eldress Phelps said so doesn't mean it's true," he repeated. "Charles may have said that but meant to return to you."

"No," Lydia said, shaking her head. "He married me for the child, so she would have her father's name. I always knew he thought the connection between us was sinful, that he would return to the ways of the Church. I didn't want to admit it. And I daresay he expected me to feel the same."

"And did you?"

"Not then. I wouldn't give up my daughter. Now?" She stared over Rees's head, seeing something invisible to him. He held his breath. "I don't know. I gave up everything for him. If I return to Zion I'll be the woman who sinned. The prodigal daughter. A living moral to a lesson. But Eldress Phelps did invite me to return to the fold so I will always have somewhere to go."

Rees wondered cynically if Eldress Phelps knew of the marriage and the estate Lydia Jane would inherit.

"Someone shot at us," he said. "He ambushed us as we went to the bluff and shot at us. He meant to kill me." Lydia blanched and her hand crept to her throat. "The man who murdered Charles and Ira is still in Durham."

"What will you do now?" she asked.

"Tomorrow I'll drive into town and speak to the sheriff. No one else knows about the remains, Lydia. Just you, me, and David." She nodded uncertainly. "I don't know who to trust. Very few people knew David and I were planning to drive down to Surry. But he found us."

Lydia took in a deep breath. "Maybe he was watching the bluff. I would, if I knew I had something to hide."

Rees stared at her and then slowly nodded. "Of course," he said. "He might do that, especially after I began poking around." He lapsed into silence, thinking hard. "After I speak to the sheriff, I'll give the remains to Elder White for burial." He managed a lopsided smile. "Perhaps, once the killer knows Charles Ellis's body has been found, he'll stop trying to kill me."

She smiled faintly. "I don't know, Mr. Rees. You seem to

annoy a large number of people." She paused. "I should go with you. I need to bring my marriage lines to Mr. Golightly." Rees hesitated, quelling his first impulse to shout a loud no.

"What if the killer is out there, waiting, and shoots you by mistake?" he said, perfectly reasonably, he thought.

"Will it make a difference if we travel tomorrow or Tuesday or Wednesday?" she asked. "Or a week from now? The only course of action that will make us safer is catching him. To do that, we need to go to Durham." Rees hesitated again. "If we drive the Surry road early, we'll be among many other wagons," Lydia said. "We'll be safe enough."

Rees shook his head unhappily. "Very well," he said. "But I'll take my rifle, just in case."

After several seconds of silence Rees realized she was waiting for him to leave. He bowed his way out and started down the flagged path. Pausing a moment to adjust his stocking, he heard the sound of weeping begin again.

Rees returned to his room. To the background of the singing and chanting emanating from the Meetinghouse, he finished warping his loom. He loaded the shuttle and began to weave. He fell automatically into a familiar twill pattern, his legs pumping the treadles up and down as he threw the shuttle back and forth. The rhythm calmed him. As the patterned blocks began to line up on the cloth, the events of the last few weeks squared up in his mind. Unfortunately, he found more questions than answers. But he was certain of one thing: he needed to talk to Henry Doucette.

Rain swept in overnight and Rees awoke to the sound of water dripping from the eaves. The journey into Durham would not be a pleasant one. The somber gray skies and steady drizzle affected the mood of even the phlegmatic Shakers; when Rees joined the Brethren in the waiting room he found them restless and agitated. Some of them even whispered to one another. Turning to William, Rees said, "What's the matter?"

"The Maine Ministry arrives this morning." Worry creased his brow. "They can disband a Family if they feel it necessary."

"Surely not," Rees said in surprise. William nodded glumly.

The atmosphere of simple contentment Rees had come to expect had disappeared. Some of the Brothers at table with Rees could not eat. The tension affected one of the Sisters serving breakfast so badly she dropped a dish and fled sobbing from the room. And Elder White, who usually presented a smiling face to all, looked worried. Rees gladly escaped the tension as soon as he was finished.

After her day's rest, Bessie was eager for some exercise. Rees harnessed her to the wagon and drove over the bridge at the southern end of the village. Lydia, bonneted and with a hooded cape over one arm, waited under the trees. Today she wore her burgundy dress with a white bertha over the shoulders. She looked pale and tired, purple ringing her eyes like bruises. As usual, Rees jumped down to assist her and, as usual, she climbed into her seat without his aid. The pulled out onto the Surry road and joined the procession toward Durham.

Rees tried to initiate a conversation but, although Lydia smiled and responded, he soon realized she was too preoccupied to engage in chat. They rode the rest of the way in silence.

He pulled the wagon in the stable yard. Today the back door was open; they took advantage and walked through it into the store. "Now what?" Coulton said, teasing, from his post at the counter. "What problem do you bring me today?" Then he saw Lydia's expression and his rallying tone disappeared. "What's the matter?"

"My son and I found Charles Ellis," Rees said and put the sack upon the counter.

"Oh no," Coulton said. "Oh no." He stared at the sack as though afraid to touch it. "Are you sure? I hope you're wrong." Rees carefully reached in and pulled out the ragged remains of the hat. Coulton read the name inside and paled. "I hoped he had gone somewhere else to start a new life," he said. Raising anguished eyes to Rees, he added, "I knew it wasn't likely but I wanted to believe it. It would be better than this." He shook his head, struggling to control his emotion. "Why Charles? He was a good man."

"I know," Rees said. "We found the body off a bluff on the Surry road. The remains had fallen to a ledge."

"I know that bluff," Coulton said, looking genuinely grieved. "Was he knifed also?" He spit out his toothpick.

"Not that I could tell," Rees said. He pulled out the cut harness. "I think he might have been strangled. After some . . ." He stopped and glanced at Lydia. "He wasn't killed immediately." After a faint sound of anguish, Lydia walked to the other side of the store.

"Very nasty," Coulton said grimly. "This killer deserves to hang."

"Ira was killed and dumped; he was of no use to the killer. But Charles . . . the killer took his time. He wanted something from him." Coulton's face went white. "There's something else. Someone shot at us, Sheriff. Charles Ellis's killer is still out there and he tried to kill me." Slowly Coulton raised another toothpick to his mouth.

"Do you know who it was?"

"Of course not," Rees said. What an odd question. "I couldn't see him. But it would have taken a lot of physical strength to toss Charles Ellis off the cliff." Coulton nodded and Rees saw something flash into his eyes. Click, click, click: something was adding up and the conclusion horrified him. "What? Do you know something?"

"No. It's just so . . . ugly." Rees didn't believe him, but although he waited Coulton did not elaborate.

"One other thing," he said. "I just learned Jane Doucette saw a man riding a black horse galloping down the Surry road on Saturday afternoon. She thought he was suspicious. Do you know anyone hereabouts who owns a black horse?" Coulton stared into space for a moment.

"Not solid black. There's Blackie, but he has four white stockings. Mrs. Doucette would have seen the white when the gelding went past." Coulton rolled his toothpick back and forth for a moment. "Most of the horses around here are your common farmer's nags, fit only for the plow. I can't imagine any of them galloping but I'll look into it." Both men stood in silence for a moment.

"What will you do with them now?" Coulton asked, gesturing to the canvas sack.

"Give them to Elder White for burial."

"Yes, Charles would like that." Coulton sighed. "He . . ." The soft click of a closing door distracted them. Rees glanced up just in time to see a bit of Mrs. Coulton's blue skirt. How long had she been eavesdropping? When he looked back at the sheriff, Coulton said, "I'll send some men around to look for black horses." Rees was almost certain that Coulton had intended to say something different. "And please ask Elder White to send word when he holds the service for Mr. Ellis. I'd like to attend."

"I will," Rees said. He looked around for Lydia, finally spotting her hovering over a box of candles. He lowered his voice. "One other thing. Elder White asked after Brother Michael's remains. He wants to bury the boy with the Shakers."

Coulton hesitated a moment and then said with a stiff smile, "Please extend my apologies to the Elder. Michael Languedela'or has already been buried."

"And who paid for that?" Rees asked. Coulton was silent a beat too long.

"He was buried in a pauper's grave," he said. "Is that all, Mr. Rees?" Rees recognized a dismissal when he heard it. He nodded at the sheriff and joined Lydia. They walked through the back door of the store to the yard beyond.

"What's the matter?" Lydia asked, noting Rees's expression. He forced a smile.

"Just surprised by the sheriff's reaction to Brother Charles's passing."

Lydia smiled slightly. "Everyone liked Charles; that is why Elder White sent him on selling trips. He was both charming and honest. You would have liked him too." Rees doubted it. From the beginning, he had pegged Charles Ellis as a selfish and opportunistic charmer and nothing he'd discovered had persuaded him otherwise. But he was honest enough to admit to himself some of his antipathy might be due to jealousy.

Chapter Twenty-one

Slowed by the muddy road, it was twenty minutes and more before they reached Mr. Golightly's house. Mrs. Baker, a smear of flour streaking one cheek, opened the door and stared at them in surprise. "Well," she said, "I didn't expect you until Wednesday."

"There have been . . . developments," Rees said.

"Mr. Golightly is in his office. I think he'll be glad to see you; he's taking an interest in these proceedings." She preceded them down the brick-floored hallway to the room at the back.

"Come in, come in," he said when he saw them, painfully levering himself to his feet. He wore a blue jacket and black breeches with lace at his throat tied in the style from thirty years ago. "I didn't expect to see you for several days yet." He gestured them to the chairs. Lydia sat down but Rees couldn't. He paced restlessly.

"I'm afraid I have sad news," he said. Mr. Golightly pinned him with those bright blue eyes.

"Please sit then, Mr. Rees. I expect I know the nature of your news. You've found Mr. Ellis, haven't you?"

"Yes," said Rees and put the hat upon the desk. Mr. Golightly picked it up and turned it over so he could read the name inscribed inside. He sighed.

"He died violently."

"Yes."

"I see. Well then, Mrs. Ellis, do you have your marriage lines with you?"

Rees experienced a shock at hearing Lydia referred to as Mrs. Ellis. She took the papers from her bag and handed them to Mr. Golightly. He looked them over and handed them back.

"They seem in order. I'll schedule a formal reading of the will with all the interested parties in attendance."

"I don't want the farm," she said in a low passionate voice.

"Hmmm. Well, you can refuse it after the will is read and the estate is settled," he said. Clearly he believed she would come to her senses in a few days. "In the meantime I pulled out the survey for you." He pulled out a loose roll and with hands that resembled chicken claws unrolled it upon his desk. Rees peered over the elderly lawyer's shoulder. The Ellis property stretched all the way to one end of the paper, five times or more larger than the Doucette farm, and well marked by streams. The man who owned this would be wealthy indeed.

As Mr. Golightly carefully rerolled the map, Mrs. Baker brought in the tray with tea and cake and put it down upon the desk. Lydia moved forward to pour.

"Did you tell that other gentleman the details of these wills?" Rees asked. Mrs. Baker hesitated and began fussing with the cups, the china cups clinking as she moved them around.

"Of course not," Mr. Golightly said, offended. "I took them out of my files and read them over, so as to familiarize myself with them. And when he returned the second time, I informed him of the older Mr. Ellis's wishes. But that will is a matter of public record." He looked at Mrs. Baker. "Mrs. Baker, please. Less noise." She smiled at him and turned to look at Rees and Lydia with an intense meaningful stare before exiting through the door. Mr. Golightly did not speak again until she had closed it behind her. "Sometimes that woman is too curious," he muttered.

Ignoring this bit of domestic drama, Rees asked, "Does the name Catherine Parker sound familiar to you?" When Mr. Golightly shook his head Rees added, "Sister Chastity?"

"No. Why?"

"That is the name of the young Shaker woman killed a month ago. I am trying to find a connection, because Ira's remains turned up on Chastity's brother's farm, where Charles's cousin Patrick O'Reardon also used to work."

"Perhaps she knew Charles Ellis." Mr. Golightly sighed. "I am glad my old friend is not here to see the death of his grandson." Rees and Lydia drank their tea, Rees so distracted by his thoughts he didn't even realize it was tea in the cup. "Do you know yet who killed the boy?"

"I'm close," Rees said. He tried to refuse cake but relented when Mr. Golightly's mouth drooped in disappointment. "I'll tell you all about it when I know everything."

He ate his cake in three bites and rose to his feet to leave. Lydia looked at him disapprovingly. "Manners, Mr. Rees," she said.

Mr. Golightly flapped his hand at them. "Go ahead. I understand. I was young once too. Send Mrs. Baker in to clear, would you?"

Lydia put her half-eaten treat aside. "I'm sorry," she said apologetically.

Mrs. Baker was waiting for them outside in the hall. "I wanted to tell you," she said. "Mr. Golightly tires easily, as you've noticed. Sometimes he falls asleep, just for a moment, a little catnap, you might say." Rees nodded. He'd already witnessed that. "Well, when that Mr. Doucette came, I went in to clear and found him standing over Mr. Golightly, looking over his shoulder at the papers on the desk. So he probably knew something of both wills."

"Thank you, Mrs. Baker," Rees said. "I think that will help."

When he and Lydia stepped out upon the porch, she said, "What does it mean?"

"That Mr. Doucette probably knew Charles Ellis was married." Rees looked at her sharply, understanding all at once the connection to Catherine Parker. "But he did not know your name." Lydia thought for a moment.

"So he realized he would not inherit anything," she said.

"Once you're out of the way, I can imagine two possibilities. He is married to one of the Ellis granddaughters. With both Roger and Charles Junior dead and Patrick missing, the estate would be split among the girls."

Lydia shook her head. "I won't believe Jane is involved."

"What if Henry Doucette pretends to be the missing Patrick O'Reardon?" Rees asked. "Once he read the wills, he must know that Patrick inherits it all." Rees was silent for a moment, thinking. "When I told the sheriff about Charles Ellis being tossed off the bluff, he thought of something. I could see it in his eyes. And I think he would have confided in me but for his sneaky eavesdropping wife. He's figured something out and I'd wager my soul it has to do with Henry Doucette. I must speak to Coulton again," Rees said. He helped Lydia up into the seat.

"It's all about greed, isn't it?" she said.

Although the rain had stopped for the moment, the Rumford road remained wet and muddy, deep ruts and puddles scoring the surface. The wagon lurched from side to side and the dirty slurry sprayed out in sticky sheets. Rapid travel was not possible and Rees thought this leg took longer than twenty minutes.

Visible from a distance, Mrs. Coulton was out on the front porch sweeping away the mud. Rees did not turn into the stable yard, but pulled over to the side and paused. "He's gone," she told him, her voice loud and harsh.

"Do you know where?"

"No. He didn't tell me. I thought it was after you." She nodded at Rees and he tried not to recoil from the dislike rolling from her. Turning her back upon him, she resumed her sweeping. Rees did not think it an accident that several of the mud clots shot toward the wagon.

"What an unpleasant woman," he muttered as he picked up the reins.

"She's worried," Lydia said. "She thinks you'll lead her husband into danger. And you probably will."

Rees swung automatically into the left fork, toward Zion. As they approached the Doucette farm, he considered the advisability of stopping. Too dangerous, he decided. If Lydia had not been sitting beside him he might have tried to speak to Mr. Doucette, but the farmer was too volatile. Rees wouldn't risk Lydia's safety as well as his own. He glanced up the driveway as they passed. No one seemed to be about.

By the time he'd dropped Lydia at her cottage, put the wagon into the stables, and loosed Bessie into the paddock, only an hour remained before dinner. He picked up the sack of remains and went in search of Elder White. He hoped to finish this chore before the meal. But as he crossed the street toward the Dwelling House, William came flying out of the Blacksmith's, calling for him. Rees turned. The young man panted up to him. Uncomfortably stroking his chin, Brother William said, "Mr. Rees, the Maine Ministry wishes to speak to you." Sudden apprehension sent a spike into Rees's belly.

"What do they want?" he growled.

"I don't know," William said. "I know you're busy and don't want to involve yourself in our affairs, but it will look worse for Elder White if you don't come."

"Very well," Rees said. He looked down at the sack in his hands. "Let me put this in my room." William nodded and Rees quickly darted into the Dwelling House. He flung open the door to his room and found Mouse making the bed, tears running down her cheeks. She glanced at him and fled, sobbing. Elder White's trouble was unnerving everyone. He quickly concealed the sack behind his loom and returned outside to rejoin William.

They crossed the street to the Meetinghouse. "Please wait here," William said. "I'll see if they're ready for you." He clattered up the wooden stairs and Rees heard the low buzz of conversation. Moments later William returned, flushed and sweaty and looking wretched. He pointed to the stairs.

Rees climbed the stairs with deliberation, entering this private space with as much dignity as he could muster. The stairs ended at a small landing with doors on either side. Directly in front of Rees was another room, a large central hall, with a large table in the center. Lined up on the side facing him were the four members of the Maine Ministry, two women and two men.

"Enter, please, Mr. Rees," said one of the men. His deep resonant voice rolled over Rees like velvet. "Sit down." Although no gray threaded his brown hair, Rees thought he was probably the same age as Elder White.

Feeling like a schoolboy called to account by his teacher, Rees did as he was told. For a moment he and the four Believers stared at one another. Finally the Elder who had first spoken said, "I am Elder Hutchins." He gestured to those beside him. "Elder Cooper, Eldresses Milner and Brand." Rees nodded at them in turn. Elder Cooper looked at Rees expressionlessly from mud-colored eyes. Eldress Brand, a woman of perhaps fifty years, offered him a brief nod. Only Eldress Milner, a young woman with a high white forehead and round blue eyes, returned his gaze with one of her own. "We understand you have lived here among the Believers for several weeks," Elder Hutchins continued.

"That is true."

"Are you planning to sign the Covenant?"

"No."

"Why you are here then?"

"My son joined the community. I came to visit. After the death of Sister Chastity, Elder White asked me to stay on and look into the circumstances surrounding it." He saw from their expressions that they knew this.

"You have experience in such matters?"

"Yes. In the Continental Army and other places."

"What of your son? Does he intend to sign the Covenant?"

"Perhaps," Rees said although he doubted it. "That is his decision." Surprise registered on all four faces and the atmosphere warmed slightly.

"Clearly the murderer is from outside," Elder Hutchins said confidently. "We do not need sheriffs or jails."

"Perhaps so," Rees said, stifling his impulse to argue. Brother Michael had been a member but he knew better than to remind them of that. Elder Hutchins smiled slightly as though reading Rees's thoughts.

"How much longer do you expect your investigation to take?" He leaned across the table.

"Not very much longer," Rees said. "I have a few more knots to unravel."

The Ministry regarded him in silence for a moment longer,

then Elder Hutchins said, "Thank you for speaking with us, Mr. Rees." They regarded him in silence as he rose to his feet and retreated down the stairs. Although he heard no sounds of conversation, he sensed the currents swirling about him. The Ministry was here to make important decisions, some of which he would never know. Sympathy for Elder White and Eldress Phelps flashed through him. Once kings in this tiny domain, they were now in the dock.

Chapter Twenty-two

Dinner was a somber meal. Although none of the Ministry joined them in the Dining Hall, the Shakers clearly felt their presence lying over the village like fog. Elder White and Eldress Phelps were in attendance, trying hard to behave as usual, but both looking tired and anxious. Rees noticed that White pushed his food around his plate, eating little.

He was not the only one who looked nervous. Mouse's eyes were almost swollen shut from weeping. Those among the Family who had already been interviewed by the Ministry wore expressions of guilt and relief. Their fear seemed out of proportion to the cause, at least in Rees's view, but he did not question the depth of their apprehension. He regretted the need to tell Elder White, to tell all of them, his sad news, but knew he must.

At the end of the meal, as the Brethren left the room for afternoon chores, Rees approached the Elder. White looked at him almost as though he didn't know him. "Elder White," Rees said, "I have disappointing news." The Elder motioned Rees to one side. Although Rees meant to tell him in private, Eldress Phelps hastened to join them. "Brother Michael has already been interred in Durham." Elder White sighed.

"Very well." He made as if to leave but Rees stayed him with a hand upon his arm. This would not be easy; better to say it quickly and finish it.

"I found the remains of Charles Ellis," he said. Eldress Phelps went pale.

"Are you sure?"

"We found a hat with his name inside."

"How?" Elder White asked hoarsely, his eyes reddening with unshed tears.

"Strangled, I think," Rees said.

"Who could be so wicked?" Elder White cried. "Charles was a good man."

"What about his property?" Eldress Phelps asked. "I believe he owned a farm . . ."

"I am not sure," Rees lied with a smile on his face. Of course Eldress Phelps knew Ellis owned property. "My sad duty is to convey the remains to Elder White so they might be buried."

"He would want to go home to Mother," White agreed. "I so hoped he would return to us someday."

Elder White followed Rees to the Dwelling House and into his room. Rees fetched the canvas sack. "Such an undignified carrier," White said, looking at it a moment before taking it from Rees's hands. "Charles deserved much better." Shoulders bowed, he trudged from the room. Even if the Maine Ministry made no changes in Zion, White was a beaten man.

The rain had diminished to alternating drizzle and breezy cloudiness. Although it was perfect weather for staying indoors and weaving, Rees decided to visit the Ellis property instead. With the arrival of the Maine Ministry and their questions a sense of urgency had taken hold of him. He knew he would not be allowed much more time to find the killer.

He hitched Bessie to the wagon and they drove down Piper

Lane. He parked on the road and walked in on the track. It had once been wide enough for a wagon but the vegetation encroached on either side, narrowing the space to a lane. Water dripped from the leaves into the silence. Rees looked around. Regular piles of horse droppings indicated recent four-footed traffic so he followed them. When the track split, one arm curving away to the abandoned house on the right, he stayed straight, following the lane as it curved left to the pasture beyond. The track was overgrown; the house, even occluded by trees, looked derelict. But the lean-tos that served as stables and the fencing around the pasture were so new the wood was still green. And although no horses remained inside the paddock, Rees knew they'd only just been removed. The outlines of iron-shod hooves imprinted in the mud were knife-sharp, unblurred by the rain.

After a few moments of thoughtful study, he turned back, taking the fork toward the house. Only the faintest path marked the way. Rees fought his way through the undergrowth, the clinging wet branches soaking him almost to the chest. He approached from the back, through what had once been a field and a barnyard. Although red blooms identified some of the brambles as roses, they had gone to briar with long sharp thorns. The barn had weathered to gray but the roof looked intact. He paused by the house and inspected it. The back stairs listed to one side, in danger of imminent collapse. Rees slowly circled to the front. The shutters were closed but several hung askew. Rees saw the shine of window glass behind them. He climbed the front stairs. Gaps in the porch roof gave entry to the rain and the porch floor was rotting, in some cases clear through. The porch floor creaked underneath him as though threatening to give way. He tugged on the front door but it was either locked or swollen shut, perhaps both, and would not move.

A sudden faint pattering of rain warned of another downpour. Rees hesitated, considered waiting it out. The light drizzle increased, becoming a steady downpour. It did not look as though it would stop, and since the storm could trap him here for the night, Rees decided to hurry back to the wagon and return to Zion. He could use a change of clothes anyway; he was already wet to the skin.

When he plunged into his room, eager to change to dry clothing and anticipating a quiet hour or so of weaving before supper, he found Mouse working inside. She had just finished making his bed and she turned from smoothing the counterpane with a start. Although she'd stopped weeping Rees thought the red-rimmed eyes in her bloodless face looked even more tragic than tears.

"Sorry," she mumbled from behind her shielding hand. "I didn't mean . . . I didn't finish before and I want to do a good job."

"Don't worry," Rees said. "You look . . ." He considered and discarded several words before settling upon one. "You look dark." She nodded.

"What will I do if the Ministry closes Zion?" she whispered.

"I'm certain they will not," Rees said, trying to be reassuring.

"You don't understand," Mouse said. "Elder White argued with some of the other Elders. And every Family is required to have two Elders, two Eldresses. Elder White and Eldress Phelps do things differently here."

"Surely such politics won't affect you," Rees said.

"If they close Zion I'll be moved to another community. My Family is here. My cousins are here. I'll be forced to start over . . ." She dropped her hand a fraction and he understood; she would be an object of pity and scorn all over again.

Rees did not even suggest she leave the Shakers; she had

nowhere else to go. At least with them she had a place and a purpose. "Don't trouble trouble," he said gently. "We don't know what will be decided, but I am certain, absolutely certain, Mouse, that it will not be so terrible as you fear." She looked at him for a moment and then nodded, but Rees knew she didn't believe him. When she left he heard the sound of her quiet sobbing disappearing down the hall.

Breakfast the following morning was as somber a meal as the supper and dinner that had preceded it. Elder White waited until the end of breakfast before announcing Charles Ellis's death. Shock gave way to sorrow and audible sobbing could be heard throughout the hall. White set the interment for the following afternoon, a sensible decision, Rees thought. Delay would only extend the grief.

"I know we should rejoice," William muttered over his plate of pancakes. "Brother Charles will be going home to Mother. But I can't. He did not die in the fullness of life, as an old man. Someone struck him down." Rees nodded. Elder White glanced over reprovingly but he did not have the will to reprimand them for talking.

The Sisters began collecting the plates. Rees looked around for Mouse. He suspected she had been at least one of those weeping. Still seated at the table, she was surrounded by Sisters, all of them holding hands. Wonderful, he thought grimly. Now she can grieve for her cousin at the same time she worries she will be turned out to beg on the road.

He rose to follow the Brethren leaving the Dining Hall. As the men moved to the door a woman screamed, her cry cutting through the soft shuffle of footsteps like a knife. "Where is my husband?" Rees looked around, trying to pinpoint the direction, but it was not until the Brethren parted that he saw her— Mrs. Coulton. Her fine brown hair sifted down around her face, loosed from the tight bun she wore. She staggered and at first Rees wondered if she were drunk. "You!" she cried, seeing Rees and pointing her finger at him. He stared at her in consternation. "Where is my husband?" Everyone turned to stare at him.

As Eldress Phelps bore down upon the emotional woman from the opposite side of the room Elder White gestured at Rees with unmistakable command. He followed the Shaker out of the Dining Hall. Elder White did not speak as he preceded Rees up the stairs to the office. A few moments later Eldress Phelps shepherded Mrs. Coulton into the room.

Although her emotional storm had abated somewhat by the time she arrived, her eyes were swollen and red with weeping. "Where is he?" she demanded of Rees.

"I don't know," he said. "When did you see him last?"

"Yesterday. He didn't come home last night." Alarm burned down Rees's spine like acid.

"Did he say anything before he left?" he asked. "Anything at all? Where he was going? When he'd be back?" She shook her head, her eyes sliding away from his. She's lying, he thought. He stared into space, thinking. Something he'd said to Coulton had triggered a realization and the sheriff had rushed out, probably into the arms of the killer. "We need to search," he said. And because several things now seemed to point to the farm on Piper Lane, he added, "We should start with the Ellis property."

"No one has lived there for four or five years," Elder White objected.

"I know," Rees said. "What better place—" he stopped abruptly, conscious of Mrs. Coulton's frightened regard. "Maybe you can stay with Mrs. Doucette," he said. He wanted Mrs. Coulton out of the way, in case the search came to a terrible conclusion.

"No," she said defiantly. "I want to help look for my husband."

"We'll help," Elder White said. "I'll ask my Family to begin now."

"We'll find him," Rees promised Mrs. Coulton. She nodded, sniffling.

"Come and wash your face," Eldress Phelps said, leading the other woman across the hall to the women's side. Rees stared after them, surprised by the Eldress's sudden thoughtfulness.

"Do you believe we will?" Elder White asked.

"Find him? Oh yes. Eventually. I just pray we find him alive. I'd give anything to know what he realized."

They left the office and descended the stairs. As Elder White hurried away to gather his community, Rees paused under the portico. He planned to visit Lydia but didn't want to make his intentions too obvious. Eldress Phelps and Mrs. Coulton came out of the women's door and Mrs. Coulton climbed into her buggy. She drove south, not north to the Doucette farm, and Rees noticed that she handled the reins with professional skill. Eldress Phelps cast Rees a sour glance and returned inside. Rees sprinted across the street and hurried up to the path to Lydia's cottage.

Within thirty or so minutes, a cavalcade of wagons left Zion, Rees's among them. Lydia had insisted upon joining him and he had put up only a token protest. He found her company comforting. In fact, as he glanced at her sitting on the seat by his side, he realized he would find it a struggle to leave her behind when he left Zion. She caught his glance and offered him an anxious smile.

Once the wagons reached Piper Lane they began to separate; some remained at the southern tip of the Ellis property while others drove north, toward the Rumford road. The Brethren planned to search in a grid, working toward the center, and effectively covering the entire farm. Rees parked midway on Piper Lane, at the end of the driveway leading to the house. He wanted to take a closer look at it. Although he didn't want to admit this even to himself, he feared the sheriff was already dead. The abandoned house would make a good hiding place for a body. Mrs. Coulton's buggy was parked by the drive, but she was nowhere to be seen. Rees pulled up beside her buggy and jumped out. Lydia joined him with alacrity.

Although untended for several years and choked with weeks, the drive was still clearly visible. A faint silvery trail through the wet leaves marked the passage of another searcher, probably Mrs. Coulton. Rees and Lydia immediately set off after her.

They approached the house very quickly from this direction. It did not look any different than it had the day before; Rees saw no signs of trespassers. He climbed the stairs to the porch and hesitated, pondering the advisability of breaking through the front door.

"He's here. He's here." Rees heard the shout, communicated from one searcher to another. He took off at a run, pelting back down the driveway to the road, and leaving Lydia far behind. A short distance to the north he spotted a crowd of Brethren, thickening in size as more and more men flocked to the scene. Rees ran full speed toward them. When he reached the throng, they parted to let him through. Rees saw Elder White's bright white hair, shining at the center, and went straight toward him.

Coulton lay faceup by the stream, Eldress Phelps kneeling beside him. Blood spotted her white apron. Panting with exertion, Rees dropped to his knees on the other side of the sheriff, mud oozing wetly through his stockings. "Someone find Mrs. Coulton," he said. Focusing all his attention upon the other man, he asked Eldress Phelps, "Did you move him?"

"No. I lifted his head a little. I think he has a head wound." Rees looked at the Shaker woman, wondering for the first time how she had come into the Church. She smiled faintly. "I had many brothers; their scrapes have given me a familiarity with minor wounds. He's been hit at least once with something heavy."

He turned his attention back to the sheriff. Mud streaked Coulton's hands and knees as though he'd fallen several times and his coat and legs wore a second skin of spiky brown burrs. The scrapes on his knuckles and a bruise on his left cheek bore mute witness to a struggle. One of his shoes was missing, the stocking coated with mud up to the ankle.

Turning his attention now to the wound, Rees gently tipped Coulton's head forward. "There is a lot of blood," Eldress Phelps warned him. Rees slid his hands underneath the sheriff's skull. He felt a large swelling and his hand came away red and sticky. He turned the sheriff over so he could examine the wound more carefully. Although the swelling blurred the edges of the wound, Rees felt no sharp cuts. Like the wounds on Sister Chastity and Brother Charles, the wound appeared to have been made with something smooth and round. Rees sat back on his heels and took out his handkerchief to wipe his bloody hands.

"Did you find the weapon?" he asked, glancing around him.

"No. Nothing," Elder White said.

"Ask everyone to search all around," Rees said. "Especially for anything stained with blood or hair." With a nod, the Elder began directing his Family into different directions. Rees didn't expect them to find anything but he couldn't breathe with the crush of people standing around him. Already all these booted feet had obliterated the footprints of anyone who had walked here before.

"He's been lying here all night," Rees said, touching Coulton's dew-wet jacket.

"Thank God the weather is warm," Elder White said.

"His color is good," Eldress Phelps said. Rees looked at Coulton's face again. Pink touched his cheeks and his breathing was smooth and regular.

"Still, he shouldn't be left here. Has anyone found Mrs. Coulton?"

"She is coming now."

Holding up her skirts, her eyes wild, she was running toward them. Her large body did not inhibit her speed. When she saw her husband, her mouth opened and a thin high shriek poured from her mouth. Rees thought she probably did not even know she was screaming. She slipped and fell and rose to her feet to keep running. Her black dress was already stained with large dark patches of moisture. Flinging herself down by her husband, she took his head into her lap. He opened his eyes.

"Wh-what?" Turning his face away from her, Coulton threw up into the grass.

"Who hit you?" Rees asked. Coulton went to shake his head and retched again.

"He needs to be put to bed," Mrs. Coulton said firmly. "Lying on the cold wet ground is not healthy."

Rees helped the sheriff stand. He vomited twice more and muttered, "What happened? I have such a headache."

"You don't remember?" Rees asked.

"No," Coulton said.

"You met someone," Rees said. "Maybe you'll remember soon. I'll come by and we'll talk."

Coulton started to nod but stopped, his hand going to his brow. "I will bring him home now," Mrs. Coulton announced, directing an angry scowl in Rees's direction.

With Rees on one side supporting Coulton's weight, and the surprisingly strong Mrs. Coulton on the other, they managed to support the sheriff into the buggy. His face ashen, Coulton leaned back as Mrs. Coulton took up the reins. The throng of searchers, mostly Shakers but with a few others mixed in, watched the buggy rattle northward to Durham. As the Shakers began streaming to their own wagons, the number of people dwindled rapidly to just three: Rees, Lydia Jane, and Mrs. Doucette. He hadn't even known the women were beside him.

Mrs. Doucette, her expression grim, nodded at Rees and Lydia and set off across the road toward her home. Rees suddenly realized he had seen no sign of Mr. Doucette at all.

Chapter Twenty-three

A fter a few minutes of clambering through the long grass, Rees and Lydia reached the road and began walking up to the wagon. She smelled faintly of lavender and honey. Rees inhaled deeply, with pleasure. "Did you notice Mr. Doucette was not among the searchers?" Lydia asked. And when he did not reply at once, "Will?"

"I noticed," he said, snapping back to the problem at hand.

"But Mrs. Doucette was there."

"Perhaps he is sick," Rees suggested, recalling Doucette's previous drunken behavior.

"I doubt she'd have left him in that case," Lydia said, and Rees had to nod in agreement.

"Maybe he is avoiding me and my questions," he said.

"Was the sheriff able to tell you who hit him?"

"He's lost his memory. I've seen it before. Sometime the victim recovers in a day or two, sometimes it takes months."

Lydia shook her head incredulously. "I can't believe this is happening here," she murmured.

"The roots were planted several years ago," Rees said. Lydia nodded thoughtfully and for a moment they walked in silence.

"When are you planning to visit the Doucettes?" She asked.

"You are not joining me," he said firmly.

"Of course I am. You need my help. Mrs. Doucette will speak more easily to me than to you."

"That may be true," Rees said, "but it's too dangerous. Mr. Doucette is a little too eager to use his rifle. And I'd wager my last farthing he is the killer."

"We don't know that for sure," Lydia argued. "Anyway, I doubt he'll shoot me; he has no reason to."

"I wouldn't be so certain," Rees said, recalling the balls flying at him from the Doucette drive. "Mr. Doucette is well known to be of choleric temperament."

"I'll visit her on my own if you won't allow me to accompany you."

"Don't be foolish. I plan to bring my rifle. Besides, I'm taller and heavier, not a defenseless woman . . ." As his mind took a sudden leap of thought, he pulled on the reins, bringing the wagon in a complete circle.

"Where are we going?" Lydia asked in surprise.

"Durham." Rees slapped down the reins on Bessie's back. "I need to speak to Simon Rouge immediately."

"The deputy?"

"Yes. Coulton is home with none but his wife to protect him. It's possible Mr. Doucette . . ." He did not finish the thought. Lydia nodded, her expression horrified.

Although Rees pushed Bessie forward as rapidly as he dared, they did not catch up to the others until they turned on to the Rumford road. And then Rees couldn't make his way around the knot of wagons and buggies traveling into Durham. Grumbling, he slowed and pulled in behind the rearmost wagon with its cargo of Shaker lads.

"Why are they even here?" he muttered.

"Patience, Mr. Rees. You asked for their help, remember? Once they have assured themselves of the sheriff's condition, they will drive back to Zion. Sometimes even they appreciate a break in the routine." Rees turned to look at her. Despite the reproof in her voice and her muddy dress and cap, her eyes sparkled with excitement.

The Coulton buggy turned into the stable yard and, one by one, the Shaker wagons followed. Finally Rees was able to pull around to the right and pass the clog. He drove rapidly to the corner and spun around it, taking it at such a speed Lydia clung to the side with a gasp. Rees pulled up in front of The Cartwheel.

All of the shopkeepers, and Mr. Rouge too, were lined up on the plank walk watching the activity across the street. From this vantage, little could be seen, and several gentlemen were ambling over to take a closer look. Rees jumped down and halted Rouge with a shout. "Mr. Rouge. A word if you please."

The burly tavern keeper paused with one foot suspended. Seeing Rees, and correctly assuming he knew the details, Rouge quickly returned to the sidewalk. Rees offered a hand to assist Lydia to the ground. Rouge's eyebrows rose when he saw the Shaker garb. "This is Miss Farrell," Rees said. "She was left behind so I have undertaken to return her to Zion."

"Of course. Come inside," Rouge said, adding for Lydia's benefit, "No one is inside at present. It will be cooler." They followed him into the dark and shadowy interior.

"Why are all the Shakers over there?"

"They joined the search for the sheriff. Didn't you know? We were looking for him."

"No one told me," Rouge said in annoyance.

"The sheriff went missing yesterday," Rees said. "I'm surprised Mrs. Coulton did not approach you."

"Damn—" Remembering Lydia's presence, Rouge bit off the rest of his epithet. "We rarely see eye to eye," he said. "She loathes anyone who argues with her husband. You found him, I suppose?"

"Yes. On the Ellis property. Someone struck him on the head and left him for dead. He doesn't remember the attack yet and so can't identify the one who struck him."

"I see. And all the Shakers brought him back?"

"I know that seems unnecessary," Rees said. "But there is a benefit. The sheriff's attacker may try again, especially if he hears the sheriff is still alive. I wondered if you would keep an eye on him, especially tonight."

Rouge nodded. "I will. But it may have to be from out here, on the street. Mrs. Coulton will not permit me in the house. She's very protective of her husband. Are you married?" Rees shook his head. "She is a shrew of the first degree with a tongue that can etch glass."

"Will you be able to see someone entering from the back?" Lydia asked, sounding doubtful.

Rouge glanced at her as though she were some kind of talking dog and turned to Rees. "If I sit on the bench outside I can watch both entrances, both the front door and the gate from the stable yard." Rees looked at Lydia. She grimaced as though she'd bitten into a sour lemon.

"Would you like something to drink?" Rouge asked. "Ale?"

"Tea for me," she said firmly. He looked at her, really seeing her for the first time.

"Would you like to wash up first?" Without a word she rose to her feet. "Eliza," he bellowed, so suddenly and so loudly Rees jumped. "Please show Miss Farrell where she might wash up. And get her some tea. Mr. Rees and I will drink ale." A plump woman of no more than sixteen bustled out. For a moment she looked at Lydia, in her mud-splashed Shaker clothing and grubby cap. Lydia returned the stare, her eyes inspecting the cocked mobcap sitting askew on brown curls and a food-spattered apron swaddling generous curves. They smiled cautiously at each other.

"It's just back here," Eliza said.

As soon as they disappeared down the hall, Rouge said, "All right, tell me what happened to the sheriff." Rees hesitated. He detected a certain gloating tone in the deputy's voice.

"I don't know much more than what I've said already," he said. "We found him by the side of the road, his head bloodied. The attacker must have carried away the weapon; we found nothing beside him." Rouge fetched two mugs of ale.

"He was probably struck elsewhere and dumped there," Rouge said. Rees agreed.

"Yes, I thought of that. And you have no idea what Coulton knew?"

"No. He wouldn't have told me anyway," Rouge admitted. He lifted his mug and drained half in one long swallow. Rees stared at the street beyond the open door for a moment.

"You know the people around here well?"

"The men anyway."

"Would you say Henry Doucette could be the sheriff's attacker? As a theory?"

"Yes. He's a brawler. I've had to throw him out more than once. And his property abuts the Ellis farm. Do you think he did it?"

"Rumors about horse stealing?'

"Yes." Rouge stared at Rees. "He always had an eye for a good horse. I've heard Doucette got caught stealing in Boston and almost killed a man. He wouldn't shy away from a bit of thieving if it earned him a few pennies. Of course, not too many horses around here worth stealing but the good'uns all disappeared. Including the blue roan over at Zion."

"He didn't join the search," Rees said.

"Could be any number of reasons for that," Rouge said. "What else do you have?"

Rees drained his glass. "Where's Miss Farrell? We need to leave for Zion."

"Here," she said, coming through the curtain. Rees expected an expression of resentful pique but she greeted him with a smile.

"I'll get word to you if I see anything," Rouge promised.

Rees and Lydia climbed back into the wagon and Rees turned toward home. Most of the Shaker wagons were gone.

As they left Durham behind, Lydia turned to Rees. "Eliza told me Mr. Rouge claims the sheriff is dirty." Rees's initial denial died on his lips as he thought about it. Up to two days ago he would have denied it without hesitation but now? "Mr. Rouge used to be the sheriff," she said. Rees whistled softly.

"That explains Rouge's antagonism," he said. "I wouldn't put much stock in it."

"Eliza says the sheriff bought the election, passing money around like water."

"I hope that's not true," Rees said, feeling the poison sink into his thoughts. But what if it was? It could explain why the shooter always kept pace with Rees's travels and always knew what he was doing. No, he didn't want to believe it. But the sheriff knew something.

"We are approaching the Doucette farm," Lydia said. "We should stop now." Recalling Mr. Doucette firing his gun at him and David, Rees almost drove on. But the sense of urgency, and the question of exactly why Mr. Doucette had not joined the searchers this morning, involuntarily tightened his hands upon the reins. Bessie halted at the base of the driveway and Rees stared up at the house. "I don't see Mr. Doucette," she said.

Suddenly Oliver and Mrs. Doucette popped out upon the porch. They had heard the sound of wagon wheels and they eagerly stared down at the passengers. Their shoulders slumped with disappointment. Cautiously, ready to turn and bolt, Rees drove up to the porch.

"Oh, it's you," Mrs. Doucette said. Rees had not mistaken the disappointment on both faces. Oliver carried an elaborate whip with a silver knob in his hands; he caressed it for comfort. "I don't want to talk to you now, Mr. Rees."

"I was hoping to speak with your husband," Rees said.

"He's not here." Mrs. Doucette's eyes filled with tears. "He drove to Surry early this morning." Rees stared at her.

"To Surry," he repeated. She nodded, her eyes shifting to the side. "Why Surry?"

"He had business," she said.

"Very well," he said. "Maybe we can talk about the horse and rider you saw, a few nights ago. Remember?"

"I can't talk now," she said. Bursting into tears, she fled inside.

"Go away," Oliver said, his eyes reddening as though he were going to cry as well. He followed his stepmother inside and slammed the door shut.

"Well," said Lydia. Rees slowly turned the wagon about and they drove out onto the sunny road.

"She's lying," he said.

"She didn't see a horse and rider?"

"I don't think so. Coulton couldn't identify any all-black horses. But that is not what I meant. I think Mr. Doucette has run away." Lydia turned to stare at Rees. "She knows he was at the bluff; she knows he shot at me. He may be the murderer. This story of a black horse is an attempt to deflect suspicion from him." Lydia remained silent for a moment as she worked it through.

"Mr. Doucette struck the sheriff?"

"Exactly. And then he ran away. That's why he wasn't searching with us this morning."

"Oh dear," Lydia said in distress.

The happy sense of accomplishment left by the successful conclusion to the search lasted only through supper that day. When Rees went to breakfast the following morning, the atmosphere was glum. Elder White looked gaunt and ill. At breakfast's end, when Elder White rose to his feet to address his Family, Rees understood why.

"Before I send you all out to do God's work," he said, "I have an announcement." Except for the scrape of a shoe upon the floor, everyone held themselves stiffly silent. "The Maine Ministry will be meeting with the entire Family in the Meetinghouse immediately at the close of dinner. Everyone is required to attend with the exception of the sick and the children, and those who care for the children." Any other group but this one would have burst into excited questions. As it was, a chorus of gasps and a low murmur of whispered exclamations betrayed the alarm. "They are waiting for you now."

As one, everyone, including Rees, rose to their feet and hastened for the doors. Rees joined the Brethren as they crossed the street and entered the Meetinghouse. He went through the Men's door automatically. He'd lived here long enough now that he no longer thought it strange or unusual.

He slid into the wooden pew closest to the wall. Since he had left the Dining Hall among the first group, he had to wait for the rest of the Family to arrive. Mouse sat directly across from him. Too terrified to return his smile, she simply stared at him, her eyes huge with apprehension. As the Family streamed in, Rees realized Elder White and Eldress Phelps were not among them and knew they were the subjects of this meeting.

The four members of the Ministry sat quietly on the chairs in the center, waiting for everyone to settle themselves. Finally the doors shut. After a few moments, Elder Hutchins rose to his feet.

"Brothers and Sisters," he said in his velvety resonant voice, "the Ministry has made its decision." A faint susurration rippled through the hall as the members tensed themselves for the worst. Mouse squeezed her hands over her face. "Several violent deaths have occurred in and around the community, shocking and disturbing in any community but particularly damaging to one for whom harmony is a pillar of the faith. However, we elected not to consider those deaths in our decision." He fixed his gaze upon Rees. "We expect that matter to be resolved and in any case we are certain the causes of those deaths reside outside our Family.

"We concentrated upon the . . . irregularities in the management of the community. One Elder? One Eldress? One Deacon? One Deaconess? Two of each are required by our Church. Greed for power is as dangerous as greed for material goods." He paused. Rees shifted one leg and the click of his shoe on the wooden pew sounded like a shot. "However, the farm is established and productive, the Family labors in harmony. 'Hands to work, Hearts to God.'

"This will be our recommendation to the Council." Time crashed to a halt. Rees watched the men around him tense even further. "Our Brother, Elder White, to be transferred to a community in Kentucky. Our Sister, Eldress Phelps, to move to a community in New Hampshire. Two new Elders and two new Eldresses will come to Zion to oversee the Family here." Surprise and relief whispered through the congregation. But as Rees looked around at the faces, he saw fear, shame, guilt, and pity mixed in with the relief. He understood. Most of this Family would remain intact here at Zion. Only Elder White and Eldress Phelps would lose their places. Yes, it was a blessing they were not here to witness this very public humiliation.

Rees suddenly realized *he* was here, witnessing the shame of the village. Even without the sudden sharp glance from Elder Hutchins's dark deep-set eyes, Rees realized he was an intruder. He was not one of this Family, and would never be, so he shouldn't be sitting here listening. Rising to his feet, he tiptoed as quietly as he could into the brilliant sun outside.

He expelled his breath in a gasp of relief. He had not felt so much an outsider since his first few days here in Zion. It was clear that, whatever the outcome of his search for the killer, his sojourn here was coming to an end. Footsteps thudded behind him. Rees turned. David, his straw hat pushed back on his red hair, clattered up behind him.

"Shouldn't you be in there?" Rees asked. David shook his head emphatically.

"I will never sign the Covenant." David glanced at his father. "You didn't hear what that Elder had to say about non-Believers taking advantage of Zion's hospitality."

"Did he say it like that?" Rees asked in surprise.

"No. But I knew what he meant." Rees looked at his son. During these last few weeks, David had shot up, his legs lengthening by inches. His eyes were almost on a level with Rees's. "I am only fourteen; I can remain here if I wish but—"

"Do you wish to?" Rees interrupted anxiously. David shook his head. "I've been thinking. Maybe we should return to the farm? I'll be around through the winter, at least until spring. After that maybe we can hire a manager. Or something." He stopped abruptly. Joy shone out of David's eyes.

"Do you mean it?

"Yes. The farm will be yours someday anyway. No point leaving it vacant . . ." David's sudden impulsive hug drove the breath from Rees's body.

"I have so many plans . . ." David stopped and some of the light went out of his eyes. "But Miss Farrell . . ."

"What about Miss Farrell?"

"She may be asked to leave Zion."

"What?" Rees looked at David in horror. "Elder White allowed Charles Ellis to live here for years."

"It will all depend upon the new Elders," David said. Rees shook his head in dismay. "Where will she live?"

"I don't know," Rees said. He looked at Dolly's steady gray eyes in the sunburned face. David's cheeks were losing the childish roundness, the bones realigning into a narrow angular length like Rees's own face.

David waited expectantly and when Rees said nothing, he said, "You should tell Miss Farrell then. She doesn't know."

As the boy turned away, clearly disappointed, Rees said, "I will." He stared after David for a moment. The boy didn't understand. Lydia wanted to settle down and Rees knew he couldn't, not for more than a few months at a time. And he didn't want to give another woman the misery he'd caused Dolly. With a sigh, Rees turned to the Blacksmith's. He would not enjoy sharing this terrible news with Lydia. It seemed that bad news was all he brought her.

Chapter Twenty-four

When he reached the top he saw her, standing among the flowers. She was curved over them protectively, almost as though she were saying goodbye. "Lydia," Rees called. She looked up, the marks of tears still visible around her eyes and on her cheeks. "What's wrong?" As if he didn't know.

"That Ministry was here," she said. "Poking around the hives, sneering at my flowers."

"Did they say anything?" Rees asked.

"The young Sister said she was sure my honey was delicious," Lydia said. "But she didn't mean it." As Rees continued to look at her, she added, "I know that sounds promising but I just got the impression . . ." She turned and surveyed her wildflower garden. "I'm worried."

"Let's go inside and sit down," Rees said. Lydia paled.

"What happened? Oh no, please don't tell me Sheriff Coulton has gone home to Mother!"

"No. The Ministry . . . The Ministry called everyone together this morning after breakfast," Rees said. Lydia pressed her hand to her chest.

"Oh no."

Rees gestured her toward the cottage. With another anxious glance, she preceded him into the cottage and sat down at the table. "You are frightening me," she said, clenching her hands tightly together.

"Zion will remain," he said. "But Elder White is being sent to Kentucky and Eldress Phelps to New Hampshire." Lydia blinked, remaining silent as she thought about that.

"They won't like it," she said.

"No. New Elders are being sent to take their places." Lydia looked at him, her expression lightening.

"But that is good news for the Family. No?"

"David said, and this is his interpretation, you understand, that all who are not Believers, and who have not signed the Covenant, will be asked to leave." Lydia stared at him, her smile slowly fading.

"That can't be true."

"Perhaps not. But he sounded confident. He suggested I bring this news to you."

"The Shakers have always permitted workmen to live nearby," Lydia said, as though he were arguing with her. "They can't mean me."

"Why don't you ask David?" Rees suggested. "Or Mouse or one of the other Shakers. Someone should be able to tell you . . ." She did not reply. Instead she rose to her feet and walked to the hearth. She poured herself a cup of tea, moving automatically as she carried it to the table.

"I suppose I knew this," she gestured around her, "could not last." Tears pricked her eyes. "I can't lose my home. I'll sign the Covenant, if that is required."

Rees, who'd expected to comfort her and promise to sort this out, felt the pit of his stomach drop away.

"Sign the Covenant," he repeated hoarsely. He had not expected this response. Lydia nodded.

"I must. This is my home," she said.

"But you want children."

"I have my garden and my bees." Her gaze lighted on the line of cups on the mantel, the bright quilt smoothed across the bed, the carefully made built-in cabinet on the wall behind Rees.

"But they don't belong to you," Rees said, arguing now.

"Mine as much as anything could be." She paused. Rees said nothing, too shocked to think of the necessary words. He didn't know if he could say them anyway; his tongue felt thick and heavy. Lydia looked at him for a moment before leaning over the table and touching his wrist.

"Try to understand," she said. "I can't take to the road as you do. Females don't. And I wouldn't, even if I could. I am a homebody at heart. I have nowhere else to go, no other home but this. Besides, my daughter is buried here. I have no choice."

"The new Elders will allow you to remain, at least for a while," Rees said, finally finding his tongue. "Of course they will."

Lydia smiled slightly. "I am already . . . besmirched," she said. "I am not sure I would enjoy the same courtesy from them as I have from Elder White. He loved Charles too. And David, well, David is still a boy, not old enough to sign the Covenant."

"I think you do not trust the Shakers enough," Rees said. He sighed. "Promise me you won't sign anything yet, Lydia." She hesitated. He turned his arm over and caught her small hand in his large calloused paw. They sat thus for a moment; then she withdrew her hand and nodded in agreement.

"Very well," she said. "But I don't think anything you do will make any difference in the end."

A clatter of footsteps on the stones outside heralded the arrival of a visitor. Rees and Lydia jerked further apart, Rees flushing guiltily. He turned just as David came into view. His cherry-red cheeks accused his father and Lydia of more than an intimate conversation.

"Come in," Lydia invited. "Coffee? Tea?" She took several large sugar cookies out of the jar and handed them to the boy. "Your father tells me you and I are in a similar situation." David nodded, his mouth full. "I am considering signing the Covenant," she said. David stared at her in surprised dismay, his gasp segueing into a coughing fit. Rees did not want to discuss this with David, or even in his son's presence.

"Why are you here?" he asked his son.

"Elder Hutchins wants to see you," David said. "The Brethren are combing the farm for you. I thought you might be here." Rees thought he detected a hint of pride in David's tone.

"I suppose I'd better meet with him," Rees said. He looked at Lydia. He wanted to say so much but couldn't find the words, especially in front of an audience. "Don't forget your promise," he said finally. She nodded. Rees fell into step behind his son and they walked down the path together.

"I've been thinking," David said. Rees looked at him warily. "I know you think me too young to manage the farm. But I can do it if I have help. After you go on the road again, I mean."

"Whom do you have in mind?" Rees asked. A sudden suspicion made him turn his gaze upon his son. "What are you planning?"

David smiled guilelessly. "Nothing. What could I be planning? It's just that if Miss Farrell has no place to go . . ." He paused. Since Rees had been considering that as well he couldn't scold or argue. But to hear it from his son, how diminishing.

"Let me think about it," he said. They rounded the corner by the Blacksmith and Rees hurried to the Meetinghouse. Since the meeting room was empty, he went up the narrow steps to the rooms above. The scene was exactly as before: the four Ministry members sat on the other side of the table waiting for him. Elder Hutchins gestured to the chair facing them. "Mr. Rees," he said. "You were present at the gathering this morning?"

"Yes," Rees said. Of course they knew to the second when he'd left.

"So you are aware we are asking our guests to find other accommodations for the present?" Rees inclined his head. "The laxity exhibited in this community is so great we must turn all our attention to it," Hutchins said. "Once Zion is operating as directed, non-Believers may be welcomed in once again. But of course, we wish the matter of the murders to be resolved first."

"I'm still working on it," Rees said cautiously.

"And how much longer do you anticipate it will take?" Elder Hutchins leaned across the table, his expression one of sincere interest.

"Maybe a few days," Rees said. "I'm searching for Brother Charles's cousin now. And of course there is the matter of the attack upon the sheriff."

"The sheriff's attack is a worldly matter," Hutchins said. "Tragic to be sure but still not our concern. And Brother Charles's cousin is, I daresay, miles away by now. However, we have no wish to be unfair. And of course Sister Chastity was one of this Family." He paused for a long moment. Rees waited anxiously. "Do you believe either Elder White or Eldress Phelps are involved in any way in these deaths?"

"No," Rees said. He might have given Elder Hutchins the same answer even if he thought they were—Elder White had been kind—but fortunately he could tell the truth.

"Tomorrow is Saturday and after that we celebrate the Sabbath. We expect this search of yours to be complete by Tuesday morning at the latest." Rees felt the blood draining from his cheeks.

"There is no way I can be ready by then," he cried.

"I do not mean to be uncaring but you must do your best, Mr. Rees," the Elder said. "Other matters demand our attention. We need to put our own house in order." Rees understood. But he made one final objection.

"A murderer may go free."

"I regret that," the Elder said. "We all do." Although he said nothing more, Rees heard the rest of his thought: the murderer was of Rees's world, not of the Shakers', and so was not their concern.

Nodding glumly, Rees rose to his feet. Whether or not he could pull everything together by then, he didn't know. But time had run out.

As he thudded down the stairs, the dinner bell began to clang. Here, in the Meetinghouse, it was deafening and Rees put his hands over his ears. When the reverberation subsided, he crossed the street to the Dwelling House. A momentary stop in his room to wash his hands and he joined the other men in the waiting room. After dinner he would drive to the Doucette farm. If Henry had returned, which Rees doubted, he would question him. Otherwise he must press Mrs. Doucette and Oliver for the truth.

It was almost two when Rees set out and past three when he reached the farm's drive. Again he saw no one; the property was beginning to take on an abandoned and uncared-for air. Rees drove up to the porch and when a fusillade of knocks on the front door brought no one forth, he walked around to the back. He could hear the children shouting and playing somewhere about. When he looked through the back door he saw Mrs. Doucette sitting at the table, a cup of cooling tea before her.

"I'm sorry," Rees said, knocking once as he entered the kitchen. "I must talk to you."

"Henry is in Surry," she said but with no conviction. "On business. I don't know when he'll be back."

"When did he leave?" Rees asked. Her mouth opened but she did not speak. "Right after the sheriff came to speak to him?" She looked down at the table and Rees knew he surmised correctly.

"He would never hurt Sheriff Coulton," she said through stiff lips. "They are friends and more."

"It looks as though he's run away," Rees said. Her face contorted.

"He's gone south for business. I'm telling you the truth. Please leave." Rees sighed and sat down next to her.

"I want to help you, Mrs. Doucette, but I can't unless you tell me the truth."

"I am telling you the truth."

"No, you're not." He paused and waited for a moment. When she said nothing, he continued. "Mrs. Doucette, at least four people are dead including a young woman."

"He didn't kill her," she cried. "He was at a farm meeting. You know that. You were staying in the barn that night. He didn't kill anyone. He just went south on business."

"Oh, I believe your husband is not here. But I don't think he rode to Surry on business. Tell me what happened." When she did not speak, he added, "The sheriff came to see him, didn't he?" Tears began leaking from her eyes and she nodded. "When was that?"

"The day before the sheriff was found injured."

"What happened then?"

"I don't really know." She heaved a heavy sigh. "I was in the kitchen. But I heard them arguing."

"What did they say?"

"I couldn't hear the words." A faint smile touched her lips. "Not most of them anyway. But I did hear the sheriff call Henry a fool."

"Then what?"

"They walked up to see the horses, I think. Oliver may know; he was in the barn."

"How long were they gone?" Rees asked. Coulton had figured it out.

"Twenty or thirty minutes? Less than an hour." Long enough to go to the Ellis property.

"Did they return?"

"Henry did, not the sheriff. And only for a few minutes. He went upstairs . . ." She broke into tears. "What's going to happen now?"

"It will be all right," he assured Mrs. Doucette, patting her hand. "I'm going to talk to Oliver. Don't worry."

Rees went out the door and up to the barn, but it was empty. He saw a flash of movement in the pasture behind and went toward it. Oliver was leaning on the fence watching the few cows in the pasture.

"My father went south," he said when he saw Rees approaching.

"When the sheriff visited your father the other day," Rees said, "were they arguing? Please answer me, lad. I know the sheriff was here. Your stepmother confirmed it."

"Yes. But that doesn't mean much. They argue all the time."

"How did this argument seem to you? Worse than usual? Not serious?"

"Maybe a little worse," Oliver said. "My uncle was really angry. His face was red and he kept shaking a finger at my father. But they always make up." After a moment's silence, Oliver suddenly burst out, "My father didn't run away. No matter what he did, he wouldn't run away. He would never leave me. And he wouldn't hurt the sheriff either." Rees thought of his sister, Caroline.

"You would be surprised what family will do," he said.

"Not my father!" Oliver cried passionately. "He would never leave me. And he would never hurt Uncle Coulton. Never." Oliver's words pursued Rees down the slope to his wagon. About halfway down the hill he paused and turned back.

"Do you remember living in Surry?"

"Not really," Oliver said, adding with the superiority of a twelve-year-old, "I was a baby then."

Rees walked on, regret sweeping through him. Maybe he was wrong and Henry Doucette had some innocent explanation for his absence. But he doubted it and he feared even greater sorrow lay ahead for this family.

Mrs. Doucette, rousing herself, had brought water for Bessie. Rees put the half-full pail on the porch and climbed back into the wagon. The two men had argued and walked together toward the Ellis property, both Mrs. Doucette and Oliver admitted that. And despite the impassioned defense of husband and father, Rees thought it almost certain Doucette had attacked the sheriff and fled. Rees just couldn't see any other explanation.

Allowing Bessie her head, which meant they returned to Zion at a slow walk, Rees reflected upon the fragments floating through his mind. He didn't yet understand how they all connected into a coherent whole, but at least he thought he knew most of the pieces now.

He arrived in Zion with twenty minutes or so to spare before supper. Rees unhitched Bessie from the wagon and was brushing her down when William found him. "I've been looking all over for you," he said. He pushed his hat back on his head so the white forehead gleamed above the sunburn. "Deputy Rouge rode in to Zion looking for you. Sheriff Coulton has begun to remember the attack. He's asking for you. He wants to see you first thing tomorrow."

Rees almost—almost—hitched up Bessie to the wagon once again. He had his hand on the bridle when William said, "It will be dark in a few hours." Rees didn't fancy driving home from Durham after sunset so he reluctantly reconsidered and followed William inside.

Chapter Twenty-five

The next morning Rees ate a quick breakfast and willed Elder White to dismiss the community so he could hurry off to see Coulton. Everything seemed to take twice as long as usual but finally he was free. Rees ran for the stables. Lydia Jane was waiting under the portico. "I thought you might be going to the Doucette farm again today," she said, adding, "I didn't want you to go without me."

"I'm going to Durham," Rees said. "Coulton's memory is coming back." Rees did not tell her that he had visited Mrs. Doucette the day previously; he knew she would be both hurt and angry. "I am just on my way to the stables. Would you care to join me?" She nodded. Of course she would.

While she waited outside, he quickly harnessed Bessie and they started out. Lydia was very quiet and finally Rees looked at her in alarm. "Is something the matter?" She smiled faintly.

"Just disturbed by the looks I received while I waited for you," she said. "So disapproving." She shuddered. "So much like when the Family discovered I was having a baby."

The way into Durham was now so familiar to Rees that he seemed to reach town in no time at all. Soon they were pulling into the yard behind the store. When they walked up to the back door they found Rouge there before them, arguing with Mrs. Coulton.

"Your husband sent word asking for us," Rees said. Still Mrs. Coulton hesitated.

"Maybe we could enjoy a nice cup of tea together," Lydia said, leaning forward and smiling. "You and I, while the men talk." Mrs. Coulton stared at her. Still smiling brightly, Lydia stepped forward. The other woman retreated, one step, two steps and finally yielded, drawing back into the shadows to allow them entrance. Lydia did not give the other woman a chance to change her mind but quickly followed her inside.

"I'll show Mr. Rees upstairs," Rouge said, peremptorily gesturing at Rees to follow him.

With the ladies in the lead, they walked through the darkened store and through the door behind the counter. A staircase on the right led up to the second floor, bundles and casks occupying the space underneath the risers. Mrs. Coulton directed Lydia through the second door at the foot of those stairs, and with an anxious look after Rouge and Rees, followed Lydia inside.

"No trouble last night?" Rees asked Rouge as they went up the stairs. Rouge shook his head.

"All quiet," he said.

At the top of the landing he turned right and they went into a room. Despite the bed in which Coulton lay, the room was fitted out as an office. In the light streaming in from two large uncurtained windows Coulton looked pale and battered. Bruises stained his left cheek purple and without the toothpick rolling around in his mouth his face looked naked. "Please, help me sit up," he said. Rouge and Rees carefully propped him up on two pillows. While the sheriff struggled to control his dizziness and nausea, Rees looked around. The windows overlooked the stable yard and if Rees inhaled he smelled horse. A desk piled high with bills sat in front of one window and horse equipment decorated the walls: silver spurs, a decorated bridle, and a silver-headed whip. As Rees moved forward to examine the whip more closely Coulton said, "It was Doucette. He hit me."

"You suspected him of stealing horses?"

"I have for a long time. But now murder . . ."

"What happened?"

"We were arguing. I accused him. He denied it, of course. I said I wanted to see where he kept the horses. He followed me over and as we went to the house he struck me from behind. My wife says you found me by the road; I suppose I walked back there."

"Did you see what he struck you with?" Rees asked.

Coulton started to shake his head, winced, and said, "No." Rees looked at him uncertainly. Coulton must have seen the weapon; it would have been too big to hide.

"Did you see any horses?"

"No. He probably moved them days ago." He paused and into the sudden quiet Rees recalled the horse tracks in the mud, sharp and clear. The horses couldn't have been moved days ago; instead it was probably the same day Coulton was attacked. Why was he lying? "I daresay that young Shaker girl knew something, that's why he killed her," the sheriff continued. "So now all my deputy here needs to do is ride out and pick Henry up."

"He can't do that," Rees said. "Mr. Doucette is missing. His wife says he rode down to Surry on business."

"Missing?" Coulton repeated. "Are you sure?" Some fear darkened his expression.

"Of course," Rees said.

"He's run away," Rouge said baldly. "He's probably in Boston by now." Coulton nodded, almost in relief. Rees glanced at the sheriff in puzzled speculation.

"Then the murders will stop," Coulton said. "They have to," he added, half under his breath. Stung by such curious remarks, Rees stared.

"You suspect your brother-in-law is the murderer and you're protecting him," he blurted.

Coulton did not protest, but looked pained. "Charles Ellis was my friend."

"What will happen to the Ellis property now?" asked Mrs. Coulton from the door. Rees turned to look at her. She couldn't stay away from her husband.

"I'm not sure," Rees lied. "Pass to the next of kin, I suppose."

Mrs. Coulton nodded and said with ferocious courtesy, "Gentlemen, it's time for you to leave. My husband requires rest."

"Of course," Rees said, sweeping off his tricorn and bowing low. He allowed Rouge to precede him and, before leaving the room, he paused by Coulton's bed to examine the whip upon the wall. He thought it might be identical to the one owned by Henry Doucette.

"It is an interesting piece," Rees said.

"Many men own them," Coulton said indifferently. "A good coachman can earn one in Philadelphia." He looked up at Rees apologetically. "Will, I—"

"Mr. Rees." Mrs. Coulton stepped inside and stared at him until he said his goodbyes.

This time he followed her down the stairs. Rouge had already gone and Lydia was waiting for Rees in the hall. She looked as though, but for good breeding, she would be rolling her eyes. Mrs. Coulton urged them through the back door, slamming it behind them with finality. Rees and Lydia went into the heat. Although Bessie stood in the shade under the overhang, the wagon seats baked under the hot sun. When Rees climbed into the seat, he felt the heat burn through his breeches.

"Thank you for distracting Mrs. Coulton," he said. "How was tea?" Lydia remained silent for a moment, struggling to find the words.

"She is not the most well-mannered woman I have ever met," she said at last. "She talked all the while of the wonderful character of her husband, drank her tea in three gulps, and raced upstairs to participate in the conversation as soon as she could, leaving me alone in the kitchen." Rees burst out laughing.

"I'm sorry," he said. "I suppose it isn't funny to you."

"Well, it wasn't, not at the time." Lydia smiled. "But I see the humor in it now." Rees chuckled a few moments longer before sobering.

"I'd like to stop again at the Doucette farm," he said. "I want to take a look at something."

"Of course. And your conversation with the sheriff?"

"Troubling. Coulton identified Doucette as his attacker."

Lydia nodded. "That's no surprise." She looked at Rees's expression. "Something is bothering you."

"Coulton claimed the horses had been moved long ago but I know that's not true. And he was relieved to hear Doucette ran away."

Comprehension flared into her eyes. "Simon Rouge is right," she said. "The sheriff is dirty."

Rees nodded in reluctant agreement. "He's in on the horse stealing. And so is his wife," he said, recalling her smile. "That explains why he was so evasive about Michael. Coulton must have paid for Michael's grave himself. I suppose he feels guilty."

"Do you think he murdered Sister Chastity and Charles?" she asked in a very quiet voice. Rees didn't know what to say.

This time they swept up the farm drive right to the porch. Mrs. Doucette and Oliver again hurried out to the porch, exhibiting disappointment when they recognized their visitors. "I'm sorry to intrude upon you once again," Rees said. "And I won't stay long. I just wanted to take a look at Mr. Doucette's whip."

Mrs. Doucette hesitated. "Very well," she said at last. "Come inside."

Rees and Lydia followed her into the house. As Mrs. Doucette and Lydia went to the kitchen Oliver disappeared up the stairs. Rees waited in the hall. He heard the boy's footsteps thudding overhead. A moment later Oliver returned with the whip. "My father was a very good coachman," Oliver said proudly. "He didn't run away, Mr. Rees. He wouldn't abandon me. And he wouldn't leave this whip behind. He was so proud of it."

Rees took the whip. It was surprisingly heavy; the short hilt was made of some sort of black stone, the silver knob on the end solid to provide a counterweight to the long lash.

Rees closed his hand around the silver ball. He thought it was the exact shape and size of the wound upon Chastity's head. He held it to the light, examining it closely. He saw no signs of blood but it had probably been carefully cleaned. "Thank you, Oliver," Rees said, handing the whip back to the boy. He raced back up the stairs to put it away. Rees sighed. He was almost certain that whip had struck down Sheriff Coulton and Sister Chastity. He could feel the noose tightening around Henry Doucette.

Rees and Lydia drove back to Zion, Rees thinking furiously. "I'm almost positive that whip struck down both Sister Chastity and Sheriff Coulton," he told Lydia. She shook her head sadly. "So now, the question is, how did the whip return to the farm?"

"Do you think Chastity saw her killer?" Lydia asked.

"Probably not," Rees said. "She would never permit a man to approach her so closely."

"Let's hope not," Lydia said with a shudder. "Coulton must have known Doucette was involved in the murders. Why didn't he say something?" Lydia asked. Rees frowned.

"I'm not sure he did know, not until recently anyway." He could almost identify the exact second when the sheriff began adding up the pieces. "I wish he'd told me then."

Rees spent the rest of the day distracted. He wove, almost without any awareness of his activity, and was surprised to find he'd finally used all of Mrs. Doucette's yarns. He walked around Zion in a state of preoccupation and finally went to bed with questions still buzzing in his brain. He dreamed about the problem, waking up with snatches of memory still clinging to his thoughts.

"My father would never abandon me, never."

"He's my brother."

"He only married me because of the child."

And finally his own voice, "You don't know what family will do."

Today was Sunday. After breakfast, he waited in his room

until all of the Brethren had disappeared into the Meetinghouse. Then he hitched up Bessie and drove to the Ellis property for a final search, a final tying up of loose ends. He parked at the driveway and walked up to the house. This time he ignored the front entrance and walked around to the back. He expected he would have to break in but discovered the shutter over the mudroom window could be pushed aside. This window, frequently used, went up smoothly and he climbed in.

Boots and a variety of horse leathers hung on hooks hammered into the walls. All of them, although heavily used, were well-cared-for and recently oiled. As he'd suspected, this house had been used as the headquarters for the horse-stealing ring.

The door into the house proper led into a kitchen, a room so large it occupied the rear quarter of the house. Although Rees expected cobwebs and mouse droppings the room was tidy and very clean. Ashes filled the grate but they were only a week or so old. The kettle on the hook still contained an inch or two of water.

He walked through to the parlor. Sunlight streamed in around the edges of the shutters so, although shadowy, he had light enough to see by. Empty spaces betrayed missing furniture and paintings, candlesticks and other possessions, stolen from the house and probably sold, Rees thought in disgust. Although everything wore a coat of dust he saw no signs of damp. The ubiquitous mouse droppings clustered in the corners but none of the upholstery exhibited signs of chewing.

Rees climbed the stairs. Several shutters hung askew and sunlight streamed in. He quickly walked through the empty rooms. In the final chamber, tucked in the rear at the back of the stairs, the window overlooked the large kitchen garden. A pile of earth and a shovel looked freshly abandoned, as though the gardener had just left. Of more interest to Rees was a pallet made up in one corner. A Shaker's straw hat lay beside it. Rees picked it up, certain this belonged to Brother Michael. He may have been shot but someone had cared for him here. Coulton? Had Michael died? No, no grave, Rees thought, recalling the sheriff's awkward story about a pauper's grave. Michael must have recovered and been spirited away to safety.

Sheriff Coulton had lied again. Michael Languedela'or had not been shot to death. Wounded, yes, but cared for and protected. How many other lies would Rees uncover?

He descended the stairs and exited through the window. With his eyes glued to the ground, he walked northeast, searching for signs of a struggle. On the east side of the house he found disturbed earth, where toes had dug into the soil, and a splash of blood. A few feet beyond he found more blood; he was following Coulton's staggering steps to Piper Lane. The footsteps wavered from side to side and crushed vegetation testified to frequent falls.

Rees wondered where he was going. To his horse? To the Doucette farm? He followed the path all the way to Piper Lane. Only Coulton's footsteps, one shod foot and one clad solely in a stocking, marked the trail. Doucette had not followed Coulton. Why not? Perhaps Doucette had taken Coulton's horse and fled. Rees shook his head. Coulton's horse had mysteriously reappeared in the stables.

Rees turned around and walked back to the house, circled around, and approached the outbuildings. Fresh horse droppings, not more than a few days old, marked a spot just outside the barn door. A buzz of certainty ran through him. Running the last steps, he flung open the door.

As soon as he stepped inside, the metallic tang of blood hit him. A lot of blood. He looked around. Coulton's shoe had tumbled across the floor, fetching up against a nearby bale of hay. On one side someone had piled straw into a large stack, right in the middle of the floor. No farmer would put his hay right in front of the doors. Rees went down on his knee and carefully began brushing aside the straw. Blood, he found blood. This was the location of the battle, the place where Doucette struck Coulton down.

But as Rees stared at the large blood pool, he realized that this amount could not have come from a head wound. There was too much. And a body must have lain here for some time, leaking its life's fluid into the straw. Rees rose to his feet and examined the floor again. This time he noticed faint lengthwise marks, stretching from the dusty floor to the track outside. Drag marks.

"Oh no," he said, his belly clenching with trepidation. "Oh no." Afraid of where these drag marks would lead, he followed them outside to the garden, and the fresh heap of earth he'd noticed from the upstairs window. He knew as he approached the disturbed soil what he would find, a body. He'd smelled the penetrating stench of death too often before.

Maybe Michael had died? Or was it Henry Doucette?

He took only a few grim minutes to clear away the light soil, revealing two broken and hard-used boots: Doucette's boots. Stealing himself, Rees cleaned the soil from the other end, uncovering the face. He had found Henry Doucette.

He sprinkled a layer of dirt over the remains and began walking back to the wagon. Working backward from Henry Doucette's murder and rethinking everything he'd heard and thought, he finally reached Sister Chastity's death. Now he knew why she had not been skittish when her killer approached her. He rubbed his forehead, regret and grief sweeping over him. Maybe he was wrong; he could still be wrong. Why couldn't he be wrong this time? But he knew he wasn't and he hated the answer he'd found. Without conscious volition but desperate for companionship, he headed for Lydia's cottage, praying she was inside.

Chapter Twenty-six

After supper that night, much calmer after a conversation with Lydia, Rees approached Elder Hutchins and told him he'd solved the case. "Who is the guilty man?" Hutchins asked.

"I'd prefer to tell everyone together," Rees said. "I thought we could draw all the interested parties together tomorrow afternoon in the Meetinghouse." When the Elder did not immediately respond, Rees said, "These deaths do not only affect the Believers." Hutchins heaved a sigh.

"Very well. Three o'clock."

"May I ask some of the Brethren to ride out and invite all those who are involved?"

"You take advantage," Hutchins said, looking put out. "But if that will finally end this business, I agree."

Rees slept poorly that night. He went over everything in his mind, over and over. The next morning several of the Brothers drove out of Zion to invite the sheriff and Mrs. Coulton, the Lewises, Mrs. Doucette, Mr. Golightly, and everyone else with an interest. Rees visited first with Brother Levi to ask two questions. Then he followed the Brethren into Durham. He went directly to The Cartwheel to speak to Deputy Rouge. As soon as the tavern keeper saw Rees, and Rees's expression, he breathed, "You've figured it out."

"I may need your assistance," Rees said. "Will you come?"

"I wouldn't miss it," Rouge said. "But you don't look pleased. You don't like the answer?"

"I never do," Rees said. "Too many innocent people are always hurt."

"Too many in Durham have already been hurt," Rouge said. Rees nodded in agreement.

Elder White and Eldress Phelps were the first to arrive, taking places on the respective male and female sides of the hall. Rees, who'd spent the last hour pacing the Meetinghouse, greeted them almost with relief. Lydia arrived next and almost immediately after all four members of the Maine Ministry. Mr. Golightly and Mrs. Baker entered a minute later, taking places together on the male side. The Shakers stared at them in consternation but said nothing and made no move to interfere. Sheriff Coulton, supported by Simon Rouge and Mrs. Coulton, entered a few minutes later. They too sat on the men's side. Brother William made a step toward them but both Elder White and Elder Hutchins deterred him with tiny shakes of their heads. Mouse and Marguerite came in and sat behind Eldress Phelps.

Although it was now past three, neither Mr. and Mrs. Lewis nor Mrs. Doucette had arrived. Rees couldn't wait any longer; the story was ready to burst from him. "I'll begin now," he said. He would try to stretch out his announcement; it was critical the others were here. "My involvement in this investigation began with Sister Chastity, née Catherine Parker. But the murders began over two years before with the deaths of Charles Ellis and Ira." Rees looked around. No one spoke. "Charles Ellis Senior, Brother Ellis's grandfather, owned a large farm on Piper Lane. When he died, he left the entirety of his estate to his grandson and namesake, Charles, on the condition he not sign the Covenant and join the Shakers. Should he do so, the farm would revert to one of his other grandsons, first Roger Bristol, who died shortly thereafter in a suspicious 'accident,' and after him, Patrick O'Reardon. The granddaughters would inherit nothing unless all of the grandsons had passed away."

Mr. and Mrs. Lewis suddenly hurried through the women's door. Rees waited until they were settled before he continued.

"What most of you don't know is that Brother Charles married and had a child." Gasps and murmurs seethed through the room. Only Mouse, Eldress Phelps, and Elder White looked unsurprised. "Charles could have signed the Covenant after the marriage of course. But in the interim, he made a will leaving all his possessions to his wife, Lydia Jane Farrell." Everyone turned to stare at her. Turning scarlet, she shot a fiery glare at Rees before turning her gaze to her clasped hands. "Once I knew this, I understood that all the deaths occurred because of the Ellis property." Rees glanced around again. Sheriff Coulton's face was the color of wax.

"But Catherine was not related to the Ellises," Mr. Lewis burst out. "She didn't even know them. Why would anyone kill her?"

"And it is not entirely true Charles inherited everything," Mr. Golightly interjected. "The will does include some bequests."

"What are they?" Rees asked.

"Each of the girls inherited a piece of their grandmother's jewelry," the lawyer answered. "And the blue roan horses were left to Patrick O'Reardon."

"So Charles took the horses as his own, giving them to Zion as part of his good faith," Rees said. "I don't wonder that his cousin Patrick was angry and wanted them back." He paused again, looking at each person in turn. "Charles Ellis and his companion, the innocent boy Ira, were murdered so that Patrick O'Reardon would inherit the estate." Everyone looked around him. Rees heard a chorus of whispered questions about Patrick O'Reardon.

"But nobody came forward to claim the estate," Mr. Golightly protested.

"No. The bodies were hidden. But the killers knew where they were. And Charles's body was hidden with a piece of identification so that, at the right time, after a few years, his remains could be produced and the estate claimed. In fact, efforts to claim the inheritance were begun fairly recently. Mr. Doucette visited Mr. Golightly and discovered, through no fault of Mr. Golightly's, that Charles Ellis Junior had left a will of his own, leaving the entire estate to his wife. All Mr. Doucette knew about this wife, however, was that she was a Shaker and had red hair and a child. I'm very sorry," Rees said, turning to Mr. and Mrs. Lewis. "Catherine was killed because she was mistaken for Lydia Jane Farrell." Tears rushed into Mr. Lewis's eyes and he turned away to hide his face in his sleeve. His wife gently laid her hand upon his.

"But who is Patrick O'Reardon?" Elder White said, looking around him. "What name did he take to live among us? Was he Henry Doucette?"

Before Rees could reply, the women's door opened and Mrs. Doucette entered. She stood for a moment, blinking in the shaft of sunlight striking her eyes through the window. She moved forward, into the dimness, and saw the size of the gathering for the first time. "Please forgive me," she said. "I know I'm late . . ." Then she saw Sheriff Coulton and his wife.

"You!" she shrilled. "You. Where is my husband?" She launched herself toward the sheriff, her hands outstretched. Astonishment froze everyone, and Mrs. Doucette almost reached the wounded man. Then Mrs. Coulton lurched to her feet and grabbed Mrs. Doucette. Rees leaped up and thrust his arm between them. Mrs. Coulton's furious grimace promised injury to the other woman and she was strong enough to do serious hurt. Simon Rouge grasped Mrs. Coulton and struggled to tug her backward.

"Ladies, ladies," Elder White cried. Mrs. Doucette broke down into wild sobbing. Lydia rose to her feet and came forward, gently leading the other woman to the bench.

"Your husband is a horse thief and a murderer," Coulton said angrily. "I did nothing to him; he's run away."

"The sheriff was just doing his job," Mr. Golightly said. "Please sit down, woman, and allow Mr. Rees to finish his long and perhaps overly complicated tale."

"Shall I continue?" Rees said.

"So, is Henry Doucette Patrick O'Reardon?" Elder White asked.

"Of course he isn't," Mrs. Doucette snapped, bewildered.

"No, he isn't," Rees said. "But Patrick is your cousin. You know him." He saw understanding flash upon her face and she stared across the room.

"Why are you torturing this poor woman," Lydia cried.

Rees looked at Sheriff Coulton.

"Will you tell me who Patrick O'Reardon is?" he asked. He held Coulton's gaze for a long moment. Finally the sheriff dropped his eyes.

"I am Patrick O'Reardon. But I did not kill my cousin Charles or that boy or the Shaker girl," he shouted through the rumble of surprised comment. "I admit I engaged in a scuffle with Henry. He struck me with his whip handle. I hit him back and knocked him down. But he was still alive when I left." Coulton looked at Rees and added fiercely, "I didn't know about the will. I moved to Durham to take back my horses. Charles knew our grandfather meant for me to have them."

"That is so," Mr. Golightly said.

"But Charles didn't even hesitate; he just took them. And then I found a place here . . ."

"I don't understand," Mouse said tentatively.

"I made a new life," Coulton said. "I wouldn't have risked that and certainly not by committing murder."

"I assume Michael is still alive somewhere?" Rees asked. Coulton nodded.

"I couldn't take the chance of you questioning him. He knew who I was, you see." He looked at Marguerite. "I'm sorry. He didn't want you to know. I took care of him until he could travel. I think he went to Portland." She uttered a little scream of joyful relief.

"I believe you," Rees said with a sigh. "You've been lying to me all along, though. You figured out the identity of the murderer after I found Charles and you've been protecting her. Your wife, Henry's sister."

"No," Coulton said in protest.

"You have it all figured out, I suppose," Mrs. Coulton said viciously.

"Most of it," Rees said. He paused and when she did not speak he continued. "When you and your brother realized Patrick could inherit that large farm, you hatched a plan to remove all the others in his way: Charles, Roger Bristol, Lydia . . ."

Coulton stared at his wife in horror. "All of them?"

"You helped your brother murder the boy Ira and your husband's cousin, Charles."

"He wouldn't promise to sign the Covenant," she said. "That's all he had to do. But he refused." Rees glanced at Lydia. Joy that Charles had not planned to leave her mingled with grief and she sobbed aloud.

"But you killed Catherine Parker," Rees said. "Henry couldn't do it; he and the sheriff were both at a farm meeting. I asked an impartial witness. Catherine would never allow an unfamiliar man to approach her. You took your husband's whip and struck her down." Mrs. Coulton shrugged.

"So where is my husband?" Mrs. Doucette asked.

Rees turned to her. "I am very sorry to tell you he is dead, murdered, as well."

Mrs. Doucette began sobbing, Rees thought as much from horror as from grief. Mouse leaped to her feet and tried to lead her cousin outside. But Mrs. Doucette wouldn't go. Still weeping, she sat down. Rees understood; she had to know the rest of it. He turned back to Mrs. Coulton.

"When Henry kept most of the money he stole from Charles's dead body to buy his farm, you didn't care. But when he struck your husband, with his own whip I might add, and almost killed him, you retaliated. I think you already suspected what had happened and were prepared. As the rest of us searched for Patrick, you found Henry unconscious in the barn. You killed him, didn't you? Struck him down with the fancy whip Henry intended to return to you. You killed your own brother, the brother who followed your orders from beginning to end."

"Not all the time," she said. "He shot at you, all on his own. Twice. But the stupid fool missed both times." Coulton still stared at her, his expression one of horrified incredulity.

"I scolded him for shooting at Mr. Rees and he never betrayed you. Your own brother . . ."

"He would have killed you," she snapped. Coulton shook his head disbelievingly and turned to stare wretchedly at Rees.

"That night you slipped out, drove to the Ellis farm," Rees said, "and buried him. Mr. Rouge would not have noticed you; he was looking for a man." Rouge, who already looked as though he'd been clubbed, turned to look at the woman next to him in stark disbelief.

"I did see you," he said.

Rees glanced at Coulton and quickly away again. He was staring at his wife in such anguish Rees couldn't bear to see it.

"It's jail for you," Rouge said to Mrs. Coulton. "At least until I decide what to do with you." He grasped her arm but she wrenched away and, carrying herself with dignity, preceded him through the door and out.

"Maybe house arrest," protested Coulton faintly. Struggling to his feet, he pursued his wife, staggering a little with dizziness.

Lydia hurried to Rees's side. Although she'd wiped away her tears, her eyes were still wet and they shone with relief and gratitude. Under cover of the noisy bustle of the others, she said, "Thank you." Rees nodded. Her eyes turned to the sheriff, tottering after his wife and the deputy.

"She would escape in five minutes," she said. "I hope Mr. Rouge doesn't feel sorry for this specimen of the fairer sex."

Rees heaved a sigh. "I know," he said. "But maybe that would be for the best." Lydia turned to look at him in astonishment.

"She'll kill again, you know."

"Hanging a woman is an ugly business." He fell silent as Mr. and Mrs. Lewis approached.

"Thank you," he said to both Rees and Lydia, reaching out to clasp Rees's hand. "We appreciate what you've done for Catherine. You and your . . . assistant." He forced a smile and bestowed it upon both of them. "We'll be holding a memorial service; we hope you'll come. Both of you." As Mr. and Mrs. Lewis walked away, Mr. Golightly, leaning upon Mrs. Baker's arm, tottered toward them.

"You must come in for the reading of the will," he said to her. "And we'll discuss your inherited property."

"I don't want it," Lydia said in a fierce undertone.

"Selling is always an option," the attorney said, and nodded meaningfully at the Shaker Elders standing quietly together.

Mrs. Doucette slowly picked herself up from the bench. She looked around uncertainly, as though not quite certain what to do next. Rees hesitated and then moved to intercept her. "Thank you," she said, offering a gloved hand. "At least I know where Henry is and that he didn't abandon us." Rees nodded. He didn't think he would be as gracious as she under similar circumstances.

"What will you do now?"

"I don't know." For a moment she looked terrified and then her expression smoothed out. "I'll worry tomorrow." She walked toward the door. Mouse joined her and they went out arm in arm.

Once everyone else had left, Elder Hutchins approached Rees.

"Thank you," he said with a stiff incline of his head. "You resolved the problem most neatly and before the deadline I set you. Of course this is a lesson that we Believers have learned; it is best to own nothing, to covet nothing, and to love only God."

Rees thought of Sister Chastity's silk stockings, and the reason she wore them; of Michael, the dog set among the sheep; and of Charles. He was the most interesting of all. Despite his hunger to live with the Shakers, he would not surrender the blue roans that belonged to his cousin, Lydia, or the property his grandfather left him. "I'm afraid I see, despite your many good works, human frailties in all men," he said. Elder Hutchins looked at him in startled wonder.

"Yes, of course," he agreed. "Only God is perfect."

Rees and Lydia left the Meetinghouse last. They separated to pass through the proper doors but met again outside in the long afternoon shadows. "It should have been me," Lydia said. "Mrs. Coulton should have killed me. Not Sister Chastity."

"I'm grateful she didn't," Rees said. "Ironic isn't it? By Shaker standards, you sinned and were banished from the community. Because you no longer lived here, that punishment saved your life." Lydia frowned at him and continued with her own thoughts.

"I own the land because Charles would surrender nothing, not the horses, not the farm. He was not the man I thought he was and certainly not the man I loved."

"Don't decide anything hastily," Rees said. "Give yourself some time."

"And where will I live while I'm thinking?" she asked tartly. "Elder Hutchins will not permit me to stay in my cottage. Remember?"

"I have the answer," Rees said. His heart speeded up, thrumming inside his chest. "David will farm my land, the property he will inherit from me when I die. We've agreed. But he is just a boy. No matter how knowledgeable he is, few men will take instruction from him. But if you were there . . ."

"Me?" She stared at him. "What do I know of farming?

What exactly are you asking, Mr. Rees? To live with you out of wedlock?"

"No. I know you'd never . . . There's a cottage, my grandmother's cottage. You can live there with your flowers and your bees. Serve as my housekeeper. While you think."

"Housekeeper? Everyone in town will think me your fancy woman," she said. Her voice was soft with disappointment.

"Mr. Golightly has Mrs. Baker," Rees said, sharp with hurt and disappointment.

"He is an old man. And besides, there is a Mr. Baker somewhere."

"Well then, marry me." The words escaped Rees's lips before he knew it and he regretted them as soon as he spoke them. Although he loved her, he knew better than to torture another woman as he'd tortured Dolly. She examined his face searchingly.

"You don't mean it," she said, the words escaping on a soft sigh. "You're not ready. I suspect you still love Dolly. And I am not sure I would agree even if you did." Because of Charles? Rees suppressed a flash of jealousy.

"I just want to give you time to think," he said. "You don't have to stay if you don't wish it. I won't even be there all the time. I travel from town to town weaving." She said nothing. Although only a few moments passed, Rees felt the hopes and dreams he'd barely admitted to himself begin to wither. She walked alongside him in silence for several moments.

"I don't know," she said. But she sounded like she could be persuaded.

"It's a business arrangement," Rees said, growing desperate. "To give you time to think. So you don't have to sign the Covenant immediately." She did not reply. As they approached the Blacksmith's, she veered right, toward the path. Rees felt his heart breaking. But she paused.

"Very well," she said at last, turning to him. "This is a business arrangement. I shall keep house for you as if I were your sister. Nothing more. And if I elect to return to the Family, you will not try and stop me."

"I understand," Rees said, relief and trepidation rushing through him. "Thank you." Tentatively he extended his hand. After a beat she grasped it and they shook.